FRIEND LIKE ME

Jamie Millen

ALSO BY JAMIE MILLEN

CLAIRE WOLFE THRILLERS

YOU DID THIS

YOU MADE ME

YOU ARE NEXT

FRIEND
LIKE ME

JAMIE MILLEN

This book is a work of fiction. Names, characters, organizations, places, events, and incidents are either products of the author's imagination or used fictitiously. Any resemblance to actual events or actual persons, living or dead, is purely coincidental.

jamiemillen.com

ISBN-13: 978-1-950139-21-7 (ebook)

ISBN-13: 978-1-950139-22-4 (paperback)

ISBN-13: 978-1-950139-23-1 (hardcover)

ISBN-13: 978-1-950139-24-8 (large print)

ISBN-13: 978-1-950139-25-5 (audiobook)

FIC031080 FICTION/Thrillers/Psychological

FIC030000 FICTION/Thrillers/Suspense

Cover design by 100 Covers

First edition

Chapter 1

Amy Walker never imagined she'd lose everything. Not again. The injustice tormented her. She'd done nothing wrong. She'd worked hard and played by the rules. Somebody else had screwed up. But none of that had mattered. The fatal mistake hounded her, snapping at her heels and forcing her, time and again, to move on and start over. Four years as a fugitive had taught her life's single bitter truth. *The fairy tales lied. Nobody's riding out to save you. No magic wand can fix things. You're on your own, kiddo. The universe just doesn't care.*

But one chilly April morning in Manhattan, Amy could run no further, and she had nowhere left to hide.

Josh Wesner leered at her from his leather manager's chair when she entered his fortieth-floor corner office. The crown of ginger curls on his prematurely balding head clashed with the royal blue of his Armani suit. His eyes darted to the takeout coffee in her hands. A tall cappuccino. Heavy cream. Dry foam. Extra hot. The way he liked it. But his smug grin had nothing to do with his daily caffeine fix.

A playful lilt slithered into his voice. "I made some inquiries about you."

A black pit of dread opened in her stomach. *He knows.* Would he fire her—or worse, call the police?

Josh licked his lips. "Don't worry, babe. Your secret's safe with me." He beckoned with his fingers. "Come here."

The pit deepened. He wouldn't rat her out. He'd blackmail her. *What does he want?*

Amy took two hesitant steps forward.

"Closer. C'mon, don't be afraid."

She rounded the large oak desk and neared his chair. Amy focused on the paper coffee cup in her pale hands.

Josh twisted his lips into a sickening smile. "We're friends, aren't we? Friends help each other."

In Amy's experience, men who promised friendship never had her best interests at heart. Her boss was no different. He ran his clammy hand up her leg and underneath her skirt.

Amy froze. Her breath caught in her chest. Was this really happening?

Why are you surprised? She'd heard the rumors. A coworker had tried to warn her. *Josh's girls never stay long.* Had her boss harassed his other assistants? His father owned the agency. Josh knew he'd get away with it. And this time, he'd cornered easy prey.

His fingers traced the hemline of her panties.

No, you don't! Amy relaxed her grip, and the cup slipped through her fingers. The plastic lid separated from the paper container, and the steaming latte poured onto his lap.

Josh yelped and launched to his feet. "What's the matter with you?"

Amy dropped to her knees to hide her smile and collected the empty vessel. "I'm so sorry. I'll clean this up."

But her revenge was short-lived.

Her boss wiped the froth from his thousand-dollar suit. "Leave it. Go back and get me another." His sickening smile returned. "We'll continue our...*conversation* soon. Then, you'll make this up to me. Big time."

Amy hurried from his office. She dumped the ruined container into the kitchenette's trash can, grabbed her jacket, and took the elevator downstairs.

Her heart pounded. Sweat trickled down the back of her neck. She should never have asked Josh to pay her in cash. The unusual request had triggered his curiosity and invited trouble. *You should know better by now.* It was time to pack up and move on again...as soon as she got her money.

She stepped into Midtown's chaos of sounds and smells. Amy zipped her jacket against the morning chill and ordered another coffee to go on her work phone's Starbucks app.

The pungent scent of freshly ground coffee greeted her in the store. Amy pressed her hands to the polished wooden service counter to steady her trembling fingers. People surrounded her. Their carefree chatter buzzed in her ears. But she'd never felt more alone and vulnerable.

Her phone vibrated twice in her hand. A text message had arrived. Had Josh grown impatient, eager to continue their "conversation?"

She swiped the screen. Josh hadn't sent the text. The sender had used an unknown number, and the message consisted of three words.

You deserve better.

Amy scoffed. *Understatement of the year.*

A sudden wave of fear washed over her. Had the sender witnessed her interaction with Josh? Was somebody watching her—following her? She studied the other waiting customers. A young unshaven man chatted up a brunette in skinny jeans and platform heels. Four other patrons hunched over their phones. Two women gossiped with enthusiasm at a sit-down table. Amy recognized none of them. Did the eavesdropper know about her past, too? She shook the paranoid thought from her head. Work had provided the phone. Only Wesner & Morgan employees had her number. Was Josh messing with her?

She thumbed a quick reply. "Who is this?"

The response arrived instantly. *Message failed to send. Invalid number.*

"Excuse me, ma'am?"

Amy looked up from her phone. A man stood behind the counter, his green apron stained with coffee.

He smiled at her. "You're Lisa, right? Your order's ready."

Lisa. Lisa Smith. Amy had used that name for the past two months. *Pull yourself together.*

She forced an apologetic grin. "Sorry. I was somewhere else."

The barista chuckled. "No problem. Sometimes I wish I was somewhere else, too."

He slid the steaming drink toward her. The coffee had arrived. Josh was waiting for her in his office. How would she get through the day? How low was she willing to fall to buy his silence?

The barista leaned on the counter. "I've seen you around. Do you work nearby?"

Amy parted her lips to answer his question. Had *he* sent her the message to brighten her day? She snatched the drink and left.

The human torrent on Broadway Street swept Amy along the sidewalk. She hated acting like a jerk. The barista hadn't deserved the ghosting even if he had stolen her number from the Starbucks customer database. But she'd fled to Manhattan to disappear in the crowd. *Keep your head down and avoid small talk. Unwanted attention can be fatal.* Amy sighed. One thing was certain. She'd need to find another Starbucks for her daily pickup.

With each step closer to the office, her pulse sped up. Wesner & Morgan had seemed like a haven—a comfortable job in a fancy building with coworkers who minded their own business. The simple office chores gave her a taste of the normal life she might have enjoyed if her world hadn't gone to hell. But today that haven had become the lion's den of an entitled pervert who preyed on vulnerable women.

Amy stopped at the red light. The large glass doors of the office building loomed fifty feet ahead. Once she passed beneath that stone arch, she'd seal her fate.

The disposable cup trembled in her grasp. Her eyes moistened. *I can't do this anymore.* She'd carried her burden for too long. The lies and constant fear had worn down her soul to a paper-thin wafer. Was her life still worth living?

A bus whooshed by. The gust of hot air in its wake blew loose strands of her hair. One small step forward and she could end her suffering, here and now. Death was the only solution to her problem. *Don't even think that! You can't quit. Not yet. This isn't only about you.*

True. Someone needed her—someone she loved. Amy had to soldier on. She had no choice. But she was broke, too. Tomorrow, she'd collect her pay and start over. *Be strong. One more day. You can do this.*

The lights changed. She charged across the street ahead of the crowd. A plan formed in her head. *Don't let him get you alone.* She'd find an excuse and drag someone into his office—one of the other assistants, Tanesha or Eddie. But how would she explain her sticky situation without exposing her secrets?

Her vision blurred. A bundle of clothing fell from the heavens and hit the sidewalk at her feet. Amy stopped dead in her tracks. *Not a bundle of clothing—a man.* His body slammed into the concrete with a wet splat and a sickening crunch of breaking bones. The corpse bounced once, then lay limp.

Behind her, a man gasped and swore. A woman screamed. A ghostly chill swept through Amy, lining her skin with clammy sweat. She gaped at the dead man. Blood and gore speckled his royal-blue designer suit. From beneath the crown of ginger curls, the crushed head's single eye stared at her.

"Oh my God."

Josh Wesner—her boss—was dead.

Chapter 2

Amy's legs turned to jelly at the sight of the corpse on the sidewalk. Hands gripped her arm and prevented her collapse. "Are you okay?" a man said.

She nodded but barely understood him. He guided her toward the wall of the building for support and hurried away. Amy slid to the ground and placed the Starbucks cup beside her. She inhaled a deep breath and suppressed the urge to vomit.

What just happened? Josh fell from...up there. But I saw him a few minutes ago. He can't be...

This was the second violent death Amy had witnessed. Both had shaken her to the core.

Tears welled. A crowd of onlookers blocked the body from view. Amy had despised Josh. Her boss was a scumbag. His sudden demise had saved her from his sexual manipulation. But nobody deserved to die *like that*.

Police cruisers arrived at the scene, followed by an ambulance. None used their sirens. Josh was beyond saving. Officers dispersed the spectators, and men in Tyvek suits erected a white tent over the corpse.

Amy's tears flowed again. A creeping premonition needled her conscience. Had Amy somehow contributed to his death?

You deserve better. Her skin crawled at the memory of the text.

Had Josh sent the message? Had he regretted his behavior and, in a fit of remorse, leaped to his death from his office window? *No way*. Josh had shown no signs of depression or moral qualms. Over the past two weeks, he'd ordered Amy around like his personal slave, often while munching energy snacks and belching without apology. He'd behaved as though his family owned not only the advertising agency but the world and its population.

Who, then, had sent her the text? Had the anonymous sender played a role in Josh's death? Had he killed her boss to protect her? A shudder sped down her spine.

A mustachioed cop lumbered toward her. Amy stiffened. Uniformed officers triggered her flight instinct. But the cop didn't cuff her. He crouched before her.

"Ma'am, I need you to leave the area. Don't you have somewhere to go?"

The police were already at Wesner & Morgan when the elevator doors opened on the fortieth floor. Amy gripped the Starbucks coffee like a shield. Miraculously, she hadn't spilled a drop.

She pressed her employee card to the sensor and entered. The reception desk stood vacant. Two police officers crossed the area. She lowered her gaze and hurried away from them.

Her first impulse had been to flee to her apartment, toss her clothes in a suitcase, and escape the city. It had taken every ounce of her self-control to return to the agency. Running away would draw unwanted attention, and tomorrow was payday. She'd collect her money and disappear. Which reminded her... Amy needed to ask the finance department to do her a favor.

Clumps of office workers lingered in the corridors and whispered among themselves. They watched her as she walked by.

Act normally. You've done nothing wrong.

Amy made for her department, Client Servicing. Glass walls lined the offices of the account executives, spacious rooms with tall street-facing windows. The warren of cubicles opposite the glass walls housed the assistants and interns. But this morning, her coworkers had abandoned their desks, too.

At the far end of the corridor, a beefy police officer with a blond crew cut spoke with Debbie, the curly-haired front desk attendant.

Behind them, yellow crime scene tape blocked the door to Josh's corner office, the blinds still closed. The tape validated Amy's assumption. *Josh fell from his office window.* But how?

Debbie and the cop eyed her. The attendant said something, and the cop scribbled on his notepad.

Amy's heart skipped a beat. Would they think she'd killed him? Amy was Josh's only assistant. She'd dropped a cup of steaming coffee on him that morning—on purpose. Would the incident make her a suspect? Had anyone seen her confrontation with her boss that morning? *But I have an alibi. I was on the sidewalk. CCTV will show I was there.*

She ducked into her cubicle and slung her pouch on the chair's backrest. Sitting, she placed the drink beside her keyboard.

Two men occupied the office opposite her cubicle. A uniformed officer stood before the desk and talked with her hands. Mark Davis leaned back in his manager's chair and steepled his fingers. The executive appeared calm and collected. His gray suit failed to conceal his muscular shoulders. His aura of understated power mesmerized her. Amy often stole glances at him through the glass wall—he always kept the blinds open—but he never seemed to notice her. Now his attention drifted from the cop, and the blue eyes beneath his slicked-back, sandy-blond hair focused on her. Amy returned his stare, hypnotized by his steely cobalt gaze. Then, he smiled at her. She looked away quickly, her cheeks warming, and nudged her computer to life.

Had Mark heard the rumors about Josh, too? Had *he* sent her the text—and pushed Josh to his death?

Don't be ridiculous. The shock had made her paranoid—more paranoid than usual. The text meant nothing. Amy searched for a rational explanation and found many. The sender had intended the message for someone else—the simple case of a wrong number.

Or a bored kid had pranked her. Better yet, an automated marketing system had spammed her by accident. Wesner & Morgan
used mass messaging tools in their ad campaigns. The text was the
harmless ricochet of a misguided algorithm. *You deserve better.* The
message probably belonged to one of the high-end lifestyle brands
the agency managed. *See?* Amy's fugitive brain had overreacted.

"Ms. Smith?" a man said in a thick Brooklyn accent.

Amy jumped.

The beefy cop peered over her cubicle divider. "Sorry, ma'am. I
didn't mean to startle you."

"That's okay."

"Are you Lisa Smith?"

Take it easy. Stay calm. "Yes. Can I help you?"

"I'm afraid I have some bad news." He studied her, his expression stern. What was he hunting for?

Don't say anything. You saw nothing. But the silence sucked on
her conscience and loosened her tongue.

"I know. I was downstairs when it happened and saw the…police
cars and ambulance." *Good. You've made it clear you weren't in the
office when he fell.*

"So, you know what happened?"

Amy chose her words carefully. "I know Mr. Wesner died."

The cop seemed confused. "Mr. Wesner?"

"Joshua Wesner. My boss. I started working here two weeks ago."

She clamped her lips shut. *Stop babbling. Don't offer so much
information. You sound nervous.*

Amy *was* nervous. His passing had truly shaken her. Wasn't
anxiety the natural and expected response? She'd given the police
no cause to dig into her background. Amy had nothing to do with
her boss's death. Or had she?

The officer flipped the page of his spiral notepad. "I need to ask
you a few questions."

"No problem."

"What's your full name?"

Hadn't they already covered that? "Lisa Smith."

"How long have you worked here?"

Ditto. "I joined the agency two weeks ago."

He scribbled. "Did you know the deceased before you started working here?"

"No. We first met at the interview."

Josh had been terse and businesslike during that first meeting. Amy hadn't sensed his deviant side. Why did the creeps always slip through the cracks in her intuition?

The cop nodded. "When did you see him last?"

"This morning."

"Did you notice any change in his behavior today?"

Besides feeling me up and threatening to expose me?

Amy swallowed her tongue and shook her head.

"What were you doing downstairs?"

She glanced at her Starbucks cup. "Getting him coffee."

"That was for him?"

She nodded.

He read the time off his wristwatch. "Ten o'clock. A bit late for Starbucks, isn't it?"

"I went out much earlier."

"What time was that?"

"I don't know. About eight-thirty."

"And you only got back now?"

Was he trying to place her in Josh's office at the time of his fall? Her mouth dried up. *I'm a suspect.* He'd led with the simple questions to lower her guard.

Should I mention the spill? Would that incriminate her? Didn't investigators always look for signs of a struggle?

"I couldn't get inside the building with all the emergency teams outside. I saw his body, and I was in shock. The coffee's cold by now. Here, see for yourself."

"It's okay. I'm sorry you had to experience that. This must be very difficult for you."

"Yes, it was."

The cop seemed to sympathize with her. Had he used a routine line of questioning? Had she panicked for nothing?

He scribbled again on his notepad. "Can anyone confirm what time you left?"

Geez. Was Amy supposed to secure witnesses every time she left the office?

"I don't know."

"What about your receipt?"

"My receipt?"

He raised an eyebrow. "From Starbucks. You picked up the coffee, didn't you?"

"There's no receipt. I order online and pick up the drinks."

He grunted. "Okay. That's it for now. Detectives will be here soon. They'll take your full statement."

Detectives. Amy swore under her breath. The investigation hadn't even begun. She should have fled while she had the chance. Had coming back been a terrible mistake?

The cop frowned sympathetically and closed his notepad. "My condolences for your loss."

"Thank you."

He strolled off.

Amy sagged in her seat. She should have told him about the spilled first coffee. The police weren't idiots. They'd find the two Starbucks orders and think she was a liar. Amy was an honest person at heart. The fake identity was just a survival strategy. *Crap!* How would she keep that secret?

Her email inbox displayed on the computer monitor. Josh's emails from yesterday were the last he'd ever send her. None of them mattered anymore. An awkward but urgent question formed in her mind. With her boss gone, had Amy become redundant? She grabbed the coffee and stood. She needed answers.

In the kitchenette, Tanesha and Eddie nursed steaming drinks. The two assistants ended their whispered conversation when she entered. Amy smiled cautiously and rubbed her arm. As usual, she'd kept to herself. Now she wished she'd befriended her coworkers. She could do with some insider information.

On Amy's first day, Tanesha Williams had spoken to her in her proud, standoffish way.

"Good luck," she'd said. "Josh's girls don't stay long."

Amy had discarded the comment on the spot. Men gravitated to her. She couldn't control them. She did nothing to encourage them either. But women always resented her. Beneath the full-bodied black woman's veneer of female camaraderie, Amy had sensed that familiar knee-jerk jealousy. *Don't worry. Male attention is the last thing I want here.*

Maybe Amy had misread the situation? Had Tanesha only tried to warn her?

Amy tossed the Starbucks cup into the trash. *Wait a minute.* She pushed the swing top lid open with her hand. She'd dumped the spilled cup into the same trash can after the spill. Now the liner was empty. Had housekeeping cleaned up already?

Tanesha and Eddie watched her, probably wondering why the trash bin interested her so much.

Amy released the lid and folded her arms. "I just talked with the police officer."

Tanesha's eyelids drooped with sarcasm. "She speaks."

Eddie elbowed his friend. "Be nice, T. She lost her boss today."

Edmund "Eddie" Vega had grinned at Amy foolishly throughout their first introduction and at their every encounter since. *Don't bother, Eddie,* Amy had thought. *We'll never date, and that's a compliment.*

Amy had terrible taste in men. She only fell for bad boys. Even if her life on the run had left room for romantic entanglements, Eddie's effeminate silky shirts, pencil mustache, and overeager attitude ruled him out.

Her conscience twinged. She'd looked down on him, but Eddie had defended her. *I'm a crappy person.*

His mustache twitched. "Don't worry, Lisa. People don't die here every week."

Her pent-up tension escaped in a quick burst of laughter. She covered her mouth. A man had fallen to his death. They shouldn't joke around.

Tanesha pouted. "I can't believe he killed himself."

Amy pounced on her words. "Is that what happened?" *Please let it be true.*

Tanesha shrugged. "So I hear. How else does a man fall out the window? Those suckers are hard to open. He must have climbed on a chair, too. That's a lot of work."

Eddie raised both his arms like a swimmer on a springboard and sniggered. "Or he dived through."

Tanesha swatted him but smiled. "Cut that out, you psycho."

Amy's body relaxed. They were right. Josh had died by suicide. There was no other reasonable explanation. The text message meant nothing. The police weren't searching for a murderer. They wouldn't investigate her too closely.

Eddie sobered. "He must have really hated himself."

Tanesha grunted in agreement.

Amy read between the lines. *Nobody here liked Josh.* The owner's son had been an entitled jerk and sexual predator.

Eddie nodded. "Poor Harry."

Their distaste didn't extend to Josh's father, the agency's founder. She'd seen Harry Wesner only twice in the office, and he seemed like a friendly, decent man.

Tanesha dropped her empty cup in the trash and turned to Amy. "I'd polish my résumé if I were you. Looks like you're out of a job."

Eddie followed her out of the kitchenette. "Sorry, Lisa."

Amy forced a brave grin and digested their verdict in gloomy silence. *They're right.* Tanesha worked for Mark, Eddie for Wesner senior. The agency no longer needed a third assistant. *There's your answer, Amy. Happy now?*

She wasn't. Until this morning, she'd pictured a career at Wesner & Morgan beyond two weeks. No point brooding on it. She'd better send out job applications right away.

"Don't listen to them, Lisa," a woman said.

Pudgy and with a ponytail of mousy hair, she filled a water bottle from the cooler. "We're always short of assistants here. I'm sure you'll stay on."

"I hope you're right." She searched her memory for the woman's name. "Bethany, right?"

The woman beamed at her. "You remembered me!"

Amy grinned. "It's a pretty name."

Human Resources had given her a tour of the offices on her first day and introduced her to a dozen employees. She'd forgotten most of the names on the spot. But Amy had paid special attention to the finance department. Soon, she'd need them.

"Call me Beth. Beth from finance." She giggled. "You are *so* beautiful."

Amy crossed her arms instinctively. Why did compliments about her physical appearance unsettle her? But her instant rapport with the woman might open doors, and she seized her opportunity.

"Beth, I need to ask you something."

"Go ahead. Ask me anything."

"Everybody!" a man called from the corridor. "Over here. Please can I have your attention?"

Amy glanced at Beth, who shrugged. They stepped out of the kitchenette toward the voice.

Three suits commanded the hallway. The bald leader stood with his hands on his hips and a gold badge of office clipped to his belt. He considered the gathering employees with a domineering stare that implied he was used to delivering orders. His associates were both in their late twenties. The man had a boyish mop of black curls and an easy smile. The shorter woman had a pixie cut and angular features. They scrutinized the crowd with the intense, eager stares of sheepdogs sizing up their flock.

The bald man spoke again. "I'm Sergeant Adrian Blank of Midtown South Precinct. I know you've already had a difficult morning. But we need a little more of your time. None of you are to leave the offices without our permission."

The employees groaned.

Sergeant Blank plowed on. "My colleagues, Detective Brandon Cooper and Detective Mindy Scott, will collect statements from each of you. Detective Cooper."

The boyish detective stepped forward and grinned with enthusiasm. "We'll make this quick and painless." His gaze settled on Amy, and his cheeks dimpled. "Thank you for your cooperation."

Chapter 3

Amy stared at the detective across the conference room table while he arranged his notepad and papers. Her pulsing heartbeat drummed in her ears. The police officers had let her stew for two hours before her interview, and the tension was boiling over. Was she the last employee on their list? Did that mean she was in the clear or the opposite? The female detective remained standing. She leaned against the wall and watched Amy closely. What had the other workers told them? How much about her and Josh did they know?

Relax. Sit up and breathe. You've done nothing wrong.

Detective Brandon Cooper placed a digital recorder between them on the table.

"Do you mind if I record your statement?"

As though I have a choice. "No."

"Thank you."

Amy remained vigilant. She'd learned her lesson from the beat cop. The detective seemed friendly. He was handsome in a safe, reliable sort of way. Not her type. But his disarming smile and polite chatter meant nothing. He was here for business, not pleasure, and his job was to catch killers.

Her phone buzzed twice on the table. Amy tensed her shoulders. Who could that be? *Josh is dead.* Had the anonymous contact sent another text?

Detective Cooper glanced at her. "You can check that if you like."

"It's okay."

"Please, go ahead. We'll all feel more comfortable."

Her mouth twitched. "Thanks."

She picked up her phone and swiped the screen. The message had originated from a different number, also unknown. Again, the message contained no greeting or names. But this time, she'd received five words.

Stay calm. You've got this.

The hairs on the back of her neck bristled. Did the sender know she was sitting with the police? Was he watching her right now?

"Is everything all right?"

Amy set the phone to Silent and put it down again. "Yes."

It's a coincidence, Amy. A message bot happened to send her two generic texts, which she'd interpreted to fit her current situation. *They're like horoscopes. Just relax.*

Detective Cooper turned on the recorder. His fingers shook slightly. Was he nervous, too? Did the involuntary movement mean he was attracted to her or anxious to trap his suspect?

He read out the date and their names for the recording.

"Where do you live, Ms. Smith?"

"Yorkville."

"Upper East Side. Nice."

"It's an old building. The rent is cheap for the area, and it's only one subway to work."

He nodded. "And where are you from?"

Why did he need to know that? Had he noticed an accent? Why was he suddenly interested in her past?

"Out of state."

She hadn't intended to snap at him. Amy blamed her frayed nerves. But her evasive reply didn't seem to annoy him.

"What brought you to New York?"

"Work."

His smile broadened with amusement, and his cheeks dimpled again. "Have we met before?"

"No."

"Are you sure? You look familiar. Have you been on TV or street ads?"

Men used that line often. Was he hitting on her or trying to throw her off-balance? His female partner's scornful huff implied the former explanation.

Amy tucked a stray lock of hair behind her ear. "No. I guess I have one of those faces."

He glanced at his notes on a blotter pad. "You're new at Wesner and Morgan."

She nodded. "I started two weeks ago." *That's it. Repeat what you told the first cop. Keep to your original story.*

He studied his notes again. "You left the office this morning at around eight-thirty AM to get coffee. Is that correct?"

Amy swallowed hard. They knew what she'd told the street cop. Had they checked the Starbucks account, too?

"Twice," she blurted out.

"Excuse me?"

"I went out twice."

"Twice?"

Amy laughed nervously. "I dropped the first cup and had to go back for another."

The detective studied his notes. "You didn't mention that to Officer Kramer."

"I should have. I'd just come back from the street where I'd seen..."

Tears choked her up. Amy wasn't faking. The stress of the death scene and the drawn-out wait for her police interview had taken their toll.

Detective Cooper lowered his voice. "It's okay. I understand. What time did you go out the second time?"

"Nine-fifteen, maybe?"

"So, you weren't in the office when he..." The line of questioning betrayed his true goal—to determine Amy's whereabouts at the time of Josh's death.

"I told you. I was on the street. He landed right in front of me. Check our Starbucks account. Or...or ask at the counter. I spoke with a barista. He'll remember me."

She wanted to kick herself. *Yeah, he'll remember the stuck-up jerk who cut him off.* Amy made friends wherever she went.

The detective raised his palms to calm her down. "That won't be necessary. A coworker saw you leave." He read from his notes. "Edmund Vega. We wanted to hear it from you."

Amy parted her lips. Eddie had vouched for her. She was in the clear, and her secrets were safe. *Thanks, pal.*

"We're almost done. Did Mr. Wesner display any unusual behavior this morning?"

She shook her head. *Not unusual for him.*

"Did you notice anything else suspicious or out of the ordinary?"

The text messages rose in her memory. *They mean nothing.*

"I don't think so."

The detective turned off the recorder. "Thank you for your time, Ms. Smith. Please accept our condolences."

They stood, and he escorted her to the door.

He handed her a business card. "Call me if you remember anything else. We'll probably need to speak with you again, so don't leave town."

Chapter 4

"Don't leave town?'" Mindy said in the elevator. "Are you kidding me? You can't stop her."

Detective Brandon Cooper chuckled. "True. But I've always wanted to use that line."

He'd expected Mindy to tease him. She loved breaking his balls, and he looked forward to it. Their playful banter brightened every day. At least she'd waited until they'd left Wesner & Morgan.

Mindy's emerald eyes flashed. "You let her off the hook too easily."

"Give her a break, Minds. Her boss hit the tarmac right in front of her."

Mindy snorted. "C'mon, Brand. Admit it. You like her."

As usual, she'd seen right through him. But even Mindy didn't realize how badly he'd fallen for the assistant. Brandon had met many beautiful women in his life, but Lisa Smith was a sucker punch to the heart. Men killed without question for women like her. He'd barely survived the interview without drooling all over her. But he couldn't admit that to his long-time partner.

He shrugged. "Maybe. Why? Are you jealous?"

She blew a raspberry. "Jealous? Why would I be jealous?"

"Be honest, Minds. Secretly, you've always wanted to date me."

She scoffed. "You know my golden rule. *Never date cops*. One officer in a relationship is more than enough. Trust me."

Mindy had adopted the rule as a teenager after her parents' nasty divorce. The rule hadn't stopped her from enrolling in the Academy.

Brandon grinned. "That's a crying shame." He liked to break her balls, too.

Their brown unmarked cruiser waited for them in the building's visitor parking bay.

Mindy got behind the wheel. She always insisted on driving, in part, Brandon assumed, to make up for her sex and small stature. His partner was one tough cookie. But his deflection tactics had failed.

She said, "I'd stay away from her if I were you."

"Yeah? Why?"

"Because she's a witness. Duh! Romantic relationships are strictly forbidden. Even you know that, knucklehead."

"That's not what you meant, Minds."

She shrugged. "Her body language was all over the place. She's definitely hiding something."

"Do you think she lied to us?"

"Oh, yeah. They all did. They work for a freaking advertising agency, Brand. These people eat, sleep, and breathe lies. They're worse than lawyers."

He chuckled. Lisa Smith had rubbed Minds the wrong way. He understood why. The universe had blessed Lisa Smith with uncommon beauty. But was she a criminal?

"I don't know. She seemed genuinely shaken. But you're right. She's...mysterious."

"Oh my God, Brand. You're in love."

He turned up the air-conditioning. *Geez, it's hot in here.*

"Not in love, Minds. Intrigued."

He gazed at the pedestrian traffic on Broadway to hide his blush. The emergency teams had cleared the sidewalk quickly. People hurried along, unaware that, hours ago, Joshua Wesner's corpse had cracked the concrete under their feet.

His phone rang on the hands-free speaker, and he answered. "Afternoon, Sarge."

"What do we have on Wesner?"

"There's no sign of a struggle in his office. No witnesses to the deed either."

Sarge grunted. "A man falls from the sky, and nobody sees a thing. Welcome to New York. What about CCTV?"

"The IT department will send it over any minute."

"Good. So, what's the verdict? Suicide?"

"That's how it looks."

Sergeant Blank sighed with audible relief. "Great. I'll notify the press. I need your report ASAP. But be thorough. Go over the video feed with a fine-tooth comb. Request a full toxicology analysis from the ME's office, too. Wesner's dad is loaded, so people are going to ask questions. Who knows what Wesner junior snorted before he jumped? These rich kids drive me nuts."

"Yes, sir."

By the sergeant's standards, anyone under forty was a kid.

Brandon ended the call. "This suicide's landed us with a lot of paperwork."

Mindy flashed her devious smile. "Us? Aren't you forgetting something?"

"What?"

"You lost our bet about The Gizmo Murder. The paperwork is on you."

He groaned. "The Gizmo Murder. I almost forgot. Sucks to be me."

Mindy laughed.

He stared out the passenger window, and his thoughts drifted back to Wesner & Morgan's intriguing new assistant. The suicide cause of death had deprived him of an excuse to renew contact with her. On the other hand, once they closed the case, she'd no longer be a witness. This was one loose end he'd love to tie up.

Lisa Smith, what are you hiding?

Chapter 5

The sun sank over Midtown. Skyscrapers cast gloomy shadows, plunging the streets into twilight. Amy slipped into the torrent of rush-hour foot traffic. The bustle and noise comforted her. Swallowed by the crowd, Amy became a nameless commuter heading home. The day's flood of tension had dried up, leaving a thin sediment of grief...and relief. Josh was dead. He'd never expose her secrets. The homicide detectives hadn't pried into her past either. For now, she was safe. She'd dodged the bullets, and for that she was thankful. *Thankful to whom?* A heartless universe? The same blind wrecking ball that had destroyed her life in the first place?

The flow of commuters funneled her down the subway stairs.

Amy brushed aside her philosophical musings to focus on an urgent practical challenge. She needed to find another job, pronto.

She reached her subway platform and waited by the tracks for the next train to arrive. The other travelers craned their necks and studied their phones. Amy had broken that habit. Life on the run meant no smart devices with their GPS chips. No social media either. Digital footprints made people easy to locate. She had no news feeds to scroll and no video reels to binge. Only the demands of her new job had forced her to accept a company phone, and today, the device had plunged her back into her screen addiction.

Amy joined the herd. She opened her Messages app and viewed the recent cryptic texts. *You deserve better. Stay calm. You've got this.* The timing of the two messages had sent her paranoia into overdrive. For a while, she'd believed somebody had murdered Josh—*to help her*. But the longer she pondered the texts, the more her new conviction hardened. The punchy, nurturing statements were the hiccups of a self-help artificial intelligence engine designed to boost self-esteem. Had Wesner & Morgan used their employees' phone numbers to test an automated messaging product for a big-brand customer? Or had a third-party tool selected her number at random? Either way, the texts resulted from pure coincidence.

You deserve better. Stay calm. You've got this. Read in the correct context, the texts were harmless, even comical.

She laughed at her own stupidity. *You crazy idiot.* Her giggles won her annoyed and amused stares from the other commuters, but Amy didn't care. She could breathe at ease again.

A Josef Heller quote tumbled through her head. He'd compared history to a whirlwind ripping open a garbage bag of chance events. Heller had been diplomatic. Amy preferred the imagery of cesspools ruptured by earthquakes.

She read the texts again. The words had shed their ominous overtones completely.

"Come on," she muttered at the phone. "I dare you. Send me another."

What self-affirmative nonsense would the message bot concoct next? "Believe in yourself?" "What doesn't kill you makes you stronger?"

A familiar cliché lodged in her mind, and the fun bled out of her game. Her mother had used the expression often, but Amy's life story had disproved that starry-eyed claim, too.

The phone vibrated, startling her. A message had arrived from a third unknown number. Amy had asked, and the message bot had delivered. Her cheer returned. *What will it be this time?* Amy could do with a pick-me-up.

She opened the message, but the three-word text had the opposite effect.

You look sad.

The chilly finger of terror traced her spine. *He can see me right now. He's watching!*

Amy spun around and shot suspicious glances at the commuters. Some, like her, stood at the yellow safety line. Others hovered by the subway walls and leaned on pillars. Most stared at their phones. None made eye contact. Any of them might have sent the text.

An unshaven man with a black beanie scowled at her. "What's your problem?" he seemed to say, then returned his attention to his phone.

Amy faced the tracks again. Staring at people in the subway tunnel bought you a one-way ticket to trouble.

Her breathing came fast and short. A marketing bot had not sent that message or the others. A living, breathing human being had contacted her, and now the sender was following her. Amy had a stalker.

Her panicked thoughts rushed back. *Did the sender kill Josh? What does he want from me? Am I in danger, too?*

High heels clicked on the hard tiles, and a woman in a beige business suit stepped up beside her. Amy inhaled her lavender perfume. Nobody would attack her here—in public and surrounded by witnesses. Would they? She had to lose him.

Think, Amy. The stalker had found her at work. He had the number of her company-issue phone. But she'd recognized none of the commuters from the agency. Did the stalker belong to a different department?

Her train arrived, the brakes squealing as it decelerated. Did the sender know where she lived? Unlike her phone number, her home address didn't appear on the internal corporate website.

The train ground to a halt, and the doors opened. People streamed into the subway car. Amy remained frozen to the spot. If she got on now, the stalker would follow her home. *Don't let that happen.*

The subway tunnel had almost emptied. Most of the commuters had packed into the train, including the perfumed woman. Amy stood alone by the open doors.

She hazarded a quick look over her shoulder. A handful of men lingered behind her, Beanie Man among them. She swore under her breath. Amy didn't want to spend another second on the platform. She longed for the security of her apartment. But she'd have no peace of mind if the stalker discovered where she lived.

A whistle blared. Pneumatic mechanisms hissed, and the doors shifted. Amy leaped between the closing metal plates, slipping through a split second before they shut.

She faced the window, her body trembling. Beanie Man glared at her. The subway car accelerated, and the stranger watched her leave without him.

Amy had done it. She'd shaken her stalker. He knew the general direction in which she was heading but not where she'd get off or lived. She'd dodged another bullet. *Or have I?*

She found a vacant seat and stole glances at the other passengers. They gripped the plastic ceiling handles and swayed with the train's turns. Amy knew nothing about her stalker. Had she escaped an innocent bystander only to flee into the murderous embrace of a killer?

A man with a gray hoodie glanced at her from the other end of the compartment. Amy leaned back, hiding behind an old man in a checkered jacket. Was Hoodie following her?

The train slowed to a stop, and the doors parted. The old man exited along with a dozen others. Hoodie remained. He stared at her. Amy averted her gaze. *Ignore him, and he'll go away.*

The doors closed, and the train sped up again. Hoodie stood and stepped toward her. *Crap.* Had she drawn his attention, or had he been following her all along?

Amy tucked her phone into her pouch and dug around for her small canister of Mace. *Where is it?* Had she left the pepper spray at home? How could she be so careless? She grasped her house key, positioning the sharp edge between her knuckles. If the stranger attacked her, she'd slash his face and run.

Hoodie stopped a few steps away from her. Amy kept her head down. Brown smears of mud soiled the edges of his Nike trainers.

The compartment slowed again. Amy gripped the key tightly and braced for a confrontation. But the filthy Nikes passed her by and walked out of the train.

Amy slumped against the backrest. Hoodie wasn't her stalker. Or he'd decided to let her go.

The subway car reached her station, and Amy emerged on Yorkville's darkened streets. Frequently, she glanced over her shoulder, but nobody seemed to be following.

I made some inquiries about you. Josh's words gnawed on her nerves. How had her boss exposed her secret? She'd paid good money for a solid new identity. Had he hired a private investigator to dig into her past? Had the freelancer developed an unhealthy interest in her, too, and turned against his client? Would he be waiting for Amy at her apartment?

She entered her red-brick building and climbed two flights to her floor. The corridor stood empty. Amy hurried down the carpeted hallway and pressed her ear to the front door. Hearing no movement within, she turned the key in the lock and slipped inside. With a series of quick, well-practiced motions, she secured three bolts and latches. She had installed the extra protective measures within hours of moving in, and their presence alone enabled her to sleep at night.

She dropped her pouch on the scratched kitchen table. The one-bedroom rental wasn't home. Amy had no home. Everything in her life was temporary, to be abandoned at a moment's notice. But the place had heat, and the landlord hadn't asked too many questions.

Amy found the Mace in her bedside drawer and slipped the canister into her pouch. She stripped and showered. The jet of scalding water massaged her neck and shoulders. Reliable water pressure was another feature Amy appreciated. The day's experiences flashed in her mind's eye. Josh's leering face. *You deserve better.* His lifeless body bouncing on the sidewalk. His single unseeing eye staring at her.

She shuddered. Josh had tried to hurt her, and now he was dead. Amy should feel lucky. But no matter how long she soaped her body, she still felt dirty.

Amy put on her pajamas and wrapped her hair in a towel. She poured herself a glass of tap water and settled on the worn upholstery of the pull-out couch.

Before her fugitive years, she'd enjoyed red wine and dining out. Now she had no money for luxuries. Amy diverted the bulk of her salary to her secret project. The venture would never repay her investment, but the mission kept her sane and made her shaky existence bearable. *Almost bearable.*

Two loud knocks on the door startled her, and she spilled water on the table. Had her stalker tracked her down?

Amy padded toward the door in her slippers. *Take it easy. It's probably nothing.* She put her eye to the peephole. A pot-bellied man with a Mediterranean complexion and white polo shirt stood on her doorstep. Mario had stopped by for an unscheduled visit. Her Greek landlord's real name was Lucas, but his thick eyebrows and mustache reminded her of the Mario Brothers games. The fish-eye lens of the peephole perfected the caricature. What did Mario want now?

She unlocked the door, dislodged the bolts, and cracked the door open as far as the security chain allowed. The cool welcome was her hint to Mario—now is not a good time.

Mario opened his mouth, then bunched his ample eyebrows and seemed to forget what he'd planned to say. "Did I approve a chain?"

Mario was very protective of his rented property. Every nail required his written approval.

Amy held his gaze. "In case you didn't notice, Mar—Lucas, I'm a single woman living alone. My personal security is non-negotiable."

Mario grunted. "Okay. But they stay when you go. I don't want any ugly holes in the woodwork."

Amy had moved in two months ago, and already he was preparing for her departure.

She made to close the door. "Fine."

He jammed his shoe in the door. "Rent is due tomorrow."

"I know."

He whined softly like an injured dog. "I don't want a repeat of last month."

"I'm sorry about that. It won't happen again. I promise. You'll get your money. Goodnight."

Amy locked the door and closed her eyes. She hated dodging landlords and making promises she probably couldn't keep. *What other choice do I have?*

At least she'd pay on time this month. If she couldn't get cash, she'd sign her paycheck over to Mario. Another side effect of the fugitive life was no bank accounts. Her fake identity had fooled Wesner & Morgan, but she didn't dare mess with the US banking system.

What about next month? Her boss was dead. Tomorrow, Wesner & Morgan might let her go. She needed a new job. Failing that, where could she turn? Loan sharks? *No, thank you.* A women's shelter might take her in. But Amy wasn't fleeing an abusive husband, and her presence might endanger the others. She ran her hands through her hair. The walls seemed to close in on her from every side.

Slow down. Take a deep breath. She'd faced the risk of homelessness before. Each time, she'd pulled through. Why should tomorrow be any different?

Her phone vibrated twice in the pouch on the kitchen table.

Amy opened her eyes. Her financial troubles had overshadowed the more imminent threat to her wellbeing. What did her stalker want now? Had he located her? Would he bait her to leave the safety of her apartment?

A part of her wanted to ignore the message, to pretend she'd never heard from the mysterious correspondent. But she craved answers. Burying one's head in the sand was never a successful survival strategy.

Amy stepped toward her pouch as though approaching a venomous snake. She retrieved the phone and swiped the screen with her thumb.

This message was different. The anonymous sender had reused the number of the previous text. What did that mean?

She held her breath and viewed the new message. Six words appeared on the display.

I couldn't let him hurt you.

The text froze the blood in her veins. Her stalker had left no room for doubt. The person behind this message had murdered Josh to protect her.

Amy squirmed. Josh had tried to blackmail her. He'd taken advantage of her weakness in the sleaziest way. She'd desperately needed to escape him. But she hadn't wanted him dead.

Why is he telling me this? What does he want from me—a thank you?

Amy dropped the phone on the table and stepped away. *Never. I'll never thank you.* Amy was neither a murderer nor an accomplice. She'd never condone that hateful crime.

But she had, hadn't she? On the subway, after the adrenaline rush of the death and police investigation had run its course, a tiny, secret part of her had sighed with relief. The desire to give thanks had surfaced within her. Had the stalker accessed the innermost recesses of her soul?

She grabbed her phone again and studied the messages for hidden demands. *You deserve better. Stay calm. You've got this. You look sad. I couldn't let him hurt you.* The stalker's tone wasn't threatening. The words were supportive. Nurturing. He sounded like a motivational coach, not a homicidal creep.

Was the murderer simply trying to console her? *Don't be sad about his death. Josh got what he deserved for picking on you.* Maybe there was no catch? *Dream on, Amy.* In real life there were no free lunches. The piper had eliminated a rat from her life. One day, he'd call in the favor.

But who was the sender, and how did he know Josh had threatened her? Nobody had hovered near his office either before or after their meeting. Was the killer familiar with her boss's reputation?

The second text had arrived during her police interview. Had the sender seen her sitting with the detectives?

A realization solidified in her brain. *The stalker works at Wesner & Morgan.* Only employees knew about Josh's former assistants, his death, and Amy's date with the police officers.

But who could it be? Besides Josh, Amy had interacted with only a handful of the agency's payroll: Debbie, Eddie, Tanesha, and Beth. None of them seemed like cold-blooded killers. Had someone else been watching her from the shadows?

Why only make contact now? And why subject her to this one-way conversation?

A second realization bloomed. Her stalker had killed for her. But what did he know about Amy? Could he trust her? What if she told the police? His first two messages had tested her loyalty. He'd used vague language and garbage phone numbers. The texts could never incriminate him if she proved unfaithful.

But Amy had told nobody about the messages, not even the detectives. She'd taken one step toward the killer, and now he'd responded in kind. This number was unlike the others. He'd used it twice. This number was real.

Amy stared at the phone and steadied her breathing. A self-righteous rage empowered her. She'd end this right now.

She dialed the sender's number and pressed the phone to her ear. *Trust me now? Want my gratitude? Come and get it.*

The call rang. The phone's metal casing trembled in her grasp. "Come on. Pick up."

Enough hiding behind text messages. Amy had never desired Josh's death. She wanted no part in murder. Once she learned her stalker's identity, she'd send the detectives an anonymous tip-off. No psychopath would drag her down a criminal sinkhole ever again.

A woman answered the call. "Hello!"

The voice threw Amy off-balance for a split second.

"The number you have dialed is unavailable. Please try again later."

The lifeless monotone did not belong to her secret helper. The stalker had screened her call.

Amy paced the room. The sender had chickened out. Had he guessed her true intentions? What had she expected—that he'd hand over his social security number?

"Fine. Don't speak to me. I can text, too."

Amy typed her message. "Who are you?"

She hit Send.

This time, her gamble didn't fail. Three dots danced beneath the message list. The killer was composing a response.

The phone jittered twice as the new message arrived. Her secret admirer had replied with two words.

Amy's heart skipped a beat. Terror chilled her body. Amy had been wrong. The killer didn't work for Wesner & Morgan. She'd uncovered the stalker's identity, and now she wished she hadn't. The two words could mean only one thing. Her worst nightmare had come true.

Chapter 6

*A*my wheeled her suitcase to the doorway of the apartment and pressed the buzzer. A tailwind of good vibes had carried her there. She stood on the threshold of a new chapter in her life. But with change—even for the better—came uncertainty. Was she asking too much?

Leo Santiago answered the door in a tank top that showed off his tats.

He glanced at the bag. "Is that it? This is all your stuff?"

Amy shrugged. "I'm a simple girl with simple needs. Low maintenance. You don't have to splurge on me."

Leo grinned. "I want to splurge on you, babe."

That's my Leo. Her boyfriend had a generous heart.

He kissed her and held her tight. Amy melted in his arms. She ran her fingers over the solid curves of his muscular abdomen. The generous heart wasn't the only thing she liked about him. Leo was a gentle lover and attentive friend. The tattoos and tank tops didn't fool her. Despite the bad-boy act, her boyfriend was a romantic. But was she taking advantage of him?

Amy disengaged from his body. "Are you sure about this?"

"Hundred percent, babe." He waved a hand at the apartment behind him. "But this place is temporary. One day, I'll buy us a fancy house in a good neighborhood. With a garden and swings."

Amy raised her eyebrow with amusement. "Swings?"

"For our kids."

She giggled. "One step at a time, Leo."

He wheeled her bag inside. "I'll help you get undressed—I mean, unpacked."

She slapped his bicep playfully and followed him into the bedroom. Their bedroom.

At long last, Amy had escaped the Underhills. Moving houses was second nature. She'd switched orphanages and foster homes every other year. She didn't get sentimental about places or possessions.

Leo hefted her suitcase onto the king-size bed, sat beside it, and pulled Amy toward him. He snuggled her breasts and squeezed her behind. Amy closed her eyes and groaned with pleasure. Leo knew how to get her juices flowing. She wanted nothing better than to climb onto him and spend the day in bed together.

She kissed his head and pushed him away. "I've got to study."

Leo pouted. "All work and no play?"

She stroked his hair. "I've got an exam tomorrow, remember?"

Amy had worked hard for her place in med school, and she wasn't about to drop the ball.

He sighed. The generous heart won out again. "Okay. Okay. Make love to your books instead."

"Thank you."

Amy unzipped the suitcase and extracted her anatomy textbooks and notepads. Moving in with Leo wasn't all about romance. She had a better chance of building a future as a pediatric surgeon without her foster father groping her body.

A framed photograph lay on top of her clothes.

Leo followed her gaze. "Are those your folks?" His tone had become solemn.

"Yeah."

"May I?"

"Sure." She handed him the photo.

He gazed at the family portrait and grinned. "You've got your mother's smile and your dad's eyes."

A ball of powerful emotion lodged in Amy's throat. "Yeah."

"You look so young. When was this taken?"

"Ten years ago. A few months before the accident."

The accident. *The words made her parents' sudden deaths sound less devastating.* No big deal. It was just an accident. *Amy had stopped smiling that terrible day...until she'd met Leo.*

In the photo, a young boy with curly hair hugged Amy.

Leo traced the curve of the boy's smiling face with his finger. "So this is Daniel."

Amy nodded. "He's sixteen now."

She'd met Leo a month ago and wasn't sure how Daniel would react to the new man in her life. Her conscience needled her. One day, she'd explain why she'd left their foster family. Would he understand?

"He's the reason I'm at college."

"Your brother?"

She nodded. "I'll be able to support him and put him through college, too."

Leo gazed at her. "You're amazing."

She was working two jobs to pay off her student loans, but she wouldn't leave her little brother behind.

Leo's eyes sparkled. "Don't worry about money, babe. I'll provide for you both."

She smiled. "Is that right?"

Leo dabbled in many small-scale business ventures. But judging by his apartment and ancient, beat-up Volkswagen, he hadn't hit the jackpot yet.

"I told you. This is temporary. I'm working on something big. Soon, we'll be drowning in money."

Amy had never asked for riches or fame, only a safe, quiet corner of the world to share with the people she loved.

She kissed his forehead. "That's my dreamer."

"I ain't dreaming, babe. This is for real."

"I know."

Amy tucked her study materials under her arm. "Time to hit the books."

She settled on the living room couch. Leo's onto something big. *One day, they wouldn't need to hustle to get by. Maybe she'd devote her energies to medical research once she'd completed her studies? Together, they'd make a difference in the world. The sunny optimism she'd known before her parents' death warmed her again. Her life had taken a turn for the better.*

Chapter 7

Amy stared bleary-eyed at her computer monitor early Tuesday morning. She paged through the Wesner & Morgan employee directory. Ten profile photos loaded on the screen. None of them matched Beanie Man, Hoodie, or any of the other subway travelers. *Tell me it's one of them. Please let it be a stranger!* She was grasping at straws. But last night, the stalker's final text message had delivered a devastating revelation—one she still refused to accept.

"Who are you?" Amy had asked, and the stalker's two-word answer had paralyzed her with dread.

Your BFF.

Only one person had ever claimed that title, and he was not her "best friend forever." She'd spent the past four years running from him.

Amy had curled up on her couch in terror. Her "friend" wasn't above stalking a woman—or murder. She knew that for a fact. The fateful day had arrived. He'd found her. But why had he killed Josh? Did he know where she lived? Would he break down the door and slaughter her, too?

No! It can't be him.

She'd analyzed the stalker's messages again, searching for contradictory evidence.

You look sad. He'd been watching her at the subway platform. But she'd spotted no familiar faces.

I couldn't let him hurt you. He knew Josh had threatened her. The sender must be a Wesner & Morgan employee.

Her panic had eased slightly. Her deadly BFF wasn't her stalker. Amy would have noticed him at work or at the subway.

She microwaved a frozen lasagna for dinner.

Her violent past hadn't caught up with her. No. This stalker was a random stranger. Her imagination had run away with her. The word BFF meant nothing. Everybody used it. This killer might have wasted her boss, but he meant her no harm.

She brushed her teeth, hid a kitchen knife underneath her pillow, and lay awake in bed.

A flaw appeared in her assumptions. The killer from her former life didn't work for Wesner & Morgan. But could he still have sent the messages? Had he spied on Amy through the agency's glass walls and windows? Her skin crawled. What were the odds that *two* unrelated psychopathic murderers pursued her?

The panic returned, banishing sleep from her eyes. *It's him. It must be.* She gripped the handle of the knife. Had he followed her home? Would he attack her tonight? No kitchen knife would save her from his wrath.

More questions tortured her. How had he found her? She'd sacrificed so much to remain undetected. Why had he murdered Josh? Why the messages? Was he toying with her? Did he derive sadistic pleasure from controlling her?

At six AM, she packed a travel bag and dressed for work. She headed downtown, glancing over her shoulder every few steps. The lights were on at Wesner & Morgan, but few employees had hit the office yet.

Amy settled at her desk and browsed the employee website. If one of the subway travelers appeared in the agency's directory, she'd have her answer. *Please let him be here.* The long shot was her only hope of identifying her stalker and calming her nerves.

She yawned and clicked Next. A fresh batch of profile photos filled the display. *Still nothing.*

Next. She had to work fast. Keyboards clattered softly down the corridor. People were arriving at the office. Any moment now, she'd lose her access to the agency's network along with her job.

Next. The page of results contained only three photos. She'd reached the end of the directory. Her quest had failed. Her stalker didn't work at Wesner & Morgan. But was Josh's murderer the shadowy killer from her past?

"Lisa?" a man said.

Mark Davis stood in the doorway of his office. "Do you have a minute?"

He'd spoken to her. His voice was deep and soothing. She could listen to that baritone all day...and all night. But his sudden interest in her existence meant one thing. *Time's up.* Had management told him to fire her?

Amy swallowed hard. "Sure."

She approached Mark and entered his office, savoring her last moments as a Wesner & Morgan employee.

"Please have a seat."

Amy complied, and he closed the door behind her. She searched for an upbeat thought. *At least now he knows my name.* Not that it mattered. After today, she'd probably never see him again.

Mark perched on the edge of his desk and clasped his hands. "I wanted to say how sorry I am. Josh's sudden passing must have been very disturbing for you."

"Yes, it was."

He smiled grimly. "You're new in town. If you want to talk about it, I'm here for you."

Amy blinked at him. "Thank you."

Her skin tingled. Her name wasn't all he knew about her. Had the death of her boss aroused his curiosity, or had she caught his eye from the start? A girlish hope nestled in her heart. Was a completely different topic on his mind? He'd spoken gently and expressed his concern for her. Had he called her over to fire her or to ask her out?

He cleared his throat. "With Josh gone, you're probably wondering about your future at Wesner and Morgan."

Amy blushed with embarrassment. *Of course, this is about work.*
Her boss had fallen to his death yesterday. Nobody was thinking
of romance. *What's the matter with you?*

Thankfully, Mark didn't appear to notice her inner turmoil. "I
spoke with Mr. Wesner last night, and he agreed you should stay
on."

Her mouth dropped open.

Mark seemed to interpret her silence as hesitation. "If you still
want the job."

"Yes. I do. But who will I work for?"

"We'll hire another executive. Until then, you'll work under
me."

She stared at him. The turn of events had left her speechless
again. Amy could stay at Wesner & Morgan. She'd keep her apartment, too. But Mark's choice of wording had winded her a second
time. *You'll work under me.* She liked the sound of that. Had he
selected the double entendre on purpose?

He curled his lips into a smile. "Would you like that?"

She averted her gaze. Her cheeks were on fire. "Yes. I don't know
what to say. Actually, I do. Thank you." She rose to her feet and
offered her hand. "Thank you, Mr. Davis. This means a lot to me."
Her voice sounded too formal and awkward to her own ears. Was
she overcompensating for her dirty thoughts? She wanted to kick
herself.

He shook her hand. His touch was warm, his grip firm.

Mark held on to her hand. "There's one condition."

She froze again. Josh had tried to extort sexual acts for his silence.
Was Mark a secret pervert, too?

He grinned. "You have to call me Mark."

She released her pent-up breath. "Okay, Mark. You won't regret
this."

He let go of her hand. "I know."

She turned to go, then remembered the favor she needed. "There's one thing..."

Amy shut her mouth in time. *Not him.* Asking Josh to arrange payment in cash had led him to dig into her past. *Don't repeat that mistake.*

Mark raised his eyebrow. "Yeah?"

Amy grinned. "It's nothing. Forget about it."

He smiled at her quizzically. "Okay."

Amy left his office before she could shove her foot in her mouth again. She marched down the corridor with a spring in her step. *He likes me!* Mark had ensured she'd stayed at the company. Lisa Smith had received a second chance at the agency, and this time, she'd be more careful.

Seconds later, she'd left the office hubbub of Client Servicing for the silent tomb of Finance. Offices lined the passage of white plaster.

Amy knocked twice on the door labeled Bethany Lewis, Bookkeeper.

"Enter," Beth said in a cheerful singsong.

She glowed with joy when Amy appeared on the threshold. "Lisa! Come on in."

Beth's office was far smaller than Mark's and filled with plants. Ferns and Ivy climbed tall rods from garden pots along the wall. Nature prints adorned the walls: tall, chiseled islands rising from turquoise oceans, and sun-drenched beaches of white sand and palm trees. The vibrant scenery clashed with the sterile corporate decor of the other offices.

Amy settled on the vacant chair. "I love what you've done to the place."

"Thank you! We spend most of our lives at work. Might as well feel at home."

The bookkeeper offered Amy a jumbo bag of Lays potato chips she'd been hiding in a drawer. "Salt and vinegar?"

"No, thanks."

Beth shrugged and dug her hand into the bag. "I'm hooked."

Amy pointed at the nature prints on the walls. "Did you take these?"

"Me? Oh, no! I never go anywhere. But a girl can dream, right? Have you heard the good news?"

"What good news?"

"Didn't Mark tell you? You'll be working with him now."

Amy almost choked. "Right! Yes. Amazing news. I was sure they'd sack me after yesterday. How did you know?"

"Everything goes through finance, honey. We know everything about everyone. I'm so glad they've kept you. We need more good people here." She lowered her voice. "Some of the others are true psychos. But don't get me started about HR. Between you and me, Josh wasn't a saint either. I shouldn't speak ill of the dead, but his female assistants never lasted—if you know what I mean. They ran for the hills, every last one. Ha! Look at me, blabbering away. You didn't come here to shoot the breeze. Tell me, Lisa, how can I help you?"

Beth had cut to the chase, and Amy followed her direct approach.

"I need to get paid in cash."

"Cash?"

Beth studied her with renewed interest. Was she searching for dilated pupils and needle marks? Only addicts demanded cash. Addicts and criminals. Amy was neither. But the truth was a bottomless pit that might swallow her and the bookkeeper whole.

Amy shrugged with girlish embarrassment. "I have a phobia of banks."

The line had worked on male bean counters in the past. But would her quirky female charms fall flat on this bookkeeper?

The plump woman poked Amy's forearm. "Me, too! I hate them. Banks are so impersonal and intimidating. Thank the gods for the Internet. I haven't set foot in a bank in years. But I wish

you'd told me earlier. We don't usually carry large amounts of cash.
Right! Let's see what we can do."

She rubbed her hands together. The opportunity to help Amy
animated her. Beth studied her computer screen and fired off a
rapid series of mouse clicks.

She beamed at Amy. "We're in luck! Wait here."

The bookkeeper launched from her seat and left the room, leaving her guest alone.

Amy checked her phone. *No new messages.* Her excitement over
her continued employment had distracted her from a stark reality.
A cold-blooded killer was stalking her. Her life was in jeopardy.

Beth returned, shut the door, and dropped an unlabeled white
envelope on the desk. She flopped into her chair and grinned mischievously. "Feels criminal, doesn't it?"

The bookkeeper seemed to relish the idea. Handing over a large
amount of cash was probably the closest she'd ever come to illegal
activity in her life. But Amy had found nothing romantic about
living on the lawless fringes of society.

She accepted the envelope and its reassuring wad of banknotes.
"Thank you, Beth."

"You're welcome, Lisa."

Amy grinned playfully. "Hmm. Where to hide it—bra or
panties?"

The bookkeeper rubbed her chin. "Go with the bra. A bulge
down there will attract the wrong kind of attention."

Amy giggled. "I think I'll just hold it in my hand."

Beth winked. "Hiding in plain sight? I like it."

Amy strolled back to her cubicle. She had rent money and funds
for her secret project. But more than that, she'd found two more
allies: Mark and Beth. The dark clouds of loneliness parted.

Tanesha was waiting for her in the cubicle. She folded her arms
when Amy returned. *Uh-oh. This looks like trouble.*

Amy smiled. "Good morning, Tanesha."

The assistant scowled. "I know what you're trying to do."

Tanesha always seemed to have a stick up her butt, but this morning her tone was openly aggressive.

Instinctively, Amy hid the envelope behind her back. "What are you talking about?"

"Don't deny it. I saw you getting cozy with Mark."

Tanesha had witnessed their chat in his office. Did she think Amy was trying to steal her job?

The assistant leaned closer. "I've worked hard to get here and even harder to stay. One day, I'll make partner, and no small-ass little white girl is going to take that from me."

Amy gasped. "You've got this wrong. Mark invited me—"

"Save it! I'm onto you, Lisa Smith. You better watch your back."

Chapter 8

A sea of humanity surged around Amy as she hurried down Broadway. She placed a protective hand on her pouch. Today, she was a pickpocket's bonanza. Amy wouldn't normally carry a thick wad of cash around Midtown. But one thing alone had enabled her to survive these past four years. The special project gave her suffering a purpose. She had to see her private mission through, whatever the risks.

She glanced over her shoulder. Nobody seemed to notice her, but still she felt the press of watchful eyes. *Is that all in my head? I hope so.* If her BFF followed her movements today, she might lose something far more valuable to her than the lump sum in her bag or even her life.

Tanesha's threat rang in her ears. *I'm onto you, Lisa Smith.*

Amy's secretive ways drew negativity. Coworkers dismissed her as antisocial and let her be. She'd welcomed that reaction. But Tanesha had mistaken her for a rival. She'd be trouble.

An ironic laugh escaped Amy's lips. *I'm not climbing the corporate ladder.* She'd worked hard to *avoid* standing out. But Tanesha wouldn't believe her, and her jealousy might drive her to dig deeper into Amy's past.

Amy halted at a red light and shot another quick look behind her. If the black assistant was tailing her, she'd hidden well.

The light turned green. Amy marched on until she arrived at the United States Postal Service. This branch wasn't the closest to Wesner & Morgan. She'd purposefully walked an extra quarter mile to avoid bumping into people from work.

Three people waited in the line. She stepped behind Number Three, a young black man with dreadlocks. *You're almost there.*

A wave of déjà vu washed over her. She'd visited post offices countless times. The fortnightly ritual was the only consistent milestone in her fugitive life. Like a devoted pagan, she offered her sacrifice at regular intervals, each time expecting the fickle gods to strike her down with a bolt of lightning.

The line progressed quickly. Amy approached a vacant service window and spoke through the holes of the reinforced glass divider.

"I need to transfer cash."

The attendant smiled at her over the black-rimmed glasses that sat on the edge of her nose. She was young, probably fresh out of high school. The job hadn't jaded her yet.

"Cash?"

"Yes."

She pulled half the money from the envelope and dropped the crisp bills into the secured service tray. The attendant shifted the tray toward her and slipped the cash into a counting machine.

"Who's the recipient?"

Amy recited the account details by heart. She'd destroyed her only written record of the numbers. Those details could lead back to the recipient and her old identity. Amy had to avoid exposing him at all costs.

"And who is the sender?"

Amy muttered her name, her real name.

The attendant cupped her ear. "Excuse me?"

"Amy Walker."

She looked behind her. Two other customers waited behind her, both strangers. Nobody she knew had overheard her true identity.

The attendant pecked at her keyboard to process the transfer. The parting down the crown of her head exposed the roots of her hair. Decades from now, the follicles would thin and turn gray. Her smile would fade. Would Amy be here, too, transferring money, hoping to launch a little warmth into the black, uncaring void?

"Do you want to add a message?"

The question choked Amy up. Of course she *wanted* to add a message. *How are you, Daniel? How's college?* Her brother would be in his second year by now. If only she could see him again, hug him, and be a part of his life. *You can't possibly understand why I had to leave. But can you forgive me? Are you even still alive?*

The attendant gazed at her. "Ma'am? Do you want to add a message?"

Amy steadied her voice. "No."

The woman hit a key with a flourish and grinned. "Can I help you with anything else?"

Amy shook her head and made for the exit. Her pouch had grown lighter, her heart heavier.

She trudged down the Midtown street. *Mission accomplished.* She had a two-week breather until the next payment. If Tanesha's bark was worse than her bite, Amy could roll along her current path indefinitely.

Her future unfurled before her...and chilled her to the bone. *Keep your head down. Collect your paycheck. Repeat.* Was there no way out of this recurring nightmare? Would she ever know a life without fear? Amy knew the answer. So long as her BFF drew breath, no, she wouldn't. She'd run and hide. The alternative was a brutal death. Judging by the recent text messages, that alternative stepped closer every day.

Long into her exile, optimistic thoughts had visited her. *Is he dead? Am I running from a ghost?* How would she know? She'd created a Google Alert for his name but received no notification of his arrest or demise. Small-time criminals didn't make the news. She couldn't risk more active tracking measures. If they led him back to her, the years of underground living would go up in smoke along with her soul.

Should she call the number again to find her answer?

No. Don't get careless. Never let down your guard. Daniel was depending on her. Curiosity, like despair, would only get her killed.

Amy slowed down. Lost in thought, she'd traveled too far. She doubled back and almost collided with a familiar pencil mustache.

"Eddie! Geez, I almost walked right into you. What are you doing here?"

Her question was ridiculous—he had every right to be there, just like her—but the glimmer of guilty panic in his eyes strengthened her suspicions.

Eddie rubbed his arm, as though unsure what to do with his hands. "Lisa, I was hoping I'd see you."

Amy studied him, searching his body language for the truth. Had he followed her? Did Eddie know about the transfer? *What does he want from me?*

"What?"

"I-I thought we could get a bite to eat."

Eddie wasn't stalking her. He wanted a lunch date.

Amy sighed. "I'm going to grab a quick sandwich."

He flashed his stupid grin. "I know the perfect place. It's on our way back to work. Best wieners in New York City. You have to try them."

Amy prepared a mental list of excuses. But she'd skipped breakfast and was running on fumes. Her stomach decided for her.

"Okay."

Eddie led the way but didn't seem to be in a rush. "You're from out of town, right?"

"Maybe?"

He grinned. "Always so mysterious. I couldn't find you on Instagram or TikTok. Why the secrecy, Lisa?"

She tensed her shoulders involuntarily. Eddie had searched for her on social media, and now he was prying into her personal life. Why had she accepted his lunch offer?

She snapped at him, "I value my privacy."

"It's okay. I respect that." He cleared his throat. "There are so many good joints I could show you here."

They walked in silence. She avoided his gaze.

Amy's conscience acted up again. Eddie had defended her at work yesterday. He'd offered her friendship and company. In return, she'd given him the cold shoulder because she *thought* he'd followed her. *Don't be such a hard-ass. You're staying on at Wesner & Morgan, remember? You'll never make friends like this.*

Amy swallowed her reservations. "Have you lived here long?"

"All my life. The city's a part of me—like a brother."

She raised an eyebrow. "Manhattan is your family?"

He chuckled. "Cities are living creatures, too."

Amy didn't hide her skepticism. "Really?"

"Sure they are. They grow and change. Sometimes, they die." He pointed at the skyscrapers ahead. "Take Times Square, for example. Bright lights. Big screens. Tourists. But in the seventies, Times Square was a hive of sex shops and peep shows. The hookers lived in fear of serial killers. Nasty time to be here."

The talk of killers dulled Amy's desire for conversation.

Eddie seemed to notice her expression. "I'm sorry. I shouldn't have mentioned that. Not after yesterday."

She softened. "It's okay, Eddie. Life goes on."

They reached a red-and-yellow hot dog cart, and the aromas of sizzling meat and fresh buns made her mouth water. Amy ordered a double hot dog with extra mustard and a diet soda. She sank her teeth into the meal and moaned with pleasure.

Eddie brightened. "What did I say? Best wieners in New York City. Am I right or what? Tell her I'm right, Mack."

The vendor, a chubby man with salt-and-pepper curls, chortled. "The check's in the mail, Eddie."

They laughed.

She and Eddie strolled through Times Square as they ate. An enormous lion's head peered down at them from an electronic billboard. The advertisement for *The Lion King* reminded Amy what Eddie had said about human predators.

"Serial killers, huh?"

Eddie nodded toward a high-end sneaker store. "The Travel Inn used to be over there. In nineteen seventy-nine, somebody set a room on fire. The police found the charred remains of two women. They called him The Torso Killer because—"

Amy raised her hand for him to stop. "I can guess."

"Sorry. Too much information."

She evicted visions of dismembered female bodies from her mind. "Did they ever catch the guy?"

"Yeah. Richard Cottingham. He killed at least eleven women and girls here. Now he's rotting in a New Jersey prison."

Amy found comfort in that fact. "Maybe there is justice in the world."

Eddie shrugged. "Not for everybody. One of them is still unidentified."

They munched their hot dogs in gloomy silence.

Eddie sipped his soda. "Speaking of serial killers, Josh Wesner isn't the only person who died suddenly at Wesner and Morgan."

Amy straightened. "What happened?"

"Two years ago, Peter Morgan died, too."

"Morgan. As in Wesner and Morgan?"

Eddie folded his empty hot dog wrapper. "Mm-hm. Peter Morgan was a founding member of the agency but much younger than Harry Wesner. He was in his forties when he died."

"What killed him?"

"Corned beef on rye. Choked on his lunch at his desk. There were some nasty rumors at the time."

Eddie grinned. He was teasing her, feeding her gossip in dribs and drabs, and forcing her to ask for more.

"What rumors?"

"Josh Wesner resented Morgan's hold on the company, which he considered his birthright. Word on the street was Josh poisoned him and moved into his corner office."

Amy's jaw dropped. "Morgan died in Josh's office? Geez."

Josh had tried to extort sexual favors. Had he poisoned a rival partner, too?

Eddie chuckled. "I know. Maybe Peter Morgan's ghost pushed him out the window?"

Amy's brain processed the information. Eddie was kidding around, but he'd supported Amy's working theory. Josh hadn't killed himself. Someone had murdered him. But ghosts didn't shove people out of windows. They didn't send text messages either. People did, and this killer had attacked Josh in his office under the noses of the other employees.

She gazed at Eddie and his pencil mustache. His grin no longer seemed stupid but sinister. Two men had died mysteriously in Josh's office, two years apart. If the deaths were connected, they probably had nothing to do with her past. An invisible weight lifted from her shoulders. Her old BFF hadn't caught up with her. She'd stumbled into the crosshairs of another killer. But who was the anonymous sender? And if her secret admirer didn't intend to harm her, what did he want?

Chapter 9

*A*my stared into the empty sugar jar and swore under her breath. *The white ceramic container had hidden two hundred dollars. She resisted the urge to throw the jar across the kitchen and smash her boyfriend's TV. He'd found their grocery money again.*

"Leo. Leo!"

She stomped across the apartment, her blood boiling. "Don't worry about money, babe," *he'd told her.* "I'll provide for you." *But Amy worried about money all right, and Leo only provided excuses.*

Leo wasn't in the bedroom either.

"Where are you?" *She'd kill him when he got home.*

Amy slumped on the bed and cradled her head in her hands. This is your own fault. *She hadn't rushed into the relationship blindly. She'd been careful. Amy had searched for obvious warning signs: alcohol, drugs, and controlling behavior.*

Gambling addictions were harder to spot. What was it this time? Fantasy football? Texas hold 'em?

Leo had let her down...again. Amy didn't have the time or the disposable income for this. She had to study and build a future. Daniel was depending on her, too. But if she left Leo tonight, where would she sleep? Crawling back to the Underhills wasn't an option.

Amy inhaled a deep breath. Don't be hasty. Let things be until you find another place. *She couldn't crash on a friend's couch. Between Leo and her overloaded work schedule, she'd had no spare time to build relationships with her fellow students.*

The front door opened and closed.

Amy rose to her feet. Calm down. *Yelling at him hadn't worked before. She needed a new strategy. She'd explain the stakes. If he cared about her, he'd agree to therapy. Failing that, she'd issue an ultimatum. If the threat of losing her didn't wake him up, she'd have to move on.*

Confident in her new plan, Amy exited the bedroom...and froze. A wiry man in a black t-shirt stood in the living room. Taller than Leo, the stranger had the shaved temples and braided blond hair of a Viking raider, as though he had traveled through time to rape and pillage.

He fixed her with his icy blue eyes. "Who are you?" *He spoke with a strong cockney accent.*

His question enraged her. The Brit had invaded her home, and he had the nerve to ask her who she was?

"I live here."

He scoffed. "You're Leo's girlfriend?"

The intruder swaggered toward her and scanned her body with his predatory gaze. A large hunting knife swung in a leather scabbard at the belt of his faded jeans.

"Aren't you a pretty thing?"

Amy stiffened with fear. Leo acted tough, but this man was the real deal—a truly evil man.

The stranger stopped inches from her, breaching her personal space. He reeked of Old Spice and pressed his hand to the wall, trapping her with his arm.

"Don't worry, love. I don't bite. Unless you're into that."

Amy quaked. Would the raider force himself on her? Her anger at her boyfriend evaporated. Come home, Leo. Please! Make him leave.

The stranger dropped his arm and straightened. "Where are my manners? I haven't introduced myself." *He bowed his head and waved his hand with a flourish.* "Steve Hamlin, at your service. My friends call me The Hammer."

Amy released her pent-up breath. He wouldn't attack her. But what did he want, and how was Leo mixed up with him?

Steve "The Hammer" Hamlin raised his eyebrows. "And you are?"

"Amy."

He flashed a cruel, toothy smile. "I have a good feeling about us, Amy." He traced her cheek with his rough fingers.

She flinched.

"You and I are going to be the best of friends. What do you Americans call it? Oh, yes. Best friends forever.*"*

Chapter 10

Wednesday afternoon, Brandon glanced at the cell phone on his desk in the NYPD squad room. No missed calls. No new messages. He clicked through the murder book of a fresh homicide on his computer. Garbage collectors had stumbled upon a trash bag of human body parts. Brandon stifled a yawn. Crime scene carnage no longer induced horror, only professional curiosity. *Organized crime, probably. The feds will want this one.* His thoughts drifted back to Lisa Smith. Her unfathomable dark eyes refused to leave his head. Not even a sack of severed limbs could distract him from the memory of her hypnotic gaze. *What's gotten into you?*

He checked his phone again. Two days had passed since their first meeting, and like an addict, he itched for another fix. He willed the attractive advertising assistant to contact him. Brandon would take anything: a clue, a question, a confession—even a wrong number. He didn't care. So long as he heard from her again.

I'd stay away from her if I were you. Mindy was right. Lisa's beauty was dangerous. Ten minutes in her presence had bewitched him for days. A second meeting would enchant him forever.

Brandon shook his head free of obsessive thoughts. *She's only a human being, not a sorceress.* He was perfectly capable of interacting with a gorgeous woman without falling to pieces.

He clicked to the next crime scene photo. The Wesner case was closing. He should call Lisa to see how she was holding up. Wasn't that his responsibility—to serve and protect? A polite and professional inquiry would prove he hadn't lost his mind.

Mindy hunched over the desk opposite him. She chewed gum and clicked her mouse rapidly.

"Brand?"

"Mm-hm."

"Have you read the ME's report on Wesner?"

"When did it get in?"

"A minute ago."

He searched his work email for the link to the document. "Anything interesting?"

"Plenty. Start with the cause of death."

Brandon opened the PDF, read the ME's verdict, and swore. "Sarge won't like this."

He was right.

"*Asphyxiation?*" Sergeant Adrian Blank repeated the word, ten minutes later.

Brandon and Mindy stood by his desk at the other end of the squad room, and he scowled as though they'd peed in his beer.

"Joshua Wesner fell from the fortieth floor. The autopsy should indicate polytrauma."

Mindy shrugged. "That's what we thought, too. But corpses don't lie. There's visceral congestion, petechial hemorrhages of the conjunctivae, and—"

Sarge cut her off. "The impact can explain those, too. You saw the body. We're talking shattered bones and a crushed skull."

She handed him a printout of an autopsy photo, a closeup of the decedent's neck. "The ligature marks match his necktie. He was dead before he hit the sidewalk. There's no way he jumped out that window."

Their boss ran his hand over his bald head. "So much for suicide. Who was the last to see him alive?"

"The assistant, Lisa Smith."

"The pretty one?"

Sarge had noticed her, too. Adrenaline tore into Brandon's bloodstream. Their homicide investigation would focus on her now. Lisa couldn't have strangled her boss. She'd been on the sidewalk at the time of his death. But had she played a role in the murder?

Mandy handed him another printed photo. "There's more. Wesner's trousers were soaked at the crotch."

Sarge huffed. "Peed himself?"

"No, sir. Coffee. Ms. Smith told us she dropped his Starbucks order and went out to get more. She didn't mention she'd emptied the first cup on her boss's lap. Maybe she helped him out of the window, too?"

Their boss frowned. "Wesner was taller and heavier than her. She couldn't overpower him."

"She didn't have to. Toxicology found Flunitrazepam in his bloodstream."

Sarge grunted. "Rohypnol, the date rape drug. That gives us means and opportunity. All we need is motive."

Brandon could remain silent no longer. "This is all hypothetical. Ms. Smith was downstairs when Wesner hit the sidewalk. She couldn't have killed him."

Their boss frowned. "Does the agency's CCTV corroborate her story?"

Mandy said, "They haven't sent it over yet. I'll follow up. But even if we place her outside at that moment, it doesn't matter. The blade of Wesner's necktie showed signs of tearing inconsistent with his fall, and fibers collected near his office window match the tie."

Sarge rubbed his chin. "She suspended him from the window using his tie, both suffocating him and giving her time to create an alibi before the fabric tore under his weight."

Mindy beamed. "Exactly."

Brandon's mouth dried up. The scenario seemed bizarre but accounted for all the facts. The net was closing around Lisa. *This must be a mistake. She's no murderer.*

He spoke up again. "Sarge, about the means. Rohypnol isn't legally available in the US. We'd have to prove she had access to the drug."

Mindy grinned. "Unless we find some at her place."

"We don't have enough meat for a search warrant. No judge will give us probable cause. Tell her, Sarge."

Sarge gazed at his warring detectives with mild amusement.

"Scott, what about the coffee? She could have poured it down the drain and gotten rid of the evidence. Why the mess?"

Brandon relaxed. Their boss had taken his side and played Devil's advocate.

Mindy folded her arms. "I figure Wesner dropped the cup when the Rohypnol kicked in, soiling his fancy suit. Smith hooked his tie on the window lock, shoved his body outside, and ran downstairs."

Mindy smirked at Brandon. She'd won.

Sarge eyed him. "What do you think?"

Brandon shook his head. "It sounds far-fetched to me. Coworkers saw her leave twenty minutes earlier. Somebody would have noticed a man dangling from the window."

Their boss frowned. "People often get the times wrong. Twenty minutes might be much less. Have the Starbucks cup tested for residue, too. That'll clear things up."

Mindy shook her head. "Forensics found no Starbucks cups in the office. Ms. Smith said she cleaned up the spill. Looks like she took out the trash on her way down, too." She turned to Brandon. "Still think she's innocent?"

He shifted on his feet. The net tightened further. There had to be more holes in Mindy's theory. *Lisa isn't a killer.*

"What about the coffee?"

Sarge squinted at him. "We've just been through that."

"I mean the coffee content. Forensics found milk and coffee on his trousers, right? Did they find traces of Rohypnol, too?"

Mandy's victorious grin faded. "No. I'll double-check. But who said she spiked his coffee? She could have handed him a glass of water, too."

The enthusiasm had drained from her voice. Brandon had found a fatal flaw in her theory, and she knew it.

Sarge smiled at them. Why was he smiling?

"Maybe there's a third angle?"

Brandon took the bait. "What do you mean?"

"Suicide and murder aren't the only options. What if his death was an accident?"

Mindy snorted. "'Sorry, Officer, I didn't intend to kill him?'"

"Not exactly. Rohypnol is a party drug, too. Maybe Wesner popped a few pills to lower his inhibitions and choked himself with his tie?"

She sniggered. "You're kidding, right? Why on earth would he do that?"

Brandon smiled, too, as understanding dawned.

Mindy scowled at the two grinning men. "What's so funny?"

He eyed his boss.

Sarge chickened out. "All yours, Cooper."

Brandon cleared his throat. "Oxygen deprivation can cause...sexual arousal."

Her mouth dropped open. "You mean, he was..." She pumped her hand in a masturbatory movement.

Sarge helped him out. "Autoerotic asphyxiation results in hundreds of accidental deaths every year, and they're often mistaken for suicides."

Mindy wrinkled her nose. "Josh Wesner, you sick, sick puppy. Now we know why he closed his blinds. But wouldn't we have found him, you know, exposed?"

"Not necessarily."

She grunted. "So Josh jammed his tie in the window and slipped to the floor. He hanged himself by mistake. Smith played no part in it."

They'd done it. They had painted Josh Wesner's death scene in all its deviant color.

Mindy placed her hands on her hips. "Wait a second. If Wesner hanged himself from the window, he would have passed out in his office. How did he get outside?"

Brandon deflated. She was right. Accidental suffocation would have incapacitated Wesner. But Sarge's smile widened, and all at once the veil lifted on the investigative masterpiece.

"We're both right," Brandon blurted out.

Sarge nodded slowly. He was on the right track. Completing the picture required only a few extra brushstrokes.

Mindy pouted. "Hello? Feeling a little left out here."

Brandon explained, and a mischievous grin spread over her lips, too.

"Now we're talking."

Sarge leaned back in his chair. "You've got your work cut out for you. Go get 'em."

Brandon nodded. "Yes, sir."

He and Mindy returned to their desks and planned their next move. This was not quite how he'd hoped to resolve the case, but the new angle had provided an opportunity to feed his new addiction.

Lisa Smith, we'll meet again soon.

Chapter 11

*A*my opened her empty suitcase on the bed that evening and tossed her clothes inside, venting her anger on the shirts, jeans, and underwear. Leo had lied to her for the last time. Their relationship was over.

The money wasn't the issue. She'd forgiven Leo for wasting her hard-earned cash. Their problem was trust. Leo had apologized. He'd promised never to betray her again, and she'd believed him. But this morning his dishonesty had reached a whole new level, and she was done with him.

She slammed a hefty textbook into the bag. Amy blamed her wishful thinking. She should have seen this coming. How could I be so stupid?

The front door opened. Leo had received her text message and rushed home. Amy had wanted to avoid a face-to-face confrontation. But a part of her was glad he'd returned before she left. She'd give him a piece of her mind. He'll get what he deserves.

Leo stood in the bedroom doorway behind her. "Don't be like this, Amy."

He spoke teasingly as though they were playing a game. Leo still thought he could talk her out of leaving. Not this time.

She shoved her red heels into her suitcase, resisting the urge to slam them into his face.

Leo stepped closer and wrapped his arms around her. He crooned in her ear.

"We're so good together, baby. C'mon. Don't be mad."

She shook free of his embrace. "Don't touch me."

He groaned with mock surprise. Everything about him was fake. "What's the matter, baby? At least tell me why you're upset."

"You know why."

"No, I don't."

Amy turned on him. "I found it, Leo."

"Found what?"

"Your little bag of...white powder."

"What are you talking about?"

She lost her cool. "Enough! I'm sick to death of your lies. I'm not an idiot. The gambling was bad enough. Now you're dealing drugs?"

His sense of humor evaporated. "Whoa! Keep it down, girl."

"Why? Aren't you proud of what you do for a living?"

He raised his finger and lowered his voice. "First of all, I don't deal anything. That bag wasn't even mine. I was keeping it safe for a friend."

Amy scoffed. She'd met Steve "The Hammer" Hamlin. His friends were criminals.

Leo mistook her seething silence for acceptance. "Secondly, I got rid of it. You'll never see that again."

She placed the framed photo of her family on top of the clothes. "I'm done, Leo. You'll never see me again either."

Leo grabbed her photo and hugged the frame to his chest. "No. I can't let you go, Amy. I won't."

"I don't need your permission."

Amy tore the portrait from his grasp. That was Leo—all bark and no bite.

"You don't understand, baby. I'm onto something big this time."

She zipped the suitcase shut. "Don't you get it, Leo? I never asked for fancy cars or houses. I need someone I can rely on. Someone I trust. But that isn't you."

Three loud knocks on the front door startled them both. Three more followed.

Leo swore under his breath. "He's here."

"*Who is?*"

Leo's face paled. "*He wasn't supposed to get back until tomorrow. You need to hide.*"

"*What? No! I'm leaving.*"

"*Listen to me!*" *he hissed.* "*Steve's going to be pissed. Give me a few minutes to calm him down, okay?*"

A dark hole opened in the pit of her soul. "*Leo, what have you done?*"

If he'd screwed over that Viking-like criminal with the pillaging eyes, he'd messed with the wrong man.

"*Nothing. I'll take care of it.*"

The loud knocking continued, and the violent blows rattled the front door.

"*Just a minute,*" *Leo yelled.* "*I'm coming!*"

He herded Amy toward the closet. "*Get in there,*" *he whispered.* "*Don't come out until I tell you, understand?*"

Would Steve attack her to teach Leo a lesson? His hands were clammy on her skin. He was in serious trouble this time, and so was she.

Amy relented. She stepped into the closet, and Leo closed the doors. Through the slats, she could see the bed and suitcase. Leo ran into the en suite bathroom and flushed the toilet.

More knocking.

"*I'm coming!*"

He exited the bedroom, but too late. Bang! Wood splintered, the sound of a metal bolt tearing through a doorframe. Amy pressed the photo to her chest. The invader had broken into the apartment.

Leo raised his voice. "*What's the matter with you? Look what you did to my place. The landlord's going to—*"

He groaned, and something thudded to the floor. Amy couldn't see out of the bedroom doorway. Had Steve hurt him? Leo, are you okay?

Her boyfriend gasped. "*What was that for?*"

Steve spoke, his British accent crisp and cruel. "'*What was that for?*' *The same reason as this.*" *Another thud.* "*And this.*" *Thud.*

Amy clapped her hand over her mouth to muffle her sobs. Leo cried out. Steve, his friend, *was kicking the crap out of him.*

"Where is it, Leo? Where's my money?"

Amy forgot her anger. Give it to him, Leo. Whatever you took, give it all back. Just make him stop.

Leo wheezed. "I don't have it."

"Where is it then?"

"Somewhere safe."

"Oh, wonderful! But if it's all the same to you, Leo, I want it back right now."

"That's a bad idea."

Steve laughed incredulously. "Oh, really? Why?"

"Because I've invested it."

"You've *invested it? Why didn't you say so. Now I'm happy.*"

Leo didn't seem to hear the deadly sarcasm in Steve's voice. "We're going to be rich, Steve. Filthy stinking rich."

Footfalls echoed from the living room. The Viking was circling Leo like a tiger stalking a lame deer. Talk of future riches hadn't comforted his attacker.

The footfalls grew louder. The doorway darkened, and Steve entered the bedroom. Amy recognized the black skull-and-crossbones t-shirt and the wiry body. Steve ran his hand over his mohawk of blond braids and rested the other on the leather scabbard at his waist.

The criminal stared at the suitcase on the bed.

"What's this, Leo? Are you going somewhere?"

He gazed at the closet. Amy held her breath. Her body quaked. Can he see me?

Leo wheezed. "It's not how it looks."

Steve drew the hunting knife from its sheath. "Here's what I think, Leo. You invested *my* money *in a romantic holiday with your lady love.*"

"No, Steve. I'd never stiff you."

Amy shuddered. Oh, yes, you would.

Steve ignored Leo's words. "Truth be told, Leo, I don't blame you. She's quite the catch. What was her name? Amy. Yes. Lovely Amy." *He plunged the knife into the suitcase and sliced a square in the fabric. Then, he peeled away the ruined cover and rummaged through her clothes.* "She's a beauty, isn't she? You don't want her to suffer for your mistakes, do you, Leo?"

Amy's blood ran cold in her veins. Leo had been right to hide her from the thug. Any second now, he'd open the closet and execute his threat. She wanted to scream.

Leo grunted. "Leave her alone. She has nothing to do with this."

"Oh, but she does, Leo. She does."

He pulled Amy's clothes from the bag and dumped them on the floor. He overturned the empty suitcase and sliced open the linings.

Steve roared with frustration. He turned on his heels and stormed out of the bedroom, knife in hand.

"Where's my money, Leo?" Thud.

Leo moaned with pain. "I don't—"

"Where's. My. Money?" *He punctuated each word with a vicious kick.*

Amy needed to call the police. Her phone was in her back pocket. But the smallest rustling movement might expose her hiding place.

"You gave it to the girl, didn't you?"

Sweat stung Amy's eyes. Tell him, Leo. Tell him I don't have his money!

But Leo said nothing.

Steve yelled, his voice an inhuman bellow. "Isn't that right, you lying bastard? Well, guess what—I'm going to find her. And when I do, I'll cut her, Leo. I'll rip her into a hundred pieces. Just like you."

A blade sang in the air, and Amy's heart skipped a beat. He's going to kill him. He's going to kill Leo.

A sickening wet sound curdled Amy's blood, the noise of a butcher knife burying itself in a chunk of meat.

Amy pressed her knees together to prevent them from buckling. She closed her eyes.

The killer delivered more savage blows and ranted. "You. Lying. Bastard."

A deathly silence followed, punctured only by Steve's labored breathing.

The killer clambered to his feet and swore. "Look what you made me do. What a mess."

Steve staggered into the bedroom. Blood spattered his clothes.

He swore again. "You shouldn't have done that. Now what?"

Steve glanced around the room and stared at Amy. She trembled, expecting him to drag her from her hiding place to her death. But he didn't. He wiped his blade clean on her pink t-shirt. Then, he washed his hands and face in the bathroom sink and walked out. The front door clattered. Has he left?

Amy strained her ears, hoping to hear Leo move, but only her heartbeat thumped in her ears.

Slowly, she pushed the door open and left the closet. She stepped over the bloody pink shirt and out of the bedroom.

Leo lay flat on his back and stared at the ceiling.

She kneeled beside him. "Leo?"

He didn't respond.

Amy touched his shoulder. "Leo, he's gone."

Blood soaked his torn, gray t-shirt. She pressed two fingers to his neck, testing for a pulse. Nothing. Leo's dead...and you're next. Get out of here!

Amy climbed to her feet. Her hands were sticky with Leo's blood, which stained the knees of her jeans, too.

She washed her hands in the bathroom sink and changed into a fresh pair of jeans. Then, Amy shoved her family portrait into her shoulder bag and fled into the night.

Chapter 12

The distant sounds of laughter snagged Amy's attention at her desk on Thursday morning. She'd been preparing a spreadsheet of cold leads Mark had sent her for a mass emailing campaign when carefree voices floated from the kitchenette. She was in the mood for some fun.

Amy saved her work and rose from her seat.

Three days had passed since Josh's death. She'd received no more mysterious text messages. No murderous BFFs had attacked her. The homicide detectives hadn't hounded her either. Amy had emerged from Monday's trauma without a scratch. The entire episode seemed like a bad dream.

She had buried herself in her job. Mark had not lied. There was more than enough work to go around. The handsome executive had inherited Josh's accounts. Her former boss had neglected many of the luxury clothing brands, and Mark was breathing fresh energy into their campaigns. Life went on.

As usual, Eddie and Tanesha nursed plastic cups of water in the kitchenette. The woman's smile faded when Amy entered, and the room's temperature dropped. Tanesha was still angry at her. Had she turned Eddie against her, too?

Amy smiled at him and poured water from the cooler.

"Hey. I heard you guys laughing. What's going on?"

Tanesha glared at her. After her street hot-dog lunch with Eddie on Tuesday, Amy was betting he'd include her in his circle of work friends, and her gamble had paid off.

His pencil mustache shifted as he grinned. "It's a game we play."
Tanesha shot him a sharp, shocked look as though he'd revealed
state secrets to the enemy.

Eddie ignored her. "One of us picks a song, and the others have
to guess the title and artist. Got it?"

Amy shrugged. "Sounds easy enough."

"There's a catch. No singing or humming. No lyrics either."

"Then how do you identify the song?"

"Get creative. Paraphrase. Talk around the subject."

She grinned. "So this is like Taboo for music?"

"Exactly. The first to answer right wins. Want to play?"

Amy sipped her water. "Sure."

"Here we go. 'The knowledge I seek is the mystery of romance.'"

She thought a moment, then pounced on the familiar idea. "'I
Want to Know What Love Is' by Foreigner."

His face lit up. "Right!"

Tanesha pouted. "That was way too easy."

"Was not. It's an eighties song."

Tanesha huffed. "Everybody knows that one!"

The clouds lifted from Amy's head. *I'm in. Thanks, Eddie.* This
was exactly what she'd needed. Would the game soften Tanesha's
attitude toward her, too?

"Give me another. Tanesha, your turn."

Tanesha eyeballed her. Her expression said, "How dare you use
my name in vain?" But she relented.

"Okay, skinny ass. You asked for it. 'If you desire to get it on with
me, you'd better butter up my buddies.'"

Amy stared at the fridge and searched her mental music library.
I know this one! The details were on the tip of her tongue.

Tanesha snapped her fingers. "Ticktock, girl."

Eddie objected. "Give her a chance."

Amy rephrased the words of the riddle. Switching out "desire"
and "get it on" gave her "if you want to have sex with me?" That
sounded too direct. But if she used the word "lover"...

"Spice Girls," she blurted.

An encouraging smile split Eddie's face. "Yes!"

Tanesha frowned. "She didn't get the title yet. And *don't you dare* help her."

Eddie gazed at Amy expectantly. "Think of the chorus. Ouch!"

Tanesha had elbowed him. "*I said*, don't help her."

Amy closed her eyes and hummed the song.

"'Wannabe!' The title is 'Wannabe!'"

Eddie punched the air. "Right again!"

Tanesha tossed her cup in the trash. "Beginner's luck." But a creeping smile hinted that Amy's jealous rival was warming to her.

Amy shrugged. "I love eighties songs. My dad used to play them in the car all the time."

The cozy scent of her father's Subaru station wagon filled her nostrils. Her fingers caressed the furry backseat upholstery. They were going to see Mom at the hospital and meet Amy's baby brother for the first time. The sun warmed the world outside her window with beams of promise.

Amy choked up. Eddie and Tanesha watched her in solemn silence. The talk of Dad in the past tense had sucked the cheer from the air.

She blinked back a tear. "That was a long time ago."

A bulky woman entered the kitchenette. "Hey, everybody. Am I late to the party?" The bookkeeper chuckled at her own joke.

"Hi, Beth."

Eddie and Tanesha filed out without a word. *What's that about?* Amy waited for the mousy-haired newcomer to explain.

Beth waved away the blatant insult. "Don't mind them. I'm used to it." Her fleshy chins trembled, undercutting her declaration. "I guess I'm not one of the cool kids."

Amy's heart went out to her. Nobody deserved to be shunned. "Their loss."

Beth's eyes glimmered with appreciation. "If only everyone was as accepting as you."

She shifted her gaze toward the entrance.

Mark poked his head into the kitchenette. "Lisa, do you have a moment?"

"Yeah."

He tilted his head for her to follow him and left.

She touched Beth on the shoulder. "I've got to go."

Beth shrugged. "See you later?"

"Sure."

Amy joined Mark in his office. He usually sent emails when he needed anything. Had she done something wrong? Had management changed their minds? Were they letting her go?

He closed the door but didn't offer her a seat.

"Mr. Wesner asked me to speak with you."

Mr. Wesner. Harry Wesner. The owner. They were definitely firing her.

Nervous tension moved her lips. "How is he?"

The question threw Mark off track for a moment. "Um, devastated. Josh was his only child and his protégé. But he's strong. Thank you for asking."

His protégé. Was Harry Wesner aware of his son's reputation? How far had the apple fallen from the tree?

Mark interlaced his fingers. "Mr. Wesner has invited you to attend a small ceremony in Josh's memory."

Amy hid her relief. Josh had tried to abuse her. She had no desire to honor the creep's memory. But anything beat losing her job.

"When is it?"

"This Saturday, at Wesner Estate in Westchester."

Wesner Estate. Harry Wesner didn't have a street address; he had an *estate.* The Wesners lived on a different level to most people. Was that why Josh had felt comfortable preying on girls who lacked his power and connections?

Mark misinterpreted her hesitation. "It's far from the city, I know. But you can ride with me if you like."

Ride with me. Amy's cheeks warmed. The phrase had a sensual edge.

Her throat dried up, making her voice raspy. "I'd like that. Thank you."

He smiled at her. "You're welcome."

Was he being polite, or had he created an opportunity to spend time alone with her?

She searched his eyes for the answer. "Is there anything else?"

"Nope. That's it."

He reached out, and for a moment, she thought he'd touch her face. But he only opened the door for her to leave.

Amy snapped out of her brief romantic fantasy. "Okay."

She hurried back to her cubicle. *Was that awkward? Who cares!*

Amy had kept her job, and she'd hit it off with her coworkers. Even Tanesha was warming to her.

But Amy's joy died suddenly.

Two suits waited for her at her desk.

Detective Brandon Cooper smiled at her. "Ms. Smith. Do you have a minute? We'd like to ask you a few more questions."

Chapter 13

*A*my nursed a paper cup of hot sweet tea in both hands and shivered. A chill had seeped into her bones, and her body shuddered uncontrollably on the hard plywood chair of the interview room. Shock. You're in shock. *She needed a warm blanket. Most of all, she needed protection. Why were they taking so long?*

After leaving Leo's apartment, she'd hurried on foot to the nearest police station, Precinct 9. The details of her boyfriend's murder poured out of her in a confused babble. The female desk officer had offered her a drink and led her to the small, undecorated room to wait for a detective.

Amy simmered in panic. The traumatic sights and sounds of the attack looped in her mind. She'd just stood there, in the closet, and done nothing. What was I supposed to do? *She couldn't stop Steve. He would have killed her, too.* I did the right thing. *She had saved her life, and her testimony would put Steve behind bars and find justice for Leo.*

Her thoughts turned to more practical concerns. Where will I sleep tonight? *Steve was looking for her. No place was safe for her while he roamed free. Returning to the Underhills was out of the question. The killer had threatened to hurt Amy to make Leo talk. Would he use Daniel as leverage, too? Steve must never learn of Daniel's existence. Amy had nowhere left to go. Would the police arrange a safe house? If the officers arrested the killer soon, that wouldn't be necessary.*

Her phone rang in her back pocket, and the sudden sound startled her. Was Daniel calling her? They hadn't spoken in days. She had to warn him. No! Say nothing. *If he knew she was in trouble he'd rush over to help, and joining her might be fatal.*

She put down the empty cup and pulled out her phone. Her heart skipped a beat. Daniel wasn't calling her. The name of the display read: Leo.

That's impossible. You're dead. *Then, it hit her. Leo wasn't at the other end of the line. Steve had stolen his phone, and he was trying to track her down.*

The device rang in her hand. Should I answer? *Amy had no idea what Leo had done with Steve's money. But would the killer believe her?* No. *Steve had tortured Leo to death, and she'd receive the same treatment—or worse. Steve's cruel voice echoed in her mind.* I have a good feeling about us, Amy. You and I are going to be the best of friends.

There came a knock on the door, and an Asian man in a cheap gray suit entered the interview room carrying a clipboard.

"Sorry to keep you waiting, Ms. Walker. I'm Detective Kim."

The ringing phone drew his attention. "You can answer that if you like."

Amy hit Cancel, and the phone fell silent.

Detective Kim placed his clipboard on the table and sat opposite her. Pockmarks covered Kim's fleshy cheeks, but his expression was sympathetic.

"You reported a homicide earlier today. Is that right?"

Amy nodded.

He glanced at the clipboard. "Did you know the victim, Mr. Leonardo Santiago?"

"He was my boyfriend."

The detective nodded. "We sent a squad car to the address you gave us, and our officers discovered the body."

Her shoulders drooped with relief. The call from Leo's number had undermined her trust in her senses. But the fearful events had not been a bad dream. *If only they were. Leo would still be alive, and Amy wouldn't be reporting his murder at the police station.*

"*The killer is Steve Hamlin. He's British. He also goes by the name The Hammer.*"

Kim scribbled notes on his clipboard. "*Would you be able to iden-tify him?*"

"*Easily. He has blond Mohawk braids. You know, down the mid-dle of his head.*"

The detective stopped writing. "*Shaved on the sides?*"

"*Yes.*"

Did Kim know him? Steve probably had a criminal record. The police might round him up sooner than she'd thought.

But the detective had more questions. "*How do you know him?*"

"*I don't. He came by the apartment once when Leo was out.*"

"*What's his connection to Mr. Santiago?*"

Should she mention the drugs? Would the detective ask why she hadn't reported them to the authorities?

"*I don't know exactly. They seemed to work together. Steve said Leo owed him money. That's why he...why he killed him.*"

"*How did you come to be at Mr. Santiago's home today?*"

"*I moved in with Leo two months ago.*"

The detective nodded. "*We found a suitcase of women's clothing at the scene. Is that yours?*"

"*Yes.*"

"*Where were you going?*"

"*I'd decided to leave him. I was about to go when...when Leo died.*"

Kim grunted. "*I see.*"

He scribbled more notes. This didn't look good. Leo had chosen the worst possible moment to get killed. Perfect timing, Leo.

"*How did Leo react to you leaving him?*"

"*He tried to talk me out of it.*"

"*Was he angry? Did he get violent?*"

"*No. Leo couldn't hurt a fly.*"

Did they think Leo had torn her suitcase with the hunting knife to stop her?

"What was his mood, then?"

Amy shrugged. "Sad, I guess. Disappointed."

Why were they talking about Leo's mental state? The detective should be searching for his murderer.

"Were you wearing these clothes when Leo died?"

They'd found her bloodstained jeans and shirt. "I changed before I left the apartment."

"Why?"

"I got blood on them when I checked Leo's pulse. There was blood everywhere. Steve beat him up and stabbed him with a hunting knife."

The pen scribbled. "Where were you when this happened?"

"In the closet. Leo told me to hide while he got rid of Steve."

Detective Kim held her gaze. "Why didn't you call nine-one-one?"

Amy sobbed. "I was scared. It all happened so fast. If Steve heard me, he'd kill me, too."

"At what point did you check Mr. Santiago's pulse?"

"When Steve left, I got out of the closet. Leo was dead. I came straight here."

"Why didn't you wait there for the police?"

"Steve told Leo he was going to find me and hurt me. He could have come back any second."

"But you changed your clothes before coming here."

"I couldn't walk around covered in blood."

The tears flowed again. Why was he grilling her? Did he think she was lying?

Detective Kim softened. "I know this is difficult. But I need to get the facts straight for our investigation."

She nodded. He handed her a tissue, and she wiped her face.

"Can I get you anything?"

"Water."

"Okay. Stay here. I'll be right back."

He left the room.

Amy collected herself. Did he think she'd killed Leo? No, of course not. He'd recorded her statement, that's all. Detective Kim had to be thorough. This was a murder investigation. But would he protect her from Steve? If he learned she'd witnessed Leo's murder, he'd kill her for sure.

She needed to pee. Amy strapped her bag on her shoulder and stepped into the corridor. She followed the bathroom sign and passed the closed doors of offices. The workplace background noise of ringing phones and human voices buzzed in her ear. One voice broke through the hubbub—a male laugh. The hearty cackle nailed her to the spot.

No, it can't be. Amy followed the sound, which had dissolved into eager chatter. She peered around a corner into an open-space work area. A man stood at the far end, beyond the rows of desks crammed with computers and folders. Tall and thin, he talked excitedly with a uniformed female police officer. He shoved one hand into the pocket of his navy trousers. The black edge of a tattoo peeked from the neckline of his collared shirt. His workplace casual wear clashed with his braided blond mohawk.

It's him. She'd never forget that voice. Steve "The Hammer" Hamlin had changed his clothes, too. *He'd followed her to the police station and was mingling with the officers.* Amy opened her mouth to shout, "That's him! He's the killer. Stop him!" But another man approached him.

Detective Kim cut into Steve's conversation. But he didn't arrest the murderer. He whispered in his ear. He knows him. The smile dropped from Steve's face, and he ran his hand over his shaved temple. The detective pointed in Amy's direction, and she ducked behind the wall just in time to avoid being seen. But in the split second before the men had turned to look at her, she had spotted something else. Steve had clipped a shiny badge to his belt—the familiar silver shield of a police officer.

Chapter 14

"Is there a problem?" Detective Brandon Cooper asked her.

Amy stood on the threshold of Josh Wesner's corner office and clutched her phone. Housekeeping had removed the yellow police tape and cleared the desk of his personal effects. But Amy hadn't set foot there since his death. Returning to his room felt like treading on a fresh grave.

The detective stared at her from within the office.

"Ms. Smith?"

Amy forced a polite smile. "The conference room is available. Won't that be more comfortable?"

"We'd like you to walk us through your boss's routine on Monday morning to set our minds at ease. This is the perfect place for that."

Had they selected Josh's office to unnerve her? *No.* Their visit was a formality. The media had labeled Josh's death a suicide and moved on to juicier stories, but the detectives had reports to file. They had no reason to dig into her past. *Don't give them one.*

Amy stepped into the middle of the room. "How can I help?"

Detective Mindy Scott followed her inside, closed the glass door, and stood by the side wall to observe her.

Brandon placed his digital recorder on the desk. "You don't mind if I record our conversation again, do you?"

"No."

He pressed a button, then stated the date and place of the meeting and the names of those present for the recording.

"Ms. Smith, did you notice any change in Mr. Wesner's behavior on the day of his death?"

He'd asked her the same question on Monday. Did they doubt her story? Were they trying to catch her in a lie?

"No. But like I told you before, I hadn't known him for long. I only started working here two weeks ago."

Brandon grinned apologetically. "I'm sorry to drag you through this again. But some new information has come to light and changed the big picture."

Amy's pulse accelerated. "What new information?"

"I'm not at liberty to disclose the details, but we're now investigating Mr. Wesner's death as a homicide."

"Oh."

A homicide. Josh hadn't killed himself. The detectives were searching for a murderer. Did they suspect her? Did they know about her stalker?

Brandon continued. "You brought Mr. Wesner a Starbucks order every morning. Did you do so on the day of his death?"

They know I did. "Yes."

"Did you deliver it to his office?"

"Yes, of course."

"What time did you return with the coffee?"

"I left around eight-thirty, so I must have got back by nine."

"But you went out a second time that morning."

Amy's phone buzzed in her hand twice. Her spine tingled. Mark usually sent emails. Had the stalker texted her again?

Brandon eyed her phone. "Go ahead. It might be urgent."

"Excuse me."

She swiped the screen. Her premonition was right. The text had originated from her stalker's number. She opened the message.

Don't worry. They have nothing on you.

The hairs on the back of her neck bristled. *He knows the police are here again. He's watching you right now.* She looked over her shoulder. The blinds were open. A man in gray trousers and a white sleeved shirt hurried past the office and disappeared down the corridor. *Is that him?* Amy almost turned on her heels to chase after him. But fleeing her second police interview would raise questions she dared not answer.

Brandon cleared his throat. "Is everything okay?"

Amy smiled. "Yes. Sorry. Where were we?"

"On Monday, you told us you left the agency that morning to pick up a second Starbucks order."

Is that what this is about? "Correct. I dropped the first cup, so I went back for more. I told you that last time, too. Check the agency's Starbucks account. You'll find two orders."

A note of confidence had entered her voice.

"We checked with Starbucks, and they confirmed what you told us. But here's the thing. Forensics found coffee stains on Josh's clothes and chair. If you dropped the first order, where did he get the coffee? Was he cheating on you?"

The detectives laughed, but the joke's sexual innuendo triggered Amy's defenses. They couldn't know Josh had threatened her, could they? Was the detective fishing for a murder motive? *Don't worry. They have nothing on you.*

"I have a confession to make."

The detectives exchanged quick glances. But if they thought she was about to admit to killing her boss, she'd disappoint them. *Two can play this game.*

"I spilled the first coffee...on Josh."

"And how did that happen?"

"By accident. Clumsy old me. I was too embarrassed to mention it before."

The detective nodded slowly. "I see. Help us picture Monday morning. You came in here with coffee number one. Where was Mr. Wesner?"

Amy pointed. "In his chair."

Brandon moved behind the desk and sat on Josh's seat.

"Then, you approached the desk?"

"Yes."

The detective gestured for her to act her part. "Please."

Amy stepped toward the desk.

"Perfect. Then what—you tripped, and the coffee slipped from your hand?"

"Something like that."

Brandon frowned. "The thing is, if that's what happened, we'd have found traces of coffee on his desk and shirt, too. But the coffee landed on his crotch."

Cheating on you. His crotch. Josh's smug sneer flashed in her mind, and Amy shuddered.

She inhaled a deep breath to clear her head. "My mistake. He was sitting to the side of the desk."

Brandon slid the chair on its wheels. "Over here?"

Amy nodded. "When I walked over, the cup slipped through my fingers and landed on his lap."

Brandon winced. "Ouch. That must have hurt."

"I guess. He jumped up. I apologized and cleaned up. Then, I went out to get another."

"He didn't drink any of it?"

"No. Why do you ask?"

Do they think I poisoned him? That made no sense. Josh had fallen from the window.

"We're just trying to understand the sequence of events. Did he get angry? You'd ruined a good suit."

Josh's voice echoed in her mind. *What's the matter with you?*

Her voice quavered. "I don't think so."

"Did he threaten to fire you?"

You'll make this up to me. Big time.

Her body trembled, and her earlier confidence shattered.

"No. I... I..."

Brandon stood down. "Hey, it's okay. It's all right. Returning to that day must be difficult. Take your time."

The female detective scoffed. "Did you often spill coffee on your boss?"

Amy glared at Mindy. Did she think she'd faked her emotional response to escape questioning?

"No. Only once."

The detective raised her eyebrow. "Minutes before he happened to die?"

"Yes."

Brandon changed the subject. "Ms. Smith, how did you get the job?"

"I answered an ad on Craig's List."

"Craig's List? Wouldn't an upmarket agency like Wesner and Morgan use professional recruiters?"

Good point. Had Josh sidestepped the headhunters so his prey couldn't report him to a third party?

Amy shrugged. "I was happy to find a job. I didn't ask questions."

Mindy grunted to express her dissatisfaction with the answers. Why were they so interested in the recruitment process?

Brandon continued the interview. "Did you enjoy working for Mr. Wesner?"

She felt Josh's clammy hand on her leg but stifled her disgust. "I like it here."

"But his former assistants never stayed long. Why is that?"

Amy swallowed hard. Had Tanesha shared the rumors with him? Had the other assistants complained about Josh? Claims of sexual coercion gave Amy a motive for killing her boss.

"I don't know. You'll have to ask them."

"We will. Have *you* been in contact with his other assistants?"

"I don't think so. I wouldn't know who they are."

They know something's off. They'd dig deeper for sure. Had the detectives already blown her fake identity? *I'm screwed.*

Mindy fired off the next question. "Ms. Smith, was your boss into kinky sex?"

"Excuse me?"

"You know? Whips. Chains. Leather thongs. That sort of thing?"

Was the detective trying to get under her skin—to shock her into revealing compromising details?

"I know nothing about that."

"Did you ever have sex with him?"

Amy clenched her fist. "No. Never."

Mindy shrugged. "There's no harm if you did. Neither of you were married. We don't care if you had a fling."

Yeah, right. But I might have a reason to kill him. "We didn't have an affair."

"What about choking? Did he get off on suffocation?"

"What?"

"Maybe he took things too far? If he died by accident, it's no-body's fault."

Amy gasped. "I have no idea what you're talking about." She glared at Brandon. "Is there anything else?"

He frowned. At least he seemed ashamed of his partner's sick line of questioning.

"That's all for now."

Amy marched out of the office. *Don't worry. They have nothing on you.* Her stalker had been right.

She lingered at the doorway to deliver a parting shot. "Detective Cooper, should I stay in town?"

He grinned meekly. "I'd appreciate that."

The wistful note in his voice said he wished they'd met under different circumstances. Mindy scowled at Amy and folded her arms. Apparently, she didn't share his sentiment.

Amy returned to her cubicle and spreadsheets while the detectives showed themselves out of the agency. Their fishing expedition had failed. Who else had they interviewed?

The skin on the back of her neck tingled, and a familiar self-conscious sensation washed over her. *Somebody's watching me.* She glanced up from her computer. Mark lounged at his desk. He smiled at her through the glass wall of his office. Amy smiled back. He turned his gaze back to his monitor. Two days from now, she'd ride with him to Harry Wesner's estate. Never had Amy looked forward to a memorial service.

She focused on her work. Mark emailed her to thank her for doing a good job on the mail merge campaign and followed up with more assignments. Amy ordered a chicken salad for lunch and joined Eddie and Tanesha for another session of Guess the Song in the kitchenette. That afternoon, she toured the agency corridors and peeked into the rooms but found no sign of the man she'd glimpsed walking past Josh's office. Beth wasn't in her room either.

Amy took the subway train home and checked her phone. *Don't worry. They have nothing on you.* The stalker's message had creeped her out, but the words had also reassured her. Somebody was guiding her. Amy wasn't facing the detectives alone.

But how did the sender know the police couldn't tie her to the crime? Was her stalker so sure he'd committed the perfect murder, or did he have inside information? Was he in law enforcement?

Like Steve. The thought threw Amy back in time to that terrifying revelation at the 9th Precinct. Staring across the room at the killer and Detective Kim, Amy had realized two things. *Steve is a cop.* Amy wouldn't find justice for her dead boyfriend. Steve would frame her for Leo's death. The second realization had changed her life forever. *To stay alive and free, you must disappear.*

Now Amy understood something else. *Steve didn't send the messages.* He wasn't her secret helper. She'd witnessed Leo's murder. Steve wanted her dead.

The subway car shook while negotiating a bend in the tracks.

Her head swirled with the day's events. The police were investigating a homicide, and Amy appeared on their suspect list. *I couldn't let him hurt you.* Her stalker claimed he was protecting her. But by exposing Amy to police scrutiny, he'd only replaced one threat with another. Had he killed Josh to help her, or did he have his own dark agenda?

Amy got off at her station and walked to her building.

Some new information has come to light. What had the cops discovered? Amy reviewed the detectives' questions for hints. Had somebody poisoned Josh? Eddie's grapevine had suspected Josh of poisoning Peter Morgan. Had Morgan's killer murdered Josh, too? Did a serial killer prowl the agency's corridors? Amy shivered.

Other details contradicted that theory. Brandon and Mindy had mentioned kinky sex and Josh's former assistants. Josh had tried to abuse Amy, and according to the rumor mill, he'd preyed on women before. Had one of his victims killed Josh in revenge? But if the murderer was an outsider, why had the detectives grilled Amy again? Did they think she'd teamed up with the killer? Would they accuse her of involvement in yet another murder she hadn't committed?

Amy rode the elevator to the third floor. She entered her apartment, engaged the locks and security chain, and dropped her pouch on the kitchen table.

"Welcome home," a man said.

Amy spun around in terror. She'd never forget that cruel voice. The killer strode toward her.

"Amy Walker," Steve said. "Aren't you a sight for sore eyes?"

Chapter 15

B randon stared at the brainstorming diagram on the squad room's whiteboard that evening and scratched his head. The more evidence they gathered, the more mystifying the case became.

A circle with the name "Josh Wesner" dominated the center. Three lines radiated upward from the decedent to bubbles labeled "fall," "asphyxiation," and "Rohypnol." Together, the facts ruled out suicide. But certainty about the homicide ended there. The crime refused to fit into a convenient box, and the grueling day of detective legwork had only added to the confusion.

He added a line from the decedent to a new circle labeled "Lisa Smith."

This morning's gambit had failed spectacularly, and Brandon had cringed with embarrassment. He and Mindy had presented the suspect with their working theory of how Josh Wesner had died. But instead of inducing a confession, the bizarre sexual scenario had seemed to surprise Lisa, and she'd denied playing a role in her boss's death, even an accidental one.

Her reaction relieved him. *Lisa Smith is no killer. Your instincts are still good.* The thought of her affair with the executive had riled him, too. But his relief quickly transformed into shame. Their implication that she'd engaged in kinky sex with her boss and tossed his dead body out the window had insulted her, and she'd stormed out of the corner office. Their gamble had destroyed any rapport they'd built with her. *So much for hooking up with her later.*

Brandon should have listened to his gut's mantra. *Lisa Smith is no killer*. But did that voice originate in his gut or lower down? Either way, Brandon had emerged from the meeting with renewed purpose. He'd crack this case and prove her innocence. Maybe then she'd agree to have a drink with him?

Mindy joined him by the whiteboard and drew a question mark beside Lisa's name.

"Don't fall for her crocodile tears. Did you see how she turned on us? She's definitely hiding something."

Brandon didn't argue. He'd sensed Lisa was holding back, too. *No harm there.* Guarding one's privacy was no admission of guilt. But did Lisa know more about her boss's death than she'd let on?

Mindy added a bubble with the words "former assistants."

"Any luck with them?"

He'd queried the agency's HR department about Wesner junior's former subordinates to prepare for their meeting with Lisa. The long list of brief stays appeared to support their theory. Had his sexual advances chased the girls away? But when Lisa's interview had dead-ended, a more ominous significance enveloped her many predecessors. Had Wesner's victims taken the law into their own hands to avenge the abuse?

Brandon consulted his pocket notepad. "Heather Brody hasn't returned my calls. Nicole Truman was reported missing a year ago. The other six are unreachable. No known employers either. They must have moved out of state."

Mindy scoffed. "They all ran for the hills. Except for Ms. Smith."

"There's no record of harassment charges either. I checked."

"Come on, Brands. Many incidents go unreported. Rapes, too. The churn rate says it all. But this time, Wesner picked on the wrong girl."

Brandon shook his head. "The churn rate only proves he was a pain in the ass. If that were a felony, half the city would be behind bars."

Mindy chuckled. "Only half? You're generous. One thing is sure. Josh Wesner was a creep."

"Yeah. Whoever offed him did the world a favor. What did the security cams give us?"

His partner inhaled a deep breath. "Ms. Smith shows up at the elevator on schedule. Otherwise, zilch. The cameras in Client Servicing are offline."

"Offline?"

"Mm-hm. Have been for years. Convenient, right?"

Brandon folded his arms and stared at the whiteboard. Was the agency's IT department involved in the crimes as well?

"This case stinks. I keep returning to the same question. Strangle him or shove him out the window. Why do both?"

"Sarge already answered that. He choked during their hanky-panky. She shoved him out of the window to make it look like a suicide. Nobody had to know what they'd done together. But his tie was still attached to the window and delayed his fall."

Brandon huffed. "I can't see her doing any of that. What if we're wrong? Shouldn't we consider other possibilities?"

"Like what?"

He wrote another name in a new bubble.

Mindy furrowed her brow. "Peter Morgan. As in Wesner and Morgan?"

Brandon nodded. "Harry Wesner's partner. He turned up in my research. Get this. He choked to death two years ago—at the agency."

Mindy's eyes glimmered. "You think the deaths are related?"

"Think about it. Both were Client Servicing executives. Both died of asphyxia. Smith joined the agency two weeks ago. Maybe she isn't the entire story?"

"What are you thinking?"

Brandon wrote another name on the board. *Mark Davis.*

Mindy's eyes widened. "The hunk? What? Don't give me that look."

"I didn't think he was your type."

"Trust me, he's most women's type."

"But you have no objections to searching him?"

"If it's a strip search, hell, I volunteer."

Brandon connected Mark Davis's bubble with those of Josh Wesner and Peter Morgan.

Mindy studied the relationships. "Do you think they did it together?"

"Who?"

"Smith and Davis. Her sleazy boss dies. The next day, she's working for Mr. Hunk. Maybe something's going on between them?"

Brandon chewed his lip. A sudden gust of jealousy fanned the flames of his curiosity. *Had Mark seduced Lisa?*

"Let's find out."

Chapter 16

A my gaped at the killer in disbelief. Her voice stuck in her throat. Steve "The Hammer" Hamlin charged toward her, a hunting knife in the sheath of his belt.

Run, Amy! Get out of here. She sprang toward the front door and unlatched the security chain. But the killer was already upon her. He grabbed her arm, spun her around, and slammed her against the door. Then, he closed his fingers around her throat.

Steve snarled in her face. "That's no way to greet an old friend."

Amy couldn't breathe. The canister of Mace was in her bag on the kitchen table and out of reach. *It's over. He's found you. You're dead meat.* Or worse.

No! She clutched at his hand. When that failed to loosen his grip, she dug her nails into the soft skin of his wrist.

Steve hurled her away from the door. Amy collapsed by the couch and sucked in air. The killer towered over her, blocking her escape route. He wore the same torn jeans she remembered and the black shirt with the skull and crossbones imprint. But he'd grown his blond hair out, trading his shaved temples and Viking braids for a menacing white-trash mullet.

"Pro tip. Latches are useless when you're out, dear. Getting in here was a piece of piss." He studied her like a hungry animal. "Your security measures speak of a guilty conscience. So tell me, where's my money?"

Amy rubbed her tender neck. "I don't know what you're talking about."

Steve tutted. "I thought we were besties, Amy. Haven't you heard? Friends don't lie. Where's my money?"

She glanced at her bag on the kitchen table. If she could get to her Mace, she might escape.

Steve followed her line of sight. He stepped toward the kitchen and emptied her pouch on the table. Her phone and personal items clattered on the plywood surface.

He picked up the pepper spray canister and sniggered. "Looking for this?"

Steve pocketed the Mace, then pulled the hunting knife from its sheath. "Tip number two. Never bring pepper spray to a knife fight. I'll ask you one last time. Where is my money?"

Amy sobbed. "It's the truth. Leo didn't tell me anything."

The killer pouted. "Poor old Leo. He could never resist a good score. He let both of us down. But if you didn't take the money, Amy, why did you run?"

"Because I knew you wouldn't believe me."

He stared into her eyes. A muscle in his jaw bulged. "I believe you, love."

Amy blinked at him. *Is this a trick?*

He slid the knife back into its sheath and jerked his head toward the couch. "Have a seat. Go on."

Keeping her gaze on him, Amy moved to the couch. Steve had murdered Leo for the money. He'd waited four years and tracked her across a continent. He wouldn't back down now. *What does he want from me?*

Steve sighed. "Ninety thousand dollars. That's what Leo owed me. But you knew that. You were hiding in the closet when Leo and I...had our disagreement."

He knows I'm a witness. Had Detective Kim told him? Would Steve let her live?

"I won't say anything, Steve. I promise. Please, just—"

The killer shushed her. "I'm not worried about that, Amy. You see, Chicago PD wants *you* for Leo's murder. The evidence is overwhelming. Your suitcase, ready to go. His blood on your clothes. The neighbors heard you arguing, too. Ha! The case is open and shut. One word from me, that's all it'll take. I'll be the hero, and you...well, you'll die in prison."

Amy had known he'd frame her for Leo's murder. She'd been right to run. But Steve hadn't killed her or reported her. Not yet. She was at his mercy. But she couldn't help him retrieve the money. What did he want from her? Terrifying answers popped into her mind, and she quaked with fear.

Steve pressed his palms together and touched his fingers to his lips. "But I don't want to rat on you. Friends should help each other."

Amy didn't like the sound of that. A devastating thought almost stopped her heart. *Does he know about Daniel?* Would he bend her to his will by threatening to hurt her brother? She couldn't stand the tension, but she didn't dare ask either.

The killer chuckled. He seemed to savor the control he exercised over her.

"You've done well for yourself, Amy. Cozy apartment. Steady job at Wesner and Morgan." His smile widened. "Oh, yes. I've been watching you, Amy. Or should I say, Lisa Smith? Pity about your boss. Not a pleasant way to go."

Had Steve killed Josh? Was he the stalker? *No.* That made no sense. Amy hadn't seen him at the agency or the train station.

Steve finally got to the point. "But why dwell on the past when we can look to the future? Here's what we're going to do. I'll let you keep your life, your freedom, and your job. But from now on, you work for me. Until you repay your boyfriend's debt—a hundred grand."

"A hundred? You said Leo took ninety thousand."

"Ninety plus interest. It's been four years, Amy. Count yourself lucky it isn't more."

A hundred grand. It would take years for Amy to pay the sum back. She'd have to suspend her transfers to Daniel, too. But when she was done, she'd be free.

Steve smirked. "I'd get moving if I were you. You've only got a week."

Amy gasped. "A week? I need more time. That's a lot of cash."

He flared his nostrils. "One week."

"But how am I supposed to get that kind of money?"

"I don't care. You're a clever girl. Use your imagination. When you settle your debt, we'll go our separate ways. No hard feelings. But if you screw me over or run again, you'll regret it."

Amy nodded. "Okay. I'll do it." What else could she say?

"Good. One week. And remember, I'm watching you."

The killer turned and let himself out.

Amy held her head in her hands. Her breathing sped up. *This is insane.* Where was she supposed to get a hundred grand—in a week? Did Steve still think she was sitting on Leo's treasure chest? What was she supposed to do?

Calm down. Breathe! Amy filled her lungs slowly. Panicking wouldn't save her, and neither would running. Steve had tracked her down once. He'd find her again. Or he'd tip off his police contacts about Leo's fugitive murderess. *There's no other way.* Amy had to fulfill her end of the deal.

Focus. A hundred thousand dollars. You can do this. Banks were out of the question. Loan sharks would only delay her violent death. Amy had no inheritance, no trust fund, and no property to sell.

Or did she? Amy had a healthy body. How much did the black market pay for a kidney? She'd sacrifice a cancerous organ to save her life, wouldn't she? Was selling a kidney any different? She wouldn't even miss it. But how did one offer a body part for sale? Was there a Craig's List for harvesting organs? How sanitary were the operating rooms? A tear dripped from her eye. *I'm seriously contemplating removing an internal organ for money. God help me. It doesn't get worse than this.*

On the kitchen table, her phone buzzed twice.

Amy stared at the device. Did Steve have her number? Was he stalking her? Had he killed Josh only to extort money from her?

She rose to her feet and neared the kitchen table. Part of her wanted to delete the unread message. But ignoring the text might have consequences. Hope fluttered in her heart. The stalker's previous text had boosted her confidence during her meeting with the detectives. Would this message help her, too?

Amy picked up her phone and swiped the screen. The message had originated from the stalker's number. She opened the text. Steve wasn't her stalker. That much was clear from the four words.

He looks like trouble.

How did he know about Steve's visit? Her breath caught in her chest. *Did he see him here? Is he watching my flat?*

The curtains were open wide. Amy moved to the closed window. Amber light glowed in a dozen apartments in the building facing hers. Most of the blinds were closed. The manic flicker of television screens projected on some. A woman with curlers in her hair chatted on her phone in a kitchen. No mysterious figures returned Amy's stare. On the street below, a white stretch limousine pulled off from the curb, and a teenager walked a Jack Russell terrier.

Where are you? Show yourself, you coward.

Her phone buzzed again. Had he seen her at the window? Would her stalker finally reveal himself?

She opened the text—another message from the same number. But nothing prepared her for the emotional dynamite hidden in the three simple words.

Need a friend?

Chapter 17

"Nervous?" Mark asked Amy on Saturday morning.

She shot him a terrified glance from the passenger seat of his large black Audi. Was her guilt written on her forehead? Did her boss know about her exchange with her homicidal stalker or the awful crime she planned to commit?

"Nervous about what?"

Mark laughed. "About visiting Wesner Estate?"

Relief washed over her. *He doesn't know. How could he?*

"A little."

Amy had barely said a word since Mark had picked her up outside her apartment building. The scent of new leather mingled with the spicy fragrance of Mark's expensive aftershave—the aromas of wealth and security. The luxury sedan's soft upholstery pampered her body. Last week, Amy had looked forward to this private journey with the handsome executive. But romance and creature comforts were the last thing on her mind. Amy clutched the strap of her new shoulder bag and stared out the window.

Need a friend?

The stalker's text on Thursday night had chilled Amy to the bone. This seemingly innocent message conveyed a wicked proposal. The sender had eliminated Josh to protect her. Now he'd offered to dispatch Steve as well. But had Amy read too much into his words?

She'd shot off a quick reply. "What do you mean?"

Her heart had palpitated. The answer had arrived five seconds later.

Bye-bye trouble.

Amy had understood perfectly well. The stalker was talking murder. One word from her, and her "troubles" would disappear forever.

The Audi crossed a bridge and turned onto I-87 toward upstate New York. The madcap city streets gave way to thick wooded hills. They had left behind the bustle of civilization and entered unfamiliar territory.

Mark made another attempt at small talk. "I was nervous on my first visit. Fourteen acres of private property is intimidating. But you get used to it. You realize Harry's just like you and me."

Amy doubted that. The world she inhabited differed starkly from that of both Mark and Mr. Wesner.

That night, her thumb had trembled over her phone's on-screen keyboard. *Say yes!* Steve deserved to die. Leo's decomposing corpse demanded justice. So did the purple bruises on Amy's neck. She'd had to cover the wounds with a gauzy leopard-print scarf for to-day's ceremony. Who knew how many other innocents the dirty cop had slaughtered?

Amy didn't need to pull the trigger either. Like Josh, Steve would simply disappear from her life. She wouldn't need to risk her health by surgically removing a kidney in an underground op-erating theater. But Josh had been different. Amy hadn't commis-sioned the hit. She'd known nothing about the crime beforehand. This time, she'd be responsible for murder, and once she crossed that Rubicon, there was no way back.

But this is self-defense. Steve posed a clear and present danger. Amy had no choice. Would a judge buy that justification? Forget the courts. Could Amy look herself in the mirror every day know-ing she'd willfully snuffed out another human being's life?

Amy had typed "No" and hit Send. Then, she'd punched her couch repeatedly and cursed her unbending conscience. This was her stalker's fault. Why had he asked permission? Couldn't he act independently like last time—without involving her?

A desperate idea had popped into her head, and she'd typed furiously: *I need 100K.*

Her thumb had hovered over the Send button. The stalker had killed for her. He'd offered to repeat the crime. Surely, he'd give her money, too. But what if he didn't have a hundred grand? Would he rob a bank—or murder—to fulfill her wish? She'd be responsible for that, too. Could she plead plausible deniability? Even if he supplied the cash without hurting a soul, she'd owe him a debt of gratitude. *What will he ask in return?*

She'd pressed Delete, and her unsent message disappeared.

What now? How was she supposed to get the money? Steve's cruel voice had replayed in her mind. *I don't care how.*

And Amy had found her answer. She'd bought the shoulder bag the next day. Harry Wesner was loaded. He lived in a freaking private estate. A hundred grand was small change for him. During the ceremony on Saturday, Amy would fill the bag. Cash. Jewelry. Rare stamps. Collectors' items. Whatever she could grab and pawn. A single diamond-studded necklace might cover the full amount.

The car floated over the bumps in the road.

This wasn't exactly stealing. Josh Wesner had abused her, and his father—his legal heir—owed her compensation.

Who am I kidding? I'm a petty thief. An ungrateful one, too. Harry Wesner had kept her on the payroll even after his son's death. She'd still rob him blind. But compared to premeditated murder, the crime seemed like a lesser evil. She'd pay him back, too. Every penny. If it took a lifetime.

But she was getting ahead of herself. *Steal first, compensate later.* Amy knew next to nothing about the agency owner. She'd passed Harry Wesner in the corridor twice but never spoken with him. To pull off the heist without getting caught, she'd better educate herself.

"Is there a Mrs. Wesner?"

Mark steered the leather-padded wheel with a light touch. "Melinda passed away five years ago. Leukemia. Harry lives alone now."

Amy's heart sank further. *Perfect. I'm stealing from a widower.* His marital status had a silver lining. Harry probably wouldn't notice that his late wife's jewelry had gone missing. Did he keep her diamonds in a safe? If so, Amy was screwed.

"What's the place like?"

"High walls. Green lawns. Servants."

Amy swallowed. She'd have to watch out for the house staff, too. "I bet there's a lot of security."

"Not really. Why? Are you thinking of robbing the place?"

Her shoulders tensed. *Take it easy. He's teasing you.* She kept her eyes on the scenery and forced a laugh.

"Yeah. I'll hot-wire the Rolls-Royce while you crack the safe."

He chuckled. "He drives a Bentley limousine, by the way. Well, his chauffeur does. There's no ignition lock cylinder, so those babies are impossible to hot-wire."

She shot him another shocked glance. "How do you know that?"

Mark grinned playfully. "I tried to steal his car on my first time there. Set the alarm off and everything. Very embarrassing."

His banter relaxed her. "I'm surprised he didn't fire you on the spot."

"Harry can't fire me. He'd never manage without his best executive."

Amy shook her head at his mock self-importance.

Mark cleared his throat. "I'm sorry. I shouldn't joke around like that. We're on our way to a memorial service."

Amy had almost forgotten their trip's purpose. She'd become too lost in her own troubles to think about others. How had Mark gotten along with Josh? Had his death moved him?

"Were you and Josh close?"

Mark snorted. "I couldn't stand him. He treated Wesner and Morgan like his personal property. We handled separate accounts and had little interaction, which suited us both fine."

Amy shared his opinion of Josh but sealed her lips. If the homicide detectives interviewed Mark again, they never learn she'd badmouthed her late boss.

Detective Brandon Cooper's black curls and dimpled cheeks projected in her mind's eye. He'd gone easy on her—to the annoyance of his female partner. But Amy couldn't bank on special treatment or risk getting too close. She had to keep her hands perfectly clean until she'd paid Steve off. Even then, Amy Walker would remain a ghost. Lisa Smith, with her fake identity, had to stay away from cops.

They left the highway. Forested hills lined the two-lane road on either side.

Mark broke the silence. "I can't believe he killed himself."

"He didn't."

This time, he gazed at her with surprise.

She continued. "The detectives told me they're investigating his death as a homicide."

Mark's knuckles whitened on the steering wheel. "Do they have any leads?"

"They wouldn't tell me anything."

Should she mention the detective's hints at poisoning? The talk of kinky sex made for spicy gossip, too, but both seemed glaringly inappropriate.

They passed a signpost for Croton River. The road meandered through a small village, then hugged the Hudson on their left.

"Almost there," Mark said.

He turned into a paved driveway. Black iron gates blocked the entrance. Mark rolled down his window and pressed an intercom button on a steel pole.

"Wesner residence," a woman said. A servant?

"Mark Davis and Lisa Smith."

"Thank you."

The gates parted silently. They passed through expansive gardens with tidy flowerbeds and water features of white stone. The driveway ended in a large circle around a central fountain. Mark parked among the visitor's cars, mostly high-end sedans and SUVs. Mr. Wesner had kept the guest list short and affluent.

Amy's stomach cramped. With her simple black dress and plain shoulder bag, Amy felt painfully out of place. *I don't belong here. I can't go through with this.* Mr. Wesner should never have invited her.

Mark got out of the car and put on the black suit jacket he'd draped on the backseat. Amy bit the bullet. She joined him, and they made for the tall white columns of the mansion. With its triangular roof and decorated cornices, the house resembled a Greek temple.

The large double doors swung open as they approached, and a white-gloved doorman greeted them. They passed through a spacious hallway with high ceilings and polished hardwood floors that opened onto a larger sitting room. By the French windows at the far end, an oil portrait of Joshua Wesner sat on a large easel.

Clumps of guests in dark suits and evening dresses occupied the earth-toned leather couches.

Amy scanned the graying men for Harry Wesner. She recognized some faces from news reports. They glanced at the newcomers, then continued their whisperings. *Nobodies. Nothing to see here.*

Mark led her to a pair of padded foldable chairs at the back. He jerked his head toward a black man in an official peaked hat and uniform and spoke into Amy's ear.

"That's Ernest Singleton, the New York City Police Commissioner." He gazed at a gray-bearded bald man who chatted up a well-preserved but unsmiling woman. "Senator Norman Leaky. Supreme Court Justice Jennifer Harper. We're in good company."

Amy wished she could crawl under the Oriental rug and disappear. The event was far more intimidating than she'd expected.

"Remind me why I'm here."

"*We* actually knew Josh. The rest are business—high-level agency clients or the heads of institutions Harry supports. People that rich have few real friends."

She nodded. *We have that in common, Harry.* Amy would gladly part ways with two of her so-called friends.

Colorful abstract paintings decorated the walls. Pedestals displayed sculpted pieces: an angular marble girl holding a ballerina's pose and a series of bronze blobs. Harry Wesner enjoyed modern art. Or his late wife had. The items must be valuable, but none would fit in Amy's bag. Besides, she couldn't steal the artwork in full sight of the police commissioner. She'd have to wait until after the ceremony and fill her bag on her way out.

Beyond the tall French windows, rolling green lawns beckoned. A large swimming pool invited her to dive into the clear blue water. The world seemed to burst with endless possibilities. But soon she'd become a criminal, and once she crossed that red line, she'd no longer be Amy Walker or even Lisa Smith. She'd be someone else. *It isn't too late to back out.*

Footfalls on the hardwood floor behind her turned the attendees' heads. Harry Wesner entered the room in an expensive suit. A young, collared priest with greasy black hair followed, and they made their way toward the portrait.

The priest gripped the lectern. "Welcome, friends and family. Please be seated. The ceremony will commence momentarily."

Two more suits entered the room behind them—Detective Brandon Cooper and Detective Mindy Scott. Brandon met her gaze and inclined his head. Amy didn't reciprocate. The officers settled in chairs at the other end of the row. *What are they doing here?*

Amy leaned into Mark. "Those detectives are here."

Mark didn't turn to look. "Yeah, I saw them."

The priest scanned the crowd with an intense, solemn expression. "To lose a loved one is devastating. When that loved one is a talented young man in the prime of his life, the tragedy is twofold." Were the detectives paying their respects? Amy's heart rate climbed. Now she had to dodge the police chief *and* two of his officers. *Wonderful.* If she got caught stealing, they'd arrest her on the spot. Amy had already burned two days since Steve's visit. This was probably her only opportunity to meet his demands.

The priest read from his Bible. "I am the life and the resurrection."

She zoned out. Why had the detectives attended the ceremony? Had Steve outed her already? Had they connected her to Leo's murder? They'd never believe her side of the story. A panic attack threatened to overwhelm her. *Calm down. Pull yourself together.* Steve wanted his money. He wouldn't expose her. For now, she was safe.

The priest concluded his words and called the bereaved father to the lectern. Harry Wesner thanked the priest and the other attendees.

"Children should outlive their parents. That's the way of the world." His voice cracked, and he cleared his throat. "Pastor Green tells me everything happens for a reason. Faith is for when those reasons escape us. Mel believed that, too. I wish I shared their convictions."

Amy shifted in her seat. His words pierced her heart. Her parents' sudden and pointless deaths had shattered her belief in Divine plans, too. Leo's murder had trampled the remaining shards of hope to dust. She and Harry Wesner might live in separate worlds, but their anguish united them.

Harry blinked back tears. "Mel and I tried our best with Josh. I can't say we succeeded in every aspect. Josh was his own man. He did things his way."

His disappointed tone surprised Amy. Was Harry aware of his son's reputation? Did he know he'd raised a sexual predator, or did he simply regret his failings as a parent?

He shook his head. "But I never imagined I'd stand here and speak of him in the past tense. Not in a million years. I'm only thankful Mel didn't live to see this day."

Harry reached out and touched the portrait.

The priest launched into action. "Thank you for honoring the memory of Joshua Wesner. Mr. Wesner invites you to a reception in the adjoining room."

Amy's gut clenched again. The ceremony had concluded. Her time was running out. She had to act fast.

New York's rich and powerful filed past Harry to offer their condolences. Mark and Amy joined the line and muttered words of sympathy. Harry smiled and nodded but seemed to hear and see nothing.

They entered the dining room. Platters of caviar, crayfish, and smoked salmon adorned the long central table and sideboards. A violinist in a glittery evening dress played classical music.

"I'll get drinks," Mark said.

"Okay."

The distinguished guests dug into the savories and engaged in lively conversation, but the thought of eating turned Amy's stomach. She needed an excuse to leave the room, or her secret mission would fail.

"I didn't expect to see you here."

Detective Brandon Cooper had materialized beside her. He sounded pleasantly surprised.

Amy replied curtly. "Mr. Wesner invited me."

Brandon glanced toward the bar where Mark waited for their drinks. "Just you and Mr. Davis?"

She shrugged. "I'm the only one who worked directly for Josh."

Was he making conversation or pursuing his investigation?

Brandon cleared his throat. "Lisa, I want to apologize for Thursday morning."

Lisa. Usually, he addressed her as Ms. Smith. Was he trying to soften her up with his casual tone?

She said nothing, so he continued.

"The things my partner implied about you and Mr. Wesner were...out of line. Sometimes we push the boundaries to get at the truth. But I never believed for a moment you'd do anything so...unprofessional."

A vindictive impulse flared. "Unprofessional? You mean like acting out twisted sexual fantasies with my boss?"

He pulled at his shirt collar. "Exactly."

He was sweating. *Good.*

"Apology accepted, Detective Cooper."

"Call me Brandon. Please."

Amy twisted the knife. "Shouldn't your partner be apologizing? She's the one who did the talking."

They both knew Mindy had no intention of begging her forgiveness. But his anxious expression was priceless.

Brandon recovered quickly. He nodded at the buffet table where Mindy piled savories on a plate.

"I wouldn't come between her and the buffet. She's a sucker for caviar."

Amy laughed.

Mark returned and handed her a yellow-green cocktail in a martini glass. "Detective Cooper, good to see you again. Have a drink?"

Brandon straightened his tie. "No, thanks. I'm on duty."

"Could have fooled me." Mark winked at Amy and sipped his cocktail. "That's too bad. The bartender makes a killer margarita."

Amy stifled a grin. Testosterone wafted in the air as the men competed for her attention.

Brandon's smile faltered. He tipped his head. "Enjoy yourselves. Drive safely."

"We will." Mark watched the detective join his partner at the snack table. "What did he want?"

"Nothing."

Mark raised his eyebrow. Her evasive answer had piqued his curiosity. "Nothing?"

She gulped her drink to avoid further questioning. *Keep 'em guessing.* "Mm. You're right. This is good."

The detectives headed for the exit.

Mark knocked back his cocktail. "If I never see another homicide detective again, it'll be too soon."

She grinned.

Mark gazed at a white-haired man. "I need to say hi to someone. Join me?"

Amy seized her opening. "No, I'll find a bathroom."

She wandered off. Waiters passed her in the corridor balancing large trays of dishes and drinking glasses. In an enormous guest bathroom, Amy washed her hands, splashed water on her face, and stared into the mirror.

"Do you know what you're doing?"

She didn't. But the margarita injected her with false courage. One small misdemeanor stood between her and freedom. True freedom. Harry Wesner had insurance. This was a victimless crime. *Almost.*

"Let's get this over with."

Amy gripped the bag on her shoulder and left the bathroom. She strolled down a hallway, away from the ambient sounds of the reception. She'd skipped the snacks, but she wouldn't leave empty-handed.

The first large wooden door she tried opened onto a spacious study. Shaded lamps burned beside the heavy oak desk, which dominated one side of the room. A carved antique grandfather clock ticked ominously at the other end. The log fireplace between them remained dark and cold. Steel forks and prods hung from ornate hooks. Baroque paintings in thick gold-leaf frames covered the walls. Did the artwork hide safes packed with his beloved wife's jewels? Amy didn't bother to check.

The air was thick with a reverential quietude. By entering the den, she'd violated a sacred space. Harry Wesner collected his innermost thoughts at that desk. He wrote his private checks with the fountain pen.

A reddish statuette drew her closer. Tongues of bronze ore rose like flames from the central mass. Features emerged from the seemingly formless hunk of metal. Tufts of hair. Cheekbones. A nose pounded flat. A small, hesitant mouth. Two hollow eye sockets with invisible soul-penetrating eyes.

Amy opened her shoulder bag. She extended her hand and touched the cool, hard surface. Both tortured and strangely defiant, the human likeness moved something within her.

"Mesmerizing, isn't it?" a man said behind her.

Amy jumped.

Harry Wesner stared at the sculpture with sad, defeated eyes. "Sorry. I didn't mean to startle you."

She searched for a suitable excuse for invading his study and found none. But her presence in his holy sanctum didn't appear to offend her employer.

"I didn't care for it much, at first. Mel had wanted it. 'The thing's butt-ugly,' I told her. Repulsive. Doesn't even look like a woman's head. Picasso, Shmicasso."

Amy gasped. "That's a Picasso?"

Harry nodded.

You crazy idiot. You almost swiped a freaking Picasso! The statue must be worth millions. No pawnshop would touch it. Attempts at fencing the masterpiece would send her straight to prison. *Do not pass Go. Do not collect two hundred dollars.*

A weak grin curled the edge of Harry's mouth. "But it grows on you, doesn't it? It sucks you in. For all its grotesque ugliness, you can't stop watching, and after a while, you see the beauty. That's the story of existence, isn't it? The universe is a random, brutal mess. But sometimes, if we're lucky, the chaos shows us a human face." He blinked at her. "Sorry. I'm a rambling old man."

"No, not at all. I know exactly what you mean." She studied the sculpture again. "It's both horrible and strangely reassuring."

His eyes glimmered. "You worked for Josh, didn't you?"

"Yes, sir."

"Harry."

"Yes, Harry."

He searched for the right words. "Josh had a difficult management style. His assistants never lasted long. I feel the need to apologize to you on his behalf."

Amy's heart ached. Harry Wesner had deserved a better son.

"I'd joined the agency under two weeks before he passed. I hardly got to know him."

He nodded. "Got to treat people right. All this..." He waved his hand at his den, his mansion, and his material wealth. "It means nothing. In the end, we all die. The only thing that matters is what we do with the time we have left."

Amy swallowed hard and nodded. "You're right."

The words were hauntingly appropriate to her own situation. At that moment, she came to a decision. Amy wasn't a killer or a thief. She had to find another way.

She swore under her breath. *I'm as good as dead.*

Chapter 18

"What the hell did you think you were doing?" Sergeant Andrew Blank yelled.

Brandon and Mindy stood at attention in the NYPD interview room. First thing Monday morning, Sarge had called them aside for a dressing down. Brandon had never seen his boss so angry. The suggestion he'd planned to put forward would have to wait.

A vein pulsed in Sarge's temple. "Who authorized you to gate-crash a private ceremony at Wesner Estate? Because I sure the hell didn't."

So, that's what this is about. Brandon had expected some push-back for poking around but not from his superior officer.

Mindy squirmed beside him. Beneath the tough exterior, she yearned for their boss's approval. Brandon had convinced her to work on the weekend, and now he'd landed her in deep trouble.

"Did Harry Wesner file a complaint?"

Brandon doubted that. He and Mindy had interviewed the decedent's father on the day of his son's death. The agency owner had cooperated fully, and he didn't seem to mind their presence at the ceremony either.

"*The commissioner* complained to Chief Anderson, who complained to Captain Heller. You're lucky he's off-site this morning, or he'd crap all over you."

Brandon shifted on his feet. This kind of negative attention could have them directing traffic until retirement.

"Sir, we had no intention of disturbing the ceremony. We were following a lead."

He explained their suspicion that Josh Wesner's homicide was related to Peter Morgan's choking death at the office two years ago.

Sarge placed his hands on his hips. "You think Harry Wesner murdered his son?"

"No, sir. We were investigating Lisa Smith."

"But she only started working there two weeks ago."

"You're right." Brandon glanced at Mindy. "But she knows more than she's let on. Lisa works for Mark Davis now, and we wanted to explore their possible collusion. He picked her up on Saturday morning. We had no idea they were heading for the ceremony."

"What's your angle?"

"Mark Davis and Josh were the only executives in Client Servicing under Peter Morgan and Wesner senior. Their deaths cleared Mark's path to promotion, and the security cameras in their corridor have been offline for years. The entire department smells fishy."

Sergeant Blank worked his jaw. "I see. Keep going. We've burned a week since the homicide, and we need results, pronto."

"Yes, sir."

"How was Wesner Estate?" Had jealousy fueled Sarge's anger, too?

"Big."

Mindy smirked. "The caviar was heavenly."

Sarge shook his head at her ballsy teasing. "Next time, I expect takeout."

The promise of fancy treats lightened his mood, and Brandon seized his opportunity.

"Sir, as far as we know, Lisa Smith was the last person to see the decedent alive. Now, she reports to Mark, and it appears she's close to Wesner senior, too. She's the key to the case."

"What do you need, Cooper?"

Mindy eyed him quizzically, too. Brandon hadn't discussed this plan with her. He knew how she'd react. *Here goes.*

"She seems comfortable with me, and I think I can win her trust. With your approval, I'll get closer and find out what she knows."

Blank raised his eyebrows. "You want to go undercover?"

Brandon shrugged. "We're treading water. This could help us close the case quickly."

Their sergeant grunted. "Okay. Go ahead. But no more surprises—from either of you."

They returned to their desks.

Mindy snorted. "*Undercover*. Seriously?"

"What?"

She rolled her eyes. "You want to go *undercover* with her? Could you be more obvious?"

Her sarcasm rankled him. "She's our only lead."

"Let me guess. You'll be the knight in shining armor, and when you clear her name, she'll fall into your arms?"

"It's not like that." She'd seen right through him.

Mindy blew a raspberry. "Whatever, Brand. But don't say I didn't warn you. Mark's rich *and* hot. You don't stand a chance."

Chapter 19

Mark gazed at Amy that afternoon, and his cobalt-blue eyes brimmed with concern.

"Are you okay?"

Her edgy behavior had triggered the question. At their window table at Risotto, she scanned the Midtown crowds and fidgeted with the sugar sachets. Steve's deadline loomed three days away, and she was no closer to raising the ransom money. Her only hope for survival would jeopardize the best development in her new life. Amy was not okay.

"I'm still...processing everything."

He nodded solemnly. Mark had saved her job. He treated her with respect and consideration. She felt safe in his presence, and today, he'd asked her out to lunch. *Is this a date?*

In another world, Amy would have welcomed romantic interest from her work crush. Mark was successful, intelligent, and attractive. But circumstances had doomed their relationship from the start. She'd met him under a false identity and lied to his face every day. She was risking his life just by sitting with him in public. Mark deserved better. And to make things worse, soon he'd think she was after his money.

A waitress with pasty skin and a red apron approached their table. "Are you ready to order?"

Amy studied the menu. She opened her mouth to answer, but Mark spoke for her.

"We'll both take the Gnocchi Alla Rosa and mineral water."

The waitress collected their menus and left.

Mark grinned. "Their gnocchi is famous. You'll love it."

Amy shrugged. "Sounds great."

He'd ordered their drinks at the ceremony without asking her opinion, too. She didn't mind. The foster system had cured her of picky eating habits, and after struggling on her own for so long, letting go felt liberating. Mark had taken charge. He'd look out for her. But would he lend her the money she so desperately needed?

Mark seemed to like her. The executive could probably afford to loan her the cash, too. But he was also her boss. Begging for money would strain their relationship and require more lies. Why did she need the money? Was she in trouble? Amy couldn't answer those questions honestly. But a few white lies beat stealing or trafficking human organs on the black market, didn't they?

Amy had rehearsed the conversation over the weekend. Her mother needed the money for life-saving surgery. Mom had no health insurance, and the banks had rejected Amy's loan requests. Amy would pay Mark back with interest. The last part, at least, was true. *Get it over with already.*

"Mark, I need to ask you something."

His grin faded. Could he tell she wanted something from him?

"Me, too. A confession, really."

A confession. Would his secret make her task easier or harder? *Let him show his cards first.*

The waitress returned with two bottles of mineral water and filled their glasses. Mark waited for her to leave.

"The thing is, I've had my eye on you since you arrived."

The expression unsettled her. Did he mean he found her attractive or that he'd been stalking her?

"What do you mean?"

Had Mark sent the anonymous messages? Had he murdered Josh?

He chuckled. "Don't look so frightened. It's nothing creepy, I promise."

She giggled nervously. "Sorry. I didn't mean... Of course not."

The suspense was killing her. *Spit it out already!*

He licked his lips. "I like you, Lisa, and I want to get to know you better."

Amy relaxed. The feeling was mutual, and she'd feel more comfortable asking favors.

He continued. "But dating coworkers is tricky, and now that I'm your boss...well, it wouldn't be right."

She sagged her shoulders. He wasn't asking her out. Mark was letting her down gently.

"I understand."

Amy admired him even more for his integrity. Strangely, the cooling of their relationship made her request seem easier.

She opened her mouth to speak, but again, he cut her short.

Mark shifted his chair back. "Bathroom. I'll be right back."

"Okay."

He grabbed his phone and walked off. Amy watched him wistfully. Had he fled their awkward conversation? Was he giving her time to digest his words?

Outside the window, a man with a blond mane marched toward the restaurant. Amy gripped her pouch and launched to her feet, ready to escape the restaurant. Then, the crowd shifted, exposing the man's face. He wasn't Steve.

Amy had almost bailed on Mark. How would he have interpreted her sudden disappearance? What could she do if Steve showed up in the middle of their meal?

This is a bad idea. What was I thinking? Would Steve hurt Mark, too, if she failed to deliver the money? *How could I be so selfish?*

Her phone vibrated twice, and the now familiar sense of dread gripped her. Amy had been so occupied with Steve's demands that she'd almost forgotten about her secret admirer. She fished the device from her bag and swiped the screen. Her stalker had texted her again. *What does he want now?* She opened the message.

Stay away from him. He's bad news.

Amy scanned the pedestrian traffic again. She turned around and studied the restaurant's patrons. *He's nearby. He saw you with Mark.* She fought the urge to sprint out of the restaurant. *That's exactly what he wants.*

She sucked in air. *Focus. What does this mean?* Did the sender know Mark, or was he jealous of a potential rival? Was the stalker afraid of him?

She sent her reply. *Who are you?*

Would the sender stop hiding behind the messages?

Her phone vibrated again.

A friend.

She swore under her breath. *Coward.* He refused to show his face. Compared to Steve, her stalker no longer appeared so threatening. Had he really killed Josh or merely taken credit for the crime? Was the offer to eliminate Steve hot air, too? Was her admirer a glorified Peeping Tom?

Don't anger him. People reacted badly to rejection—sometimes violently. *You have no idea what you're dealing with.* Evolution had selected women who let suitors down softly for survival. Amy longed for answers, but she'd better choose her words carefully to avoid this wild card's wrath.

She tapped her reply on the touchscreen with trembling fingers. *My friends don't kill people.*

Her message set out her code of conduct. *Want to be my friend? Stop hurting people.* But she regretted the text the moment she hit Send. Had she insulted him? *What have I done?*

The phone shuddered again. Her stalker had responded. Amy hadn't angered the sender or dissuaded him from violence. But the message showed no sign of remorse either, and her skin crawled.

You have no friends like me.

Chapter 20

A my gazed mindlessly at her computer monitor that afternoon, unable to focus on her work. She'd blown her last
opportunity and, like a condemned convict on death row, she
watched her execution draw closer every moment.

At lunch, doubt had paralyzed her. *Stay away from him. He's
bad news.* Had her stalker smeared Mark's name to isolate her? Did
the killer want to control her? But he'd identified Josh and Steve as
threats to her wellbeing. Was he right about Mark, too?

When Mark had returned from the bathroom, her resolve had
crumbled. Her boss shared anecdotes about the colorful characters
behind the luxury brands he managed for Wesner & Morgan. Amy
had nodded and smiled and chased her potato dumplings around
her plate with her fork. She hadn't mentioned the loan.

Stay away from him. He's bad news. Did her new boss have dark
secrets, too?

One thing seemed certain. Mark wasn't her stalker. He'd never
sabotage himself. *Or would he?* Suspicions bounced around her
skull. Did the stalker know she needed money? Had Mark texted
her from the bathroom to dissuade her from asking for a loan?

Amy banished the crazy thought from her head. *That's ridiculous.* Her paranoia had ballooned out of control. Mark was a gen-
tleman, not a twisted killer.

"Hello, beautiful!"

Bethany Morris poked her head into Amy's cubicle. She held an open Tupperware container filled with large chocolate chip cookies. "It's Cookie Monday."

Amy selected one. "Thanks, Beth."

The bookkeeper lowered her voice. "How was the ceremony?"

"How do you know about that?"

"Are you kidding me? Everybody's talking about it. *Architectural Digest* is the closest any of us will get to Wesner Estate, and they printed that edition five years ago. But you were there in the flesh."

Amy groaned inwardly. The Wesner & Morgan rumor mill worked overtime.

Beth gazed at her expectantly. "So? How was it?"

"Um, okay."

"*Okay?* That's it?"

"I'm clueless about interior design."

Beth grinned mischievously. "Forget the house. How was Mark?" Her singsong tone pleaded for the spicy details.

Amy felt hot in the face. "He, um, drives well." She took a bite of the cookie to avoid further questioning.

Beth winked. "On the road or in bed?"

Amy almost choked. "Nothing happened. We're not dating, and we never will."

The bookkeeper deflated. "Seriously? You look so good together."

"Beth, he's my boss. I hitched a ride with him to the ceremony. That's all."

The woman waggled a chubby finger at her. "You aren't holding out on me, are you?"

"Nope. But if anything happens, you'll be the first to know. Promise."

Beth shrugged. "Okay. That's probably for the best. He's not the settling-down type, if you know what I mean. Every week, it's a different actress or lingerie model." She shuddered at his scandalous promiscuity.

The gossip wounded Amy. *Is that why he nixed our relationship?* Had Amy failed to meet his high standards?

Beth continued. "You, on the other hand, aren't just a pretty face. You've got brains, too, and balls." The bookkeeper winced. "I didn't mean..." She pointed at her nether regions.

Amy smiled. "I know what you meant, Beth. Thank you."

"You're welcome."

The administrator waddled back to her department with a contented grin. But Amy stewed in hurt. *Apparently, I don't respond well to rejection either.* She glanced across the corridor. Mark manned his desk and spoke on his phone. *Not good enough, hey?* Beth was right. *This is for the best.* With Steve and a stalker breathing down her neck, Amy couldn't afford romantic entanglements.

The sounds of laughter in the kitchenette roused Amy to her feet. She needed a break and a light-hearted distraction to clear her head.

Eddie and Tanesha didn't seem to notice her entrance.

Tanesha raised her paper cup. "'We were three, but now we're just a pair.'"

Eddie rubbed his chin. "Three is a trio. Pair is two." He grinned. "'Can You Feel the Love Tonight?'"

Amy had identified the song, too. "From *The Lion King.* Right?"

The assistants stared at her, and their expressions darkened.

Tanesha pouted. "What's up, Cinderella? Mingling with the peasants today?"

Amy squirmed. The rumor had reached them, too. Did they think she was climbing the corporate ladder at their expense?

Once again, Eddie rescued her. "We're doing animated movies. You up for it?"

Tanesha answered for her. "Cinderella doesn't have time to play with us. She's too busy living her fairy tale. Isn't that right?"

"Come on, Tee. Ease up already."

"Would you ease up if she was sleeping with *your* boss?"

His face slackened with shock.

Amy spoke up. "That's not true. Nothing is going on between me and Mark."

Tanesha scoffed. "Yeah, right."

"Listen to me. I need this job. I'd never do anything to mess this up."

Eddie grinned weakly. "See, Tee. We're all good. Lighten up. I've got another one. But this song's for Amy."

Something in his tone was off.

He turned to her. "'You've got no ally like me.'"

Amy blinked at him. Eddie stared back, unflinching.

Tanesha snickered. "Ha! That line's got her name all over it!"

You've got no ally like me. Amy had identified the song immediately by replacing "ally" with "a friend" and adding "never" after "you." She hadn't missed his words' double meaning either. *We're not your friends.* But the challenge packed an added significance that Amy alone understood. She'd read an eerily similar sentence at lunch today...in her stalker's ominous text message. *You have no friends like me.* But Eddie couldn't possibly know about their chat unless...

Her mouth popped open. Eddie had eyed her strangely from day one. Had he sent the messages? Was Eddie her stalker?

Tanesha glared at her. "Go on, girl. That one's easy enough. What's the matter? Cat got your tongue?"

Amy studied Eddie. Had he killed Josh? The murderer had warned Amy to stay away from her boss. Was he jealous of Mark, too?

Eddie bared his teeth in a phony smile. "Come on, Lisa. You've got this."

You've got this. He'd quoted another text message. *It's him! There's no other explanation.*

Amy stood there like a stunned fish. *You have no friends like me.* When the message had arrived, the musical guessing game had been far from her thoughts. But now the answer to the quiz popped into her head effortlessly.

She swallowed. "'Friend Like Me' from *Aladdin*."

Eddie glowered at her. "That's right. The genie's song. It proves he can make Aladdin's every wish come true."

Amy gazed at him in shock. Did Eddie see himself as her demonic helper like the genie in the lamp? *You are so wrong, pal.* The pathetic assistant with the pencil mustache and stupid smile was neither omnipotent nor all-knowing. He couldn't hurt a fly, never mind Josh. He couldn't deal with Steve either. Eddie had been messing with her mind.

She lunged at him. "Did you send the messages? Have you been stalking me?"

Eddie stepped backward. "Huh? What are you talking about?"

Amy grabbed his shoulders. "Have you been following me?"

"What? No!"

She shook him. "Then how do you know those words?"

"It's just a song. What's wrong with you?"

Tanesha slapped Amy's arm, releasing her friend. "Get off him, you crazy-assed bitch!"

Confusion washed over Amy. She gaped at her scowling coworkers. Eddie seemed genuinely rattled by her accusations. *Did I get it all wrong?*

She turned from them and ran.

Chapter 21

Tanesha lit two cigarettes that afternoon and handed one to her friend. "What was that all about?"

She'd invited Eddie to the roof for a smoke after the kitchenette blowup. Lisa Smith was up to no good. Tanesha would whip her skinny ass, and Eddie would help her.

He took a drag and stared at the Manhattan skyline. "Beats me."

"Don't give me that, Eddie. What was she babbling about?"

Tanesha knew the new assistant was trouble the moment she'd laid eyes on her. She had experience with Lisa's type. Stuck-up pretty girls thought they could get away with murder.

In high school, Taylor West had cheated on her mid-term exams. She'd tried to bully Tanesha into writing her history assignments, too. But when Tanesha reported her to Mrs. Banks, the teacher chided her for "besmirching a fine young lady." When the "fine young lady" found out Tanesha had snitched on her, she stole her boyfriend just because she could. Alone on prom night, Tanesha had sworn an oath. Stuck-up pretty girls would never trample her again.

Lisa Smith was an older version of Taylor West. Unlike Mark and Eddie, Tanesha didn't fall for her girly smile. The wily bitch wouldn't steal her promotion either. *No, sir.* Tanesha intended to keep her promise. She'd fight back with every weapon at her disposal.

Today's heated argument had handed Tanesha some valuable intelligence. *Lisa is hiding something.* A war strategy formed in Tanesha's head. She'd uncover Lisa's secret and destroy her.

Eddie ignored her question. But they'd worked together for years. She'd learned his every quirk and habit. She knew how to open him up.

Tanesha exhaled smoke through her nostrils like a fire-breathing dragon on a rampage. "You've been following her, haven't you? Dirty little perve."

The taunt brought a smile to his lips. *That's my boy. You can do it.*

"I wasn't following her, okay?" An admission hid between his words.

"What were you doing, then?"

"Just forget it."

"I won't forget it, Eddie. That little bitch is hitting on my boss. I've worked hard, man. Finally, they're looking for a new executive. You're happy where you are, but I've got dreams. I can't let that little snake slither into Mark's bed and steal my promotion."

Eddie snickered. "She isn't a snake, Tee. She's just a girl."

Tanesha rested her hands on her hips. "I heard the way she spoke to you. She's a snake. This is the USA, Eddie. You can sue her ass for calling you a stalker."

Eddie cringed at the word. "I'm not stalking her."

Bingo! We're getting somewhere. "Then where'd she get that idea?"

He sighed. "I bumped into her on the street."

"When?"

"Tuesday. She went to the post office at lunch."

"Post office? What did she want at the post office?"

"How should I know? Probably nothing. She was only there a few minutes."

Tanesha grinned. "You dirty little liar. You *were* following her!"

Eddie rolled his eyes. "It's not like that. I was hoping we'd meet up, and we did. We grabbed hot dogs and had a good chat. I thought we'd made a connection. Then she ignored me."

Tanesha shook her head at him. "You sad little man. Don't waste your time on her. She's set her sights much higher. We're not good enough for her."

Eddie grinned. "She'll come around in the end."

Tanesha tutted. "Poor fool."

She unpacked the new information. Why had Lisa visited the post office on her lunch break? What was she hiding, and how could Tanesha find out?

"Eddie, was that the post office on forty-second?"

"No. East thirty-fourth."

"East thirty-fourth? Why so far away?"

Eddie shrugged.

Wait a minute. East thirty-fourth? The heavens opened. Tanesha grinned in ecstasy. This was almost too good to be true.

Eddie frowned at her. "What are you so happy about?"

Tanesha exhaled two plumes of dragon smoke. "Nothing."

Lisa Smith, you're going down.

Chapter 22

Amy hurried along the subway tunnel that evening. She looked over her shoulder. Commuters rushed toward their destinations, ignoring her. No menacing strangers followed in her tracks. But one invisible tormentor did pursue her now—shame.

You ain't never had a friend. Eddie and her stalker had used the same words. Both were jealous of Mark's closeness to her. Eddie had followed her to the post office, too. He'd spoken excitedly about serial killers and Peter Morgan's suspicious death. The conclusion had appeared rock-solid. *It's him.* Eddie had sent the messages. He'd invaded her privacy. But his shock and confusion at her accusations demolished her certainty. Either Eddie deserved an Academy Award for best actor, or he wasn't her stalker.

The crowd thinned as people exited the tunnels to reach their platforms.

You idiot. What if she'd confronted a serial killer in the kitchenette? Eddie seemed harmless, but vicious predators might hide behind unthreatening exteriors. Josh's murderer claimed to care for her. But if she unmasked the psychopath in public, would he slaughter her and any unlucky witnesses without hesitation to avoid capture?

Footfalls echoed ominously off the tunnel walls. Amy glanced back. Three strangers walked behind her—a middle-aged woman in high heels and a trench coat and two men. The gray suit held a briefcase. The burly older man pulled his flat cap over his nose.

High Heels made eye contact briefly, then looked away. The men stared past her.

No. Eddie wasn't her stalker. He was no killer. Her secret admirer was methodical and cautious. He wouldn't risk exposure with such an obvious hint. Still, the uncanny coincidence astounded her. Was Eddie's selection of the quote a one-in-a-million fluke, or had the stalker somehow primed him? Had Eddie heard the lyrics recently, the song getting stuck in his head? Amy's heart raced. Her musings reinforced her earlier suspicion. *The stalker works at Wesner & Morgan.*

Amy cursed her stupidity again. A killer lurked at the office, and Steve's deadline drew closer. She needed allies and information more than ever. Eddie had supplied both, but she'd burned that bridge. Tanesha hated her guts. Mark liked her, but the stalker's warning had raised doubts about him, too. The only friendly face left was Beth. Did the bookkeeper have a spare hundred grand tucked beneath her mattress? *Unlikely.* Amy swore under her breath. *Who can I turn to?*

High Heels exited the tunnel along with Briefcase. Only Flat Cap's heavy steps followed her now.

Amy sped up. Flat Cap kept pace.

Her breathing accelerated. *Is he following me?* Was the burly man her stalker? Or an accomplice? She'd never considered that possibility. Had Josh's murder required multiple conspirators working together?

She broke into a sprint and burst into the women's bathroom. An elderly Asian lady washed her hands in the sink and gazed at her with mild annoyance. Amy smiled politely. She wasn't alone. *Good.* Company meant security. But the woman dried her hands under the air blower and left. The toilet stalls stood empty.

Amy faced the door. She reached into her pouch but couldn't find the Mace canister. *Steve stole it.* She should have bought a replacement.

The bathroom door remained closed. Had Flat Cap walked off? Would he risk entering the women's bathroom? Was her tail a figment of her paranoid imagination?

The door swung open violently, and a man stormed inside. Steve glanced at the unlocked toilet stalls, then glared at her.

"Do you have the money?"

Amy pressed her back to the wall. Her knees shook. "I've got two more days."

He slammed his fist onto the counter. "Do you have it?"

"I will. I promise."

He rested his hand on the sheath of his hunting knife. "How?"

Amy shot a quick look at the door of the cramped bathroom behind him. He'd block her escape easily, and he knew where she lived. *Sound convincing.*

"I couldn't get anything from Wesner. But I have friends at work. They're loaning me the money."

He studied her face. Did he believe her? She'd say anything to save her skin. But he'd gain nothing from her death.

"You'd better pray they come through." Steve leered at her chest and smiled wickedly. "There are other ways to pay me back. But it'll take years to work off a hundred grand."

Amy quaked. She'd rather die than let him violate her body. But she held his gaze.

"I'll be back soon, Amy. Either you'll pay up, or we'll proceed with plan B. Understand?"

He smirked and left the bathroom.

Amy took a minute to regain her composure. She washed her face in the sink and stared at the desperate woman in the mirror. *You're out of options.* Beth might help her if she had the money. Did Amy have the heart to take her friend's life savings? What if Steve came back for more?

The truth struck her like a slap to the face. *This will never go away.* Once Steve tasted easy money, he'd never release his cash cow. Her lips trembled. Tears flooded her eyes. *This will never end.* So long as Steve lived...

An ungodly idea arose in her mind. Amy pulled her phone from her bag and scrolled through her message history. *Bye-bye trouble.* The stalker had offered to get rid of Steve. Amy only had to express her wish. The genie would do the rest.

She scrolled down and typed two words. *Help me.*

Her thumb hesitated over the Send button. *Once you release that genie, there's no putting him back.* If Amy had a gun, she'd shoot Steve dead to stop him from killing her. How was this different? *Strike first and live. Don't wait until it's too late.*

Her thumb gravitated toward the button. *See? You're not really doing anything. The universe wants Steve dead, too.*

Her body convulsed, and she nearly puked. She erased the message. *I can't do this. I can't.* There had to be another way.

Amy left the bathroom and headed for her platform. A fresh batch of commuters flowed through the tunnel, and she joined them. The inner struggle had drained her strength. But she'd emerged with a clearer sense of direction.

Her train arrived, and she boarded.

Murder is never the solution. The moral fog had dissipated, revealing another path forward. This route also demanded a victim, but Amy alone would execute the sentence. *Lisa Smith dies tonight.* She'd die so that Amy Walker could live.

She arrived home. Amy locked the door, closed the blinds, and started packing. She'd head west and lie low. She'd work odd jobs for cash in sleepy towns until she saved up for a new identity. She understood the risks. If Steve caught her, he'd kill her. But if she stayed put, she'd die, too.

Amy placed her framed family portrait on top of her clothes. *Sorry, Daniel.* Her little brother would have to fend for himself until she got settled again. But he'd have a future. And who knows what tomorrow might bring?

Her phone rang. The caller ID read Detective Brandon Cooper. She'd forgotten about the police. Was he summoning her to another interrogation? He never called ahead. The detectives preferred to show up at the agency without warning. *What does he want now?*

The phone continued to ring. Did he have more information about Josh's death—details that might expose her stalker? If she ignored his call, would he pay her a visit and botch her escape?

She answered. "Hello."

"Lisa, it's Brandon. Brandon Cooper. The detective—"

"I know who you are. I saved your number on my phone." She'd done that to screen his calls.

"Oh. Okay. Um... I enjoyed bumping into you on Saturday. I mean, despite the circumstances."

He was blabbering like an awkward teenager. *What's going on with him?* After the ceremony, he'd apologized for his partner's insulting accusations. The detective wasn't all bad.

Amy softened her tone. "It was nice to see you, too, Brandon. How can I help you?"

He cleared his throat. "Maybe we can help each other?"

"With what?"

"Settling a debt."

The walls seemed to close in on her. Only Steve knew about Leo's debt. Was the detective working for the killer? *Steve knows I'm running. He's called in the police.*

"Hello? Are you there?"

Amy could barely speak. "Yes."

"You see, the last time we met, I was on duty. So technically, I still owe you a drink."

She inhaled sharply. Brandon hadn't called to threaten her or arrest her for murder. He was asking her out.

"Hello?"

Her eyes watered. "I'm still here."

Amy was safe. *For now.*

Brandon sounded relieved, too. "Great. Is tonight good?"

Chapter 23

Later that night, Brandon gazed at Amy across a lacquered wooden table. His warm brown eyes sparkled.

"What are we drinking?"

Mark had ordered for her without asking. The two men were very different. But Brandon was still an enigma. *What does he really want?*

She nearly hadn't recognized the detective when she'd arrived at The Blue Velvet in the Lower East Side. He'd traded his cheap work suit for jeans and a black t-shirt that emphasized his biceps. While a hostess led them to a cozy private booth, the voices in Amy's head tortured her. *What are you doing here? You should have left the city already. He can't help you.* Her choice of beverage hadn't crossed her mind.

The waitress looked at Amy expectantly. In her former life, she'd enjoyed red wine and vodka shots. Since Leo's murder, she'd never let her guard down. Part of her wanted to give Fate the finger and live a little. *Eat, drink, and be merry, for tomorrow we die.*

She played it safe. "A Diet Coke."

Brandon smiled at the waitress. "Make that two."

He'd followed Amy's lead and seemed eager to please her.

He rested his hands on the table. "So, what brings you to New York?"

"You've asked me that before."

"You didn't answer me the first time either. Come on. We're off duty. Let your hair down."

"My hair is down."

"You know what I mean. I want to get to know you better."

Hmm. Mark had used the same words.

She folded her arms. "I don't like talking about the past."

Their drinks arrived.

Brandon raised his glass. "Here's to the future."

Amy clinked her drink to his. "The future."

All five minutes of it. If Steve sees me drinking with a cop, I'm dead. She should have ordered wine.

Amy sipped her soda. "How's the investigation going?"

He smirked. "I don't like talking about work."

He'd copied her response again. But this time, he proved he wasn't a sucker. She'd have to open up, too, if she wanted information.

She sighed. "I grew up in Chicago. But you already knew that."

Lisa Smith's official records matched Amy's real background in the general details. It made keeping her story straight easier.

"Why'd you leave?"

"My parents died in a car crash when I was twelve. Drunk driver."

Her voice wavered. Talking about her parents still choked her up.

Brandon nodded solemnly. "I'm sorry. That must be so difficult."

Her lips trembled. "Until then, I believed that, overall, life was fair. Tragedy was a freak of nature. The day my parents died I realized the opposite is true. Suffering is the rule. Peace and happiness are the exceptions."

Empathy glimmered in his eyes. Did his upbeat mask hide a private agony, too, or did he simply pity her? *Why did I tell him that?*

She smiled bravely. "My point is nothing kept me there."

Have I said too much? Lisa Smith was an only child. Her fake identity wouldn't lead back to Daniel.

Amy changed the subject. "Aren't there rules against hanging out with suspects?"

He chuckled. She'd diverted their conversation back to the investigation.

"You didn't kill Josh Wesner."

"How can you be sure? Have you caught the guy?"

Her gut tightened. If the detectives arrested her stalker, they'd find her messages on his phone. Thankfully, she'd done nothing criminal. But would they believe she'd had nothing to do with the murder? Would they fault her for not notifying the police?

Brandon shook his head. "Not yet. I'll let you know when we do."

A crazy impulse gripped her. *Tell him. Tell him everything. About Steve and Leo. The messages. Come clean. He'll help you.*

Amy opened her mouth to confess. Brandon studied her eyes with interest. Had he noticed the surge of emotion within her and the burden she longed to share?

The words stuck in her throat. *What if you're wrong?* Steve had framed her for Leo's murder. Brandon had said he believed her, but what about a jury of strangers? Had Steve planted evidence in Leo's apartment to prove her guilt? Calling in the police might backfire terribly.

Brandon leaned forward. "What is it, Lisa?"

She shook her head. "Nothing."

He didn't give up. "This city can be a lonely place. But you're not alone."

He rested his hand on hers. The bold move surprised her. But she didn't resist. His skin was warm. When was the last time anybody had touched her with genuine affection? She needed a hug. Amy needed someone to hold her and tell her everything would be all right...and she'd believe the lie.

"Thank you."

Brandon tossed a ten-dollar bill on the table. "Want to get out of here? I know a good place."

"Sure."

He led her to a darkened nightclub. Strobe lights flickered over the dancing bodies. Three vodka shots banished thoughts of stalkers and escape. Amy raised her arms above her head and surrendered to the deafening techno beat. The bass notes pulsed through her body. Brandon danced close to her. Again, he followed her lead. But he didn't lay his hands on her.

Sweaty and exhilarated, they stumbled into the chilly night air and giggled for no reason. For once, Amy stopped looking over her shoulder. Brandon hailed a taxi, and they rode to her apartment. Nothing bad could happen to her with him beside her.

Brandon escorted her up the stairs to her apartment. At her door, Amy dug her house keys from her bag and turned to face him.

"Thank you for tonight. I had a good time."

He studied her eyes. "Me, too."

They stood inches apart. Amy inhaled the warm, heady scent of his cologne. His chest rose as he breathed in rhythm with her racing heart, and an irrepressible gravitational pull closed the distance between them.

Their lips touched and parted. Her hands explored his back and pressed his solid frame to her softness. His body responded. He stepped forward, sandwiching her against the wall. His fingers traced her thighs with urgent desire and gripped the curve of her jeans.

Amy wanted him. She needed him. But her packed suitcase lay on her bed, crowned with her family portrait. *What am I doing?*

She broke their kiss and gently pushed him away. Alcohol had overridden her better judgment. Amy liked Brandon. But he was a cop. He'd notice her brother in the photo and reveal her secrets. Would he abandon his duty and cover for her? He might lose his job. How could she put him in that situation?

Brandon gazed at her with confusion. She needed to explain. A dozen excuses buzzed in her head, but she was sick to death of lying to him.

"I'm sorry, Brandon. You're a good guy. But my life is complicated. You should stay away from me."

He grinned. "No chance."

For once in her life, she'd met a decent man. But she had to turn him away.

"I'm sorry."

He frowned. "Goodnight, Lisa."

Lisa. The name burned a hole in her soul.

She watched him walk away. "Goodnight."

Chapter 24

"Late night?" her boss said.

Amy snapped awake at her desk. Mark grinned at her over her cubicle wall. He'd caught her dozing off. This was not how she'd wanted to start the morning. Today, of all days, she needed to make a good impression. But she was running on fumes and struggled to keep her eyes open.

She swallowed her embarrassment. "Um. Early morning?"

Mark chuckled and headed toward his office. "Glad you're enjoying the city."

Amy wished she'd partied all night. The cause of her sleeplessness was far more disturbing. After saying goodnight to Brandon early that morning, she'd showered and crawled into bed. But an hour later, she'd woken up covered in sweat.

Her nightmare had seemed so real. Amy was washing her hands in Leo's bathroom, and the water in the sink turned red. She inspected her skin for cuts but found nothing. A bloodstained hunting knife rested on the counter, and when Amy looked into the mirror, crimson spatter speckled her face.

Amy had bolted upright in bed. What did the dream mean? She hadn't killed Leo. Steve had murdered her boyfriend and freshened up in Leo's bathroom. Had Steve's threat of violence jumbled the traumatic memories in her brain? Was her unconscious mind pointing an accusatory finger at her? *You're guilty, too. You stood there and watched.* Did paying Steve off make her an accessory to his crimes, too?

It's only a dream. Leo's death wasn't her fault. She'd done nothing wrong. Amy was just trying to survive.

Is the nightmare a warning? Steve could easily double-cross her once she settled the debt. He'd have nothing to lose, and charging her for Leo's murder would tie up the loose ends. But what choice did Amy have?

I should have left last night. Her date with Brandon had given her false hope, and she'd wasted time. Steve was watching. Escape became riskier with every passing minute. She had to cooperate now, and only one option remained for raising the money.

Amy tossed and turned in bed. She rehearsed her conversation with Mark. How would he react? Her future depended on his generosity.

At six AM, she'd abandoned hope of sleep and dressed for work. She'd waited for Mark to arrive, dreading the encounter, when slumber had overpowered her. Now her boss sat behind his desk. His schedule showed a meeting in fifteen minutes. *This is your window. You might not get another chance.*

She inhaled two deep breaths to calm her nerves. *You can do this.* In the worst-case scenario, he'd say no. He had no reason to doubt her cover story. Her fictitious sick mother would arouse pity not suspicion. If necessary, she'd break down in tears to dodge his questions.

Amy stood and brushed lint from her skirt. *Here goes nothing.*

"Lisa," a woman said.

Tanesha had snuck up behind her.

"Yes?" *What does she want?* Amy had avoided the other assistants since her argument with Eddie in the kitchenette yesterday.

The woman smiled. "I need to show you something."

Uh-oh. She's up to no good. "Um, I'm on my way to see Mark."

"He can wait. Trust me, this is urgent."

Amy didn't trust her. Tanesha hated her guts. But if she was scheming to get rid of her, Amy had better uncover the plot soon. Amy glanced longingly at Mark through the glass wall. She'd speak with him later. A shouting match outside his office was the last thing she needed.

She sighed. "Make it quick."

Tanesha smirked. "Oh, I will."

Amy followed Tanesha down the corridor and toward the elevators. "Where are we going?"

"Somewhere private."

Okay, she wants to chat. Amy swiped her phone's screen and opened the Voice Memos app. If Tanesha threatened her, Amy could use the recording against her.

The elevator arrived, they got in, and Tanesha pressed the button labeled fifty. She was taking her to the top floor.

The doors closed, and Amy's gut tightened. *I need to show you something.* What could be so urgent? Was the outing just an excuse to get her alone? Would Eddie be waiting for them on the rooftop? *This is a bad idea.*

Find an excuse to return to the office. You need to pee. Anything!

But the doors opened, and Tanesha stepped out of the elevator. Eddie wasn't lying in wait. The short, unfurnished corridor ended in a metal door.

The assistant glared at her. "Come on."

Amy left the elevator. Tanesha swiped a sensor with her employee card and pushed through the door. Amy followed her into the blue expanse.

The Manhattan skyline surrounded her. A stiff breeze whistled in her ears and ruffled her hair and blouse. Vertigo unsettled her. She'd never seen the city from this giddy height.

Tanesha set out along the line of rectangular air-conditioning units and toward the building's edge. The breeze strengthened, and Amy's hair whipped at her face. She slowed her pace. Would Tanesha throw her from the rooftop? Had *she* killed Josh?

The assistant stopped near the ledge and turned around. Amy joined her but remained at a safe distance from her rival. Without looking at her phone, she pressed the app's Record button. Would the microphone pick up their conversation over the wind?

"What do you want?"

Tanesha smiled victoriously. "The game's over."

Amy used her poker face. *She's bluffing.* "What game?"

She jabbed her finger at Amy. "Your game, *Amy Walker.*"

Amy gaped at her. *She knows my name. But how?* "What are you talking about?"

Tanesha lost her patience. "Don't mess with me. I've figured you out. Think Mark will let you stay once I tell him?"

"Tell him what?"

"Give it up, girl. My cousin works at the post office. You sent money last week under a different name, which means one of them is fake. How long did you think you'd get away with it?"

Tanesha didn't need proof. Even a quality false identity wasn't bulletproof. If HR dug deeper, they'd discover the truth.

Amy stepped closer. She couldn't deny the facts. But could she win Tanesha over?

"You don't understand, Tanesha. I did that for my protection. Somebody's stalking me." That much was true.

Tanesha folded her flabby arms. "Not my problem."

"He's murdered people. For all I know he killed Josh, too."

The woman squinted at her. "Josh Wesner? What are you talking about, crazy girl? Josh killed himself. Don't use him to save your scrawny ass."

Amy stepped closer. "He's after me now. If you say anything, you'll put my life in danger."

Tanesha flashed the whites of her eyes. "Girl, even if I believed you, I don't care."

Her appeal to Tanesha's humanity had failed.

"What do you want? I don't have any money."

Tanesha howled with self-righteous indignation. "I don't want your money. I want you out of here. Gone. Either you quit *today,* or I'll talk. I swear to God."

Amy's desperation bubbled over into a seething rage. She had enough problems without jealous coworkers blackmailing her. She moved even closer. A violent impulse flared in her lizard brain. They were alone on the roof. Tanesha was threatening her life. One shove in the right direction, and her rival would hit the sidewalk at terminal velocity.

Tanesha stretched to her full height. "What you gonna do, skinny ass?"

She was right. The odds favored the burly woman. But Amy hadn't seriously considered wrestling her over the edge. She'd never do that. *I'm not a killer.*

Despair settled over her. The day had started badly, but at least she'd had a plan. After Tanesha revealed her secret, Mark would never loan her the money. Amy had nothing left at Wesner & Morgan. She had to leave.

"Okay." Her voice was a defeated whimper.

"What's that? I can't hear you."

Was she rubbing her victory in? "I'll go."

"Thank you. Nice knowing you, bitch."

Tanesha brushed past her and headed for the elevator. Amy stood alone on the roof. The world shifted around her. Her chest tightened, and she struggled to draw breath. White spots dotted her vision. She leaned on an air-conditioning unit and sucked in air with tremulous gulps.

The edge of the building beckoned. *Just a few more steps, and this nightmare ends.* Steve couldn't hurt her if she died. He'd never get his money back either. Tanesha would have to live with Amy's death on her conscience.

Don't you dare! Pull yourself together. You'll get through this. You have to. Daniel needs you. Amy closed her eyes. She focused on her breathing. Slowly, the dizziness subsided. Only one option remained. Amy had to run, and she had no time to lose. Steve would be close on her heels.

She returned to the elevator and pressed the button for Wesner & Morgan. Eddie must have told Tanesha about her visit to the post office. Was that his revenge for her verbal attack the other day? She understood Tanesha's jealousy, too. Even so, the betrayal stung. *That's what you get for relying on other people.*

Amy returned to the agency, collected her pouch, and doubled back toward the exit. Tanesha had won, but Amy would surrender on her own terms. Mark raised his head from his computer as she departed, but Amy kept her head down.

She pressed the elevator button. Amy wouldn't send in her resignation. Her stalker had eyes and ears in the office. To make a clean break, she needed a head start. The longer the better. By the time the killer realized she'd fled, she'd be gone. With luck, she'd slip through Steve's net, too.

Her phone buzzed twice, and her skin crawled. The stalker's messages had conditioned her to cringe at the everyday sound. She swiped the screen. Again, he'd used the same number.

She's onto you.

Amy looked over her shoulder. She saw nobody. *How does he know?* When she stepped into the elevator, another text arrived.

I can help.

Amy swallowed hard. Again, the stalker had extended a helping hand, and again, his solution was deadly clear—murder.

She waited for the doors to open on the ground floor, then sent her response.

No.

Amy hit the sidewalk and joined the throng of pedestrians. The weight on her shoulders lifted slightly. Leaving had that effect. Her work tasks no longer mattered. Neither did Tanesha, Eddie, or Lucas, her landlord. She no longer had to deal with them. They faded into insignificance. She was going to start over, her slate cleaner, lighter.

Where would she go? *North.* Amy had never been to Maine. She'd find a small city and settle down. *Sorry, Manhattan. Things didn't work out.* The promise of anonymity had proved false.

"Amy?" a man said, a note of doubt in his eerily familiar voice. A tall stranger stared at her, but she couldn't place his wild dark curls, stubbly jawline, or large backpack. *How does he know my name?*

His dark eyes glimmered, and a wide smile broke across his face. Had the tourist mistaken her for someone else?

Amy continued walking. *Ignore him. Keep your head down. He'll realize his mistake and leave you alone.*

But the stranger didn't give up. He ran after her and grabbed her arm, laughing with delight. "Amy, it's you!"

She gazed into his eyes and gasped. *No, it can't be...*

Chapter 25

*T*he machines in the room beeped loudly. Amy hated the sound. She hated the hospital's strong chemical smell, too. She'd waited beside the bed for ages. The boy beneath the bedsheet breathed easily, but his eyes remained shut. Amy had prayed for him to wake up but secretly, she dreaded that moment. Their world had ended that afternoon, and Amy didn't want to tell him.

She leaned back on the visitor's hard chair and sighed. The stiff pajamas were too big for her and chafed her skin.

A man in blue scrubs and a surgical face mask had explained everything calmly. The surgeon had operated on her brother, but he was still asleep. He didn't know when Daniel would wake up. They were both very lucky to be alive.

Amy didn't feel lucky. She didn't remember the accident. One moment, she'd been sitting in her dad's car listening to Bon Jovi, and the next, she'd woken up in a hospital bed. Her entire body ached, especially her neck.

A nurse with a hooked nose had hovered over her. She'd said they'd thrown away Amy's clothes because of the blood—incinerated them. The woman said her parents had died instantly as though the speed of their deaths somehow made things better.

Amy didn't believe her. "Mom!" she cried. "Dad!"

She sat up, but her parents weren't in the other beds. The nurse handed her a pill and a splastic cup of water, but Amy knocked them out of her hands and slipped off the bed.

"Mom! Dad!" Where are they? *Her limbs felt so heavy. She would have fallen to the floor if the nurse hadn't hugged her.*

Amy cried into her uniform. "Take me to them. I want to see them."

The nurse held her tight. "I'm sorry, dear. I'm so sorry." *She guided her back to the bed and tucked her in. Amy stared at the hooks in the ceiling.* This can't be happening. *She seemed to float like an astronaut in the dark void of deep space. She lost all sense of direction and couldn't tell which way was up or down.*

Terrifying questions overwhelmed her. What do we do now? Where will we go? Who will take care of us?

She turned her head. Daniel lay in the next bed. Part of her stepped out of the bubble of fear and confusion. Amy was twelve years old, four years older than her brother. She was the head of the family now. She had to be strong and brave for him.

Amy spoke with the nurses. Slowly, her strength returned, and she began her vigil beside Daniel's bed.

She stared at his resting body. Amy envied him. He doesn't know. Maybe it's better if he never wakes up?

Images from that morning flashed in her head. They had waited at the red light. Amy watched her parents from the backseat of the car. Her father's clean-shaven cheeks bulged as he smiled. He winked at Amy in the rearview mirror, but she still fumed. Today was supposed to be a happy day, a celebration. But she couldn't see past the hurtful encounter at school. Mom consoled her with her favorite saying. The sentence always soothed Amy. But now, in the hospital, the words angered her. The accident had proved Mom wrong. Her mother had lied. She'd deceived Amy all her life. Amy hated her. She hated both her parents for leaving her. It wasn't fair. How could they do this to her? If they walked into the hospital room, she'd punch and kick them.

The electronic beeping sped up, and her brother stirred in the bed. Amy launched to her feet and leaned over him. "Daniel?"

He grimaced and cracked his eyes open. "Where am I?"

She gripped his hand. "You're okay now. We're in the hospital."

"Where's Mom and Dad?"

Her lips trembled. "They had to go away. But I'm here with you, Daniel. We're best friends, remember?" Her tears dripped onto the bedsheet. "I'll never leave you."

Chapter 26

Amy locked her apartment door and shut the curtains. Then, she turned to her unexpected guest, unsure what to do with her hands.

"What are you doing in New York?"

Daniel laughed incredulously. "We haven't seen each other in years. Aren't you glad to see me?"

The criticism stung. When she'd recognized him on the sidewalk, her first concern had been his safety. If Steve—or her stalker—discovered her little brother, they'd target him, too. She had to get him out of sight. Amy hailed a taxi and told Daniel to hold his questions until they reached her home. Had her avoidant behavior insulted him?

"I *am* glad to see you. But I didn't want to put you in danger."

He frowned. "Danger? What danger?"

Now I sound paranoid, too. Daniel had no clue about Leo or Steve. *Let's keep it that way.* Every second he spent with her placed his life in jeopardy. But he'd only just arrived. How could she explain the need to send him away?

"Never mind. I'll explain later."

He dropped his backpack on the floor and glanced around her cramped apartment. "This isn't how I pictured your place."

"What do you mean?"

He shrugged. "Doctors earn well. You seemed to have plenty of money."

"You got the transfers?"

"Every two weeks, like clockwork. I figured you were living the good life."

His words pierced her heart. She hadn't been able to explain her sudden disappearance to him. For all he knew, Amy had abandoned him to pursue her selfish dreams.

"Daniel, I didn't finish med school."

Her confession seemed to wound him. "But you always told me how important it was to study and build a future."

"I know, and that's still true. Dropping out wasn't my choice. I had to leave in a hurry. I couldn't even tell you what was happening or where I was going."

Hurt glimmered in his eyes. "Why not?"

Amy swallowed. She had to tell him something—enough to understand how precarious their situation was.

"I had a boyfriend, Leo. He got into trouble with criminals, and now they're after me."

"What do they want with you?"

Her chest heaved. She'd never shared that story with another living being. Now the details poured out of her in a gush of emotional release.

"Leo stole money from them. They killed him—and they think I was working with him. I've been on the run ever since."

Daniel's eyes shifted as he processed the information. "Why didn't you call the police?"

"It's complicated. The less you know the better."

"The money you sent me—was it from Leo?"

"No. I had nothing to do with that. I bought a fake ID and found work. Minimum-wage jobs, mostly, for people who paid cash and didn't ask questions. I sent you half of anything I got."

He blinked at her. "Geez, Amy. I had no idea what you'd gone through. I never understood why you just disappeared."

She stepped closer. "I'm so sorry, Daniel. But if they found out about you, they'd hurt you to get to me. It's so good to see you."

She hugged him. "It's good to see you, too."

She lingered in his warm embrace. The teenager she'd left behind had grown into a young man. They had so much to catch up on.

"Do you want a drink?"

"Sure."

"I only have water."

"Water's fine."

In the kitchen, Amy filled two clean drinking glasses. Her phone vibrated twice on the counter. Amy's heart skipped a beat. Had her stalker seen Daniel with her? Was Steve on his way, right now?

She swiped the screen and sighed. Mark had sent the message.

Are you in the office?

He'd noticed her sudden absence.

Amy typed a quick reply. *Not feeling well. Gone home. Sorry.* She hit Send and bit her lip. That wasn't a complete lie. Tanesha's threat had sickened her. Then, she swore under her breath. Had Tanesha told her boss the truth? Is that why he'd texted her?

Daniel stared at her. "Is everything okay?"

"Yeah, it's work."

The phone vibrated again.

Feel better soon.

She thanked Mark for his concern. Tanesha hadn't outed her. *Not yet.*

Amy returned to the living room with the drinks. Daniel studied the framed family photograph.

"I love this photo. I remember that day clearly. This was a few weeks before the accident, right?"

Amy placed the glasses on the coffee table and settled on the couch. "Yeah."

Her conscience prickled again. She'd taken the photo with her, robbing Daniel of the only remaining image of their happy early childhood. The family portrait had given Amy strength in difficult times. What had given Daniel the courage to carry on?

He joined her on the couch. "I used to pretend I could step into the photo and travel back in time. I'd warn Dad not to take us out for dinner for his birthday. 'Don't be silly, Dan,' he'd say, 'Burgers are your favorite,' and I'd say, 'I don't care. This year we'll order in.'"

Amy grinned. "I wish we could do that, too."

Daniel placed the frame on the table and sipped his water. "Imagine how different things would have been. We'd never have met the Underhills."

The memory of the foster family turned Amy's stomach. "Don't remind me."

They sat there in comfortable silence. Amy savored the moment, knowing it wouldn't last. Steve had located her and so had Daniel. How much longer could she cheat death?

"How did you find me?"

"The postal order listed New York."

"New York is a big city."

"I got lucky. Maybe fate is finally smiling on us?"

Amy scoffed. The universe had conspired against them from day one. Fate was taunting them with a few stolen minutes of joy before delivering another death blow. But Amy was grateful for the opportunity to see her brother and explain her actions. *Use these minutes well.*

"What have you been up to, Dan?"

He inhaled a deep breath. "Looking for you."

She laughed. "I'm serious. What are you studying?"

"I'm on the PhD track."

A thrill passed through her body. He'd done it! Daniel was making something of his life. Her hard years of sacrifice were paying off.

She slapped his shoulder. "Good for you! Where?"

"The School of Hard Knocks."

Her excitement fled. Daniel wasn't in college. "You're kidding, right?"

He rubbed his head. "I couldn't focus in high school, so I dropped out. I'm sorry I let you down."

What's happened to him? The teenager she'd left behind had dreamed of conquering the world. Who was this gloomy quitter? The blood drained from Amy's face. *This is my fault.* She'd promised she'd be there for him. But during his critical years, she'd ghosted him. Amy should have stuck it out at the Underhills instead of moving in with Leo. But staying there had been impossible.

Amy touched his shoulder. "It's not too late. Do your SATs and apply for next year."

He shrugged. "Don't waste your money."

She looked him in the eye. "Listen to me. That money is for your education. It's too late for me, but you can turn things around."

"How? I've spent everything you sent me."

"What? Why?"

"I couldn't stand the Underhills anymore, so I left. Your money covers my rent. But I'm barely getting by."

"Barely getting by? Why didn't you get a job?"

"Believe me, I've tried. Nobody will hire me. I'm worthless."

"Don't say that. You're not worthless."

Had the Underhills destroyed his self-confidence? She didn't blame him for fleeing their foster family. She'd escaped at the first opportunity. But Amy wasn't made of money. She'd worked her butt off to help her brother. But the handouts had backfired. He'd become dependent on her. Did he think she'd support him forever?

There's no easy way to say this. "Dan, I wish I could help you more, but I can't. I'm about to lose my job. I won't be able to send more money. You'll have to make your own way."

He stared at her and flexed his jaw. She'd disappointed him. Did he resent this dose of tough love? Her heart ached. They'd finally reconnected after years apart. Would their reunion end on a bitter note?

Daniel hung his head. "You're right. You've done so much, and I'm grateful for everything. I'll look for a job and as soon as I find something, I'll get my own place."

The dagger in her heart turned. "Daniel, you can't stay here."

"I have nowhere else to go."

"Leo's killer has found me. He's blackmailing me into covering Leo's debt. But I can't get the money. He'll be back here any minute. If he catches you, we're both finished."

Daniel held her gaze. "We'll fight him together."

Amy laughed. "He's a career criminal, Dan. We don't stand a chance against him. You have to go right now. Me, too."

"Then we'll leave together."

She shook her head. "That's too risky. We need to split up."

"But I just found you."

"We don't have a choice."

His eyes hardened. "Last time you left, I didn't see you for four years. Don't do that to me again. You're all I've got."

Amy opened her mouth to argue. The cogs in her brain spun wildly. Staying apart had kept Daniel safe until now. But her brother's arrival had stacked the odds against them. *Has Steve already spotted him?* Eventually, he would, and she'd lose everything.

She studied Daniel with new understanding. His stubborn defiance had rubbed off on her. Or maybe she didn't have the heart to abandon him again? Either way, the time had come for her to attempt the impossible. Amy had to stop running and start fighting.

Chapter 27

Tanesha slipped into the vacant office at the end of the corridor on Wednesday morning and closed the door. Wesner & Morgan reserved the room for visiting contractors, but employees used the space for private phone calls. Conversations with lovers. Interviews with other potential employers. Today, Tanesha added a new category to the list, and the anticipation sent a pleasant shiver down her spine.

"Promises are sacred," Momma had always told her. Tanesha eased onto the office chair and placed her phone on the table. She closed her eyes and inhaled deeply as though performing a holy ritual.

Lisa Smith—aka Amy Walker—had failed to hand in her resignation. She hadn't even bothered to show up for work today. Tanesha had promised to destroy the crooked assistant, and she'd fulfill her solemn duty.

But she'd be smart, too. Tanesha had tussled with entitled white bitches before, and she had the psychological scars to prove it. She'd learned her lesson the hard way and wouldn't repeat her mistakes.

She retrieved the business card from her pocket, typed the number into her phone, and hit Call.

Nobody likes a rat. Neither would Mark. Tanesha wasn't foolish enough to deliver Lisa's secrets to their boss directly. Besides, Mark was a man. When it came to attractive women, men didn't use their gray matter. The split brain in their scrotum did the thinking for them. Would Tanesha let Mark brush Lisa's lies under the carpet? *No, sirree.* He'd receive the information from an undeniable authority, and Lisa would be irredeemable.

The man answered on the second ring. "Cooper."

"Hello, Detective? This is Tanesha Williams from Wesner and Morgan. We spoke last week after Mr. Wesner's tragic death."

"How can I help you, Ms. Williams?"

"You said to call if I had any more information. Well, I do."

She drew out the suspense. Tanesha had planned her every word and would enjoy every moment.

"And?"

"This isn't easy for me, Detective Cooper. You see, the information relates to one of my coworkers."

"Who?"

"Lisa Smith."

"Mr. Wesner's assistant?"

"Correct. Only Lisa Smith isn't her real name."

This was his cue to ask, "What's her real name?" But the line fell silent. Had he ended the call?

"Are you still there, Detective?"

He cleared his throat. "I am. What's her real name?"

"Amy Walker. From Chicago, I think."

"How did you come by this information, Ms. Williams?"

Tanesha had anticipated the tricky question and prepared a safe response. "From a friend who prefers to remain anonymous. But there's more. When I confronted Ms. Smith about her fake identity yesterday, she started talking crazy."

"What do you mean?"

"She said people are stalking her and that they killed Mr. Wesner."

"She knows who killed Mr. Wesner?"

"Seems that way. It surprised me, too. Everybody knows Mr. Wesner killed himself. Ms. Smith's behavior is very suspicious. She's obviously unstable and, to be honest, I fear for my safety."

The detective's voice became urgent. "Is Ms. Smith at work now?"

"No, I haven't seen her. She left early yesterday. I heard she's sick, but who knows?"

"Okay. You did the right thing by contacting me. Call me if you see her."

"I will. Now you have a good day, Detective."

She hung up and punched the air. "Lisa Smith, you are history!"

Tanesha stood and danced, shaking her booty. The dominos were falling. The police would pick up Lisa for questioning and expose all her dirty secrets. Tanesha had defeated her skinny-assed rival and came out smelling like roses. *Go, girl!*

She floated back to her cubicle on a cloud of bliss.

Eddie squinted at her. "What are you smiling about?"

"Oh, nothing. But I don't think we'll be seeing much of Lisa anymore."

"Why, what happened?"

Tanesha shrugged. "You'll find out soon enough."

Chapter 28

"We've got to bring her in," Mindy said late that afternoon.

Brandon stood with her by the squad room's whiteboard. He ran his hand over his face. *She's right.* They couldn't ignore Tanesha's tip-off or the damning information they'd collected since her call. But every fiber of his body resisted the revelation. *Lisa Smith is no killer.* But what about Amy Walker?

Mindy folded her arms. "She lied to us. She lied to everyone."

Had his partner noticed his inner struggle? Lisa Smith had invaded his heart, and he had no desire to evict her. He'd thought he was playing her, but the opposite was true. Thank goodness she'd sent him home after their date on Monday night. He would have spent the night with her if she'd let him. Sleeping with a witness was bad enough. But Lisa was no longer merely a witness.

Sergeant Adrian Blank joined them. "What's the urgent update?"

Mindy's sharp glance warned Brandon not to undermine her presentation. "Wesner's assistant, Lisa Smith, is using a false identity."

She handed their boss a printout. Lisa's profile photo appeared on the four-year-old BOLO request.

"Her real name is Amy Walker. Chicago PD wants her in connection with the homicide of Leonardo Santiago, apparently her boyfriend."

Blank whistled. "Good work, Cooper. Your undercover work paid off in spades."

Brandon grimaced. "Not exactly. Her coworker tipped us off. Tanesha Williams."

Sarge chuckled. "Got to love corporate America. Always at each other's throats. What are you thinking—she's a black widow?"

"We're still working on a motive."

"There's the harassment angle, too. What did Wesner's other assistants say?"

"We're still trying to get hold of them."

Their boss grunted. "Make that a priority. We need to close this before Chicago PD takes her."

"Sir, there's another possibility."

"Yes?"

Brandon ignored Mindy's annoyed stare. "Smith told the informant she has a stalker. She claims he killed Wesner. What if she's telling the truth? That would explain the false identity."

Sarge frowned. "What's Wesner's connection to the dead boyfriend in Chicago?"

"Maybe the stalker followed her to New York? He could have attacked her perceived romantic partners out of jealousy."

Mindy's annoyance bubbled over. "Sir, Santiago was stabbed multiple times in his home. Wesner's death was staged as a suicide, and the killer had access to the agency. Lisa is the only thing they have in common."

Their boss smiled. "Good point, Scott. But that cuts both ways. If the MOs are so different, who says Smith committed both crimes?"

Mindy shut her mouth. Her objection to Brandon's theory had undermined her own.

Sarge sighed. "We've kept this homicide investigation quiet so far. The media aren't breathing down our necks yet. But once we make an arrest, the clock will start ticking. Let's not jump to any conclusions."

He handed Mindy back the printout. "Bring her in for questioning."

Brandon pushed his luck. "Sir, Smith is our best lead."

Mindy folded her arms. "Our best *suspect*."

"True. But I've managed to get close to her."

Mindy snorted. "That's an understatement."

He plowed on. "Maybe her stalker is real, maybe not? But the false identity means she's scared. If we call her in for questioning, we might spook her, and she'll run. She's evaded Chicago PD for years. We could lose her, too."

Mindy folded her arms. "*Please*."

Sarge raised his hand to calm her. "He's got a point, Scott."

The scales had shifted back in Brandon's favor, and he leveraged his advantage.

"Let me speak with her off the record. If she doesn't come clean, we'll bring her in."

Their boss gazed at Mindy. "What do you think?"

Mindy cocked her head. "I think my partner is biased."

"But is he wrong?"

Brandon's phone rang. The caller ID read, "Lisa Smith."

"It's her."

Lisa had turned to him of her own volition. Her call vindicated his approach.

Brandon answered. "Hey, Lisa."

"I need to speak with you."

His heart rate galloped at the sound of her voice. "Sure. What's up?"

"Not on the phone."

Her urgency alarmed him. *Is she in danger?* He fought the compulsion to rush out to her defense. After Mindy's accusation of partiality, he had to handle this by the book.

"Where'd you like to meet?"

Sergeant Blank widened his eyes, and even Mindy unfolded her arms. Lisa wanted to come clean. Was this the breakthrough they needed to blow the case wide open?

"Somewhere private."

Brandon needed a venue he could control. Somewhere she'd feel safe.

"I know the perfect place."

Chapter 29

Amy followed the detective into his Upper West Side apartment, and her heart fell. Discarded clothing draped the stained couch. Discarded food wrappers littered the coffee table. The bachelor pad did not inspire confidence. *Can I trust him with my life?*

Brandon collected empty beer bottles, takeout boxes, and a sweater.

"Sorry about the mess. I wasn't expecting company. Please, make yourself at home."

Amy perched on the couch. *I hope his detective skills are better than his housekeeping.*

Her hair was still damp from her shower. She'd stayed up most of the night planning her exit strategy, examining each step for unintended consequences until her head spun. In the morning, she'd told Daniel she'd meet a friend later to find a solution to her "problem" and she'd given her brother cash for sightseeing. If Steve dropped by, he wouldn't discover her brother in her apartment. With Daniel safely out of the way, the anxiety and exhaustion had taken their toll, and Amy had collapsed into a deep sleep.

She'd woken up in the late afternoon. Still in bed, she'd checked her phone. Beth had called. So had Mark, and he'd left a text asking how she was feeling. Her stalker had sent no new messages. But their last exchange still bounced around her head.

She's onto you. I can help.

Tanesha had attacked Amy unfairly and ended her career at Wesner & Morgan. But being a vindictive jerk wasn't a capital offense. Still, the threat of violence might have shut her mouth. Perhaps then Tanesha would have left Wesner & Morgan instead of her? *Don't go there, Amy.* Her secret admirer wouldn't stop at intimidation, especially if Tanesha called their bluff. *You did the right thing.*

Amy had evicted her stalker from her thoughts. *Stay focused. Steve is your problem.* She'd stepped under a steaming shower and called Brandon to schedule a meeting.

Brandon spoke to her from the kitchen. "Do you want a beer?"

"No, thanks."

"Soda?"

"I'm good."

The butterflies in her stomach had banished the desire for food or drink. This visit risked everything. Once she told Brandon her story, there was no turning back. But Daniel had forced her hand. She had to protect her little brother. Running was no longer an option.

Offense is the best defense. Coming clean was the only way to fight Steve and remove the threat to their lives. But the move could boomerang terribly. Amy was a fugitive from the law. Steve was a police officer. Would Brandon believe her?

During their date on Monday night, the detective had spent freely on her. His generosity didn't mean he had deep pockets. His grubby apartment proved that. He liked her. His choice of meeting place probably wasn't random either. Did he hope their discussion would lead to something more intimate? Amy wasn't looking for a lover. She needed a friend in law enforcement who would see through the incriminating evidence and accept the truth. Amy was betting everything on Brandon. Her fate was in his hands.

Her phone vibrated twice. Amy's conscience tingled. She hadn't returned Mark's text or his calls. How was she supposed to explain her absence? She could only offer him lies.

But Steve hadn't sent the message. The stalker had contacted her again. She opened the text.

I had no choice. She knew.

Amy's blood turned to ice. He meant Tanesha. What had he done? Had the stalker read her innermost thoughts and acted on his own? Had he hurt Tanesha...or killed her?

Brandon returned with two glasses and a bottle of mineral water.

Amy slipped her phone into her pouch. *I said no. I'm not responsible.* Had she misunderstood the message? Amy couldn't deal with that now. *Focus!* Steve would demand his money tomorrow. Her life hung in the balance. Daniel's, too. *Set the plan in motion.*

She gripped her knees. "Thank you for meeting me."

Brandon poured the drinks. "You're welcome. It sounded urgent."

"It is."

She inhaled a quavering breath. *Here goes.*

"I owe you an apology. I haven't been completely honest."

Brandon studied her impassively. The admission didn't seem to surprise him. Amy had evaded his questions, after all.

"Lisa Smith isn't my real name. It's Amy Walker."

The revelation didn't appear to shock him.

"Why the new identity?"

She swallowed. "Back home, in Chicago, my boyfriend, Leo, got mixed up with a drug dealer. He murdered Leo in our apartment. I saw it all. Leo hid me in his closet when the killer arrived. That's why I left and changed my name."

"When did this happen?"

"Four years ago."

"Did you know the killer?"

"Not well. I'd met him once before. His name is Steve Hamlin."

"Why didn't you go to the police?"

"I did. I spoke with an officer—Detective Kim—and told him everything. But then Steve showed up at the station. He's a police officer. That's why I ran. I knew he'd make it look like I killed Leo."

Brandon leaned back on the couch and stared at the wall. *Does he believe me?*

The corner of his mouth twitched. "Why are you coming forward now?"

Amy hesitated. *Keep Daniel out of this.*

"Steve found me last week. He said Leo took money from him and he'd kill me if I didn't pay him by tomorrow."

"How much?"

"A hundred thousand."

Brandon took out a small notebook and pen. "What else do you know about Steve?"

"He's British. He calls himself The Hammer. When we first met, he had long blond braids and shaved sides like a Viking."

Brandon grinned. "A British Viking?"

Does he think I'm kidding around? She soldiered on.

"He carries a big hunting knife in a leather holder. He killed Leo with it."

Brandon recorded the details, and his scribbling reassured her. *He's taking this seriously.*

"And your boyfriend's full name?"

"Leonardo Santiago."

"Did Steve commit any other crimes besides Leo's murder?"

How was she supposed to know? Wasn't murder enough?

"I think he used Leo to sell drugs. Maybe that's where the money came in? I'd found a bag of cocaine in the apartment that morning. It's the reason I'd decided to leave him."

Brandon jotted down the information. "Do you think Steve was involved in Josh Wesner's death, too?"

"No. Why would you think...?" Her breath caught in her throat. "She told you, didn't she?"

"Who did?"

"Tanesha."

Brandon blinked. She was right. Her confession about her name and Leo's murder hadn't jolted him...because he already knew. Amy had wrung her hands over lying to him, but he'd kept secrets from her, too.

He licked his lips. "She called us this morning."

"You could have told me."

"I can't share information about an ongoing murder investigation."

"You think I killed Josh? Is that why you asked me out—to trap me?"

Amy had trusted him. *This was a big mistake.*

"It's not like that. I'm trying to help. If you cooperate, we can protect you. But I need the whole truth. Tanesha said you mentioned a stalker and that he'd killed Josh."

Amy hadn't intended to mention her secret admirer. Her tale about a British Viking in Chicago's police force already stretched her credibility to breaking point.

"I'm not making this up."

"Nobody's saying that. Just tell me everything. Who's been stalking you?"

She couldn't backpedal now.

"I don't know. I've never seen him or spoken to him. He sends messages."

"Text messages?"

Amy nodded. "They started the morning Josh died. At first, I ignored them. They seemed harmless and generic like automated messages. But then more texts arrived. He knew where I was and how I looked. That's when I realized he was following me, and then..."

Brandon gazed into her eyes. "What?"

Why does this feel like a betrayal? "Then, he hinted that he'd killed Josh."

"Why would he kill Josh?"

She swallowed hard. "To protect me. Josh figured out my false identity. He tried to force me to..." She trailed off.

Brandon completed her sentence. "To have sex with him."

She nodded.

"Amy, do you have any idea who sent you the messages?"

"No. I figured it must be someone from work, but now I'm not so sure."

"Could it be Mark Davis?"

"No. He warned me to stay away from Mark."

"What about Steve Hamlin?"

She shook her head. "The stalker offered to get rid of Steve. I said no."

But you wanted to.

Brandon stopped his scribbling. "Can I see the messages?"

"Sure."

Amy reached for the phone in her pouch. Her story might sound crazy, but nobody could deny the clear, hard evidence of her message history.

She swiped her finger across the screen. "Each message came from a different number at first. Lately, he's been using the same one."

Brandon shifted closer to look at her phone. "Good. We'll be able to track his movements. Even if he's taken steps to conceal his identity, a forensic linguistic analysis might give us leads. We'll need screenshots, too."

"Okay."

Amy opened her Messages app, and the floor seemed to fall away beneath her feet. *Oh my God. This can't be.*

"Amy, what's the matter?"

"They've disappeared."

"What's disappeared?"

The phone trembled in her hand. "The messages. They're gone."

Chapter 30

Tanesha poured a ladle of liquid batter into the frying pan that evening, and the sweet scent of pancakes filled her kitchen—the aroma of victory.

Mark had approached her desk that morning. "Is Lisa in yet?"

Tanesha smiled innocently. "I haven't seen her. She left early yesterday, too."

Her boss bit his lip. "She wasn't feeling well. I hope she's okay."

"She seemed fine to me."

Mark frowned. "She was going to touch up the slides for my presentation at ten o'clock."

Tanesha read the time off her monitor. "Yikes. That's soon. Want me to have a look?"

"Please!"

"Your wish is my command. Send it over, and I'll do my magic."

Mark grinned. "Thanks, Tee. You're a lifesaver."

"I won't let you down."

Tanesha got to work on the presentation. She fixed Mark's typos and corrected the animation order of bullet points. Tanesha had never enjoyed her work more. Her plan had come together perfectly except for one minor glitch.

Lisa hadn't handed in her resignation. The coward had chickened out and flown the coop. *Never mind.* Tanesha adjusted her plan and called Detective Cooper. Felonies such as false impersonation meant prison time, and Lisa Smith would soon wish she'd followed Tanesha's orders to the letter. *Serves you right.* Her attempt to usurp Tanesha's throne had ended in a sweeping defeat. Lisa Smith was history, and Mark didn't suspect a thing. Order had returned to the universe, and Tanesha had tasted revenge. *Take that, Taylor West.*

She added fancy transitions and returned the presentation on time. Mark would trust no one else with mission-critical tasks again. Soon, he'd forget about that skinny-assed witch.

Only Eddie had soured at her triumph. He wheeled his chair into her cubicle.

"What have you done?"

Tanesha grinned sweetly. "I don't know what you're talking about."

His eyelid jittered. "Did you get Lisa fired?"

"How would I do that?"

"Because of what I told you."

"Since when is going to the post office a crime? Not my problem she doesn't show up at work."

Eddie retreated with his chair and fumed in silence. She'd stumped him. In a moment of anger, he'd handed her that crucial lead. But he had no idea what Tanesha had learned from her cousin or how she'd leverage the information. The poor fool had fallen under Lisa's spell, too. *He'll get over her.* Lisa would have ruined him. Tanesha had done him a favor.

Her secret victory had only one downside. She couldn't tell anyone about it. *Who cares?* Tanesha was celebrating at home with her pancakes and a bottle of red.

She turned off the stove and carried her plate to the kitchen table. Tanesha anointed the pancake tower with maple syrup and raised her wine glass.

"Here's to you, Lisa Smith. Amy Walker. Whoever the hell you are. Here's to never seeing your skinny ass again. Ha!"

Tanesha gulped her wine and dug into her festive meal. *Mm.* She savored the flat cakes' sweet, warm softness.

There came a knocking on the door. Tanesha swallowed her mouthful. She wasn't expecting any visitors tonight. Was her neighbor's kid selling brownies again? Tanesha was in a charitable mood.

She shifted her chair back, walked over to the door, and put her eye to the peephole. Her mouth dropped open in surprise.

What are you doing here?

Chapter 31

"They were here seconds ago. I swear."

A surreal terror gripped Amy in Brandon's apartment. She'd opened the Messages app on her phone to show him the stalker's texts. But her secret admirer's messages had vanished without a trace. *That's impossible.*

Brandon sat next to her on the couch. "Maybe you deleted them by accident?"

"No. I'd remember that."

"Maybe the app updated automatically and reset the message log?"

She shook her head. "The other messages are still here."

Amy studied the phone for clues. There had to be a rational explanation. But she knew how this seemed. *Does he think I lied about the stalker?*

Brandon frowned. "Does anybody else have access to your phone?"

"No."

She swallowed. *That isn't true.* Daniel was staying with her. Had he deleted the messages while she'd slept? But she hadn't told him about her stalker, and even if she had, why would he tamper with her phone? *Keep him out of this.* Amy hadn't mentioned her brother's visit to Brandon. Maybe she didn't need to?

"The last text arrived a few minutes ago. I've had my phone with me the whole time."

"What was the message?"

Amy stiffened. She remembered the text clearly. *I had no choice. She knew.* But sharing those words meant stepping onto a very slippery slope.

"I'm not sure. It was too vague."

She winced. *I understood the message perfectly well.* The stalker had killed Tanesha. *Or had he?* Why would he murder Tanesha? She'd already ratted Amy out to the police. Killing her now didn't help Amy. It only made things worse.

Brandon didn't push the matter. "Did he send any clickable links?"

"No. Why?"

"That's usually how hackers take over devices. I'll have our digital department scan your phone for spyware."

Spyware? Had her stalker invaded her phone?

"Would he be able to delete messages remotely?"

"And much more. Some malicious apps can access the phone's location, microphone, and camera, too."

The information hit her like a ton of bricks. *That's how he knows everything. That's why I've never seen him.* The stalker had hacked her phone. He'd eavesdropped on her conversations and watched her every move.

Amy shuddered. She'd undressed near her phone. Had the creep taken photos of her naked? Her so-called best friend had violated her privacy.

"Is he listening now?"

"That's possible."

She turned off the device. Had she acted too late? Did the stalker know she'd informed on him? He'd killed people for less. What would he do to her?

Brandon held out his hand for her phone, but Amy refused to surrender the device.

"I need this for work."

That was an excuse. But the phone was her lifeline. What if the stalker texted her again? Would the police think she was an accomplice? Would the stalker blame her for the murders?

Brandon grinned. "I'm sure Wesner and Morgan will understand."

Amy didn't budge. "I should get permission first."

"Okay. I'll stop by the station to see what our databases have on Steve Hamlin."

Amy relaxed. Brandon believed her. He was on her side. He'd do everything in his power to help her. *But will that be enough?*

He rose to his feet. "I'll get a Faraday bag for the phone, too."

"What's that?"

"Faraday bags block electromagnetic fields. It'll prevent your hacker from removing his spyware remotely. But we're probably too late for that. He deleted the messages, so he probably knows we're onto him. You should stay here tonight."

Amy recoiled. Daniel was waiting for her at her apartment. But how could she justify leaving without exposing her brother?

"I can't. All my stuff is at home."

"I'll get you whatever you need. You're safe here."

She stood. "Steve gave me until tomorrow. I still have time."

"What about the hacker?"

"He wants to help me, not hurt me. I'll grab my things and come straight back."

The lie weighed on her heart like a boulder all the way home. She wouldn't return to Brandon's apartment. Her plan had crashed and burned. Now Amy had two killers on her tail.

Daniel's face was ghostly pale when she returned.

"Where have you been? I was worried about you."

Amy locked the door behind her. "I told you. I went to meet a friend."

He huffed. "I thought you'd bailed on me."

Ouch. She couldn't blame him. She'd dropped out of his life without warning before.

Amy looked him in the eye. "Daniel, I'll never leave you again. Okay?"

He smiled bitterly. She'd promised him that last time, too.

Daniel brightened. "How'd the meeting go? Does your friend have the money?"

The meeting. Amy hadn't shared her plan with him, and he'd assumed she'd begged her friend for a loan. But the result was the same.

"Not well."

He stared at her. "What are we going to do?"

"The only thing we can. Run."

"What? No!"

"Listen to me, Daniel. I tried everything. Our situation is more complicated than you think. I'm out of ideas and almost out of time."

Someone knocked loudly on the front door.

Amy's heart skipped a beat. Had Steve arrived early to collect his money? Had her stalker come to murder her, too?

"Lisa?" a man said. "It's me, Lucas."

Amy snuck up to the door and put her eye to the peephole. Lucas held a phone to his chest but appeared to be alone.

She put her finger to her lips and shepherded her brother into her bedroom.

"It's my landlord. I can't have him see you here."

"Who's Lisa?"

Lucas knocked twice more. "Lisa, I know you're in there."

She raised her voice. "I'm coming!" She turned back to her brother. "I'll explain later. Wait here until he's gone."

Amy returned to the entrance and opened the door. "Lucas, how can I help you?"

The man gazed past her and wiggled his thick eyebrows. "Subletting is forbidden. It's in the contract."

"I know. I'm alone."

"Then who were you speaking to?"

"Myself. I like to...talk things out." She shrugged at her quirky habits. "What's up, Lucas?"

"Detective Cooper from NYPD called for you. He said your phone is off."

"Oh, thank you." Brandon had looked up her landlord to reach her. Was he checking up on her or had he discovered some new information?

She took the phone. "Hi, Brandon."

"Hi, Lisa—um, Amy. I thought I'd missed you."

Amy smiled at Lucas. "No, I just got back. Won't be long."

"Good. Listen, you said Steve Hamlin used the name The Hammer. Did he use any other aliases?"

The black jaws of the abyss opened beneath her. *Something's wrong.*

"Not as far as I know. Why?"

"I searched our national databases including the FBI. I called Chicago to confirm, too. There's no record of a Steve Hamlin working there."

The vertigo of the missing text messages returned.

"That was four years ago. Maybe he left since then?"

"I checked that, too. Nothing."

The jaws closed around her. The messages had disappeared. Now Steve was a ghost, too. *That's impossible.* Steve killed Leo. He'd threatened Amy in her apartment and in a public bathroom. She'd watched him interact with other police officers in Chicago.

"Speak with Detective Kim at the 9th Precinct. He seemed to know him. He'll remember."

She waited for Brandon's answer. There it was again—that momentary hesitation before he replied.

"Good idea. I'll ask."

Is he lying? Amy had mentioned Kim. Had Brandon asked already? What had Kim told him? Was Kim working with Steve?

"Amy, are you there?"

"Yeah."

"Steve Hamlin might not be his real name. Could you identify him from a photo?"

"Definitely."

"Great. I'm sending a cruiser to pick you up."

Amy's cheek twitched. *Or to arrest me?*

"Sure. I'll wait right here."

"Perfect. I'll see you soon."

She ended the call and handed back the phone. "Thanks, Lucas."

The landlord stroked his mustache. "Are you in trouble? I don't want any problems with the police."

She closed the door. "Have a good night."

Amy returned to her bedroom. "Daniel, get your things. We're leaving."

She opened her overnight bag on the bed and shoved shirts and a spare pair of jeans into the bag. A wave of déjà vu soaked her senses. The day Leo had died, she'd packed her suitcase on the bed. This time, at least, she didn't need room for bulky textbooks.

Daniel sputtered, "Where will we go?"

"North."

She marched back to the living room.

Her brother followed. "You're running again?"

"We don't have a choice. The cops will be here any minute."

"Cops? How are they involved now?"

She picked up her family portrait. "I'll explain on the way."

"I don't want to run for the rest of my life."

"Then don't."

"What are you saying? We split up? That's your solution?"

Amy shrugged. "I don't have Steve's money. The police think I killed Leo. If I stay here, I'll end up dead or in prison. We have to leave tonight, and to be honest, you'll be safer on your own. But it's up to you."

Daniel glared at her for three long seconds. "Then I'll take that with me."

He snatched the photo frame from her. A second wave of déjà vu crashed over her. Leo had seized the family portrait to stop her from leaving, too. He'd known how much the photo meant to her.

"Give that back."

"It's as much mine as yours."

He was right. The portrait had belonged to their parents. They had equal claims to it. But why was he being so difficult?

"I'll send you a copy, all right? We'll both have it."

He sneered. "The way we shared everything else?"

"What are you talking about?"

Daniel raised his chin. "Mom and Dad must have left us something. I never got my share."

Amy's laugh was short and mirthless. "Mom and Dad left us with debt. The banks took the house, and the funeral expenses cleared out the rest."

"You said nothing about that."

"You were too young to understand, and I didn't want to burden you. They'd already left us alone in the world. You didn't need another reason to hate them."

Her vision swam. Why was he fighting her? Why was he dredging up those painful memories? Daniel didn't care about the photo. He wasn't sentimental about their childhood memories. He only wanted money.

She grabbed the photo frame. "Give it back!"

He held on tight. "You don't deserve it."

"*I* don't deserve it? You ungrateful douche!"

Amy pulled with all her strength. Daniel yanked in the opposite direction. Then, her fingers slipped, and the portrait launched from their hands. Glass tinkled as the frame shattered against the wall and fell to the floor.

She ran to the destroyed heirloom. "No, no, no!"

Had shards of glass sliced the treasured image to shreds?

The impact had broken the frame in two. Amy rescued the photo from the wreckage and ran her finger over her parents' smiling faces. They'd survived this accident unscathed. But the damaged frame wasn't empty. A folded page of white paper remained where the photo had rested.

Amy drew the note from the frame.

Daniel moved closer. "What's that?"

"I don't know."

She unfolded the page and stared in bewilderment at the two lines of text.

He looked over her shoulder. "What does it mean?"

Amy blinked at the mysterious characters. "I have no idea."

Chapter 32

B randon strangled the steering wheel of their unmarked cruiser while the nighttime Midtown traffic inched along. For a change, Mindy rode shotgun and said nothing. She didn't tease Brandon or say, "I told you so." She didn't need to rub it in. That's how badly he'd screwed up. Soon, he'd rectify his mistake, but the abysmal slipup irked him. *How did I fall so hard?*

The warning signs had been abundant and clear: Amy's evasive answers; her false identity; her unlikely tales of crooked cops and homicidal stalkers. But Brandon had galloped past the flashing red lights toward the edge of the cliff.

"She trusts me," he'd told Sergeant Blank. "She'll turn herself in without a struggle. I promise."

He'd sent a squad car to collect her. But by the time the patrol officers knocked on her door, she'd fled. Attempts to triangulate her phone signal failed. Amy had kept the device off. She'd gone underground. Her earlier adamant refusal to remain in the safety of his apartment only strengthened the unavoidable conclusion: Amy had duped him.

Sarge instructed them to file a BOLO and call a judge to approve an emergency search warrant for Amy's apartment. This time, Brandon hadn't argued.

He cruised down Madison Avenue.

His bruised ego searched for reassuring explanations. Steve Jobs, the legendary Apple Inc. founder and CEO, had used his irresistible charm to convince employees they could achieve the impossible. Did Amy also radiate a "reality distortion field?" Had she wielded her striking beauty and animal magnetism not to invent iPhones but to get away with murder?

Don't shift the blame. Own it. His sex drive had overruled his better judgment, and he'd let a prime suspect slip through his fingers. *I'm an idiot.* Or had Amy's presence stirred something deeper and darker within him?

Mindy stared out of the passenger window. "To be honest, I thought she'd show up, too."

Brandon scoffed. "Sure you did."

His partner's attempt at cheering him up only highlighted his failure.

"I'm serious. She came to you before she knew Tanesha had contacted us. Maybe she truly believes she's the victim?"

He shifted in his seat. "You mean, she's delusional?"

The theory appealed to him. Amy's confession had seemed honest, and the missing messages appeared to genuinely surprise her. His suggestion that a sophisticated hacker had infiltrated her phone had shaken her visibly. *Maybe I haven't lost my touch?*

Mindy shrugged. "Makes sense. Why invent a story we'd disprove so easily?"

A few quick phone calls from the station had unraveled Amy's conspiracy theory. Steve "The Hammer" Hamlin had never worked for Chicago's 9th Precinct. Detective Kim knew nobody who fitted the cop's colorful description either. In desperation, Brandon had called the local FBI field office, too, but had drawn more blanks. Amy's alleged dirty cop blew away like a smoke screen, casting shadows of doubt on the veracity of her vigilante stalker, too.

But Mindy's words offered consolation. Maybe Amy hadn't deceived him, at least not intentionally? Her paranoid mind had tricked them both. But one brutal fact ruined this booby prize.

"Then why did she run?"

Mindy frowned. "Yep, you're right. I guess she was just muddying the investigation to buy time."

Thanks for nothing.

"For what it's worth," she continued, "I'm sorry things turned out this way. Amy is bad news. That's why I tried to warn you. I didn't want you to get hurt."

Underneath her sarcasm and competitive streak, Mindy cared about him. He should have listened to her.

Brandon swallowed his pride. "Thanks, Minds."

The landlord waited for them outside Amy's door. Lucas Stefanos asked to see their badges and search warrant, then dug a large keychain from his pocket.

He waggled his bushy mustache with dissatisfaction. "This is a respectable building, Officers. I don't want any trouble. Whatever Ms. Smith got mixed up with, I had no idea."

The landlord was fishing for information. Was he concerned his property would become a crime scene?

Brandon pulled on a pair of disposable gloves from his shoulder bag of forensic tools. "How did she seem to you tonight?"

Lucas found the key among a dozen others. "Wary. More than usual. But she was never a talker. Is this about the man who was with her?"

Brandon and Mindy traded meaningful glances. Amy hadn't mentioned she had company.

"What man?"

Did Steve attack her at home? Is that why she disappeared? He pictured Amy sprawled on the floor of her apartment in a pool of blood, and fear for her safety erased his resentment.

The landlord shrugged. "I heard them speaking before I knocked. Ms. Smith said she was talking to herself. Ha! Can't fool me. I've seen it all."

"What did they say?"

Lucas turned the key in the lock. "Beats me. But it sounded like an argument."

He made to open the door, but Brandon raised his hand.

"Thank you, Mr. Stefanos. We'll take it from here."

"Be my guest."

Brandon drew his Glock and cracked the door open. Hours ago, he'd promised Amy that he'd protect her. *Am I too late?*

"Lisa, it's Detective Cooper and Detective Scott. Are you in there?"

She didn't respond.

He stepped inside, his heart thumping rapidly. Mindy followed him, her service weapon in hand, too. Sweeping his gun from side to side, he scanned the room for intruders.

"Clear."

He rushed to the bedroom and checked the bathroom, too.

"Clear. Nobody's home."

They holstered their weapons.

Mindy opened the bedroom closet. "Her clothes are gone. Looks like she split."

Brandon nodded. "Or she was abducted?"

"Unlikely. There are no signs of forced entry or a struggle. Maybe she really was talking to herself?"

The doubts returned. *Is Amy unstable? Had she argued with imaginary enemies?*

They returned to the living room, and a glint of reflected light caught his eye. A wooden photo frame lay in the corner on a bed of broken glass.

Brandon kneeled over the shattered object. The photo was missing.

"Sign of a struggle? The landlord heard voices. Maybe she threw the frame at her attacker?"

Mindy stood over him. "She had time to collect the photo and her things. Doesn't seem like a heroic last stand."

Brandon tried to connect the dots. Had someone been here with Amy? Identifying the man would move them closer to Amy.

Lucas peered at them from the threshold. "Will she be back?"

Brandon stood. "I wouldn't look for a new tenant yet. Call us if you see her. We'll want to ask her a few questions."

He studied the living room. There were no empty drinking glasses on the coffee table or any sign anybody had lived there recently. Somebody had cleaned up before Amy fell off the radar. Either a professional criminal had captured Amy, or she had more secrets.

Brandon dropped to his haunches by the couch. A straight black hair lay on a cushion.

"Look at this. Steve was supposed to have blond hair. Did our mystery man leave this behind?"

Mindy joined him. "Could be hers."

Brandon grunted. The hair was too short to be Amy's. Maybe she wasn't psychotic after all? He pulled a paper evidence bag from his forensic kit.

"Let's find out."

Chapter 33

A my lurked on Broadway Street Thursday morning with her peaked cap angled to hide her face. CCTV cameras eyed her from every corner—the dark orbs on metal stalks above traffic lights and the slanted metal boxes atop NYPD observation towers. Getting to her destination undetected wouldn't be easy. But a puzzle stood at the epicenter of the earthquake that had ruined her life, and she couldn't complete the picture alone.

Amy joined the crowd at the intersection with 42nd Street and crossed at the green light.

Steve's deadline had expired, and Amy still didn't have his money. But the murderous crook was only one of her worries.

Last night, she'd lied to Brandon again. Instead of waiting for his officers, she'd locked the door of her apartment and fled with Daniel. The detective liked her. He wanted to believe her side of the story. But his duty as a police officer would force him to turn on her. *Sorry, Brandon.*

She and her brother had checked into The Manhattan Grand Hotel in the Lower East Side using her brother's identity card. The cops were looking for a lone female fugitive, not Mr. and Mrs. Daniel Walker. The mysterious note behind their family portrait had united them again. In the relative safety of the cheap hotel, they'd pored over the printout's contents but failed to decipher the two lines of jumbled alphanumeric characters.

"It's some kind of computer code," Daniel had said.

Amy had shaken her head. "Leo wasn't a programmer."

"You think Leo put it there?"

Her theory made perfect sense. "The night I left him, Leo grabbed the photo. I thought he'd done that to force me to stay. But now I know the true reason. He didn't want me to take the note he'd hidden there. This must be the key to where he put the money."

"Like a treasure map?"

She'd shrugged. "There are two lines of text. Could they be longitude and latitude? Maybe Leo encoded the coordinates?"

"How do we decode them?"

"I have no idea." If only she could ask Brandon. Then, another name had popped into her mind. "But I know someone who might."

She'd told Daniel her plan. Amy would meet the man alone.

Her brother had frowned. "Can we trust him?"

Amy had weighed the question. *Can we?* Tanesha had informed the police about her true identity. Had she told him, too? Would he help her anyway?

"It's worth a shot. We're out of options."

That night in their hotel room, she'd had trouble falling asleep. Her afternoon nap had left her wide awake, and now her head had buzzed with the mysterious note. But she must have drifted off because she'd woken up with a start at five AM. The nightmare had returned. Again, Amy washed blood from her hands. But this time, she wasn't in Leo's apartment. She didn't recognize the bathroom or the gory knife by the sink. *Where am I? What's going on?*

The endless tension had invaded her dreams again and scrambled her memories.

Her thoughts drifted back to the folded printout. What had Leo hidden behind her photo? Was the mysterious note the gateway to her salvation? Today, she'd try to find the answer. But to survive, she'd better stay out of sight.

On the street, Amy kept her head down and flowed with the pedestrians until a familiar building came into view. Two patrol officers lingered outside the double doors of the entrance. Instinctively, Amy stepped back. *Crap.* Had NYPD posted cops at the agency in case she showed up to work?

She remained on the opposite side of the street. Her watch read eleven fifty-nine AM. She leaned on a pole and tied the laces of her running shoes. Was he at work today? *I can't wait here all day.*

Mark Davis stepped out of the building in a gray suit. Amy relaxed. *Right on time.* He greeted the police officers and turned left. Amy kept pace with him.

Where are you eating today, Mark? She shadowed him, casting furtive glances in his direction. *He has no idea I'm here, watching.* The satisfying thrill in her core surprised her. Was that how her stalker felt? Was he addicted to the electrifying tingle of control? *Is he following me now?* She looked over her shoulder. No suspicious men pursued her. Today, Amy was the hunter, not the hunted.

Mark made another left and walked away from her. Amy waited at the red light. Her boss merged with the crowd and disappeared. *I'm losing him.* She shuffled on her feet but stayed put. *Don't do anything stupid.* Jaywalking could draw attention and ruin everything.

The light changed, and Amy ran. She pushed through the thicket of bodies.

"Excuse me. Sorry."

But Mark had vanished. *Where are you?* Had he left the street? How would she ever find him now? *Don't panic.* Amy scanned her surroundings. A hostess ushered a man to a window table in a familiar restaurant. *There you are!* The sign read: Risotto. *I should have guessed.*

Mark studied his phone and seemed unaware of his shadow. Did he have a lunch date? Amy would have to wait. A waitress arrived. Mark dictated his order and sent her away without browsing the menu. He'd ordered his usual. Mark was dining alone.

She crossed the street and slipped inside the restaurant. The hostess approached her, but Amy cut her off.

"I'm meeting someone. He's already here."

She hurried to his table and sat in the vacant chair.

"Surprise!"

Mark almost choked on his sip of water. "Lisa! I've been worried about you. Are you okay?"

Maybe Tanesha hadn't told him?

"I'm fine. I'll explain everything. I promise."

Mark glanced over his shoulder. "What's going on? People have been asking about you."

Her stomach cramped. "What people?"

"That detective called. Cooper."

"What did he say?"

"He asked if I'd heard from you. Lisa, are you in trouble?"

Her lips trembled. "No. Maybe? I'm not sure. I just need time to figure things out."

The waitress returned. "Would you like a menu?"

"No, I'm not staying."

They waited for the server to leave them.

Mark leaned closer. "How can I help?"

His openness surprised her. She'd feared he'd turn her away or call the police. He didn't seem to know about her fake identity.

Amy reached into her pocket and unfolded Leo's note. "I found this recently among my parents' things. Do you know what it could mean?"

Mark studied the rows of symbols. "I think so."

Amy gasped. Asking Mark had been the right decision. He'd supply the missing puzzle piece.

"Well, what is it?"

He frowned. "I'll need a computer to be sure I'm right. When we're back at the office, I'll—"

"I can't go back yet."

"Okay." He drummed his fingers on the table. "Drop by my apartment tonight, and we'll figure this out." He handed back the page and wrote his address on a napkin.

"Perfect! Thank you!"

"Stay for lunch? My treat."

"Thank you, but I can't. I'll see you later."

He grinned. "It's a date."

Chapter 34

B randon and Mindy ducked beneath the yellow strip of police tape. The apartment reeked of congealed blood. The stench of violent death no longer bothered him, but today a nagging doubt threatened to toss his lunch. *Is this my fault?*

The dispatch call had interrupted their meal at a deli on West 35th Street.

"You've got a one-eighty-seven," the female operator said.

Brandon rested his egg sandwich on the greasy table and reached for his notepad. "What's the address?"

With his phone pressed to his ear, he jotted down the details.

Mindy chewed her ham sandwich. "What is it?"

"A murder in East Village."

She frowned. "East Village? Why'd they call us?"

Good question.

He spoke into the phone. "There's been some mistake. We're with Midtown South Precinct."

"No mistake," the operator said. "Apparently, the decedent is a POI in a case of yours."

His heart skipped a beat. Only one person of interest had gone missing recently. *No. Not her. Please don't say it's Amy.*

"What's the victim's name?"

"Sorry. I don't have that."

"We're on our way."

Brandon discarded his sandwich, and they hurried to the crime scene. His conscience tortured him during the short ride. *Is that why Amy disappeared last night?* Had Steve abducted her and killed her while Brandon had searched her apartment and suspected her of betrayal?

"Don't beat yourself up," Mindy said from the passenger seat. Again, she'd read his mind. "I doubt it's her. And if it is, we had no way of knowing."

He gritted his teeth. "I did. She turned to me for help. I should have done something."

They parked outside a red-brick residential building and ran up the stairs. A patrol officer guarded the door of the apartment. Brandon and Mindy signed the log and pulled on disposable booties, shower caps, and gloves from boxes on the floor. Then, they followed the smell of carnage to the kitchen.

Forensic techs in full-body scrubs photographed the corpse on the white tiles. The victim wasn't Amy Walker but a thickset black woman. *Tanesha Williams.* The copious amount of blood and the gaping slit across her neck left little doubt as to the cause of death.

One agonizing question replaced another. *Did Amy kill her?*

Sergeant Blank arrived wearing forensic covers. He stepped around the pool of blood to join them and studied the body.

"Know her?"

Mindy answered. "Tanesha Williams, an assistant at Wesner and Morgan."

"Is she the one who ratted on Ms. Smith?"

"Yes, sir."

Sarge eyed them meaningfully but said nothing. Brandon's conscience spoke for him. *If you hadn't let Amy slip away, we wouldn't be here.*

Their boss called over the patrol officer with the tidy beard, tanned skin, and dark eyes.

"Officer Jamali. Where's your shift sergeant?"

"He left ten minutes ago."

Sarge grunted. "Walk us through the scene."

Officer Jamali consulted a ringed notepad. "The call came in at eleven oh-five AM. A neighbor, Melissa West, discovered the body when she noticed the door was slightly open. I arrived at the scene with Officer Bennet at eleven fourteen AM and secured the site. The ME's assistant estimated the time of death between eight PM and midnight last night."

Brandon's throat constricted. Amy had left his apartment around nine after learning about Tanesha's tip-off. Was that why she'd insisted on leaving—to murder the assistant who had outed her?

Jamali turned a page of his notepad. "The cause of death is exsanguination caused by a single incision to the neck. We're still trying to locate the murder weapon, probably a kitchen knife obtained at the scene."

"Any witnesses?"

"Mrs. West didn't hear a commotion and neither did any of the immediate neighbors. Once we identified the victim from the photo ID in her bag, Major Crimes referred the case to Midtown South."

"Thank you, Officer. We'll take it from here."

Sarge turned to Mindy. "Detective Scott, remind me. How did Walker's boyfriend die in Chicago?"

"Multiple sharp force trauma, sir. Probably a large, serrated knife."

Sergeant Blank eyed Brandon. "Your thoughts, Detective?"

His airways tightened further. Brandon could see which way the wind was blowing. Sarge was offering him a chance to correct his screwup.

He gazed at the kitchen table. A pile of pancakes towered on a single plate. Had Tanesha expected company?

"There's no sign of a struggle or forced entry. The victim probably let her attacker inside willingly. They likely knew each other on some level. The use of a knife in the murder might connect this to the Santiago homicide in Chicago. Amy Walker's recent history with the decedent makes her a prime suspect. Finding her should be a top priority."

Sarge grunted again. "Good. Then, we're on the same page."

Brandon forced a grin. The evidence against Amy was circumstantial. Unless they found the murder weapon in her possession or trace evidence placed her at the murder scene last night, the DA would refuse to press charges. There were other leads to explore. He opened his mouth to mention the short black hair they'd found at Amy's apartment, then thought better of it.

Sarge raised his eyebrows. "Anything else?"

If he thinks I'm shielding Amy again, he'll kick me off the case.

"No, sir."

"Okay, let's get to work. Interview her neighbors in the building and across the street. Somebody must have seen something. Speak with her coworkers, too. I want all CCTV footage in the vicinity. Traffic cams, too. And for heaven's sake, find me that murder weapon. Detective Cooper, may I have a word?"

They stepped to the side for a private chat.

"If you want to sit this one out, I'll understand."

Did Sarge still suspect he was under Amy's influence?

"I want to see this to the end."

"Fine. But we can't afford any more cock-ups. Do you understand?"

"Yes, sir."

"Good." He left the scene.

Brandon stared at the pool of blood on the floor. The shattered glass in Amy's apartment implied a struggle. Had Steve used Amy to gain access to Tanesha? No, that made no sense. Why would he assault Tanesha? Steve was a dead end.

What about Amy's stalker? He'd killed Josh to protect her. What if her secret admirer had witnessed her confrontation with Tanesha? Would he dispatch the assistant, too? This new direction held more promise. Last night, Amy had powered off her phone, severing the stalker's window on her life. How had he reacted to the sudden rejection? Was he angry, after all he'd done for her? Had his admiration turned to hate? Would he assault her at home? Did the black hair on her couch belong to him?

Mindy eyed him with concern. "Hey. Are you okay?"

Brandon snapped back to the apartment's bleak reality. "Yeah."

"We should get started on the neighbors."

"Right."

His phone rang. Had officers located Amy? Was she already in custody? Or had they discovered her corpse, too?

The word Blocked displayed on the screen. Was Amy calling him from another phone?

Mindy watched him. "Who is it?"

He shrugged and answered. "Cooper."

"Hi," a woman said. "This is Heather Brody. You called me last week?"

Brandon flashed his eyes at Mindy. "Thank you for getting back to me. Are you still in Manhattan?"

"Yes."

"I need to ask you a few questions about a case I'm investigating."

She didn't respond. Was she hesitant to meet a police officer or simply short on time?

"It'll take a few minutes, tops."

She sighed. "I can meet tonight after work."

He thanked her, jotted down the time and place she'd selected, and ended the call.

Mindy studied him. "Who was that?"

"Heather Brody, one of Josh Wesner's former assistants. She sounded scared."

"Scared of what? Josh is dead."

Mindy was right. Unless Heather lived under a rock, she'd heard about her boss's apparent suicide. Josh could no longer harm her for speaking out. What threat still fueled her anxiety?

"Good question."

Chapter 35

A my followed Mark into his spacious penthouse on Broadway and 28th Street and stopped dead in her tracks. The panoramic view filled her with awe.

"Wow! This is amazing."

The Hudson River glowed with soft golden light as the sun set over the Manhattan skyline. The stylish living room seemed to float above the city, insulated from the everyday hustle and bustle of the streets below.

Mark draped his suit jacket on a leather bar chair at the elegant kitchen's island of white marble. "Make yourself at home."

"I will."

Amy flopped on the gray leather couch and soaked in the breathtaking scenery. The skyscrapers returned her gaze, blinking open a thousand square, yellow eyes. At nightfall, The City That Never Sleeps came alive.

I could get used to this. Unfortunately, Mark had kept their relationship platonic. A luxury New York apartment wouldn't solve her problems anyway.

Her boss placed a glass of soda on the glass coffee table. "Diet Coke."

"Thank you."

"I'll get the laptop."

Amy sipped her drink and retrieved the folded page from her pouch. In their dingy hotel room that afternoon, she and Daniel had studied Leo's note for clues. What did the two lines of random characters mean? The location and code of a safe-deposit box? Log-in credentials for an online bank account? Leo had said he'd invested the money. Had the ninety grand grown significantly over four years? Would the balance exceed the hundred thousand dollars Steve demanded? She and Daniel desperately needed the extra money for a fresh start.

Don't get your hopes up. Leo had been reckless. He'd probably bet the entire sum on a lame racehorse, and the mysterious note wasn't worth the paper it was written on.

Mark settled beside her and opened the computer on the coffee table. "I've been thinking about this all day. Can I see it again?"

Amy handed him the note. "That's why we're here."

Mark studied the message and grunted.

A thrill passed through her. "What do you think? Secret codes for a website and password?"

"That's one option. But then we'd need the encryption cipher and keys to decode them."

Amy nodded. "I'll pretend I understood that."

"Don't bother. I think the message is to be used as-is."

"How?"

"You've heard of cryptocurrency, right?"

"You mean like Bitcoin?"

"Exactly."

She braced for another barrage of computer jargon. "I have no idea how that works."

"It's not as complicated as you think. You need two pieces of information to access a Bitcoin account: a public address and a private key. Both are long strings of characters."

"Like these?"

"Correct. Usually, they're stored digitally or using QR codes. Nobody in their right mind types these bad boys by hand. But the raw character strings will work, too. Should we give it a try?"

"Sure."

"Okay. We'll need to install a wallet app on your phone."

Amy bit her lip. She'd turned off her phone to block her stalker, and now NYPD would track her cellular signal, too. But she didn't want to open that can of worms. *Oops! Sorry, Mark. I forgot to tell you. I'm a fugitive from the law, and a deranged murderer is on my tail.*

"Um, I'm having trouble with my phone."

"We can use my laptop if you like. Everything's already set up. I'll delete your account right after we test it out. Sound good?"

"Yeah, let's do that."

"Perfect." He clicked the icon on his computer desktop for an app called Exodus.

Exodus. The Israelites' journey from slavery to freedom. The word seemed like a good omen.

When the app opened, Mark selected the menu option for adding an account.

He handed back the note. "Read the strings out to me. Start with the first one, the public address."

Amy read the characters, one by one. "One. Ee. One. One. Four..."

When they were done, Mark hit Enter, and a spinner icon rotated on the screen while the app loaded the account data.

Amy held her breath. *Princess or pauper?* In a few seconds, she'd discover her fate. She'd heard of Bitcoin millionaires and the fortunes won—and lost—with cryptocurrency. Had Leo finally bet on a winning horse? *Please, please, let it be a hundred grand. I'll settle for ninety, too.*

The icon vanished, and a number appeared in a large green circle.

Amy deflated. "Twelve thousand. That's it?"

Leo's investment had fallen flat, burning most of the ninety grand. Would the balance buy her time? Amy doubted it. *I'm screwed.*

Mark stared at the screen with his mouth open. Twelve-thousand dollars was spare change for a man who lived in a multi-million-dollar penthouse. Had the number underwhelmed him into shocked silence? Did he pity her?

"It's okay, Mark. I hadn't expected much."

Liar! Reality had hit her over the head like a debt collector's baseball bat. She'd have to beg her new boss for a loan.

Mark blinked at her. "Not dollars, Lisa. Twelve thousand Bitcoin."

"Oh." Was she out of the red after all? "How much is that in dollars?"

He cleared his throat. "Let's see."

Mark touched the mouse pad and clicked a button with a dollar-sign icon. A new number displayed in the circle.

This time, Amy's jaw dropped, too. "Holy crap."

Chapter 36

Alone at the coffee shop table, Brandon checked his watch again. 8:07 PM. Josh Wesner's former assistant had stood him up. *Story of my life.*

He understood the woman's hesitation. Few people enjoyed interviews with homicide detectives. Most harbored secrets. Heather Brody had resigned from Wesner & Morgan three years ago. She'd moved on with her life. Why dredge up the past and speak ill of the dead? But he'd sensed another emotion in her voice. *Fear.*

He waved over the waiter, a balding man in his thirties. "I'll have that espresso now."

Brandon sighed. He'd dreaded this meeting, too. If Heather confirmed the rumors about Josh's harassment, she'd provide Amy's motive for killing her boss. He'd hammer another nail into her coffin. *You're still under her spell, aren't you?*

Amy had lied to him about her past. She'd made a fool of him at the NYPD. The evidence implicating her in multiple homicides grew with every passing hour. He should despise her. But his heart refused to release the beautiful suspect. *She's innocent. I can feel it.*

An elderly couple entered the coffee shop and selected a corner table. The waiter delivered Brandon's drink along with a granola cookie.

"On the house."

"Thanks."

See? Even the waiter pities you.

Brandon sipped his espresso. The pungent scent of Brazilian coffee cleansed his sinuses of the murder scene stench.

Tanesha is dead. Yesterday, she'd exposed Amy's identity, and Brandon, like an idiot, had informed Amy about the betrayal. He'd interviewed Tanesha's coworkers and boss. None had obvious reasons to kill her—except Amy.

The murder was a wake-up call. Amy needed to confess the whole truth—not some cockamamie tale about crooked police officers and homicidal hackers.

"Detective Cooper?" a woman said.

Locks of shoulder-length auburn hair framed her pale, uncertain face.

Brandon stood. "Ms. Brody, I thought you were a no-show."

"I'm sorry. My train ran late."

"Happens to the best of us. Please, sit with me."

Building rapport was the secret to a successful interview. They'd chosen a public, non-threatening venue for their meeting. When at ease, subjects are more likely to speak freely.

Heather Brody perched on the chair but clutched her handbag. She'd need extra reassurance.

"Do you want some coffee?"

"No, thank you. I can't stay long."

The waiter approached their table, but Brandon waved him away. Then, he flashed his NYPD badge. Any cold caller might claim to be a detective. Brandon had displayed his bona fides.

"You used to work for Wesner and Morgan, right?"

"That was three years ago."

She'd distanced herself from that part of her life. Did the agency's name raise unpleasant memories?

"You worked for Joshua Wesner?"

"I was his assistant for a month."

"Why'd you quit?"

She raised her chin in defiance. "I received an offer from another agency." Was she daring him to challenge her explanation?

"I heard a rumor about improper conduct at Wesner and Morgan."

Heather bolted to her feet, and her chair chattered to the floor. The elderly couple stared at them.

"I'm sorry, but I can't help you."

"Wait! I just need information. You're not in trouble. Please, hear me out."

She shifted on her feet. A mental struggle seemed to rage within her.

The bald waiter set the fallen chair upright.

"I'm sorry about that," she said.

"No problem, ma'am."

Heather waited for him to move away, then returned to her seat and inhaled deeply. "I'm listening."

Brandon chose his words carefully. "He can't hurt you anymore. But I need to hear the full story."

The news appeared to calm her. *Maybe she does live under a rock?*

Her lips trembled. "It started slowly at first. A smile here, a compliment there. Then, he asked me out to lunch. He seemed so interested in me." She smiled briefly at the memory. "I couldn't believe my luck. He was successful and single. I was alone here. I had nobody."

She sobbed.

Brandon handed her a napkin. "You're doing great, Heather. What happened next?"

She wiped her eyes. "He invited me to his fancy apartment." Her face went slack. "He tied me up. I asked him to stop. I begged him! But he didn't seem to hear...or care. He had whips and knives..."

Brandon swore under his breath. Josh Wesner had been a monster. *Did he torture Amy as well?* The bastard deserved to die. Amy could plead self-defense. A jury would sympathize with her situation.

Heather stared numbly at the table. "When he finished, he told me to get dressed and go home. The next day, I quit my job and didn't look back."

"Why didn't you report him?"

"He said he'd kill me if I talked. With his money and connections, he'd get away with it, too. I was lucky to escape in one piece."

Brandon nodded. "You did nothing wrong, Heather. Predators prey on the vulnerable. He'd picked you because you were alone and defenseless. But you're safe now."

"Safe? If he finds out I've talked..."

"He'll never hurt you again."

"How can you be so sure?"

"Haven't you heard? Josh Wesner died last week."

She squinted at him as though he was insane. "I wasn't talking about Josh."

The ground seemed to swallow him whole. "Who, then?"

Brandon knew the answer before she spoke the rapist's name.

"Mark Davis."

Chapter 37

M ark opened a bottle of champagne in the kitchen with a loud pop. "This calls for a celebration."

Amy remained on the couch, transfixed by the number on the laptop's screen. She'd never seen an account balance with so many numbers. *My account balance. Somebody pinch me.*

She read the number out loud. "Four hundred and eighty million dollars. Four hundred and eighty *million* dollars!"

Behind her, cupboard doors opened, and wine glasses chimed. "Don't forget the twenty-seven thousand."

"That's an insane amount of money."

"You're rich, Lisa. Filthy rich. Obscenely rich. Embrace it. Your parents left you an amazing inheritance."

Amy winced. She'd lied to Mark about the account's origin. *The less you know, the better.* Leo's face materialized in her head. *I'm onto something big this time.* His gambling addiction had finally paid off. *If only you'd lived to see this day.* She'd tell Mark the truth one day once she'd paid Steve and cleared her name. But why spoil the celebration? The universe had sent her a long-needed windfall and not a moment too soon. *Maybe fairy tale endings exist after all?*

She gaped at the screen. "But how do I use it? I've never bought anything with Bitcoin."

He carried the drinks toward her. "Some stores accept Bitcoin. For everything else, convert your crypto to dollars in the app and transfer to your bank account. Easy."

Amy grunted. Her troubles were over. She'd pay off Steve. She'd hire bodyguards, too. A soothing calm washed over her. She and Daniel were set for life. *We'll be okay. Everything will be okay.*

Mark joined her on the couch and handed her a glass of champagne.

A sudden worry disturbed her peace of mind. "Wait. Can anyone with the account details access the money?"

"Mm-hm. That reminds me."

He grasped the mouse with his free hand, clicked a few buttons on the Exodus app, and the enormous account balance disappeared.

"There. I've deleted the account from my computer. Only you have the details now. Hold on to that piece of paper."

The calm returned. Her paranoia hadn't insulted Mark, and he'd set her at ease immediately.

He raised his glass. "Congratulations, Lisa. Here's to being filthy rich."

She clinked her glass to his, and they gulped the bubbly wine.

"Mm. This is good."

He grinned. "I hope so. It's a thousand dollars a bottle. I've been saving it for a special occasion."

She took another sip. Amy had never tasted a thousand-dollar bottle of wine before. *I can get used to that, too.*

Mark gazed at her intensely. "So, what are you going to do with your fortune, Ms. Smith?"

"Pay off debts. After that, I have no idea. Any suggestions, Mr. Davis?"

Amy felt tipsy already. *This stuff is great.*

"You could buy Wesner and Morgan."

"Ha! Then, I'd be your boss."

He undressed her with his eyes. "I look forward to working under you."

He's flirting with me. Mark Davis is flirting with me!

She wagged her finger at him. "I thought you don't date employees."

He shifted closer. "You don't need the job anymore."

He's right. She'd never work another day in her life. Amy was free not just from Steve and financial stress. She could do anything she wanted. The world was her playground.

Her head swirled, a side-effect of her sudden stroke of luck or the champagne, she didn't care. Amy drained her drink in one shot and placed the glass on the table. Then, she climbed onto Mark and straddled him.

"I quit. Consider this my formal resignation."

What's come over me? She'd thrown herself at her boss.

Mark didn't object. He placed his glass on the table.

"I accept your resignation."

Amy ran her hands through his hair. "I want you."

His breath came in short, urgent gasps. "I've wanted you since I first laid eyes on you."

She kissed his lips. His hands caressed her body. Amy gripped the hem of her shirt to pull it over her head, but her arms felt heavy. Her head spun with a sudden rush of vertigo, and her muscles relaxed. She toppled sideways, and her face pressed against the leather upholstery.

"I don't feel so good."

Speaking took so much effort. Was it the wine, or had the intense stress of the past two weeks caught up with her?

Mark slipped out from under her, and her legs slid to the floor.

He stood. "You got a double dose. It's hit you hard."

What was he talking about? She'd only had one glass of wine. Amy had never reacted this way to alcohol.

She mumbled into the couch, "Double dose of what?"

He walked off. "Never mind."

Amy sighed. He'd take care of her. Mark loved her. She was rich. Everything was right with the world.

Her eyelids drooped. Plastic rustled in the distance. Then, the sound drifted closer. Was he opening a condom? *I'm in no state for sex. Can't he see that?*

"No," she said, but her voice was a whisper.

Amy tried to get up, but she was too exhausted to move. *A double dose.* Alarm bells rang in the back of her mind. *He drugged me!* Mark had slipped something into her drink. He could do anything to her now, and she'd be helpless to resist. *But why would he...?*

Hands gripped her torso. Mark lifted her off the couch and dragged her away, her limp feet trailing on the rug. Where was he taking her?

He lowered her to the floor and onto her back. She tried to launch to her feet and sprint toward the door, but her limbs flopped uselessly. Something crinkled beneath her. Her fingers brushed the loose, creased surface. He'd laid her out on a large piece of thick plastic sheeting.

Who kept reams of construction material at home? Nobody. *He planned this.* He'd kill her for the Bitcoin fortune and dispose of her body. *But that's impossible!* Mark couldn't have known about the money. They'd only discovered the account a few minutes ago. Had he planned to drug her anyway?

Mark towered over her. He placed a large black toolkit beside her and rummaged inside. He extracted steel implements from the box, lifting each in the air for her to see: a handsaw, an ax, bolt cutters. Terror racked her mind. *Why does he need those? What's he going to do to me?* He wasn't just going to murder her. He'd cut up her body piece by piece.

Her boss leered at her, and his twisted smile frightened her. She'd been wrong about him. Fatally wrong. Mark was a sick and violent man. He'd violate her body and snuff out her life...and he'd enjoy every moment.

A tear dripped from her eye and slid down her temple. Her lips formed a single word. *Why?*

He scoffed. "I've had my eye on you since you started work. Trust Josh to screw things up by killing himself. The place was crawling with uniforms, so I had to behave. You should have behaved, too."

What's he talking about? A numbness spread through her brain. She could barely raise her eyebrow in confusion.

"Tanesha got under your skin. But you shouldn't have killed her. That was careless."

Amy gasped. *Killed her?* Was Tanesha dead? Did he think she'd killed her?

The assistant had exposed Amy's identity to Brandon. There was no love lost between them. But Amy hadn't murdered her. She hadn't let the stalker touch her either.

Mark sneered. "Maybe in a different life, we could have been a team? I wasn't planning on doing this now. I never work on impulse. But tonight, you gave me four hundred million reasons."

A heavy fog descended on Amy's mind. *Josh's girls never stay long.* The other assistants hadn't fled the office. Mark had killed them.

The room darkened. *I'm losing consciousness.* But one last question burned in her. Had Mark sent the messages? *Are you my friend?*

Amy strained to move her tongue, but no sound emerged.

Mark dropped to his knees and straddled her. He wrapped his hands around her neck and squeezed.

I can't breathe. He's killing me! Amy would never enjoy Leo's money. She'd never tell her brother. *Wait! What about Daniel?* Who would guide him now? *Please, help me! Somebody. Anybody!* But the cruel, unfeeling world fell silent and faded to black.

Chapter 38

A my fumed on the backseat of the family car. "I hate her!"

Daniel sat beside her and listened to stupid kids' songs on Mom's iPod. But it wasn't his attention she'd wanted.

Dad stopped the car at the red light. His stubbly cheeks widened as he smiled. "Who do you hate, honey?"

Amy hugged her chest and said nothing, so Mom answered.

"Mrs. Kramer gave her a B plus in math today."

Her mother's silky brown hair flowed in the gap below the raised headrest of the passenger seat. Mom had the most beautiful hair.

Dad winked at Amy in the rearview mirror. "A B plus? That's great."

She exploded. "No, it isn't! She gave us a pop quiz with no warning and ruined my straight-A record."

Her father chuckled. "But, honey, if she warned you, it wouldn't be a pop quiz, would it?"

Amy bawled. He was making fun of her.

"William!" Mom said. She usually called him Bill. William meant he was in trouble.

Because of me.

Dad glanced back at her. "I'm sorry, darling. You're right. Mrs. Kramer is a meanie. But don't be sad. Today's my birthday. We're going to get our favorite burgers. Doesn't that make you happy?"

Tears spilled over her cheeks. He was right. I'm twelve years old. Why am I acting like a baby? *Even Daniel didn't take things so badly.*

Her father faced the front and watched the passing traffic. "Remember what Mom always says. Come on, what does Mom always say?"

Amy clamped her lips shut. Her parents each had a favorite expression. Dad's was, "Always do the right thing."

He grinned at her mother. "Go on, tell her."

Mom craned her neck and smiled at Amy. "Everything happens for the best."

Her father slapped the steering wheel. "That's what I'm talking about. 'Everything happens for the best.' Come on, Amy. Let's hear you say it."

Amy hugged herself tighter. "How is a B plus for the best?"

"Hmm, let's see. You'll remember your mistakes and never repeat them. How's that?"

She searched for cracks in his argument but found none.

Dad didn't give up. "I can't hear you. Do you want a tickle when we get there? Is that it? Come on, say the words."

Amy pouted. "Everything happens for the best."

"That's my little girl. Say it again. Or do you need those tickles?"

She giggled. "Everything happens for the best!"

The saying cheered her up despite herself. Even bad things happened for a reason. The universe was a good place. Somebody upstairs was looking out for them.

The light turned green, and her father accelerated. "Now for the big question," he said. "Do you want the cheeseburger or—"

A deafening crunch cut him short. Glass tinkled. The car spun with murderous force. Amy screamed, but something slammed against her head, and she blacked out.

Chapter 39

Mindy cracked her front door open, stretching the security chain to its full length.

"This is a surprise."

Brandon grinned to mask the turbulent emotions within him. If he didn't share Heather Brody's revelation with somebody soon, he'd explode.

"I met the assistant. You'll want to hear this."

Mindy held his gaze. He'd never bother her at home this late if the matter wasn't urgent. Why hadn't she let him in yet?

The strap of her undershirt caught his eye. She wasn't fully dressed.

"Sorry. I didn't know you had company. We'll speak tomorrow."

He turned to go.

"Wait."

She closed the door, released the chain, and let him inside. They were alone in her small two-room rental.

Mindy brushed a stray lock of hair from her face. "I was about to take a shower. Do you want a beer?"

"Thanks."

A drink would calm his nerves. He followed her to the kitchen and sat at the table. Mindy pulled two bottles of Bud Light from the fridge and popped the lids.

"What did Heather Brody have to say?"

Brandon sipped his drink. "The rumors of sexual harassment at Wesner and Morgan are true. An executive raped her. That's why she left. But the perp wasn't Josh."

Mindy shifted her eyes as she scanned a mental list of suspects and threw out an educated guess.

"Mark Davis?"

He nodded.

She huffed. "Makes sense. Don't crap where you eat. If his assistants kept quitting, he'd come under suspicion. So, he picked on Josh's employees instead."

His partner didn't seem excited about the breakthrough.

"Minds, this changes everything."

"How so?"

"Amy had no motive to kill Josh."

Mindy smiled bitterly. "I should have guessed. This isn't about Josh or Mark, is it? You're still hung up on Amy."

"I am not—"

"Oh, wake up, Brand."

He counted to ten. Mindy wouldn't buy an outright denial, and he needed her on board to help Amy.

"Okay, I admit it. I'm a little bit obsessed with her."

"A little bit?"

"I could have handled this more...professionally."

"Ya think?"

"But that doesn't change the facts. Mark killed Josh."

"Whoa. You've lost me. Take it from the top."

He described his meeting with Heather Brody, her brutal rape in Mark's apartment, and his threat to kill her if she talked. Then, Brandon presented his new theory.

"Josh must have figured out Mark was assaulting his assistants, so Mark killed him to cover up his crimes."

His partner bit her lip. "That's motive. What about means? Did Mark drug Heather?"

"No. She didn't black out. She seemed to remember every detail."

Mindy shook her head. "I don't know, Brand. It's a long shot. Rape isn't murder."

"But he said he'd kill her if she talked."

"An empty threat. We'll need more than a one-off rape."

"There is more."

Brandon weighed his words. He was wading into speculative territory.

"Mark raped Heather three years ago. Let's assume she was his first. He got away with the rape and wanted more. But letting them go was too risky. Eventually, one of his victims would talk. So, he changed his MO."

Mindy scoffed. "He killed them all? That's a lot of dead bodies."

"Think about it, Minds. Heather is the only assistant we've reached. All the others disappeared into thin air. He lured them to his apartment, slipped them Rohypnol to avoid a struggle, and disposed of their bodies."

"Why use Rohypnol on Wesner? That could blow everything wide open."

Brandon had considered that, too. "Mark didn't see Josh coming. He'd had to move fast and slipped into familiar patterns. Then, he staged the murder as a suicide, hoping the drug would go undetected."

Mindy took a swig of her beer. "I bet nobody ordered toxicology work on Peter Morgan, the partner who choked two years ago."

"Exactly. The drug had done the job before."

Mindy nodded slowly. He was winning her over. Finally, they were a team again.

"We'll need to search his place. If Rohypnol turns up, we've got him. Sarge will want Brody's testimony on tape first. What about Amy Walker? Wrong place, wrong time?"

Brandon shrugged.

"And the messages? Did she make that part up? Why would Mark hack her phone?"

He'd thought about that, too. "Amy was Josh's assistant. He needed to figure out how much she knew. Anyone can download surveillance software online if you know where to look, and Mark had access to Amy and her phone."

"What about Tanesha Williams? Was she onto him, too?"

He nodded. "She'd worked with him for years. Tanesha was bound to make the connection."

Mindy smiled thinly. "You've got an answer for everything, haven't you?"

"Not Steve Hamlin. He doesn't add up. Maybe Amy imagined him? You were right about her. She isn't stable."

Her smile hardened. "The insanity defense. Is that how you'll get her off the hook for Santiago's murder, too?"

Brandon set his beer on the table. Had Mindy pretended to play along to see how far he'd take this? They weren't on the same team yet.

"I wouldn't know. I'm not her lawyer."

"It's a bit too convenient, don't you think?"

"What is?"

"That Mark killed Tanesha the day she ratted on Amy. He did her a huge favor. Maybe they're working together?"

"Mark and Amy?"

"Why not? They seemed to get along well enough at the ceremony. Maybe they're closer than we think?"

Brandon's skin itched at the accusation. Had Amy played him? Were she and Mark swimming circles around him?

"I doubt that. Amy only started working there a few weeks ago."

Mindy dropped her smile. "I get it. No matter what, Amy comes out clean."

His cheeks warmed. "It's not like that."

"You're cherry-picking evidence."

"Mindy, give me more credit than that."

"Okay, answer this one. She promised to turn herself in, then disappeared. If she's so innocent, why did she run?"

"She didn't run. We found signs of a struggle. What if Steve got to her—or Mark?"

Brandon hadn't considered that last scenario. Thoughts of Steve and the missing photo in the shattered picture frame had distracted him. With Josh and Tanesha murdered, suspicion would fall on Mark. Had he selected Amy as his scapegoat?

Mindy knocked back the rest of her beer and set the bottle down beside his.

"The black hair on Amy's couch isn't hers."

How could she be sure? "Are the results in?"

"We're still waiting on the full DNA analysis, but forensics released their initial findings this afternoon. The root tissue cells have Y chromosomes. The hair is from a male."

Brandon blinked at her. The color ruled out both Steve and Mark. Had the stalker visited her apartment? Had *he* abducted Amy?

Another question popped into his detective brain. *Why am I only hearing about this now?* Brandon had submitted the hair sample to forensics. Why had Mindy alone received feedback that afternoon? The inescapable deduction winded him.

"Forensics didn't notify me. Sarge cut me out, didn't he? Am I off the investigation?"

Was that why Mindy had hesitated to let him in and discuss the case? Had Sarge blackballed him?

Mindy winced. "Not yet. But he's concerned, Brand, and frankly, so am I."

"Concerned about what?"

She looked him in the eye. "Were you ever in her apartment before our search?"

That's it. They think the hair is mine. The insult burned in his chest.

"You think I slept with her?"

"That's not what I asked. Answer the question, Brand."

"No! I've never been there, and I didn't sleep with her." *But I wanted to.*

Sweat beaded on his forehead. Had a shed follicle of his hair clung to Amy when they'd kissed outside her door? Would that trace evidence place him inside her apartment, turning him into a liar? He masked his guilt and anxiety with self-righteous anger.

"I'm not an accomplice to murder either."

Mindy softened. "You can't blame Sarge for wondering, Brand. You're too close to our prime suspect in a high-profile case. He can't afford to screw this up."

Brandon wanted to throw the beer bottle at the wall. His entanglement with Amy would cost him his career. But he vented his rage on Mindy.

"We've worked together for two years, Mindy. We've trusted each other with our lives. You think I'd go rogue for some girl."

Mindy didn't flinch. "You're not yourself, Brand. I can say that because I know you so well. Step back and let Sarge handle this his way."

Brandon pointed at the darkness outside her kitchen window. "Mark's a predator. He's killed before and he'll kill again. For all we know, he's torturing her as we speak."

"We don't know that. Mark raped Heather, and he'll pay for his crime. But that doesn't make him a killer."

"But if he is, she'll be dead by the time we get a search warrant." Brandon stood. "I shouldn't have come here."

Mindy read his mind. "Don't, Brandon. You're in enough trouble. Don't make things worse."

"Thanks for the beer. I'll let myself out."

"Brand," she called after him, but he was already out the door.

He got into his car, looked up Mark's residential address in his notepad, and headed for the corner of Broadway and 28th Street.

The executive had kept his cool during his police interviews. After raping and murdering a half dozen young women, he'd grown overconfident. He'd screwed up by using Rohypnol, not expecting NYPD to run a full toxicology analysis for Josh's apparent suicide. If Sarge had been less thorough, Mark Davis would have escaped justice yet again.

Brandon cruised through the Flatiron District. Partygoers and tourists teamed the sidewalks, dressed up for a night on the town. *How did I not see through him?* The only hint of Mark's aggression had slipped out at Harry Wesner's mansion. Brandon had dismissed his talk of "killer margaritas" as male posturing to impress a beautiful woman. Was the comment the killer's way of giving the criminal justice system the finger? His possessive body language around Amy seemed ominous now, too. Had Mark pursued Amy as his prey? Had he waited only for the attention surrounding Josh Wesner's death to settle before pouncing?

But his hunting grounds had changed since then. Josh's suicide had become a homicide, and Tanesha was dead, too. Why would the executive risk exposing his evil nature now? Had his serial-killer compulsions overpowered his survival instinct, or had something else triggered his murderous impulses?

Brandon parked down the block from the upmarket NoMad condos. Reflective glass panels covered the immense structure like futuristic shields. Money and power wouldn't protect Mark from justice, not on Brandon's shift.

He stepped through the tall glass doors adorned with long golden handles into an airy lobby with high ceilings and muted LED lighting.

He approached the reception desk. "I'm here to see Mark Davis. Is he in?"

A gangly male attendant peered snootily over his round-framed eyeglasses.

"I'm afraid I can't provide that information."

Brandon flashed his gold NYPD badge. "Make an exception."

"Do you have a search warrant?"

He knew the tenants' constitutional rights. Strict privacy safeguards probably featured on the condo's glossy marketing brochures.

"Do I need one?"

"I'm afraid—"

Brandon walked off. "Never mind."

He found the elevators and punched the number forty-two on the keypad. *That was a mistake.* Would the attendant warn Mark of his arrival, giving him ample opportunity to dispose of incriminating evidence?

The doors opened soundlessly, and he stepped inside. A bossa nova tune played softly from hidden speakers. A pleasant lavender fragrance filled the air. The number forty-two glowed on the glass doorframe. *How do they do that?* He searched for digital displays and projectors but found none. He'd entered a magical realm where privileged men like Mark made young women disappear. But Brandon had a few tricks up his sleeve, too.

The doors closed. A glowing floor number incremented rapidly on another panel, and vertigo unsettled his stomach. *Do you know what you're doing?* Mindy had disapproved. Sarge would probably suspend him. But Brandon had no choice.

What if Amy's up there? He pictured her tied up and at the brink of death. Worse yet, he imagined finding nothing. Had Mark dispatched her long ago and disposed of her remains?

Brandon checked his sidearm. The magazine was full. If Mark had hurt her, he'd spend the rest of his days behind bars. No amount of money would save him.

The elevator chimed, and the doors whooshed open. The wide, luxurious corridor boasted marble floors and thick oak skirting. Muted light projected from fixtures of dark wood.

Mark's penthouse was the closest door to the elevator—all the better for the disposal of body parts without running into neighbors. Had that consideration influenced his purchase decision?

Brandon jabbed the buzzer. An electronic jingle played within. He listened for movement behind the thick wooden door but heard nothing over the thump of his heart. He pressed the buzzer again, longer and harder. Nobody answered.

He knocked on the door and raised his voice. "Mr. Davis. This is Detective Cooper."

Still nothing. Was he hiding, hoping the police would give up and go away?

Time to smoke him out. Brandon called Mark's cell phone number. If the executive was home, his ringtone would give him away.

The number rang in the receiver. Mark's phone was on. Brandon pressed his ear to the door. *Still nothing.* Either Mark had placed his phone on silent or he was out. On the third ring, the call cut out.

"The subscriber you have called is unavailable. Please—"

Brandon hit Cancel and pocketed his phone.

Where are you, Mark, and what are you doing?

He stepped back from the door. The wooden frame looked thick and solid. Goliath couldn't kick that in, and Brandon didn't carry a lock-picking kit.

If he broke in, his findings would be ineligible as evidence. A broken photo frame and a rape allegation didn't provide credible risk to life. Mark could slap NYPD with a sizable lawsuit for the unlawful invasion of his property. Never mind suspension, Brandon might face criminal charges, too.

He swore under his breath and ran his hand through his hair. Was Mark dumping Amy in the Hudson, piece by piece, at this very moment?

Brandon chose a lesser evil. He dialed a number on his phone. Lacking hard evidence, he needed to catch Mark in the act.

A woman answered the call. "Verizon Forensics Department. How may I help you?"

Brandon introduced himself and read out his badge number. "I need a current phone location."

"We'll need to receive a court order within three business days."

"No problem." He dictated Mark's cell phone number. The weekend bought him extra time. If he nailed the murderer, Sarge would sort out the red tape.

"One moment, please."

GPS coordinates were useless in the crowded jungle of Manhattan. But Mark would dump his victims' remains at an isolated location to escape detection.

"Thank you for holding. Signal towers place the device in No-Mad, Manhattan."

He's still here or nearby.

"How long has the phone held its current location?"

"Please hold." Plastic keys clicked at the other end of the line. "The past two hours."

Mark had been home for some time but wasn't answering his door or phone.

"Thank you."

Brandon pounded the door with his fists. "Mr. Davis, open the door. It's the police."

The deathly silence continued.

He tried the handle, but the door refused to open. *Is Amy in here? Is she in trouble?* To find out, he'd have to break the law.

Chapter 40

A my stirred from a deep slumber. A hard surface pressed against her back. Her head throbbed, and her mouth tasted like rubber. *Is this a hangover?* Had she spent the night drinking?

Wisps of a fading dream clung to her mind. Her parents were alive. She'd watched them from the backseat of the family car. Mom and Dad had joked around while Amy had grouched about school. That scene had haunted her nightmares for months after the accident. But this time, the flashback had felt different. The usual paralyzing dread was gone. Tragedy loomed—that certainty remained. But her foreknowledge didn't prevent her from savoring those last precious moments with her parents. Their memory wrapped her in a warm, otherworldly hug and gifted her with a soothing conviction. *I'll see them again someday, and everything will be okay.*

She blinked her eyes open. Morning rays poured through a tall window. A fancy light fixture dangled from the ceiling above her—a series of black rectangles lined with LED strips. She lay on the floor of an upmarket home. *Where am I?*

Memories fell into place. She'd met Mark at his penthouse. He'd figured out Leo's code. The Bitcoin account contained four hundred and eighty million dollars. Amy was rich. *Filthy rich.*

Mark had spoken those words. He'd opened a bottle of champagne and...a gaping hole marred her memory. *Did I sleep with him? Was he good?*

Amy giggled, and something crinkled beneath her body. She lay on a sheet of plastic. *That's weird.* Did they do it here, on the floor? She was still in her clothes. *Where's Mark?*

She turned her head. Mark lay beside her on the plastic sheet. He stared at the ceiling.

Amy touched his shoulder. "Mark?"

He didn't respond. He didn't move at all. *Is he breathing?*

She sat up. A large, red stain covered his button-down shirt, the fabric torn in a dozen places. *He's dead. Somebody stabbed him.*

Amy gasped. She covered her mouth and shifted away from his corpse. Her face felt wet and sticky. She inspected her fingers. Blood covered her right hand.

Her body convulsed. *No. This isn't real. This can't be happening.*

She hugged her legs to her chest, collapsing into a fetal position. Amy was alone with his corpse in the apartment. *What happened last night?* She strained her mind for clues, but her memory remained a frustrating blank.

Did I kill him? Why would I do that? Mark had helped her. Amy was rich. Soon, she'd be free. *This makes no sense.* But the black void in her recollection had swallowed the night's events whole. Had her brain repressed Mark's murder?

Amy scrambled to her feet. Sunlight twinkled on the windows of the buildings below. A new day was dawning. What was she to do?

Call the police. But would they think she'd killed him? She'd spent the night beside his corpse. His blood stained her hands. She was wanted in connection with two other murders. The facts pointed in only one direction. *I did this.*

Her soul rebelled. *I didn't kill him! I'm not a murderer.* Amy needed time to process her situation and recover her memory. Daniel was waiting for her. He'd be worried sick.

I can't stay here. But I can't leave like this either. She found a bathroom and washed her hands and face. Her head throbbed. The swirling red water triggered a memory. *I've been here before.*

In her nightmares, she'd washed blood from her hands. But were those dreams or memories?

The hand towel she'd used had red smears. Amy swore under her breath. Blood spatter dotted her clothes with a hundred tiny marks of Cain. She stripped to her underwear.

Under the kitchen sink, she found disposable gloves and disinfectant. She wiped away the red handprints on the plastic sheeting and dropped the filthy kitchen towels in a garbage bag along with her wine and soda glasses, soiled clothes, and the hand towel.

Amy put on a hooded sweatshirt and running pants from Mark's walk-in bedroom closet. She surveyed the living room one last time. *What have I forgotten?*

Leo's note lay on the coffee table beside Mark's laptop. Amy folded and slipped the Bitcoin credentials into her pouch. Then, she tucked the pouch and the garbage bag under her sweatshirt and made for the front door.

Her boss lay dead on the floor. *Sorry, Mark.* She pulled the hood over her head and stepped into the corridor.

The elevator was a few steps away. A bell chimed. The doors opened, and a housekeeper walked out. Amy kept her head down.

"Good morning, Mr. Davis," the woman said. She had a Latino accent.

Amy brushed past her and said nothing. The doors closed behind her. *You can do this. You've done nothing wrong.* But the lie weighed her down like an anchor in her belly. She'd fled a crime scene and destroyed evidence. *But I had to. Otherwise, they'd think...* Amy couldn't complete that thought. *They'd think what? The truth?*

She jogged through the lobby and burst onto the street. The crisp morning air chilled her face. Amy ran. A white garbage truck idled on the corner. She tossed the plastic bag into the gaping compactor and marched on.

Keep going. Don't think about it. But Mark's corpse stuck in her mind. *How could I leave him there?* He'd been kind to her, but she'd left him to rot alone. How long would it take for anyone to find him?

Amy crossed the street, stopped at a pay phone, and dialed 9-1-1. A woman answered. "What's your emergency?"

Tears rolled down Amy's cheeks. "I need to report a murder."

Chapter 41

B randon's phone rang before his alarm went off on Friday morning.

"Mindy, it's six AM."

His partner didn't apologize. "Where were you last night?"

"At your place, remember? We had beers."

"Where'd you go after that?"

Crap. Had she discovered his unauthorized triangulation request already?

"I went home."

That was true. He had gone home. *Eventually.*

He'd waited outside Mark's apartment for an hour, listening for movement but hearing nothing. The executive hadn't returned home either. A second call to Verizon placed Mark's phone at the same location, and a more likely explanation presented itself. The douche was asleep.

Feeling like an idiot, Brandon had gone home. Mindy's question had bounced around his brain. *Why had Amy disappeared?* Was she in danger or had she simply fled, knocking over the picture frame in her rush to evade arrest?

Mindy had seen through him last night, and that morning was no different.

"Don't lie to me."

"What's this really about?"

Her voice softened. "There's been another homicide."

He sat up in bed. Last night, he'd sensed Amy was in danger. He'd pictured her lying dead in a pool of blood. Had he failed to save her?

"Amy?"

"No."

Brandon exhaled. *She's alive.* Was the murder unrelated to the Wesner case? *Unlikely.* Dispatch should have called instead of Mindy. Why had she asked about his whereabouts last night? A premonition clouded his mood. His calls to Verizon's forensics department were the least of his problems.

"Who, then?"

Her answer slapped him fully awake.

"Mark Davis."

Mark is dead. Had Amy killed him in self-defense?

"Where?"

"At his home."

Brandon gasped. Was that why Mark hadn't answered his door or his phone?

He got out of bed. "I'm on my way."

"Don't bother."

"What? Why not?"

Did she think he'd killed Mark? Is that why she'd asked where he'd gone last night?

"Sorry, Brand. You need to stay away from the crime scene. Sarge's orders."

Chapter 42

"Don't do this, Amy," Daniel said.

They sat on conjoined metal chairs in the waiting hall of George Washington Bridge Bus Terminal. Commuters hurried by on their way to work.

Amy avoided her brother's stare. "It's the only way."

"I don't understand. Why won't you tell me why?"

She'd refused to answer his questions on the subway ride there. The truth was too terrible to share.

"It's for your protection."

"But you said we'd stick together. Why are you sending me away?"

How can I explain?

Amy had returned to their hotel room at the crack of dawn wearing a man's sweat suit. Daniel had fallen asleep on the couch.

She'd shaken him awake. "Get your things. We're leaving."

He'd wiped his eyes. "What? How did it go with your friend?"

"Things didn't work out. We have to go."

Amy had showered and changed her clothes. Then, she'd bundled Mark's sweat suit into a garbage bag. Mental images of that morning filled her with horror: Mark's butchered body on the penthouse floor; her hands and face, sticky with blood; washing the gore from her body at the bathroom sink. *Just like the dreams...*

A shudder had passed through her. Not dreams. Memories. *Did I kill Mark? Did I murder Leo, too?*

Her soul rejected the possibility. *No! Steve murdered them both. He must have.* But once that doubt slithered into the world, she couldn't repress the terrifying thought.

Brandon had found no trace of Steve in the police databases. Detective Kim didn't remember him either. Nobody else had been present during her interactions with Steve. Did he exist, or had her twisted mind fabricated the dirty cop to suppress an unacceptable truth?

The seismic shift in perspective provided more bone-chilling answers. The messages from her all-knowing, all-seeing stalker had vanished from her phone the moment she'd shown Brandon her text history. Was her murderous secret admirer a fiction, too, a bogeyman generated to conceal her abhorrent homicidal urges?

For years, Amy had fled from a killer. But she'd never outrun this murderer...because the monster lurked inside her.

Amy and Daniel had left the hotel without checking out and took a subway train to the bus station. By the time they'd arrived, a conviction had solidified in her heart. Amy had sacrificed everything to protect Daniel. But he'd never be safe in her presence.

At a self-service terminal, she'd bought a single, one-way Greyhound ticket. *It's for the best.*

"Talk to me, Amy." Daniel's voice snapped her back to the present moment.

She swallowed hard. *The less he knows the better. Be strong for a few minutes longer. See him off, and then you can end this.*

Her brother whispered, "Is it Steve? Did you see him?"

Amy scoffed. Her Viking tormentor seemed like a bizarre caricature now. Steve wasn't an actual human being, only a psychotic manifestation of her murderous, fractured personality. But Daniel wouldn't understand. He'd try to talk her out of this.

She shook her head. "It's not safe to be around me."

"Why not, Amy? What have you done?"

Could he sense her guilt?

She sobbed. "I don't know. I can't remember."

Amy had racked her memory for details of the crimes but failed to construct a continuous narrative. *Maybe that's for the best, too?*

Daniel gripped her arm. "I don't care what you've done. We should stay together."

She shook free. "We can't. Trust me, Daniel."

Amy read the time off the departures board and stood. "Let's go."

She walked him to the boarding terminal for his bus. Daniel stowed his backpack in the open luggage compartment, and they joined the line of passengers.

Amy handed him a pre-paid mobile phone, one of two she'd bought that morning.

"There's a single saved contact with my new number. Don't share that with anyone."

He tucked the phone into his jacket pocket. The line progressed steadily.

Daniel shrugged. "I guess this is goodbye."

"Text me when you get to Chicago."

He nodded. His sullen expression tore at her heart.

Amy touched Leo's note in her pouch. She didn't mention the Bitcoin account. The immense fortune might be a figment of her imagination, too. Besides, once Daniel learned of their sudden riches, there was no way he'd agree to leave for safety. Today, she'd split the money in half and send him his account details. She'd explain everything someday. Maybe then he'd forgive her?

She kissed him on the cheek. "I love you."

Daniel stepped onto the bus. "Me, too."

He presented his ticket to the driver.

Amy teared up. *Will I ever see him again?* They'd left so much unsaid. She wished she could give him hope, a hint of the good news that awaited him.

Daniel found a window seat in the middle of the bus. Amy waited for the doors to close, then waved for her brother to open the window. He poked his head out of the narrow slot.

She grinned. "We figured out the code."

He smiled. "And?"

"We're rich!"

"You're kidding. How much? A million?"

"Much more!"

He laughed with joy. "How is that even possible?"

The bus backed up, and Daniel's brow furrowed. Did he think she'd hoard the money for herself?

"Bitcoin. I'll send details. Everything's going to be okay."

He blew her a kiss. The bus departed, and Daniel disappeared.

Like her mother, Amy had lied. Things would not be okay. Not for her.

Chapter 43

B randon's heartbeat drummed in his ears when he stepped out of the luxury condo's golden elevator. He loosened the collar of his shirt. The air of the forty-second-floor corridor seemed hot and stifling. Sarge had banned him from this murder scene, but Brandon couldn't stay away. His future hung in the balance. *Time to break another rule.*

Yellow police tape blocked the doorway of Mark's apartment. A bearded beat cop holding a clipboard stood guard where Brandon had waited last night. Brandon flashed his badge and added his name to the log. Sarge and Mindy were already at the scene. *This will be tricky.* But he'd rather end his career today than face a murder rap. Brandon handed back the clipboard, and the officer read his name. Beads of sweat prickled Brandon's forehead. Would the guard deny him access? *Stay calm. Act like you belong here.* The officer made eye contact again, then stepped aside. Apparently, he hadn't gotten the memo.

Every contact leaves a trace. Locard's exchange principle, the bedrock of forensic science, meant Brandon's nocturnal visit wouldn't go unnoticed. His fingerprints marked the door handle. Flecks of dry skin and hair follicles carrying his DNA would show up in the filtered trap of a forensic vacuum pump. His physical presence at the penthouse last night would mark him as a key suspect in the homicide investigation. Gatecrashing the fresh murder scene was the only way to undo the damage. *Of course, you found my DNA there. I investigated the scene. The logbook doesn't lie.* But Sarge would see through his excuses. *Here goes nothing.*

He ducked under the police tape and wrinkled his nose. The sharp hospital scent of antiseptic filled the apartment. Manhattan sprawled below through the expansive French windows. But the dead body in the center of the living room could no longer enjoy the breathtaking view. Two forensic techs in full-body scrubs crouched over the corpse. One placed paper bags over the decedent's hands. The other tech dabbed a cotton swab at a blood stain. Mark stared at the ceiling. His savaged chest looked like Bolognese. Someone had vented a murderous rage on his torso. *Serves you right, sicko.* But the brutal homicide unsettled him. *Was Amy capable of doing that?*

Mindy and Sergeant Blank conducted a hushed conversation by the window, disposable blue gloves and booties preventing their DNA from contaminating the site. They didn't appear to have noticed his arrival yet. *You'd better move fast.*

Brandon leaned on the door and rested his hand on the knob.

The forensic tech with the cotton swab gazed at him and raised his bushy eyebrows. "Hey! What are you doing? We haven't dusted there yet."

Perfect. "Sorry."

Brandon squatted on his haunches and grabbed pairs of gloves and booties from the boxes on the floor. *Mission accomplished.* But his guilty conscience ruined his sense of achievement. *Did I just tamper with evidence? What's happened to me?*

His stunt drew Sarge's attention. "Cooper, what are you doing here?"

Brandon walked over, pulling on the gloves with a satisfying latex snap.

"Investigating, sir. This is our crime scene."

His boss glared at Mindy. "My orders were clear."

She blushed. "I told him not to come."

Brandon's conscience stung again. *Great. Now I've gotten her into trouble, too.* Last night, she'd warned him not to pursue Mark, but he hadn't listened. Had she told their boss about their conversation? *She will now.* Brandon wouldn't blame her. He was dive-bombing toward suspension. She'd need to protect her reputation.

He searched for a diversion and jerked his head at the sheeting below the corpse. "What's with the plastic?"

Sarge worked his jaw. Would he fire him on the spot for insubordination and contaminating a crime scene?

Mandy answered. "NYPD discovered the body that way."

Brandon shot her a furtive glance. *Thanks, buddy.* By playing along with his distraction, she'd thrown him a lifeline. Maybe she'd kept their meeting last night secret, too?

But her words agitated his detective brain. *NYPD?* Victims who lay dead in their apartments were usually discovered by family and friends, not local cops.

"Were we looking for him?"

Brandon had written up his summary of Heather Brody's interview before visiting Mindy last night. Had Sarge read his report and sent the patrol officers to round Mark up? Maybe the breakthrough had convinced his boss to let him off the hook?

Mindy didn't answer this time. She eyed their superior cautiously as though unsure whether to share more details with her partner.

Sarge broke his silence. "Somebody phoned in the murder."

Brandon inhaled with relief. He was back on the team. *For now.* "An anonymous caller?"

His boss nodded. "A woman. Dispatch traced the call to a public phone nearby. We've requested the recording, and there are plenty of street cameras in the vicinity. We shouldn't have trouble identifying her."

Had Amy called 9-1-1? Had she killed Mark, or had somebody else cut the executive down—a woman driven by a powerful desire for revenge?

Brandon scanned the apartment for signs of social activity.

"Did Mark have company last night?"

Mindy pointed at the coffee table behind her. "We bagged a bottle of champagne and one wine glass over there. But I doubt he was celebrating alone. The cleaner saw someone leave in a hurry around six AM. She thought it was the owner. The nine-one-one call took place at around the same time."

Brandon grunted. His new theory was taking shape in his head, but he needed more data.

He focused on the corpse. "Multiple sharp force trauma. I'm guessing the cause of death is exsanguination."

"Or an air embolism. The ME's assistant won't know for sure until after the autopsy. The incisions suggest the use of a single blade. There's a knife set on the kitchen counter, and the wooden holder has an empty slot about the same size as the murder weapon."

He nodded. The culprit had acquired the blade at the scene. That fact undermined his working theory unless the killer had gained access to the apartment ahead of time. Either way, she'd made a fatal mistake.

"Why take the murder weapon? It can only incriminate them."

Mindy shrugged. "Their screwups are our blessings."

"What's the time of death?"

"Between nine PM and one AM."

Brandon squirmed. Mark was probably dead when he'd come knocking. That explained why the executive hadn't answered his phone or his door. But the timing seemed off.

"Why did the killer stick around until morning?"

Mindy shrugged. "They did a thorough job cleaning up. That can take a while. The place still reeks of disinfectant."

Brandon nodded. He'd waited outside the door for an hour. Had he delayed the murderer's exit, too?

The forensic tech with the bushy eyebrows turned to them. "Sergeant. Over here." Between two gloved fingers, he held a small glass bottle containing round white pills. "Found this in his pocket. There's no label."

"Any idea what those are?"

The tech squinted at the vial and studied the pills. "Judging by the markings, I'm betting on Rohypnol, the colorless type. No drugstore stocks these."

Rohypnol. Brandon almost punched the air. That was the evidence they needed.

"Sarge, this means—"

His boss cut him off. "I know, Cooper. I read your report on Heather Brody. It appears you were right about the missing assistants. The drug also ties Mark to the Wesner homicide. Maybe he killed Tanesha Williams to keep her silent, as well? Don't look so surprised. His torture toolbox and the roll of industrial plastic sheeting in the spare bedroom gave the game away. Then, we found identity cards for three of the former assistants in a drawer. Unfortunately, Mark Davis is a victim, too, so our work isn't done. There's another killer out there. Unless you think he did this to himself."

"No, sir."

"Scott, what are you thinking?"

Mindy pouted. "Simple. Mark chose another victim, but this time the girl fought back."

"Who?"

"His new assistant, Lisa Smith. Aka Amy Walker."

Mindy stared at Brandon, daring him to disagree.

Sarge frowned. "Cooper, any objections?"

This was another loyalty test. *Will he finally commit to pursuing Amy as a suspect?* But Brandon had facts on his side, too, and a brand-new theory.

"Yes. The Roofies would have knocked his victim out. She'd never be able to defend herself, never mind..." He jerked his head at the brutalized corpse. "Do that. Whoever killed him wanted to expose what he'd done. It's why they left the plastic sheeting and the Rohypnol after cleaning up so thoroughly—so we'd piece together his evil history."

Mindy placed her hands on her hips. "You're saying Heather Brody did this?"

"Why not? Revenge is a powerful motive. Maybe she'd planned this for years and targeted anyone who aided and abetted Mark? Tanesha. Josh."

Mindy scoffed. "We have no indication Josh knew about Mark's crimes. The same goes for Tanesha. Besides, why would Heather tell you about the rape if she planned to kill him?"

Brandon didn't back down. "She thought I knew about Mark already. Yesterday, she realized time was running out, so she struck while she could."

"But you said Heather was afraid of Mark!"

Sarge stepped between them like a referee separating boxers in the ring. "Whoa! There's a middle ground. What if Heather and Amy did this together?"

The suggestion silenced them. Brandon's mind reeled. Was Heather Amy's secret admirer? Had *she* sent the mysterious texts?

Mindy snorted. "You mean Heather is her stalker? Sir, you can't seriously believe Amy's conspiracy theories."

"I don't. Her vanishing messages and dirty cops are distractions. But Heather might have contacted Amy to warn her and win her cooperation."

Mindy's eyes sparkled. "Or she recruited Amy to her cause. She needed to place somebody with the proper skill set inside the agency. Maybe that's how Amy ended up working there to begin with?"

Brandon couldn't believe his ears.

"That's ridiculous. Amy isn't an assassin!"

"Think about it, Brand. She's wanted for Santiago's murder. She travels under false identities. The Chicago crime scene matches this one almost to the letter. Now she's disappeared without a trace and probably for good."

Brandon shook his head. "Heather's accomplice must be somebody else. What about the black hair on Amy's couch? We still don't know who that is."

"Then explain this," Mindy said. "If she's so innocent, why did she run?"

He clenched his jaw. That glaring fact had stumped him before. "She didn't run. She's probably dead."

Mindy scoffed. "Right, I forgot. Her imaginary cop got her. Because Amy would never betray your trust. She'd never con you to get away with murder."

Ouch. Her words stunned him like a slap to the face. *Is she right? Did Amy fool me?*

Sarge took charge. "That's enough, both of you. I want more facts, less speculation. Bring in Heather Brody for questioning. Check her alibi for each murder. Review every camera feed within two blocks. Speak with the neighbors. We need positive IDs for the caller and whoever left this place this morning. Good old-fashioned detective work. Assume nothing. Scott, Cooper, are we on the same page?"

Mindy nodded. "Yes, sir. We're on it."

Brandon's phone rang. He slipped the device from his jacket pocket. The name Lisa Smith appeared on the caller ID. *She's alive.* "It's Amy. She's using her work phone again."

Sarge and Mindy gaped at him. Their elusive prime suspect had contacted him. *Or had somebody else taken her phone?*

Sarge flashed his eyes. "Don't just stand there, Cooper. Answer."

Brandon did. "Cooper."

"It's me."

"Amy, are you okay?"

"I'm sorry I let you down."

She sounded contrite. But she'd tricked him before. Was this another deception?

"Never mind that. Where are you?"

"I need help, Brandon."

"With what?"

Don't say you did it. Don't say you killed Mark. Please, anything but that.

Amy sobbed. "I think I killed someone."

Chapter 44

Amy studied her family photo in the hotel room late that morning. Unshielded by a frame, the print had folded in her overnight bag, and a crease line split the young Amy in half. She traced the wrinkle with her finger. Was she fractured, too?

She tore open the plastic wrapping of the cheap photo frame she'd purchased minutes ago and opened the back cover. Amy replaced the generic placeholder image of a beautiful smiling family with her damaged family portrait. She slipped Leo's note with the Bitcoin codes behind the photo, sealed the frame, and searched for hints of the hidden message from all angles. She found none.

Good. Amy would serve her time and undergo therapy. She'd stash the photo in a self-storage locker and collect the Bitcoin account on the day of her release. *If it's real.*

Her grasp of reality had once been solid and reliable. But her stalker had evaporated along with his messages. Steve, her murderous tormentor, had left no trace in the physical world either. Slowly, the twisted landscape of her life emerged from the fog of her delusions. The nightmares of bloodied hands were not dreams but flashbacks to her terrible crimes. Steve had never approached her in the presence of others because he existed only in her fragmented mind. She'd spent her adult life fleeing a murderer, but the killer lay within her. How had she missed the warning signs?

Amy perched on the edge of the bed. She placed the photo beside her and fished her work phone from her pouch. The device no longer seemed ominous, an evil genie's window into her life.

A notification icon alerted her to unread text messages. Her heart lurched. Had her imaginary stalker contacted her again?

She scrolled through the Messages app. To her relief, no unlisted numbers appeared.

Amy stared at the phone with defiance. "Message me. I dare you. You don't exist. You never did."

She flipped through the other texts, and her vision swam with tears. Yesterday morning, Mark had asked how she was feeling. That was his last message to her before his...death. Beth had reached out, too. *Are you okay? Have chicken soup. Will travel.* The offer brought a much-needed smile to Amy's face. Then, today: *Did you hear about T? Worried about you. Call me!*

T must mean Tanesha. What had happened to her? Dread filled Amy. Tanesha had ratted her out, and Amy had seethed with hatred. In her dream, she'd washed blood from her body at an unfamiliar sink. *Did I hurt her, too?*

She stared at her family photo again. Not long ago, she'd been that bright-eyed kid with big dreams and no actual problems. Her future had swelled with promise. Her brains and ambition would take her far. By now, she would have finished med school. She'd be researching new treatments and making the world a better place. But a drunk driver had smashed that future to pieces, and her stupid boyfriend had trampled the shards to dust. Under the mental strain of those injustices, her sanity had snapped.

Hot tears spilled down her cheek. "It isn't fair. I could have been somebody. I had so much potential. Now, that's all gone. My life is wasted."

The wave of self-pity subsided. Amy shoved the photo and phone back into her bag. Soon, she'd make her way to the police station. She'd promised Brandon that she'd turn herself in. There was no other solution. *I'm a danger to those around me.*

Daniel was safe. That's what mattered. On the way to the NYPD, she'd stop at an Internet café. She'd copy half the Bitcoin balance into a new account and send the access codes to Daniel, splitting the two strings of characters between his Gmail and burner phone to evade digital eavesdroppers. Amy would call Daniel to explain. Then, she'd take her first step on the long road to mental health.

Amy slipped her pouch onto her shoulder and wheeled her bag toward the door. When had the psychotic breaks begun? Had her fight with Leo triggered them? *No.* Steve had shown up weeks before her boyfriend's death. How far back did the delusions go? The car crash? The impact had knocked her unconscious. Or had the Underhills' abuse split her conscious self into two? What other phantom events and people had seeped through the cracks in her soul?

Mark's butchered body flashed in her mind, and she shuddered. A large square of thick plastic sheeting had covered the living room floor beneath him. *Did I put that there?* Had she planned to destroy his body? Amy didn't recall getting the sheeting. A metal toolbox had rested beside the corpse. Mark had carried that over, hadn't he? He'd placed steel cutting implements in a tidy row like a surgeon preparing his scalpels for an operation. Why had he done that? What was generating these images? Was her memory returning, shard by broken shard, or was her psychotic brain painting over her crimes to avoid prison?

A phone rang in her pouch. The unfamiliar ringtone, a simple electronic trill, did not belong to her work phone. She reached for the prepaid device. The number of Daniel's burner phone appeared on the screen.

Why is he calling? Chicago was many hours away. *Is he okay?* Had her hint at a million-dollar fortune inflamed his curiosity during the long, boring journey? *I shouldn't have said anything.* She'd raised his hopes. The Bitcoin fortune might be another trick of her unreliable psyche. But now was as good a time as any to explain. Who knew when she'd hear his voice again?

She answered. "Missing me already?"

Daniel spoke urgently. "Amy, don't listen to him! Run!"

Amy let go of her overnight bag. "Daniel? Who are you talking about?"

Her insides twisted in a knot. *Something's wrong. Terribly wrong.* But why didn't he explain?

"Daniel!"

There was a commotion at the end of the line, and then another voice spoke.

"Hello, pretty."

Amy stepped backward. She'd never forget that cruel voice. *But you're not real.*

Steve snickered. "I made a new friend. He likes to talk...with the right incentive."

The phone trembled in her hand. "I've got your money. The hundred grand. Please, let him go, and I'll give it to you."

The killer laughed. "A hundred grand? You're sitting on much more than that, my dear. Either you hand the account over, or I'll return your dear brother in a million pieces."

A million pieces. The blood drained from her face. Daniel had told him about the Bitcoin fortune, and Steve wanted it all.

"Okay."

"There's a good girl. No cops or he dies. Do you understand?"

Her voice was a defeated whisper. "Yes."

"Good. And don't even dream about screwing me over. If I see any transfers on the blockchain, he dies. Savvy?"

Amy didn't understand the crypto jargon, but the bottom line was crystal clear. Steve would know if she'd withdrawn any of the funds.

"Yes."

Steve grunted with satisfaction. "We'll meet tonight. I'll send coordinates later. Guess what happens if you make me wait?"

Amy swallowed hard. "He dies."

"You're a fast learner." He ended the call.

Amy's knees threatened to cave beneath her. She leaned against the hotel room's door for support.

Did that really happen? The terror in her heart was no hallucination. Steve had captured Daniel. He'd kill her brother if she didn't hand over the Bitcoin account. *What if I'm not delusional?* Amy couldn't take that chance.

No cops or he dies. Brandon would never believe her anyway, and she'd promised him she'd meet him at the station. *Sorry, Brandon. Looks like I'll have to stand you up again.*

Amy ran her hands through her hair. *Wait a minute.* If she handed over the codes, would Steve let them go? Cryptocurrency, apparently, was traceable. If she'd kept a copy of the account details, she'd still be a threat. Would he kill Daniel anyway? He'd kill her, too. But with millions of dollars at her disposal, Amy had a better chance at survival.

What am I saying? No! Amy chided herself for even considering escaping with the money and abandoning her brother to a gruesome death. *There must be a way to save both our lives.* Amy needed time to think. She needed a plan.

Someone knocked on the door, the shock waves jolting her. Amy retreated into the small hotel room. She breathed in short, shallow gasps. Had Steve found her?

"Police," a man yelled. "Open the door."

The cops had come for her. Brandon hadn't taken her word. He'd located her using her phone signal and sent officers to arrest her.

But if she didn't deliver the codes, Steve would kill her brother. *No cops or he dies.* She couldn't surrender now. Was Steve a ghost? Had she imagined the phone call, too? *Is any of this real? What am I supposed to do?*

Her work phone vibrated twice in her pouch. *What now?*

With trembling fingers and a galloping heart, she grabbed the phone and swiped the screen. The text originated from a familiar, unlisted number. Amy held her breath and opened the message.

Need a friend?

Chapter 45

B randon clenched his fists with frustration. "I should be up there."

The cramped interior of the mobile command post bristled with computer monitors and communications equipment.

Sergeant Blank lifted the headset from his ear. "What's that, Cooper?"

An NYPD driver had parked the black RV around the corner from The Manhattan Grand Hotel in the Lower East Side. A communications tech manned the equipment while Brandon, Mindy, and their boss waited on swivel seats attached to the vehicle's chassis.

Brandon cleared his throat. "I should be primary, sir. I know how to talk to her."

Two black SWAT vans had joined them, and the heavily armed officers had entered the building twenty seconds ago.

Sarge shook his head. "It's too dangerous. For all we know, she's rigged her hotel room with C-4."

"She's no assassin, sir. She's frightened."

"Walker is a suspect in four murders, three of which involved kitchen knives. We can assume she's armed and deadly."

"But *she* called us. She agreed to turn herself in."

Mindy chimed in. "She's ditched us before. The call could be another diversion."

"This time is different. She knows she's unwell. That's why she called nine-one-one."

Brandon and Mindy had identified Amy's voice from the emergency call recording.

His partner shook her head. "If she's mentally unhinged, that's another reason to be careful."

He sighed. "Amy needs treatment. But if we shove semi-automatic rifles in her face, she might snap."

The communications tech spoke to Sarge. "We're in position."

Sarge put his headset back on. "Too late. We're going in."

Brandon huffed. "What's the room number?" he asked the tech

"Three-sixteen."

Brandon opened the door and stepped out of the van.

Mindy called after him. "Brandon! Come back here."

But he'd already left the vehicle and slammed the door shut behind him.

He pushed into the hotel's shabby lobby and headed for the stairs.

Nightmare scenarios swept through his mind. SWAT officers trained for violent confrontations. They never opened fire without reason. But would they mistake a phone for a weapon? Amy suffered from psychotic breaks and paranoid delusions. How would she interpret the sudden entry of masked gunmen? Would she jump from the third-floor window to escape her attackers?

A loud bang echoed through the stairwell. Had a door slammed shut or had the SWAT officers opened fire? He leaped up the stairs in twos and threes.

"Excuse me." He brushed past a man in a hooded sweatshirt heading in the opposite direction.

In his mind's eye, Amy gasped for breath on the floor of her room while her lifeblood spilled out. He shoved the image aside. *Please be okay, Amy. Don't do anything hasty.*

Brandon burst onto the third-floor landing. Two SWAT officers in full-body armor stood outside the room with a uniformed hotel employee. One cop held a battering ram, but the doorframe showed no damage. The hotel rep must have opened the room. Had shots been fired?

A SWAT officer raised his hand for him to stop, then seemed to recognize him from the pre-mission briefing.

Brandon slipped through the open door before the guard could object.

Three SWAT officers assembled in the small room.

Brandon turned to the sergeant. "Where is she?"

He raised his helmet's visor. "Not here. There's a travel bag by the door. It appears she was getting ready to leave."

Brandon scanned the spartan room. "But her phone placed her here minutes ago."

He shrugged. "She ain't here now."

Was Sarge right? Had Amy lured them here and booby-trapped the hotel room?

"Did you open the bag?"

"Hell, no. There's no visible triggering mechanism, but we'll call in a bomb tech just in case. Otherwise, the site is clear."

Mindy entered the hotel room, panting. "How did she know?"

Brandon bristled. Did she think he'd tipped Amy off?

"Don't look at me."

He made for the window and brushed the curtains aside. The ugly backside of the neighboring building glared back across a narrow, dingy backstreet. Brandon slid the glass pane upward easily and poked his head outside.

He swore. "There's a fire escape. She must have left out the back alley."

The SWAT sergeant spoke into his mouthpiece. "Beta team, do you have eyes on the back exit? Our suspect might be on her way now."

He listened to the reply on his helmet's speakers, then shook his head. "Negative. Nobody passed that way. We just missed her."

Chapter 46

Fifteen minutes earlier, Amy stared at the message on her work phone. *Need a friend?*

Was the text a mirage, or had her stalker offered help?

The police knocked on her door again. Amy had no time for indecision. She typed a quick reply and hit Send.

Yes.

Three seconds later, another message arrived.

Window. Stairs.

Amy hadn't selected the room for its view. She'd kept the curtains drawn. Now, she slid the window open, poked her head out, and stared at the old building's fire escape above a narrow alley between aging brick walls. She climbed onto the rusty metal landing, closed the curtains, and shut the window.

What now? Two flights of rusty stairs stretched below her. She started her descent, the metal frame clanging with each step. Did the alley lead to the main street? Would the cops see her running away and give chase?

She halted on the second-floor landing. A metal lattice blocked her path. She had to lower the ladder to ground level to get down.

Amy grabbed an iron rung when her phone vibrated again.

Window.

She glanced behind her. Sure enough, the window of the room below hers hung partly open. *How did he know that?* Amy scanned her surroundings. Could her stalker see her? Amy heaved the window upward, then froze. The police were in the hotel. She needed to leave the place, not climb back inside.

The scraping sound of a window opening overhead scattered her questions. Amy tumbled headfirst into the dark room. Thankfully, the unit seemed vacant. She clambered to her feet. Cracking the door open, she peered into the corridor. The coast was clear. But was the lobby crawling with cops? Had they seen her enter the second-floor room? *Keep going.* Amy pulled the hood of her sweater over her head and hurried along the rows of closed doors. She passed the elevator and entered the stairwell, letting the door slam behind her.

A suit rushed toward her from below. Amy tensed up. *It's Brandon! Crap!* She'd escaped the cops outside her hotel room only to walk straight into the detective. She lowered her head. Turning on her heels to flee upstairs would trap her for sure. Her only hope was to slip past him and run. She gritted her teeth and continued her descent. He didn't call her name or tell her to stop. Did he recognize her?

Brandon bumped her shoulder. "Excuse me." He continued upward.

Amy said nothing and didn't look back.

No uniforms waited for her on the ground floor. She power-walked through the narrow lobby and onto the street. The sun burned overhead, casting short shadows. No police cars parked outside. They'd kept a low profile. She marched up Seventh Avenue. *I made it!*

Questions swirled in her mind. Had Brandon sent the officers to arrest her? Why wasn't he with them? She opened the Messages app. The texts were still there. She hadn't imagined them. Her secret admirer was real. Who had sent the messages? Not Mark. He was dead.

She hadn't invented Steve either. He'd called her on Daniel's prepaid phone. *I'm not delusional.* Her memory hadn't deceived her. *Maybe I didn't kill Mark?*

Her work phone vibrated in her hand. Another message had arrived from her secret friend.

Phone off.

Amy touched her thumb to the power button but hesitated. The messages had aided her escape. The phone was her lifeline. What if she needed help again?

He's right. The police must have tracked her signal to the hotel. They'd locate her again unless she turned off the device. Steve would call her on the burner phone later. Her brother's life depended on her handing over the Bitcoin codes. Tonight, of all nights, she needed her freedom.

Amy powered off the device. She'd face Steve alone. The cops and her stalker would have to wait. *If I'm still breathing.*

The beady eye of a surveillance camera perched above a traffic light. Amy faced away. By now, the police would know she'd slipped away. They'd be searching for her, and Brandon might remember the hooded figure in the stairwell.

Amy ducked into the nearest souvenir store. She selected the black cap with the words "I Heart New York" and a matching hoodie from the store's jam-packed shelves. Normally, she wouldn't be caught dead in Midtown tourist traps or wearing their cheesy clothing. But today the disguise might save her brother's life.

She paid cash at the counter and changed into her new clothes. Then, she left the store and tossed her old sweater into a trash can.

She slipped among the workers who packed the streets of Midtown on their lunch break. She'd find a park and lie low, somewhere she might linger without drawing attention.

When would Steve call? Where would they meet? The killer held all the cards. Amy had no contingency plan if things went south. Would he double-cross her and Daniel? How could he let the witnesses to his crimes live?

The weight of the looming confrontation crushed Amy. Her only ally was a homicidal stalker. In a moment of desperation, she'd accepted her genie's help. But at what price?

Did her "best friend" know Steve had Daniel? Why hadn't he dispatched her tormenter the way he'd disposed of Josh, Tanesha, and—now that she thought about it—probably Mark, too? He'd left her, covered in blood, in the dead executive's penthouse. Was he truly on her side or setting her up for murder?

Amy slowed to a stop. Her airways constricted. She couldn't breathe. The police were searching for her. Her boyfriend's killer was holding Daniel hostage. A murderous stalker was weaving murderous webs around her. *It's too much.* She leaned against a streetlight to steady herself. *Come on, Amy. You can do this. You have to. Daniel needs you.*

Her spine tingled. A man stared at her from across the street. He stood by the railing of a subway entrance, a hot dog in hand.

Amy held her breath. Eddie's cheek bulged with food. By blind habit, her body had walked her back toward the agency and a waiting coworker.

Eddie stopped chewing. He no longer smiled stupidly. The world shifted gears, grinding along in slow-motion.

You deserve better. Eddie had hovered over her ever since she'd started working at Wesner & Morgan. *You have no friends like me. You've got this.* He'd quoted the stalker's messages. *I had no choice. She knew.* Had Tanesha told him about Amy's identity? Was he her deadly friend?

Eddie gazed at her. He placed his hot dog on the low wall of the subway stairs, rose to his feet, and stepped toward her. Her stalker had told her to power off her phone. He no longer needed it because Amy was walking right toward him.

No! She turned and ran.

"Hey! Watch where you're going!" a man snapped at her.

She weaved through the sea of tourists, suits, and street urchins. *I knew it!* The truth had stared her in the face all along. Eddie had installed the spyware when she'd left her phone unattended on her desk. He'd invaded her life, watching her through the phone's camera and listening, always listening. *What does he want from me?*

Amy pounded the sidewalk with her sneakers. Her lungs burned. Sweat stung her eyes and trickled down her back. She peered over her shoulder at the chaotic mass of bodies. Was Eddie following her?

"Lisa?" a woman said. "Look out!"

Amy collided with someone, and they tumbled to the hard ground.

Bethany Morris spread-eagled beneath Amy. "Ouch."

Her body was soft and warm. Amy sprang to her feet and offered her hand. "I'm so sorry, Beth. Are you all right?"

She hauled the bookkeeper upright.

Beth slapped dirt from her thighs. "Am *I* all right? I've been calling you for days and sending messages. Where have you been?"

Amy glanced down the street. Eddie would catch up any second. She had no time to chat and didn't want to mix Beth up in her problems.

"It's complicated."

Beth leaned in close. "The police have been asking about you. Tanesha is dead. Mark, too. The agency is in chaos. People are talking about a serial killer. They're afraid to come to work."

"I know. I heard."

Did she think Amy had stayed away out of fear, too?

The bookkeeper gave Amy the once-over and bunched her eyebrows. "What's with the clothes? Are you in trouble, Lisa?"

The name jolted her. Amy hadn't been Lisa for days. She'd lied to the bubbly woman for weeks. The sudden desire to confess ignited within. But the truth would only break her friend's heart.

Amy's lips trembled. The guilt added to the crushing mental burden, shoving her psyche to the edge of collapse. "You don't want to know."

The words seemed to galvanize Beth. "Oh, yeah?"

The bookkeeper hailed a yellow cab and opened the back door. "Get in."

Amy stared at her. "What are you doing?"

"Proving you wrong."

Chapter 47

B eth looked Amy square in the eye an hour later. "I believe you."

Amy blinked at her. "You do?"

They shared the comfy old couch in the living room of the book-keeper's cozy Brooklyn apartment. Bookshelves lined the walls. The names on the spines were a who's-who of mystery fiction. Agatha Christie. Patricia Highsmith. Harlan Coben. The worn covers hinted at multiple readings. After hours, Beth escaped from her safe, boring numbers into thrilling literary worlds of crime and suspense.

Upon their arrival, she'd fixed two large yellow mugs of hot chocolate, and Amy had surrendered to her pampering. When had anyone last spoiled her like this? Beth's unexpected kindness had demolished Amy's protective walls, and the whole truth had poured out. She'd expected her coworker to react with surprise and hurt. Amy had lied to her about her identity. But her friend had listened patiently and hadn't judged her.

Beth shrugged. "Sure, I believe you. Why not?"

"Because I sound crazy. I mean, *I* don't believe me."

"Steve is real enough if he kidnapped your brother. He's proved he's capable of murder. Unlike you. I know people. You're a good soul."

"What about Mark? I think I killed him."

The mousy woman huffed. "Nonsense! You passed out. He must have drugged you. That explains your wonky memory of the events. Don't feel bad for him. Those cutting tools and the plastic sheeting weren't there by accident. He'd probably used those before to…"

Beth's eyes widened. "Josh's assistants! They all left suddenly without explanation or even collecting their paychecks. I always thought that was strange. But we figured Josh was an entitled jerk, and no one blamed them for running. But now we know why they disappeared. They didn't quit. Mark murdered them in his penthouse. Those poor girls! Who knows how many others he tortured to death?"

She shuddered. "Lisa—I mean, Amy—you had a close call with a horrible death. You should consider yourself lucky."

People kept telling her that. "But what about the dreams and the blood on my hands?"

"Ha! Dreams reflect your emotional state, that's all. The trauma of witnessing Leo's murder mixed with your guilt over leaving Daniel behind. I'd have nightmares, too. It's a wonder you can sleep at all."

Amy nodded. Beth's mystery-novel addiction had trained her to analyze the facts with a cool, rational head, and her conclusions validated Amy's inner convictions. *I'm not a killer.*

Beth gazed distractedly at the cuckoo clock on the wall. She seemed to relish the challenge of solving the puzzle of Amy's traumatic predicament.

"Your stalker said he killed Josh and Tanesha. He must have disposed of Mark, too."

Amy followed her line of reasoning. "Maybe he knew about Mark's past? He realized I was in danger. But why did he leave me there? Was he trying to save me or frame me for all the murders?"

The bookkeeper raised her eyebrows. "Could Steve be your secret admirer? He murdered Leo. Perhaps he killed the others?"

"Why would he do that? It can't be him. The stalker offered to get rid of Steve."

"And?"

"I turned him down."

"Why?"

"I'm not a murderer, Beth. Besides, he could use that against me. Who knows what he'd demand of me in return?"

"Mm. Good point. But I wouldn't rule Steve out. From what you've told me about him, he'd get a kick out of controlling you." Amy sighed. The Steve Is the Stalker theory made her head spin. Beth had clearly read too many crazy plot twists. But one detail excluded the dirty cop for sure.

"The killer knew about Josh, Mark, and Tanesha. But Steve didn't have access to Wesner and Morgan. It can't be him."

Beth bit her lip. "I guess you're right. Steve sounds like a street thug anyway. Spyware is too sophisticated for him." Her eyes gleamed. "Unless he isn't working alone."

Amy's mouth dropped open. "Eddie!"

"What about him?"

"Eddie hinted at the stalker's message, a song from *Aladdin*. 'Friend Like Me.' Maybe he's the inside man?"

The bookkeeper didn't seem enthusiastic. "People are very suggestible. Maybe you hummed the tune at work, and it got stuck in his head?"

"I didn't. Eddie knows all these random facts about serial killers in Midtown. Today, he chased me down Seventh Avenue."

Beth frowned. "I don't know, Amy. Eddie isn't serial killer material."

"He stared straight at me. I'm telling you, he's our guy."

"But what's his connection to Steve?"

"I don't know. What do you know about Eddie?"

Beth shrugged. "He's worked at the agency for five years. No promotions. Not management material, from what I hear."

"Let's look him up online."

Beth opened the Facebook app on her phone and searched her friend list. "Here he is. Edmund Vega. Not very photogenic, and that mustache is ridiculous."

Amy didn't argue. Eddie wore an old-style rower's hat in his profile photo. No wonder he was still single.

"What about his friends?"

Beth scoffed. "There's over a thousand."

She typed "Steve" in the search box, but no results returned.

"Try Leo Santiago."

Beth typed Santiago. "I doubt Eddie had anything—"

Amy pointed at the profile picture. "That's him!"

Leo hadn't smiled for the camera. He was tough. *Not tough enough.*

Beth shivered with excitement at their discovery. "Eddie knew Leo. Maybe Steve found him through Leo's Facebook page?"

"Just like us."

Had Eddie and Steve tormented Amy like a homicidal tag team? Did that explain Eddie's stupid smile—a sign of perverse enjoyment?

Beth clicked her tongue dismissively. "Facebook friendships mean nothing. They might never have met. Why would Eddie team up with a career criminal?"

"Maybe Leo was his cousin? If he thinks I killed Leo and got away with it, he'd want revenge."

Beth snorted. "Why set you up for murder? He could just call the cops."

Their suspicions simmered in pensive silence.

This is a distraction. Their speculations wouldn't save Amy or Daniel from Steve tonight. But the discussion soothed her. Maybe it was the hot chocolate or Beth's snug living room or the simple fact that, for once, Amy wasn't facing her problems alone?

"Thank you, Beth."

"For what?"

"For listening...and believing me. You're a true friend."

Beth's lips parted. "Aww. You're welcome, Amy. Do you really mean that?"

Amy smiled. "You're the best friend I've had in years."

The bookkeeper gasped and blinked back tears. "Nobody's ever said that to me."

Amy put her arms around the pudgy woman and hugged her. Their roles reversed in an instant, the desperate fugitive becoming the comforter.

Beth pulled away, and a new resolve flashed in her eyes. "You deserve that money, not Steve."

The bookkeeper had seemed genuinely happy to hear about Amy's newly discovered wealth and not at all jealous.

"I don't have a choice, Beth. If I don't—"

The prepaid phone rang in her pouch. Daniel's burner number displayed on the screen.

"It's him."

Beth reached for the sheet of paper and pen on the coffee table. "Go ahead. We're ready."

Amy swallowed. *Are we?*

She answered. "Hello."

"Ten o'clock tonight," Steve said. "Write down the coordinates." He dictated two decimal numbers. "No cops. Come alone, and don't be late."

He disconnected the call.

Beth punched the digits into her smartphone. Her map app showed New York's five boroughs and a red pin in Brooklyn.

She zoomed in. "Greenpoint."

"What's there?"

"Old factories. It's isolated."

Amy didn't like the sound of that. Did Steve want extra privacy to conduct the exchange or to dispatch both her and Daniel after he'd received the Bitcoin codes? *It's a death trap.*

Beth shared her concerns. "We need to call the police."

"He said, no cops."

"He won't play by the rules. Neither should we."

"*We?* Beth, I'm not dragging you into this."

"Nobody's dragging me."

"This isn't a mystery novel. You don't get to pick up another book if things end badly. This is life and death."

"I know. But you can't do this on your own."

She's right. They were no match for the murderous criminal and his accomplice. But Amy had burned that bridge.

"The police won't believe me. I've broken too many promises."

Beth chewed her lip. Would she find a solution to their problem in her mental crime fiction archives?

Her eyes sparkled. "I know what to do."

"You do?"

"Believe me, if I can balance Wesner and Morgan's books every year, I can do anything. But I'm warning you, it'll sound crazy."

Amy had that sinking feeling. "How crazy?"

They were in over their heads. But the clock was ticking, and Daniel's life depended on her. She'd try anything.

"Promise me two things. First, no questions until I'm done."

"Agreed. What's the second thing?"

Beth grinned deviously. "Don't freak out."

Amy's confidence wavered. Beth meant well. But Amy wouldn't bet her future on a madcap scheme. *Don't be rude. Hear her out.* Worst-case scenario, she'd respectfully decline the offer. How bad could her idea be?

"Okay. I promise. What's your plan?"

Beth told her...and Amy freaked out.

Chapter 48

Brandon pointed at Mindy's computer monitor that evening, drawing attention to the gray-hooded figure walking down a crowded sidewalk. "That's her."

He and Sergeant Blank stood by Mindy's desk in their squad room at Midtown South Precinct and looked over her shoulder. She paused the video feed. The timestamp read 12:43 PM. While they'd searched The Manhattan Grand Hotel room by room, their suspect had strolled around Midtown. Amy had played him for a fool yet again. But the sting of this betrayal hurt the most.

"Are you sure that's her?"

"The person who passed me on the stairwell was wearing the same sweatshirt. It must be her."

"Where is this?"

Mindy answered. "Corner of Seventh and Thirty-Second."

Sarge grunted. "What's she doing in Midtown? Is she messing with us?"

"She entered a tourist store a minute later and came out wearing a black sweater and cap. Seems she tried to throw us off her trail."

Mindy switched windows to the feed of Amy exiting the store.

Sarge squinted at the screen. "I Heart New York? She's got a sense of humor. But why hang around our precinct? She could change clothes anywhere."

Brandon swallowed hard. His opinion carried little weight after he'd fallen repeatedly for her tricks. As penance, he'd scanned street camera footage for hours until he'd struck gold. But the question offered him another opportunity to atone for his sins.

"Sir, she might have been meeting someone. The hotel room was registered under the name Mr. and Mrs. Daniel Walker, and a desk attendant remembered a dark-haired man with her when she signed for the room."

Their boss raised his eyebrows. "The black hair on her couch?"

Mindy nodded. "The voices her landlord overheard, too. Amy has a brother named Daniel."

"Is he married?"

"No. His last place of residence is unknown, but he'd been living in Chicago. No criminal record. His Instagram account is inactive, but this might be an old shot of him."

Mindy clicked to the image they'd copied from his feed. An unshaven young man with black curls peered unsmiling at the camera. Sadness glinted in his gaze.

Sarge grunted. "I see the family resemblance. Cooper, did she mention a brother?"

"No, sir."

The admission stung. Amy hadn't trusted him enough to share that detail. What other crucial facts had she hidden from him?

Their boss sighed. "So, her brother crashed on her couch. But is he an accomplice?"

"Unclear. He might have arrived only recently, but maybe he's helping her escape?"

Sarge turned to Mindy. "Did she meet up with him?"

"We have no visuals of the brother. But Amy shows up later, on Thirty-Ninth Street."

She clicked another file, and the video played. The woman in the peaked cap leaned against a streetlight, then she stepped backward and bolted through the crowd.

Sarge leaned in. "Looks like she saw a ghost. Where did she go?"

"We lost her, sir. But you're right. Something spooked her."

"A cop?"

Mindy shrugged.

Sergeant Blank nodded thoughtfully. "Put out a BOLO for the brother, too. Any other leads?"

"No. She turned off her phone again. We found a number for the brother, but that's also offline."

Sarge frowned. "I don't like this. Her behavior seems erratic. Cooper, maybe you're right about her being mentally unstable? Let's get eyes on her apartment and the agency. We don't want her hurting anyone else."

"Yes, sir."

Sarge walked off.

Brandon rubbed his eyes and flopped on his chair. His watch read 9:32 PM. He'd work this weekend, too. He'd keep going until he took Amy into custody.

Mindy peered at him. "I'm sorry, Brand. I know this isn't how you wanted things to go."

He leaned back and stretched his arms. "I got carried away. Thanks for not being a jerk about it."

She grinned. "There's no fun in kicking a dead horse."

"Ouch."

His phone rang. The display read: "private number." Was Amy calling again? *No more chances.*

"Cooper."

"Detective, this is Bethany Morris from Wesner and Morgan."

Brandon pouted with surprise at Mindy. "Hi, Ms. Morris. How can I help you?"

"Beth from finance."

"Yes, I remember." He'd interviewed the bookkeeper twice after the deaths of Josh and Tanesha. She'd been very helpful, and the prospect of a serial killer at the agency had seemed to disturb her. Had she reached out to calm her nerves?

"You said to call if we heard from Lisa."

Brandon straightened. "Did Lisa contact you?"

"Better than that, Detective Cooper. I know where she is."

Chapter 49

The blare of a barge horn pierced the night. Amy walked alone in the dark. Gravel crunched underneath her sneakers. The earthy scent of wild grass carried in the chill air. Corrugated iron sheets hedged the access road, funneling her toward the large black shadow of a factory building that swallowed the light. Beyond the East River, Manhattan sparkled like a distant galaxy. Amy had wandered far from civilization. *Do you know what you're doing?*

That afternoon, she'd listened open-mouthed to Beth. The bookkeeper hadn't lied. Her plan sounded crazy. She must be insane, too. Certifiable. But her scheme was Amy's only hope to save her brother's life *and* escape Steve's chokehold on her future. She had no choice.

The dark shadow loomed taller. She'd arrived on time. But the ominous silence filled her mind with doubt. *Is Steve here? Does he even exist?* Amy wished he didn't. If the killer was an illusion, then Daniel would be safe, and she wouldn't be facing a deadly confrontation.

No such luck. Beth had witnessed Steve's call and prepared Amy for battle. *This is real.* Part of Amy welcomed the fight. *No more running. No more fear. One way or another, this ends tonight.*

A chicken wire gate stood open. Bolt cutters had severed the thick steel chain, which lay on the ground beside a large padlock. A pickup truck parked on the side of the path. Her heart raced. *You're in the right place. He's here.*

Her eyes adjusted to the darkness. Two industrial forklifts emerged from the gloom alongside a towering stack of pine logs. Conveyer belts protruded from the factory toward a tall mound of wood chips.

Amy dug into her pouch and closed her fingers around her weapon.

Beth had handed her the pepper spray. "Let's be clear about something. Steve won't let you or Daniel live. Timing is everything. Preparation, too. Once he gets the codes, he'll attack, and you need to be ready."

Amy had practiced with a test canister, inserting her thumb into the trigger guard and spraying at her assailant's eyes.

Beth had nodded with approval. "Wait until he's under ten feet away. The spray won't stop him, but it will buy you a few seconds."

Amy gripped the pepper spray in her bag. The cool canister provided a pinch of much-needed confidence. *Will a few seconds be enough?*

She headed for the gaping mouth of the building's triangular facade. Pausing at the entrance, she listened for movement within but only the desperate thumping of her heart filled her ears. *Where are they? Is this a trap?*

Amy stepped onto the smooth concrete floor of the building. She hadn't brought a flashlight. Would Steve sneak up behind her and slit her throat? *This is a mistake.* She'd bet her life on the madcap plan of a mousy mystery novel addict. What had she been thinking? *Get out of here now!* But Amy had come this far, and she wouldn't abandon Daniel again.

She tightened her grip on the Mace. "Hello?"

Her voice echoed in the creepy void.

Something rustled inside the factory...and someone grunted.

Then, a lever clanked noisily, and fluorescent strips flickered on overhead, flooding the factory floor with bright light.

Amy shuttered her eyes. Untreated wooden boards lay in tidy rows on her left. To her right, a tall pile of unprocessed pine logs rose toward the high ceiling. Bulky industrial machinery and control terminals lined the factory wall of the central clearing. At the back, a man slumped on a hardwood chair, his arms and legs tied to the steel frame. A strip of cloth gagged his mouth. Now he raised his head, and his eyes bulged with fear.

Daniel struggled against his restraints and mumbled unintelligibly. Was he trying to warn her? Had Amy walked into an ambush?

A figure stepped out from behind a machine. A large, serrated hunting knife glinted in his hand. Steve slipped behind his prisoner and put the blade to Daniel's throat.

The killer grinned at her wickedly. "Hello, Amy. Say goodbye to your brother."

Chapter 50

The bulky woman answered the door of her Brooklyn apartment with a smile. She'd dressed up for the meeting, selecting a knee-length green frock and applying makeup. Brandon had a bad feeling about this. *Does she think we're paying her a social call?*

"Please come in."

Brandon and Mindy stepped into her living room. During her interviews, the Wesner & Morgan bookkeeper had seemed quirky but professional and eager to help—the classic indispensable office worker who blended into the woodwork. But her apartment opened a new window on Bethany Morris. The brown shaggy rug, overstuffed couch, and shelves crammed with crime novels hinted at many hours at home alone with her thoughts. The bookkeeper lacked only a few stray cats to complete the old maid stereotype.

He cut to the chase. "You said you know where to find Lisa Smith?"

She swept a wavy lock of mousy hair behind her ear. "All in good time, Detective. Coffee?"

The offer clashed with the urgent tone of her call. She'd refused to provide details over the phone, insisting they meet in person.

Brandon shrugged at Mindy. *I guess we'll do this her way.*

"Thank you. Black. No sugar."

Mindy followed his lead. "Make that two, Ms. Morris."

"Please, call me Beth."

She hurried to the kitchen.

Brandon and Mindy flopped on the couch.

The precinct's dedicated hotline had received dozens of tip-offs about the recent murders from concerned citizens. The callers fell into three groups: armchair detectives, crackpots, and attention seekers. Beth clearly belonged to the last group. *This is probably a wild-goose chase.*

But few tip-offs warranted home visits late on a Friday night. Bethany Morris was different. She worked for Wesner & Morgan. She knew the victims and the prime suspect personally. Would she lead them to Amy?

A kettle whistled in the kitchen.

Brandon rubbed his eyes. He'd worked long, fruitless hours. The case had sapped his energy and messed with his head. Amy's reality distortion field had blurred his red lines, too. He needed a hot shower and a warm bed. Most of all, he needed to find Amy and get answers.

Beth returned with a tray of steaming coffee mugs and a bowl of sugar cubes. He'd last seen the grainy white blocks of sweetener in fourth grade at Grandma's apartment. Had they stepped back in time?

Their hostess handed out the mugs and sipped her drink. "I know who killed Mark Davis."

Brandon and Mindy exchanged surprised glances. Beth would naturally take an interest in the murder of her colleagues. But she appeared to have mistaken the homicide detectives for members of her book club.

She didn't wait for them to respond. "Not only Mark. I know who killed Tanesha Williams, too, and it's not Lisa Smith. Or should I say, Amy Walker?"

Beth had uncovered Amy's identity, too. The mystery fiction aficionado seemed to delight in their surprised expressions and dragged out their suspense.

Brandon took the bait. "I give up. Who's the killer?"

Beth narrowed her eyes. "Killer or *killers*?"

Mindy raised her eyebrows. "There's more than one perp?"

"Two, to be precise."

Brandon and Mindy had also suspected the involvement of collaborators—Josh Wesner's former assistant or Amy's brother, Daniel. What else had the bookkeeper discovered?

Brandon didn't contradict her. "How do you know all this?"

"Amy and I figured it out here in my apartment."

"She was here?"

"Oh, yes. A few hours ago. We bumped into each other in Midtown. I hadn't seen her in days, and I was worried about her. She was very shaken, so I brought her home, and we had a nice long chat. The poor thing has been through hell!"

Mindy leaned forward. "Where did she go from here?"

"I'm getting there. Amy changed her name to get away from a murderer, Steve Hamlin. He killed her boyfriend, Leo, for stealing ninety thousand dollars, and now he expects her to pay him back with interest. Amy has no money, but he doesn't care."

"Why would Steve kill your coworkers?"

Beth stared at the far wall and sipped her drink. "That's where the plot thickens. Mark led a double life. High-flying executive by day, serial killer by night. He drugged Amy yesterday in his apartment, where he kept reams of plastic sheeting and torture implements. Josh's assistants never stayed at the agency long. They all disappeared without warning. We assumed Josh had hit on them. He was a jerk. Now we know the truth. Mark murdered them. When Josh and Tanesha found out, Mark killed them, too. 'But Mark's dead, too,' you say, 'so who murdered him?' The answer is Steve!"

Mindy objected. "But—"

Beth raised her hand for silence. "Steve tracked Amy to Manhattan. Maybe he broke into her apartment but couldn't find the money? Reporting her to the police wouldn't make him any richer. Had she spent it all? Steve bided his time and watched her. He hacked her phone and sent friendly anonymous messages to gain her trust. When Mark killed Josh, Steve leveraged that, too.

He pretended to have eliminated her boss to protect her so Amy would feel indebted to him. She couldn't turn to the cops anyway, because he'd framed her for her boyfriend's murder. But then Amy stumbled into Mark's web. If she dies, Steve gets nothing. So he saved her life but left her at the crime scene. Now he'd pin two murders on her."

Was this the story Amy had sold Beth? If she and Heather Brody had collaborated to kill Mark and his associates, they'd need an alternative narrative to cover up their crimes. The bookkeeper had swallowed the lie whole.

Brandon challenged Beth's theory. "Josh fell from his office window. How did Steve gain access to the agency?"

Beth cradled her steaming mug. "Simple. Steve has a man on the inside. The accomplice installed the spyware on her phone. He let Steve in."

"Why would he do that?"

"Revenge! Steve told him Amy killed Leo, his friend. Or his cousin. We haven't figured out that part yet. We were hoping you'd tie up those loose ends."

She winked.

Mindy scoffed. "Okay, I'll bite. Who's the accomplice?"

Beth grinned. "Edmund Vega."

Brandon didn't hide his astonishment. "Eddie?" Harry Wesner's assistant wasn't even on their radar.

"Check his Facebook. He's friends with Leo Santiago."

Brandon met Mindy's gaze. They hadn't scrutinized Eddie's social media accounts. Had they screwed up?

"Where is Eddie now?"

"With Steve, probably."

Beth glanced at the wall again. No, not the wall. The cuckoo clock. *Is she stalling to buy Amy time?* "Beth, where is Amy?"

"She went to meet Steve."

"I don't understand. Isn't Steve her enemy?"

"He kidnapped her brother, Daniel. She's trying to get him back."

Brandon swore under his breath. They'd been right about the brother. Why hadn't Amy mentioned him? Had she tried to protect him? *If only she'd trusted me.*

Mindy put her mug down. "Beth, we need to speak with her. Where is she?"

"I don't know."

"But you said—"

Beth raised her hand again. "I don't know where she is *right now.* But I know where she'll be."

Chapter 51

Terror gripped Amy. Steve held the hunting knife to Daniel's neck, and murder flashed in his eyes. He'd slit her brother's throat. He'd slaughter him before her eyes.

Don't just stand there. Do something!

"Wait. I have the codes. Take them. But, please, don't hurt him."

Beth had seriously underestimated Steve. They couldn't beat the killer at his own game. Amy had too much to lose. *Let Steve have the money.* She only cared about her brother's life.

The killer snarled at her. "I thought you were smarter than that, Amy."

What does he mean? Did he know she'd confided in Beth? Was Steve her stalker? Her pulse thumped in her ears. The killer watched her closely. But he didn't execute his captive. Not yet. Daniel was still breathing. There was hope. *Keep him talking. Find out what's bothering him.*

"I don't understand."

Steve gazed at her pouch. "Take your hand out of the bag, nice and slow."

The penny dropped. He'd expected her to play dirty. Did he think she'd hidden a gun in her pouch?

Amy let go of the pepper spray canister and grasped Leo's note. Then slowly, she withdrew her hand and raised the folded page into the air.

Steve lowered the knife. "That's better. Put it on the floor halfway between us and step away."

He was taking no chances, not letting her get close to him. At this distance, the Mace was useless. But the killer's caution strengthened her. He feared her, too. Steve wasn't invincible. Beth's plan had a fighting chance of succeeding after all.

Amy stepped forward slowly. Daniel shook his head and mumbled incoherently. She knew what he was saying. *Don't do it, Amy. You're handing over your only bargaining chip.* Steve could pocket the codes and murder them both. But what choice did she have?

She stopped in the middle of the factory floor. Keeping her eyes on the abductor, she bent her knees and placed the page on the concrete floor, then backed off.

Knife still in his hand, Steve walked over. He collected the note, examined the codes, and grinned.

"You did the right thing, my friend."

Amy balled her hands into fists. *You gave me no choice.* Steve had murdered Leo. He'd stolen years from her life. Now he'd kidnapped her brother and robbed them of a multi-million-dollar fortune. She wanted to Mace him and beat him to a pulp. But she held her tongue. Steve still had Daniel. If he killed her brother, she'd lose the will to live.

Steve slipped the note into his back pocket. "I'm a man of my word. You did your part. I'll do mine."

He sauntered toward Daniel.

Amy blinked. *This is too good to be true.* Steve hadn't checked the Bitcoin codes yet. Did he trust that she'd followed his instructions to the letter, or was he toying with her, raising her hopes only to dash them by murdering Daniel?

Is this a trap? She scanned the factory for hidden collaborators, but Eddie wasn't lurking among the bulky machinery and conveyor belts.

Steve didn't attack her brother. He sliced the ropes that secured him to the chair and returned the knife to its leather sheath.

Daniel pulled the gag from his mouth and rubbed his raw wrists. Then, he stood on wobbly legs and rushed toward her.

Amy gasped with relief. Her brother was free and uninjured. The trade had taken place so quickly. *Too quickly.* Steve would escape with the money before Beth's trap snapped shut. *Who cares?* Daniel was free. Amy had paid off her tormentor. New horizons beckoned.

Her brother ran at her, a smile splitting his face. Their family reunion would be short-lived. The police still wanted Amy for murder. She'd have to disappear again. She'd start over in another state and under a new identity. But without Steve snapping at her heels, she could put down roots. Her days of constant running were over.

Amy opened her arms to hug him. But Daniel didn't return the embrace. Instead, a grimace twisted his mouth, and he punched her in the face.

Chapter 52

"Ham sandwich, anyone?" Bethany Morris rummaged in her large black handbag on the backseat of the unmarked police car.

Brandon studied her reflection in the rearview mirror. She'd added a pink jacket to her outfit.

"No, thank you."

Outside, darkened warehouses panned by on the industrial zone's abandoned streets. The bookkeeper had refused to provide a street address for Amy's rendezvous with her brother's kidnappers, determined to ride with them in the cruiser. The excursion had started well. She'd directed Brandon to cross the East River into Greenpoint. The isolated streets were ideal venues for clandestine encounters. But now the scenery repeated itself. Was Beth lost or intentionally driving them in circles?

"I have egg mayo, too."

Does she think we're on a road trip?

Mindy lost her temper. "We don't need food. Just tell us where to go."

Beth squinted out the back window. "Turn, um, left at the next corner."

Mindy fumed. "Again? We've already gone that way."

Brandon gasped with frustration. "Listen, Beth. If Amy is in danger, we're running out of time. Either you tell us where she is *right now*, or I swear I'll arrest you for obstruction of justice."

"Okay, calm down. I'm trying to remember the way."

Mindy shifted in her seat to glare at their passenger. "You've been there before?"

"On Google Maps. We're close. Real close. Turn right."

Brandon did. "This had better not be a waste of time."

"We'll be there any second. You should call for backup."

His shoulders tensed. The bookkeeper's frequent commands rubbed him the wrong way. He wouldn't call Dispatch yet. If this was a hoax, he'd be the laughingstock of the department. Had the lonely armchair detective arranged a fun night out at their expense or a diversion to allow Amy to slip away again?

The car wobbled over a gravel access road without streetlights. Corrugated iron sheeting narrowed the alley to the width of a single vehicle. They'd have trouble backing out if this was a dead end.

The triangular facade of a factory building loomed ahead. White light escaped through the building's windows and seams. *Somebody's working late this Friday night.* Had Beth led them to the right place?

Beth perked up. "Kill the lights. No need to announce our arrival."

Grudgingly, Brandon obeyed. A chicken wire gate stood open, its heavy chain lying on the ground. Brandon pulled up behind a black Ford F-150 pickup truck.

Beth zipped her bag shut. "I'll go around the back while you take the front."

Brandon looked at her in the rearview mirror. "You're staying put."

"But Amy needs me."

"You've helped plenty. We'll take things from here. Steve is armed and dangerous. This is no place for a civilian. Stay here and let us do our jobs. Understood?"

Beth frowned. "Fine. But if you need assistance, I know karate."

"We'll bear that in mind."

Brandon and Mindy checked their service weapons and spare magazines. Then they got out of the car and approached the structure.

A thin line of light marked the sliding door of the main entrance. In the distance, the Manhattan skyline glittered in silence. Brandon's eyes adjusted to the darkness. A tall mound of wood shavings rose beside the building.

The loose gravel crunched underfoot. Brandon grimaced. But his concern over their noisy advance proved unwarranted.

A machine roared to life inside the factory, emitting a loud churning sound, and the conveyor belts leading out of the building shuddered into motion.

Mindy halted. "What is that?"

Brandon recognized the mechanical whine. "A wood chipper."

She frowned. "Why would anyone use the wood chipper on a Friday night?"

He swallowed hard. "Good question."

Answers came to mind, but none boded well for Amy and her brother.

Chapter 53

Amy sprawled on the factory's hard floor. Her cheek burned, and her shoulder ached from the impact on the concrete. Her brother's unexpected right hook had knocked her off her feet. But the shock of the sudden attack stung the most. *Why did he hit me?*

Daniel grabbed her by the hair and dragged her further inside. Pain racked her scalp, scattering her thoughts.

"Ow! Daniel! Stop! What are you doing?"

But her brother didn't seem to hear her cries...or to care. He dumped her at the killer's feet.

Steve chuckled. "You didn't think we'd let you off that easily, did you?"

We. Was Eddie there, too? What was he talking about? Her mind fought the inescapable conclusion. *Not Eddie. Daniel.* But why was her brother collaborating with Steve?

"I-I don't understand."

Steve ignored her. "Throw me her bag."

Her brother snatched her pouch and tossed the bag to the killer. *The Mace!* They'd robbed her of her only means of defense.

The killer peeked inside. "Keep an eye on her while I check the account. If she gives you trouble, beat the crap out of her."

Daniel smiled. "With pleasure."

Steve moved to a wooden worktable. He pulled a laptop from a black shoulder bag, opened the computer on the table, and retrieved Leo's note from his back pocket. Soon, he'd confirm the money was in the account. But Amy had lost interest in the Bitcoin fortune. Her head spun at her brother's heartbreaking betrayal.

She shifted onto her knees. "Daniel, why are you doing this?"

He scowled at her as though she was a diseased rat. "Shut up. I've had enough of your lies."

"Lies? What lies?" He must be mistaken.

Daniel scoffed. "That's it. Pretend you don't know."

Amy searched her memory for clues. Had she blocked some terrible crime from her past? Leo's bloodied corpse rose in her mind, and she shuddered. *Does he think I killed him?*

"Is this about Leo?"

Daniel huffed with disgust.

What could explain his sudden hatred? "I've always been good to you."

His cheek twitched. "Good to me? You deserted me!"

Was he still angry about her disappearance four years ago? "I'm sorry, Daniel. I never wanted to leave you."

His nostrils flared. "When Mom and Dad died, I thought, 'At least, I have Amy. We'll look out for each other.' But you cut me out!"

"I still tried to help. I sent you money."

He snarled. "*Scraps.* That's what you sent me. But you were sitting on millions."

He'd got this all wrong.

"I just found that out now."

He folded his arms. "Yeah, right. Tell me another."

Why wouldn't he believe her? "I was going to share the account with you."

Daniel scoffed. "Sure you were. That's why you put me on that bus. As always, you took everything for yourself."

Amy gaped at him. Did he not understand how much she'd sacrificed for him? His ingratitude kindled her temper.

"So, this is about the money?"

At least he had the decency to squirm. An ember of goodness still burned within him.

He clenched his jaw. "No. This is about justice."

"Justice for what?"

He glared at her. "Our inheritance."

"What inheritance, Daniel? Mom and Dad left us nothing."

"Whatever."

"You have to believe me."

He scoffed again. "Steve was right about you. You're a liar and a cheat."

Steve. The dirty cop had poisoned her brother's mind.

"Don't listen to him, Daniel. He's a murderer. He'll kill us both."

Her brother smirked. "He told me you'd say that."

"It's true. He killed Leo. That's how this started."

"Enough! Admit it, Amy. *You* killed Leo. *You* stole the cash Steve gave him, and you've been living off that stash ever since."

"What? No. No! How can you think that? Don't you know me at all?"

And suddenly, Amy understood. Steve hadn't turned him against her in Manhattan. He'd recruited Daniel long before. Tiring of searching for Amy, he'd contacted her brother in Chicago. Steve had told him she'd stolen his inheritance and killed Leo for money, too. Daniel had believed him. Why wouldn't he? Steve was a cop. "Let's work together," the killer had probably told him. They'd reel Amy in, recover the stolen property, and deliver her to justice. Everybody wins.

Knowing no better, Daniel had agreed. Steve had followed the money trail of her regular transfers, tracked her to Manhattan, and found an inside man at Wesner & Morgan. When threats of violence hadn't yielded dividends, Steve had used his secret weapon, the one person Amy would protect at any cost—her brother.

Daniel's eyes filled with scorn. "You sent me scraps to calm your guilty conscience. But that will never change what you did."

Amy sputtered with frustration. Arguing with her brother was like talking to a brick wall. Protesting her innocence hadn't budged him. She'd have to find proof.

"Think about it, Daniel. If I'm loaded, why do I live in a tiny old apartment?"

He glared at her. "Do you think I'm stupid? You're wanted by the police. Spending heaps of money would draw attention. That's why you used a fake name, too."

"But why take an office job when I could hang out at the beach and drink margaritas?"

He opened his mouth to answer but found no words. The question had stumped him, cracking his rock-hard certainty.

Still, he resisted. "How should I know? You're the psycho. Maybe you got bored?"

Amy pressed on. "I didn't know about the Bitcoin codes. We discovered them together."

Daniel blinked. "You knew they were there. When the picture frame broke, you just couldn't hide it any longer."

But the confidence faded from his tone. The cracks had widened. *I'm getting through to him.*

"Listen to me, Daniel. I was about to leave Leo the day Steve came over. Leo hid me in the closet. When Leo didn't have his money, Steve killed him in cold blood. I was there. He promised Leo he'd come after me, too. I went straight to the police, but Steve was there. When I found out he was a cop, I knew he'd frame me. That's why I ran, Daniel. That's why I had to leave."

Daniel stared at her. The truth was seeping in. Amy hadn't deceived him. Steve had. But there was no time for blame or apologies.

"I'm not a murderer, Daniel, and neither are you. But you have no idea who you're dealing with. Think—why didn't he call in the police? Why didn't he arrest me? He used you to get to me. You'll never get whatever he promised you. He won't share the money with anyone. He'll kill us both."

Steve swore and slammed the table with his fist, startling them. Daniel turned to his accomplice. "What's the matter?"

"There's nothing here."

"What do you mean?"

"The account is empty. She screwed us."

Empty? The floor seemed to fall away beneath Amy.

She gasped. "That's impossible. Mark checked the account on his computer. I saw the balance. It's worth four hundred and eighty million dollars."

Steve sneered. "Well, now it's zero."

Amy searched frantically for an explanation. She'd blacked out that night in Mark's apartment, leaving Leo's note on the coffee table. "Mark must have transferred the money without my knowledge."

"I thought of that. The log is empty. No transfers. It's a virgin account."

Amy gaped at the two men. *This isn't possible.*

Steve shut the laptop and stormed toward them. "That bitch lied to us."

Amy rose to her trembling feet. "The money was there. Daniel, you've got to believe me."

Steve rushed at her, and she flinched. But he didn't hit her. He passed her by and pressed three red buttons on a control panel. The factory came to life. Motors whirred, and chains clinked.

The killer picked up a severed branch the size of a baseball bat. "You see this, Amy? This is what we do to liars."

He walked over to a waist-heigh metal trough that shook rhythmically, and he tossed the branch inside. Seconds later, a high-pitched grinding sound issued from the large box at the end of the receptacle, and the machine spewed wood shavings out the other side and onto a conveyor belt. The chilling whine cut out. *What would the wood chipper do to soft human flesh?*

Steve barked a command. "Hold her."

She lunged for the exit, but Daniel grabbed her.

"Let me go! No, Daniel. Don't do this."

Her brother growled in her ear. "Last chance. Tell us where you put the money."

The empty account had plugged the cracks of doubt in his resolve.

"I told you the truth. The money was there. I have no idea what happened—"

Her eyes opened. *I was honest. But what about Steve?*

"He's lying."

"What?"

"The money's all there. He's looking for an excuse to kill us both."

Steven scoffed. "She's pathetic. See for yourself, if you like."

The killer seized her arm, twisted it behind her back, and frog-marched her toward the deadly machine.

"Game over, my friend."

Amy dug her feet into the floor, but Steve was too powerful. Her sneakers slid over the smooth concrete as he dragged her to her grisly execution.

"Daniel! Help me. Please!"

He'd feed her to the industrial chipper while her brother—her own flesh and blood—stood by.

Steve pushed her over the side of the trough, but she clung to the edges.

He leaned into her, groaning with the effort. "The hardest part...is getting rid...of the body."

Her feet lifted off the floor. Soon, he'd tip her onto the conveyor belt of death. Amy kicked with all her strength, and her foot connected with his belly. Steve grunted but didn't let go.

Daniel spoke behind them. "That's enough."

Steve ignored him.

"Hey! I said, that's enough. Let her go."

Steve growled, "Back off, Daniel."

"The account is empty. She doesn't have the money."

"She's a murderer. She deserves this."

"Then hand her over to the police."

Steve laughed. "I am the police."

"She's my sister. I can't let you do this."

The killer let go of Amy and spun around.

There was a crunch of cartilage, and the thud of a body hitting the floor. What had he done to Daniel?

Steve yelled. "I said, back off!"

Amy scrambled out of the trough, but he punched her in the gut. He gripped her waist, lifted her into the air, and tossed her into the feeder. She landed on her side. The conveyor belt swept her toward the chipper's black mouth of death. Amy scrambled onto her haunches.

"Oh, no, you don't!"

Steve jumped over the side of the trough. He shoved her backward and clamped his hands on her arms, pinning her with his body weight. The belt carried Amy headfirst toward the dark hole.

She writhed underneath him. Amy kicked her legs and shifted her shoulders, but the killer didn't budge.

Behind her, rotors spun with inhuman speed, and the shredder's knives whistled softly.

Her head entered the mouth of the chipper.

Steve smiled down at her. He reeked of Old Spice, and a maniacal evil grin split his face.

"Goodbye, my friend."

Chapter 54

The chipper wailed like a demon within the factory. Outside on the gravel path, Brandon scanned the gloomy surroundings for perps and braced for action. Wood shavings traveled along the conveyor belt toward the large mound. Then, the wail subsided to a background whine. The chipper had processed a small amount of timber. The equipment chugged along, but no more shavings followed. Amy had come here to ransom her brother from Steve. They had no reason to mess around with the factory's equipment. A chill traced his spine. The chipper's activity could mean only one thing. Amy and her brother were in mortal danger.

He stepped forward.

Mindy grasped his arm, holding him back. "We should call for backup."

"We don't have time."

"Do you trust Beth?"

His partner had raised a critical question. The bookkeeper had led them here, and her eccentric behavior had ignited mental warning lights. Was Beth a concerned citizen or a master manipulator?

Brandon shrugged. "The jury's still out."

Mindy glanced back at the cruiser. "Even if she's a straight shooter, Amy and her brother could ambush us. Who knows how many perps we're dealing with and what they're packing?"

He nodded. They had no body armor. Were they outnumbered and outgunned? To run headlong into an armed confrontation without backup was to court disaster.

"Okay."

Mindy called Dispatch and hung up. "The nearest squad car is five minutes away."

Brandon swore under his breath. Was five minutes too late to save Amy?

"Let's get closer."

"Brand, we should wait."

"We need eyes on the situation."

Mindy pursed her lips. "Okay."

They crept closer to the factory. The mechanical sounds grew louder. Snatches of human speech escaped the cacophony. Through the illuminated slit of the opening, he glimpsed a tall pile of unprocessed logs but no human forms.

He reached the wall, and Mindy joined him. There was a dull thud. Was Amy caught in a violent struggle with the captors? Was she injured—or dead? Then, the chipper noises died down, and an ominous silence reigned.

Brandon edged forward and peeked inside the sawmill. *What the hell?* He drew his service weapon. Both he and Mindy had been wrong.

Chapter 55

A my writhed from side to side, desperate to break free from Steve's death grip. But the killer's weight and wiry arms pinned her to the conveyor belt. The chipper's spinning rotors sucked in air, drawing her hair toward the deadly blades. *No! It can't end this way.*

"Help me! Please! Help!"

But who would come to her aid? Steve had beaten up her brother, and Beth hadn't arrived with the detectives yet. The bookkeeper had been right. *Timing is everything.* Had her plan failed?

Veins popped in Steve's temples. "Nobody's coming to save you, Amy."

The chipper caught a strand of her hair, plucking it painfully from her scalp. Any moment now, the rotating blades would catch a larger lock and yank her into its cruel jaws.

"No!"

With a burst of frantic energy, she rolled sideways and kneed Steve in the groin. His eyes bulged, and he loosened his grip on her shoulders.

Amy clutched the edge of the trough and raised herself up but banged her head on the chipper's steel opening. Pain dazed her. Stars danced in her field of vision.

Steve recovered. He clung to her, flattening his wiry body over hers.

"Stay down and die, you bitch!"

More strands of hair pulled free from her head, and she yelled. The black mouth of the chipper inched over her visual field. The machine chittered in her ears like a nightmarish monster. Amy craned her neck forward to stay ahead of the hungry blades.

Dad looked at her from the driver's seat. Mom, too. They smiled. Soon, she'd join them, and her struggle would be over. Tears burned her eyes. *No! I don't want to die!* She'd left so much undone. *I don't deserve this!*

Steve raised his torso, ready to spring free as soon as the chipper seized her. The crooked cop had no intention of dying with his victim.

"See you in Hell, Amy."

The cruel blades tore a clump of hair from her scalp, and Amy cried out.

Steve rose onto his knees.

Bang.

His head snapped sideways, and Steve toppled over the side of the feeder like a sack of potatoes.

Amy wasted no time. Ignoring the searing pain, she scrambled on her heels and elbows away from the chipper's opening.

The conveyor belt halted, and the machine noises wound down. Somebody had turned off the chipper. Amy tumbled over the edge of the trough and collapsed on the factory floor. Steve lay on the other side of the feeder, his body prone and still.

At the sound of footsteps, she spun around. Daniel stood over her, his nose bruised and bloody. He held a wooden plank. He'd knocked Steve unconscious, and not a moment too soon. Daniel had saved her life.

He dropped the plank, which clattered to the floor, and offered her his hand.

Amy accepted the assist. The battle had ended, and they had both survived. Daniel hung his head. Regret clouded his expression. Amy forgave him in an instant and hugged him tight.

Daniel sobbed in her ear. "I'm so sorry, Amy. You were right about him. I should never have doubted you."

"It's all right. We're okay now."

"I had no idea he'd try to kill you."

"I know."

"Police!" a woman yelled.

Amy disengaged from her brother. Two suits stepped toward them with their handguns raised. Brandon and Mindy had arrived at last. But they hadn't come to save her.

"Put your hands in the air."

Chapter 56

Brandon aimed his gun at Amy and the dark-haired stranger. The family resemblance was undeniable. Her brother had a bloody nose. Bruises marred her face. A two-by-four lay at their feet. Moments ago, they had embraced. What had happened here?

Amy smiled, and her relief at seeing him melted his heart.

"Brandon. Thank God, you're here! Where's Beth?"

The question raised his defenses. Amy knew Beth had led them there. She'd orchestrated the events, controlling him like a puppet on strings. But where was Steve, and why had they activated the chipper? Had the exchange already taken place, or had Amy and her brother invented the kidnapping to cover their tracks? *Do I know her at all?*

Mindy repeated her command. "Hands in the air."

Amy's smile faltered. She and her brother raised their hands.

Brandon didn't lower his gun. "Aren't you going to introduce us?"

"This is Daniel, my brother."

"You didn't tell me about him."

"He arrived only a few days ago. I had to keep him safe."

"Safe from the police?"

"From Steve. But I failed. Steve got to him."

Brandon gritted his teeth. How could she lie so easily?

"He seems fine to me."

She'd given him the slip twice before. He wouldn't fall for that trick again.

Mindy took over. "Keep your hands in the air and get down on your knees."

They did as she'd commanded.

Brandon holstered his Glock and reached for his cuffs. "We'll talk at the station."

Amy pleaded with him. "Fine. But arrest Steve, too. He broke Daniel's nose and almost killed me in the chipper."

Had Steve tried to murder Amy with the industrial wood chipper? Rage swelled within him. But he found no trace of her alleged attacker in the sawmill.

"Where is he?"

She jerked her head behind her.

"Back there. Behind the conveyor belt. Daniel knocked him out with a plank. He saved my life." She gazed warmly at her brother.

Brandon studied the chipper's feeder. Was she lying again? "Nobody's there."

Amy shot an anxious glance over her shoulder. "He was there a second ago. I swear to God."

"Yeah," Daniel said. "He lay right there."

Brandon sighed. *Here we go again.* The moment Brandon and Mindy turned their backs, their suspects would vanish. This time, he knew better.

Mindy joined him in the center of the factory floor. "Tell us all about it at the station. No sudden moves."

Amy panicked. "You don't understand. He was here." She pointed at a table at the back. "That's his laptop."

"I said, no sudden moves!"

Amy shuddered. "Eddie might be here, too. Beth thought—"

But she didn't complete her sentence.

Thunder rumbled to Brandon's right. The tall pile of unprocessed timber collapsed, releasing a tidal wave of tumbling logs toward him and Mindy.

"Watch out!"

Brandon sprinted out of the way, but a bouncing tree trunk swept his legs from under him. His head slammed onto the concrete floor, and he knew no more.

Chapter 57

Terror glued Amy to the spot. Kneeling helplessly on the factory floor, she watched the unfolding catastrophe. The avalanche advanced through the clearing as though in slow-motion. Brandon and Mindy dashed for their lives, but the heavy logs quickly overtook them, toppling the detectives and hiding their bodies from view. One fearful question chased another. *Are they okay? Are they alive?*

The landslide ran its course, and the ruckus settled. She scanned the chaotic factory floor, hoping Brandon would climb to his feet. He'd trusted her and tried to help despite her unreliable track record. Amy cared for him, too. She'd never wanted to put him in harm's way. *Is he dead because of me?*

Her conscience would have to wait. Dread piled in her heart. The avalanche was no coincidence. Steve was on the move. The killer had regained consciousness, and he'd neither forgive nor forget. Had he triggered the landslide?

The danger hadn't passed. With the cops out of the way, he'd come after Amy and Daniel and finish what he'd started. Like an angry, injured bear, the Viking would rain the full force of his wrath upon them.

Daniel picked up the wooden plank. He'd come to the same conclusion. Amy needed to arm herself, too. The pepper spray lay in her pouch on the worktable beside Steve's computer. She made for her bag, then stopped dead in her tracks.

Steve stepped from behind a metal machine by the table. Blood trickled from his bruised temple, and murder flashed in his eyes.

The killer growled. "I said no cops. You never could follow instructions. Neither of you."

Daniel moved in front of Amy, shielding her with his body. "She doesn't have the money, Steve."

The killer stalked toward them. "She lied to us."

"No, *you* lied to me!"

Amy searched the scattered logs for signs of life, but the detectives still hadn't surfaced.

She whispered in her brother's ear, "He's got a knife. We should run for it and take his truck."

But he didn't seem to hear. "You said she killed Leo. But all along it was you, wasn't it?"

Why was Daniel arguing with him? Did the piece of wood give him a false sense of security? They were no match for Steve. Earlier, Daniel had struck while she'd distracted the killer. This time, they might not be so lucky.

Steve halted three feet from them and sneered at Daniel.

"Don't act so holier-than-thou. You don't care about her. You're here for the money, too."

Daniel raised his chin. "That's not true. I won't let you hurt her."

Amy backed away slowly. *Don't do this, Daniel. You're messing with the wrong criminal.* A canister of Mace wouldn't save them. She needed serious firepower. Amy glanced at the fallen pine trunks. Where were the detectives when she needed them? Couldn't they see what was happening?

Steve laughed. "How touching. The little brother stands up for his sister. Are you willing to die for her, too?"

Daniel raised the plank like a baseball bat. "Leave us alone."

Steve tutted. "I'm afraid I can't do that."

Her brother stepped forward and swung the plank at the killer's head with all his strength.

Steve ducked the blow, drew his large hunting knife from its sheath, and plunged the savage blade into his opponent's belly.

Amy covered her mouth. "No!"

The plank fell noisily to the factory floor. Daniel stared at the knife in his gut and trembled.

Steve withdrew the blade. He shoved Daniel, who collapsed to the floor and onto his back. Blood seeped from his wound, staining his shirt red.

Amy fought the urge to rush to him. He needed medical attention. But she couldn't save him if Steve slaughtered her, too.

The killer crouched over her brother and wiped his blade on Daniel's jeans. Then, he gazed at her and grinned. *You're next.*

Amy sprinted toward the exit. Could she outrun him? She might beat him to the truck. Had he left the keys in the ignition? How could she leave Daniel to die? *There must be a better way.*

Steve's footsteps echoed behind her. He strolled toward her. There was no rush. Nobody was left to stop him. He'd kill Amy at his leisure.

She leaped over a log, hunting the rubble for Brandon, Mindy, or their weapons. Amy had never fired a gun, but she'd shoot Steve dead. *If I get the chance.*

A trousered leg protruded from under a large trunk. Amy sprinted toward Brandon's unmoving body. His eyes were closed, his holster empty.

She shook him. "Brandon, wake up!"

Steve's footfalls grew louder.

An electric whirring sound emanated from the entrance, and a yellow vehicle sped into the factory. The forklift charged across the floor toward the knife-wielding attacker.

Amy glimpsed the figure behind the wheel, and her mouth fell open.

Chapter 58

S teve "The Hammer" Hamlin stared at the speeding vehicle. The Hyster forklift raced through the factory's open sliding door and made a beeline for him. Surprisingly fast, the yellow buggy bumped scattered logs from its path with twin metal forks, which rose now to chest height like the lances of a jousting knight. *I should get out of the way.* But the spellbinding spectacle rooted him to the spot. The vehicle's operator fascinated him the most. The fat woman in the pink jacket hunched over the machine's controls and bore down on him. *Who the hell is that?*

The pudgy stranger posed no threat. Steve had eliminated opponents far more deadly than her. Besides, collisions with the fallen pine trunks had shifted the forklift off course, and soon the crazed woman driver would steamroll Amy's wounded brother.

Steve sniggered. *How pathetic.*

But at the last moment, the forklift swerved sharply twice to avoid Daniel's legs and almost skewered Steve. He jumped sideways, slipping between the metal forks. But he'd reacted too late. The steel mast of the forklift slammed into his shoulder, hurling him against the hard metal side of a factory machine. The impact winded him, and the knife flew from his hand, clattering out of sight. He collapsed to the floor. Luckily the forklift didn't crush him. The steel tusks lodged in the machine's body, and the buggy's electric motor whined while its wheels spun uselessly.

Steve's arm ached. His ribs and hip burned. But the adrenaline rush of battle launched him back onto his feet. *The bitch will pay for that!* He limped around the vehicle. Darts of pain stabbed his injured body, but he gritted his teeth and pushed ahead.

The crazy woman jumped from the driver's seat. She had disheveled mousy hair, rounded cheeks, and an upturned nose. Her ugly mug seemed strangely familiar. Where had he seen her before?

She grimaced with fury and hurtled toward him. "Leave my friend alone!"

Friend? Did the hag mean Daniel or—

Her handbag connected with the side of his face and knocked him off his feet. He spread-eagled on the concrete floor, his head spinning. He touched his raw and tender jaw. *What's she got in there—bricks?*

She trotted closer, and a sharp pain stung his butt. Steve swore. His head still reeling, he scrambled to his feet and faced her.

He rubbed his throbbing behind. *What was that?* Had the lunatic stabbed him with the heel of her shoe? He'd teach her a lesson. He raised his arms in a boxing stance and scanned his peripheral vision for his knife.

Steve snarled. "That all you got?"

The crazy woman swung the bag again. Steve leaned out of the way. Behind him, Daniel groaned, but Steve focused on the hag and her bag. The kid was a goner. He'd bleed out in seconds. The overweight berserker was the problem.

He bared his teeth. "What are you waiting for, Miss Piggy?"

The insult hit its mark. She scowled at him and struck again. But this time he was ready for her. He dodged the blow, lunged forward, and slugged her in the eye.

Miss Piggy squealed and staggered sideways. *This'll be fun.*

Steve landed a right jab and a left hook. She took her punishment but remained on her feet. This piggy had surprising endurance. She flailed at him wildly, but he sidestepped the bag and punched her in the kidney.

She doubled over and struggled to draw breath, then staggered toward the conveyor belt.

Great idea! Steve snuck up behind her, wrapped his arms around her girth, and hefted her over the sides of the conveyor belt. She landed flat on her back, her eyes puffy and her lips bloodied. Miss Piggy was finished.

Steve smiled at her. "Time for some bacon bits."

He staggered to the control panel and pulled two levers. The wood chipper roared to life, and the conveyor belt moved. *Four down, one to go.*

He surveyed the factory floor. Miss Piggy had distracted him from his primary target—Amy Walker. *Where is she?* Had she slipped away during the fight? *Some friend she is...and some sister.*

Daniel lay silent on the factory floor. His breathing had become shallow. A blade glinted underneath the worktable. Steve walked over, lowered his frame painfully to the floor, and retrieved his knife.

Over the din of the chipper, he heard Amy's voice. He'd been wrong. She hadn't run. He hobbled toward her. Soon, she'd regret that.

Chapter 59

Someone shook Brandon by his shoulders, pulling him from a deep slumber. He lay flat on his back on a hard surface. A migraine pounded his head, and a searing pain tore through his left leg.

"Brandon!" a woman said. "Wake up."

He opened his eyes. Amy Walker hunched over him, her hair raining on his face. *Am I still dreaming?* Purple bruises inflamed her cheek. A sloped fiberglass ceiling rose high above her. *Where am I?*

Fear flashed in her eyes. "Brandon! Oh, thank God. Give me your gun."

Did she really think he'd hand her his sidearm? What was going on?

And he remembered. The Greenpoint sawmill. Amy and her brother. The tsunami of tumbling logs. He and Mindy had tried to escape, but the deadly wave had swept them away.

"Where's Mindy?"

Amy shook her head. Didn't she know, or had his partner not survived the disaster? Brandon had to find out. He tried to get up and survey his surroundings but fell back immediately in agony. A huge pine log pinned his left leg and had probably broken the bone. *That explains the pain.* The sounds of a distant scuffle carried in the air, but the surrounding trunks blocked his view of the factory floor.

She repeated her question. "I need your gun. Where is it?"

Brandon touched his empty holster. *Good question.* He and Mindy had aimed their service weapons at Amy and her brother when the tsunami had hit. Had she caused that?

"Amy Walker, you're under arrest."

"Arrest me later. We need to stop Steve!"

"Steve?" Brandon hadn't seen Amy's theoretical dirty cop. Was this another deception?

She sobbed. "He stabbed Daniel, and now he's killing Beth. Do something!"

Beth? They'd told the bookkeeper to stay in the car. Letting her tag along had been a terrible mistake.

Amy looked toward the wood chipper and covered her mouth with her hand. "He put her in the machine!"

On cue, a high-pitched mechanical whine assaulted Brandon's eardrums. Someone had turned the chipper back on.

Amy shook him. "The gun! Where is it?"

Pain shot down his leg at the movement.

"I don't know. Get this log off me."

She shuffled away on her haunches, dug her fingers under the log, and hefted.

The trunk shifted slightly. Brandon clenched his jaw against the pain. White spots exploded in his visual field, and he nearly passed out. But the log rolled off his foot.

Free at last, he tried to climb to his feet, but his leg bent at an unnatural angle, and the pain overcame him. *Yep, definitely broke something.*

The chipper's whine grew louder and shriller.

Amy's face slackened. "Beth!"

Sickening wet noises joined the high-pitched whine as the rotating blades shredded flesh and bone. Brandon shuddered. *Beth!* Amy pressed her face to his chest and wept. Her friend was gone. After what seemed an eternity, the revolting sounds subsided. Brandon held Amy tight. He wanted to tell her everything would be okay. But this nightmare wasn't over, and both their lives were in jeopardy.

Brandon pressed his elbows into the floor, raising his torso, and peered over the log. A man limped across the factory floor in a black tank top and matching jeans. His lanky blond hair fell to his athletic shoulders. Blood spatter marked his face and the long hunting knife in his hand.

Steve. Amy's tormentor existed. He'd released the logs. Had he killed Mindy, too? Rage burned within. Brandon and Amy had to act fast, or they'd share her fate.

He whispered, "I dropped the gun."

"Where?"

"I don't know."

Steve yelled over the noise of the chipper, "Amy, my friend. My *bestie*. Where are you?"

The killer had a British accent.

Brandon fished his car key from his pocket. "I parked by the truck. Get out of here."

Amy swallowed. "I can't leave you."

"We called for backup. They'll be here any second. Go! While you still can."

She accepted the keys. He'd given her a fighting chance. It was the best he could do.

Amy kissed his cheek. "I'll come back for you."

"I know."

She positioned her feet beneath her like a sprinter on the starting block. But the race never began.

Steve called her name again. But this time, the joyful lilt in his voice lent the word a sadistic edge.

"Amy! There you are!"

Chapter 60

A my stood slowly. The killer's eyes burned a hole in her back. It was too late to run or hide. *What do I do now?*

She turned around. Steve grinned at her. Blood smeared his face like war paint. He gripped the hunting knife loosely and yelled over the chipper's whine.

"Your friends are gone, Amy. It's just you and me now."

Steve hungered for battle. He longed to destroy her. But she didn't have to fight him to win. *We called for backup.* Help was on its way. She only had to survive a little longer and keep him from killing the others. Time was on her side.

The chipper groaned. Behind Steve, Daniel lay on the floor in a puddle of blood, his chest barely moving. *Please let him live.* She balled her hand into a fist, and Brandon's car key jutted from between her knuckles. Steve wouldn't get away with this. She'd stop him. For Leo...and Beth. Her friend's plan had failed. Amy made a new one.

Distract him. Take the lead.

She stepped over a fallen log and toward the murderer.

Steve blinked at her. Her ballsy advance seemed to surprise him.

Behind him, blood dripped from the conveyor belt. Small chunks of flesh littered the floor. Amy shuddered and almost lost her nerve.

Steve followed her gaze. "Nasty way to go. You don't have to end up like her. Last chance. Tell me where you put the money, and I'll never bother you again."

He's lying. He'll kill you. Don't lower your guard. Amy had nothing to give him anyway, but he was still dangerously close to Daniel.

Steve blinked again. The struggle had weakened him. Daniel had knocked him over the head, and Beth had rammed him with the forklift. *Good for you both.* Amy had kneed him in the balls, too. *There's more where that came from.*

She halted twenty feet from him. "Okay, Steve. You win. I'll give you the money."

He grinned. "Good girl. I knew you'd come through for me. Where is it?"

Amy said nothing.

He limped closer. "Well? I don't have all day."

"In my bag."

Steve rolled his head. "Amy, Amy, Amy. I checked your bag. It's not there."

She swallowed hard. "You didn't know where to look."

He sniggered. "You want to spray me with that can of Mace, don't you? Nice try."

An emergency siren blared in the distance. Her body stiffened. Were the cops here? Steve stared at her, and his smile faded. Did he understand what she was doing?

But the siren grew distant and faded. The vehicle had rushed to another crisis, unaware of Amy's desperate situation.

Steve grinned again. "Who are we kidding? We both know there's no money. Come here."

Amy balked.

Steve sheathed his knife. "See? I won't hurt you."

Yes, you will. She shook her head.

"I said, come here. Or should I put your brother out of his misery?"

"No!"

She moved two paces forward, stepping over another log.

"Closer."

Amy obeyed. Only fifteen feet separated them now.

He shut his eyes, then opened them. "That's better."

Her time was running out. "Where's Eddie?"

"Eddie?"

"Edmund Vega, Harry Wesner's assistant."

Steve grimaced. "How should I know?"

Doesn't he know Eddie? "Who helped you in the agency?"

"Nobody *helped* me, except your dear little brother."

Eddie hadn't fed him inside information. Had Beth gotten it wrong?

"Then why did you kill Tanesha?"

"Tanesha? Who the hell is...?"

Steve wobbled on his feet. He wasn't tired. Something was overwhelming his senses.

He touched his butt. "Miss Piggy... What did she...?"

Then, his eyes filled with venom. Steve sprang at her and clamped his hands around her neck.

Amy couldn't breathe.

He growled, holding his face close to hers. "What did she do to me?"

What is he talking about? Amy didn't care. She needed oxygen. Gripping the key between her knuckles, she punched his arm. Steve yelped and released her neck.

Amy sucked in air.

Steve widened his eyes with rage. "Why, you little..."

He reached for his knife, and Amy wasted no time. She lunged forward and jabbed at his face with all her might, burying the key in his eye.

Steve howled and staggered backward. He pressed his hand to the bloody socket.

"My eye!"

Amy cringed at the damage she'd inflicted. But this was no time to be squeamish. Steve had killed Leo and ruined her life. He'd stabbed Daniel and murdered poor Beth. He'd tried to kill Amy, too. She was done running, waiting for Steve to hunt her down.

He drew the knife. "I'll rip you apart!"

Her rage exploded. Amy kicked him in the groin. Then, she shoved him away.

Steve staggered backward. His heel caught on Daniel's shoe, and he reeled like a drunkard, swinging his arms to keep his balance. Then he bumped into the feeder and toppled onto the conveyor belt.

The killer inched toward the chipper's open mouth. "Turn it off! Turn it off!"

He shifted onto his hands and knees and crawled away from the whining blades.

Amy watched, transfixed to the spot. Weak and half-blind, Steve gripped the edge of the feeder. *He'll climb out and come after you! Do something!*

The wooden beam lay at her feet. Amy grabbed the plank, raised it over her head in both hands, and slammed his fingers.

Steve cried out and let go. The feeder dragged him back. He kneeled on the conveyor belt and placed one foot beneath him. *He'll jump out the other side. Finish him now!*

Amy raised the beam again. *One blow to the head. That's it. He'll go down, and the chipper will do the rest. Nobody will blame you. Do it!*

She froze. *I'm not a killer.*

But he almost murdered you!

Amy shook her head. *He can barely walk. He's no longer a threat.*

She lowered the plank and stepped back.

Steve didn't jump out of the feeder. He didn't bark commands or beg for help either. He slumped over and disappeared.

Has he passed out? Is this a trick? If she stepped closer, would he grab her and feed her to the chipper? Amy kept her distance.

The chipper whined louder, joined by the nauseating sounds of grinding bone and meat. Steve shrieked, a blood-curdling primal scream of excruciating suffering. Amy dropped the beam and clamped her hands over her ears. The feeder shook violently. Fingers grasped the edges, startling her. Then the fingers slipped away, and all at once, the cries cut out.

Amy ran to the control panel and turned off the chipper. She rushed to Daniel and crouched over him. *He's breathing. He's alive!* Blood seeped through her jeans, wetting her knees. She pressed her trembling hands to his stomach, applying pressure to his wound.

"It's over," she whispered. "Help is almost here. I'm here with you, Daniel. You'll be okay."

And she prayed she was right.

Chapter 61

Mindy glanced at Brandon from the driver's seat. Before his injury, her gaze had radiated friendship and, occasionally, romantic desire. Now they only projected pity.

"Are you sure you're up to this?"

In the passenger seat, Brandon hugged his crutches. *Am I?*

He smiled bravely. "Yeah."

They cruised along a tree-lined street in Brooklyn. His former partner had offered to drop him off, knowing how difficult the subway had become. Mindy had gotten off lightly. Their dramatic encounter at the sawmill had left her with a fractured scapula and a mild concussion. His scars were for life.

Surgeons had stabilized his crushed leg bones with metal plates, rods, and screws. His physical therapist had promised that, with perseverance and luck, he'd get behind the wheel again someday. Three months after their brush with death, he still struggled to walk. Would this morning's meeting justify all the pain and suffering?

Five towering Gothic spires crowned Green-Wood Cemetery's entrance. Mindy maneuvered the unmarked cruiser through one of the double arches and along the graveyard's meandering streets.

Ornate tombs decorated the gardens: Greek-style mausoleums complete with Doric columns, immense obelisks, and even a miniature pyramid guarded by a stone sphinx. The grandiose efforts to secure a foothold in eternity amused Brandon. But he hadn't traveled to Brooklyn to visit the dead. His interest lay with the living.

Mindy pulled up at the address he'd given her. "Good luck, Brand."

He'd need all the lucky breaks he could get.

"Thanks for the ride."

Brandon opened the door, positioned his crutches, and climbed out of the car. Miraculously, he didn't drop the bouquet of irises.

Mindy drove off. Brandon brushed off his sports jacket, ran his hand over his hair, and set off along the footpath.

Amy had arrived early. She stood by the gravestone, a lone figure in solemn silence.

His heart rate picked up. *Ta-dum, ta-dum, ta-dum.* Day and night, her face had haunted his thoughts. Now, at last, he'd see her again in the flesh. At their last meeting, he'd tried to arrest her. Would she forgive him? Would his lame leg repulse her? *There's one way to find out.*

He drew near and cleared his throat.

Amy turned and smiled. "You made it."

How he'd missed that smile. *She's happy to see me.* They were getting off to a good start.

Brandon grinned hesitantly. "Wouldn't miss this for the world." He hobbled closer and handed her the flowers.

Her smile widened. "That's kind of you."

She placed the bouquet on the grave, and they stared at the final resting place. The temporary marker read, "Bethany Morris."

A gentle breeze shifted the shiny locks of her hair. Tall leafy trees hugged the horizon.

During the long months of his recovery, Brandon had pondered his obsession with Amy Walker until eventually he'd cracked the mystery. Black magic hadn't drawn him to her nor base sexual desire. She'd reminded him of another hypnotic beauty from the dawn of his awareness.

Brandon's mother had been a stunner. Everybody commented on her good looks. Even his father admitted she was out of his league. Brandon spent his formative years clinging to her leg and basking in her affection. But in primary school, the illness had taken Mom, and Brandon had buried a part of him with her. He'd dated girls since high school, but his relationships never lasted. He always held back emotionally, and now he realized why. Why open your heart when, without warning, tragedy might break it? Besides, what earthly woman could ever measure up to his dear departed mother?

But Amy was different. Her overpowering presence had awakened his dormant heart. Her mysterious dark aura had released years of suppressed longing. No wonder he'd fallen for her so hard. But this insight into his psyche didn't cure him of his fascination with her. On the contrary, his resolve intensified. He and Amy belonged together, and today was his one chance to become whole again, if not in body, then in soul.

Brandon searched for a compliment suitable to a cemetery visit and remembered that Amy had covered Beth's burial costs.

"It's a peaceful plot."

"Yeah. I think she'd like it."

The cogs spun in his detective brain. "This must have been expensive."

She shot him a quick, searching glance. Was he wondering where she'd gotten the money?

Idiot! Why can't you keep your mouth shut?

But the comment didn't seem to offend her.

"Beth had no living family. She left me everything in her will."

"Wow!"

"Yeah. It's not a fortune, but it's helped get me back on my feet."

"You must have been close."

Brandon wanted to kick his bad leg from under him. *Seriously? You must have been close?*

"We hadn't known each other long. But she was alone like me. Maybe I was the only one who was kind to her?"

He sealed his lips. That way he couldn't put his foot in his mouth again.

Amy turned to him. "Should we get going?"

She ordered an Uber, and they sat together on the backseat of the blue Toyota Corolla.

Brandon wiped his moist palms on his jeans in case she reached for his hand. *Whoa! Slow down, cowboy. Don't get your hopes up.*

He cleared his throat. "How is Daniel?"

"Good. He's studying for his SATs and hopes to start college next year."

"No kidding. Thanks to Beth?"

She laughed. "Yeah, thanks to Beth. I'm going back to med school, too."

"That's wonderful. Which college?"

"NYU."

"Nice."

His mood improved. Amy was staying in Manhattan. Anything was possible.

They arrived at an Italian restaurant in Brooklyn and ordered pasta.

Amy leaned back on her chair, and her dark eyes swallowed him whole. "What about you—how's work?"

"NYPD didn't fire me. That's the good news. The bad is I'm chained to a desk. Research. Paperwork. All the fun stuff."

Her face fell. "I'm sorry to hear that."

"It's fine," he lied. "I'll be back to crime scenes and car chases in no time."

Her eyes drew him in. "I never thanked you for that night."

"Thank me? I thought you might be angry. You know, for pulling a gun on you."

She pursed her lips. "I would have done the same in your shoes. But you showed up. If you hadn't, things could have turned out very differently."

He drew a tremulous breath. "I'm sorry I didn't trust you. I wanted to. But—"

Their food arrived, cutting his lame apology short. They ate and discussed Italian food and the latest film offerings. They were two friends catching up over lunch. Was this the start of a close friendship?

Amy put down her fork. "You said you had some new information?"

He wiped his mouth on a napkin. Was that the only reason she'd agreed to meet with him?

"I almost forgot. We closed the investigation, so I can share what we've learned. You were right about Steve being a cop. His real name was Dennis Pratt. He'd worked deep undercover on a DEA task force and went rogue. Steve 'The Hammer' Hamlin was his alter ego."

"But Detective Kim didn't recognize his description."

Brandon coughed with unease. "It turns out there were two officers named Kim at Chicago's 9th Precinct. We spoke with the other guy. The department fired Steve six months ago for unethical behavior. That's when he must have focused on finding you."

Amy blinked. "He needed the money and tracked me down through Daniel."

Brandon nodded. "Steve had stolen the pickup truck he'd left at the sawmill. His prints were everywhere. A forensic search discovered two knives hidden underneath the passenger seat. The blade types and trace evidence match the murders of Mark Davis and Tanesha Williams."

"He killed them both?"

"Yep. His hunting knife is a match for Leonardo Santiago's homicide, too."

Amy nodded. "Why did he kill the others?"

Brandon inhaled deeply. He'd had trouble making sense of that, too.

"He took down anybody who might expose you and lead back to him. The stash of murder weapons implies he planned to frame you for all the homicides. He needed you."

Amy relaxed her shoulders. The news seemed to relieve her. Had she doubted her innocence all this time?

"What about Josh?"

"Mark killed him. He'd murdered Josh's assistants and used the same sedative on their boss. Josh had probably found out about Mark's criminal activity and threatened to expose him."

Amy became pale. She'd experienced that drug firsthand and almost joined Mark's list of victims.

"How did Steve know about Mark and Tanesha?"

Brandon shrugged. "Beth was right. Steve must have had a conspirator inside Wesner and Morgan. Edmund Vega is the most likely candidate."

"But Eddie had worked there for years."

"True. The nature of his relationship with Leo is unclear, but they had connected on social media. Steve might have met Eddie through Leo before you arrived in Manhattan. Eddie must have hacked your phone and stalked you. Maybe Leo owed him money, too? We'll never know for sure."

"Why not?"

"Eddie disappeared the morning of the incident."

Amy flashed the whites of her eyes. "So he's still out there?"

"We're assuming Steve murdered him and disposed of his body. The crime scene was a mess. We had to identify Beth by matching the DNA in tooth fragments with that of hairs from her apartment."

Anguish crumpled Amy's face.

Too much information. Well done, Brandon. You've done it again.

"I'm sorry. That was insensitive of me."

She wiped her eye. "No. I figured that much. There wasn't much left of her to bury."

He changed the subject. "I was hoping you could help me answer a few questions."

Amy sniffed. "Sure."

"We found a note by Steve's laptop with credentials for a Bitcoin account. What was that about?"

She shrugged. "We thought Leo invested Steve's money in cryptocurrency. But there was nothing there."

"Right, the balance was empty. Was that the note Leo hid behind your family photo?"

She glanced at him, surprised.

"It's in the case files. Trading Daniel for an empty Bitcoin account was quite a risk."

Amy shrugged. "I didn't know it was empty. We'd assumed it was worth millions."

He nodded. "So, Leo never bought crypto?"

"I guess. Or he saved the wrong account details. Leo was like that."

Her phone buzzed. She swept the screen and froze.

"What is it?" he asked.

Their waiter returned. "Would you like a dessert menu?"

Amy snapped out of her trance. "I should get going."

She's leaving. His opportunity was slipping away.

"Wait. Give us a moment?"

The waiter moved off.

Brandon drew a deep breath. He'd rehearsed the pitch a hundred times, but the words never sounded right. Amy stared at him and shut her mouth tight. Had she sensed the true purpose of the meeting?

"Amy, my interest in you isn't only professional."

"Brandon, I—"

"Just hear me out, okay?"

She remained silent.

His body trembled. *Can she see that?* He lost track of his speech. What came next?

"We met under difficult circumstances, and we weren't always on the same team. But despite everything, I enjoyed spending time with you. You're smart and funny. Resilient. You have the most beautiful smile."

Amy lowered her gaze to the table. *Have I embarrassed her? Do I sound pathetic? I don't care.* He had to let her know how he felt.

"Stay in my life, even if there's no murder to solve."

He'd crafted that line for humorous effect. But Amy didn't laugh or even smile. She glanced at the window behind him. Had she heard a word he'd said?

"Amy?"

She seemed to see him for the first time. "Sorry, Brandon. I have to go."

She opened her wallet, dropped a twenty-dollar note on the table, and stood.

He tried to hand the money back. "I've got that. Can I call you? Amy?"

But she'd already stepped out of the door and onto the street.

Chapter 62

A my marched down the sidewalk. Her heart pounded. Sweat trickled down her neck. People passed her by, their carefree chatter buzzing in her ears. In the restaurant, Brandon had spoken earnestly, but his words fluttered away. The text message had scrambled her thoughts and constricted her windpipe. The three words from the unfamiliar number could mean only one thing. Brandon was wrong. Her stalker lived...and he was still watching her.

She glanced over her shoulder. Brandon hadn't followed her. *Good.* Amy felt bad about bailing on him. He'd sacrificed so much for her. She hated lying to him, too. But she couldn't put his life in jeopardy again.

Amy stopped at the red light and checked her message history. The text was still there.

You deserve better.

The meaning was clear. Her secret admirer disapproved of the company she kept. The last time she'd received that message, the man in question had fallen to his death. But today, the text packed an additional layer of meaning. The sender had repeated the words that had started their twisted relationship. Was her stalker feeling nostalgic, or had their perverse friendship entered a new phase?

The light changed, and Amy soldiered on.

The message hadn't blindsided her completely. She'd expected to hear from the mysterious sender one day. Over the past three months, the events of those traumatic two weeks had stewed in her mind, and slowly she'd pieced the clues together. Those fearful and baffling crimes formed part of a carefully executed plan. Like any complex strategy, the design had provided for every contingency. But the mastermind's endgame eluded her. *There's only one way to find out.*

Amy typed her reply and hit Send.

Where are you?

Enough hiding behind technology. They needed to meet face-to-face.

The response arrived immediately.

Message undeliverable. Invalid number.

She clenched her jaw. Her "best friend" had silenced her. The one-way conversation's subtext was clear, too. *I'm in control. I hold all the cards.*

Amy reached the next corner and waited for green. What did her stalker want from her? Had her secret admirer returned to eliminate her? *Stay calm.* Easier said than done. Amy had a life now. She had too much to lose. But did she also have a lot to gain?

"Ms. Walker?" a man said.

A white stretch limousine stopped alongside her. The black, uniformed driver gazed at her through his open window.

"Yes?"

He got out of the vehicle and opened the back door for her. Amy peered inside, but the ample seats were empty. The stalker had sent a chauffeur to collect her.

Amy looked around her. Two young women watched the interaction with interest. The witnesses reassured her. He wouldn't abduct her in broad daylight, would he?

"Um. Who sent you?"

The driver flashed his perfect white teeth. "Your secret admirer."

One woman gasped with delight. "It's a marriage proposal!"

Her friend started recording on her phone. "Oh my God! She's so lucky. I'm sending this to Jim. He'd better do this for me, too. Go on, girl. Don't keep him waiting."

Amy smiled falteringly. Would her refusal enrage her friend? Was this ride the only way to answer her questions?

She climbed into the limo. The chauffeur closed the door and returned to his seat. The luxury vehicle drove off, and the locks engaged softly. A glass screen separated her from the driver's compartment and prevented further questioning.

Amy leaned back on the comfortable white upholstery and inhaled the heady scent of new leather. If her admirer had wanted her dead, why bother with a limo? *You're safe. For now. Might as well enjoy the ride.*

They headed east through Brooklyn.

She searched the food trays, storage compartments, and magazine pockets for clues to her admirer's identity and intentions. Amy found nothing except for the winged Bentley logo.

Why the limo? Was her genie trying to impress her or buy her off?

The car took the LaGuardia Airport exit.

Amy leaned forward. "Excuse me. Driver!"

He didn't acknowledge her. Could he hear her?

She moved to the facing row of seats and knocked on the glass divider.

"Hey! Where are we going?"

He stared ahead. Was he ignoring her?

Airports, with their tearful separations and reunions, aroused powerful emotions. Was this her evil genie's idea of a romantic rendezvous? Her skin crawled.

But the vehicle passed by the terminal exit. *Not the airport, then. Somewhere nearby?* Were they heading toward an abandoned warehouse or another isolated sawmill? A shudder rippled through her body. Did Amy know too much? Was she the final loose end her secret admirer intended to prune? *This is madness. Get out of here!*

Amy grabbed the door handle. When the limo slowed, she'd tumble onto the asphalt and flag down a passing car for help. The driver turned a corner. She yanked the handle, but the door didn't budge. Amy pressed the unlock button and tried again. Still no luck. *I'm trapped!*

She dialed 9-1-1 on her phone. The limo slowed as it approached a security checkpoint. A metal gate swung open, and a uniformed guard waved them through. Curiosity lulled her fears. *Where are we going?*

"Nine-one-one," a woman said. "What's your emergency?"

Amy ended the call. She wasn't in danger. Not yet.

They drove onto the tarmac. In the distance, jetliners rolled along runways. Were they going to play chicken with a 747?

The limo sped toward a private jet. *Whoa! Is this really happening?* Whoever sent the limo had money. Lots of it.

They pulled up beside the plane, and the chauffeur opened her door. Jet engines hummed.

Amy stepped onto the tarmac. The plane's tail number read: BFF-911. *BFF. Coincidence or another hint from her secret admirer?*

A smiling blonde flight attendant shook Amy's hand and spoke over the whine of the engines. "Welcome aboard, Ms. Walker. We'll take off as soon as you're seated."

"I didn't pack any clothes."

"There's no need."

What does that mean? Was she embarking on a short trip, or did her imminent death dispense with the need for spare clothing?

"Where are we going?"

The attendant grinned. "It's a surprise."

This is insane. Amy had never flown before, never mind by private jet. But the sheer thrill of the new experience overwhelmed her survival instinct. Would her mysterious benefactor greet her on board?

Amy climbed the stairs. *Wrong again.* Aside from the flight attendant and two pilots, Amy was the only passenger. The airmen zipped their lips, too. All her queries evoked the same response. *It's a surprise.*

She surrendered to the indulgent interior of leather armchairs and polished wood paneling. After a steep, quick takeoff, the flight attendant served platters of bagels, lox, and sliced fruit. Amy lounged on a comfy couch and browsed the movie collection on a flat-screen television, but she couldn't focus.

Maybe her stalker didn't want her dead? There were easier ways to kill a girl. What did her secret admirer want from her? Friendship? Her eternal gratitude? How could she accept gifts from a murderer? What was expected of her in return for this bounty?

The penny dropped. Had Leo's Bitcoin fortune funded this extravagance? Had her genie somehow stolen millions from under her nose?

It was never your money. The ninety-thousand-dollar investment hadn't belonged to Leo either or to Steve. Could she have lived in peace with that blood money on her conscience?

Amy counted her blessings. She'd escaped Steve's death trap. Daniel had survived, too, but her brother no longer occupied the same warm corner of her heart. She'd fulfilled her duty as a sister. Daniel was an adult now. How he spent his days was his problem.

She focused on her immediate dilemma—what to say to her so-called best friend? "Thank you" was out of the question. The killer had forced her through a minefield of death and abandoned her beside Mark's bloodied corpse. Amy had thought she'd murdered her boss and doubted her sanity!

A spiteful smile curled her lips. She'd found the perfect opening line. *I deserve better.*

Amy discarded the idea. *You're dealing with a ruthless, psychopathic killer. Do not pick a fight! Read your cards first, then play your best hand.*

She must have dozed off on the couch because the flight attendant woke her for landing. They touched down on a small, forested island late that afternoon. A luxury SUV waited for her on the tarmac. Amy removed her jacket in the warm tropical air, and another tight-lipped driver shuttled her to a private mansion.

A housekeeper led Amy to a bright, spacious room. A white gift box waited on the queen-size bed. Within the box she found, wrapped in high-end tissue paper, a pink bikini and a silky white robe. The note read: "See you at the beach." Signed *BFF*.

Amy opened the closets. A wardrobe of summer dresses filled the rack. Her friend hadn't removed the tags. The collection was in her size and cost easily over twenty grand. Nausea upset her stomach. How long would she stay there? Was she trapped on the island forever?

She inhaled a deep breath to calm her nerves. *Don't panic. One step at a time.*

In the luxurious bathroom, she changed into the bikini and robe, stepped into the new pair of platform sandals, and followed the stone path outside the French windows.

Clear azure waters lapped the private beach of pure-white sand. The sun hung low above the horizon. Her friend lay on a recliner beneath a leafy tropical tree and read a book. Amy settled on the second sunbed and stretched her legs on the warm cushions. A server delivered two chilled margaritas complete with paper umbrellas.

Amy stared at the blue skies. Condensation beads hovered on the slippery surface of the chilled glass. This wasn't so bad.

Don't let your guard down! The tropical paradise belonged to a deadly and deceptive snake. Had the owner drugged her drink? Would this sunset be Amy's last?

Unable to withstand the tension, she broke the silence. "BFF. I finally get it."

Her friend lowered the book and raised her sunglasses.

Amy swallowed. "Beth from finance."

Bethany Morris smirked. "Took you long enough."

The sharp comment unnerved Amy. *Show your value. Your life might depend on it.*

"I knew you were alive."

"Really? How?"

Amy had moved into Beth's apartment after the execution of her will and skimmed her library of crime novels. Dog-ears and penciled notes marked the twists, clues, and reveals of a hundred murder mysteries. The archive had given her insight into the book-keeper's thought process.

"There were plenty of signs. But the clincher was the chipper. Steve shrieked like a banshee. You didn't make a peep."

Beth snorted. "Like the curious incident of the dog in the night-time. You've become a regular Sherlock Holmes."

"I learned from the best."

The bookkeeper sipped her cocktail. "My will gave the game away. Was that too obvious?"

"Not at all."

"I figured you'd need the cash."

"I did. That helped a lot."

The killer seemed wistful. "Steve had been eyeing the sawmill for days. The chipper had been a possibility, if not my preferred solution. I planted some suitable organic material nearby just in case and added my DNA. I knew my wisdom teeth would come in useful someday! Like I told you, Amy. Timing and preparation are everything. But putting him through the grinder was perfection. Great job!"

Amy inclined her head. She'd had no idea her actions had dove-tailed with Beth's secret plan or that the bookkeeper had kept tabs on Steve, too. Casting her net wide had paid off.

Beth crossed her legs. "But I confess, the sawmill could have gone terribly wrong. What else did you figure out?"

Where to begin?

"You planted the knives in Steve's truck. That's why you insisted on being at the sawmill."

"Not the *only* reason. I wanted to help you, Amy. Steve was too dangerous. He needed...taming."

Amy remembered the stumbling knifeman and made an educat-ed guess.

"You injected him with Rohypnol, didn't you?"

Beth raised her glass. "Now I'm impressed!"

Amy shrugged. "Detective Cooper mentioned it."

The bookkeeper huffed. "Don't get me started on the NYPD. I flooded them with tip-offs about Josh's poor girls. Do you think the cops followed through with any of them?" She laughed. "Here's a song for you. 'Sisters Are Doin' It for Themselves.' If we don't look out for each other, who will?"

Beth slurped her margarita. "I needed hard proof of Mark's crimes, so I bugged his phone. But he was cautious. I uncovered his methods, though, and gained access to his penthouse and stash of drugs. The next girl would be his last. I loaded the spyware onto her phone as well to make darn sure.

"Then you arrived. You were different from the others. You *saw* me. I couldn't let Mark hurt you, Amy. I saw through your fake identity immediately. But your troubled past made you even more interesting. When Josh threatened you, everything clicked. This was our chance to make things right. Drugging him was no problem. Josh could never resist Cookie Monday. Any homicide detective worth his salt would suspect foul play once Rohypnol turned up in Josh's bloodstream. To be super obvious, I choked Josh with his tie first. He was dead before I shoved him out the window."

She sighed. "Competent investigators exist only in fiction. The idiots didn't suspect Mark. Instead, they focused on you! But I wasn't worried. I had made no mistakes. But then Steve showed up. Talk about plot twists! I wanted to help, but you had your own plans for him, and I respected that."

Beth chuckled. "I'll admit, things got a little out of hand. Tanesha caught on to you, so she had to go. Killing her was risky. But you know I'll do anything for my friends. And as for Eddie, well, that was just…necessary."

Dear Lord. Eddie, too? Amy didn't ask for details. But her cheeks burned. The bookkeeper seemed to picture them as a vigilante tag team dealing out justice to criminals who victimized women, but she'd abandoned Amy in her time of need.

"Why'd you leave me in Mark's penthouse?"

The bookkeeper's mouth twitched. "I was angry, Amy. After all I'd done for you, you leaked our texts to the NYPD. You betrayed me, so I came to a decision. If you wanted to go it alone, I'd respect that, too. But I didn't let him murder you."

Amy fumed. "You left me there to take the blame. Between the missing messages and waking up next to his dead body, I thought I'd gone insane."

Beth shrugged. "I couldn't get you out safely, and frankly, I didn't trust you anymore. But you're smart and resourceful. I knew you'd pull through."

Amy inhaled deeply. She understood Beth's reaction and couldn't fault her for covering her back. But leaving Amy behind wasn't her "friend's" only vengeful act that night.

"Is that when you switched Leo's note?"

Beth grinned sheepishly. "You'd turned off your phone, but not Mark's. His camera didn't capture the character strings well when you showed him the note at lunch. But if Leo had invested even a small part of the ninety grand in Bitcoin four years ago, we were talking millions. I opened a fresh account and printed out the access codes. I knew Mark would strike that night. The temptation was too great. You'd fallen into his lap and were already off the grid. I slipped inside when he let you in through the back entrance. Once I'd dealt with Mark, I compared the two pages to make sure they matched in every fold and tear."

"Why'd you take the money?"

She shrugged. "Would you prefer Steve got it? What could you do with half a billion dollars anyway? Good luck explaining your sudden wealth to the IRS. Ha! Eventually, NYPD would take the codes into evidence. I'd put the money to better use."

Like buying a private island resort? Amy didn't dare voice that sarcastic thought.

Beth had moved the money offshore and created a new, clean identity beyond the reach of the law. She'd live out her days in luxury and never answer for her crimes.

Let her keep the millions. They'd talked things out, and Beth had achieved closure. But Amy had learned her secrets. Would she let her guest go free?

Amy cleared her throat. "What now?"

Beth stared at the horizon and chewed her lip. "Harry Wesner was right, Amy, and you were wrong."

Amy racked her brain. She'd barely exchanged two sentences with the agency owner, and they'd never argued. Was this a riddle?

"Right about what?"

"The Picasso in his den. He said, 'The universe is a random, brutal mess. But sometimes, if we're lucky, the chaos shows us a human face.'"

Beth had quoted Harry verbatim. She'd eavesdropped on Amy every step of the way.

"That's our job, Amy—to restore order. We're the human face. The world is unfair. The only justice out there is the justice we deliver. That's our destiny. And it's what you got wrong."

She answered Beth's expectant gaze with a shrug of surrender.

"In a moment of weakness, you said your life was wasted. Well, it isn't."

Amy remembered that pit of depression. Alone in a dingy hotel room and resigned to a life sentence in a psychiatric ward, she'd ranted against the injustice of this blind universe. But Beth had been watching.

The bookkeeper continued. "Leonardo da Vinci thought fate had screwed him, too. He was supposed to be a notary like his father and earn a comfortable living. But Leonardo was born out of wedlock, and the profession refused to admit bastards. That setback freed him to follow his genius."

Amy held her tongue. She wanted to jump into the ocean and escape to safety. Beth's manic speech had ranged from cosmic justice to the painter of the Mona Lisa. But beneath the criminally insane logic, she glimpsed an answer to her question.

"All the bad things in our lives led us here?"

"Yes!"

"So, we can use the money to punish murderers?"

"Exactly!"

"We're the da Vincis of vigilante justice?"

"Well, let's not get carried away. But there are other women out there like you and those poor girls. We can help them and bring order to the chaos." She grinned slyly. "As a wise woman once said, 'Everything happens for the best.'"

Amy forced a smile. Her mother would never have supported that twisted interpretation of her trademark expression. Summary executions didn't qualify as "doing the right thing" either.

Look on the bright side. Beth hadn't brought her here to die. She'd offered her a partnership. Amy's conscience rebelled. She wanted to save lives, not end them. But how would Beth react to another rejection? With hundreds of millions at her disposal, this genie was unstoppable. Was this an offer Amy couldn't refuse?

Her body quaked. "Beth, I won't kill anyone. I can't."

"I know. But you have other skills, and once you qualify, you'll have more."

Beth wouldn't keep Amy there against her will or force her to commit murder.

The killer gazed at her. "Well? What do you say, my friend?"

Amy downed her margarita in one gulp and faked a smile. "We've got a lot of work to do."

Beth beamed at her. "Yes, we do. I can't wait to get started."

Epilogue

Anastasiya gazed at the cracked mirror. The cramped bathroom stank of pee and despair. A young blonde woman with a painted face, puffy eyes, and torn lip stared back. Her hands trembled on the edges of the sink. *Is that really me?*

Vlad pounded the locked door with his fists, and she flinched. "Open up!"

Four months ago, she'd answered an ad in the *Kyiv Post* and attached her photo to the email. A woman had called the next day to arrange a meeting. Katya, a fellow Ukrainian her age, explained about the secretarial position in the United States. Anastasiya would learn English on the job and could quit whenever she liked. The pay wasn't high, but after two years, she'd qualify for a green card. In fact, Katya had recently completed her internship and returned home to escort the rest of her family to a new life of opportunity in the Land of the Free.

Anastasiya's mother had hated the idea. They knew nobody in the United States. It was too far away. But Mom was just afraid...and maybe a little jealous? Anastasiya would get nowhere packing groceries at ATB-Market. But in America, her youth and good looks could open doors. She'd accepted the offer, and Katya had helped fill out her passport application.

Vlad banged on the door again. "They're waiting for you. If you make me break down the door, you'll regret it!"

She shivered in her flimsy lingerie.

The job, of course, was nothing like she'd imagined. A van had picked her up at the airport along with six other hopeful young women. Their muscular driver, Vlad, had collected their passports for safekeeping and transported them to their accommodation. In the bleak hostel, he'd assigned them stage names and ordered them to change into their work clothes. By the time they'd realized what was happening, it had been too late.

Vlad changed tactics and softened his tone. "Enough, Candy! Don't be like this."

Candy. She was no longer a human being but a treat for violent men to chew and spit out as they wished.

"Open the door, and I'll give you the rest of the day off."

Anastasiya shook her head. She'd fallen for that line before. If she unlocked the door, she'd receive a heavy beating and a double shift of the vilest customers.

What could she do? For a while, the girls had whispered about escape. But without documentation they were illegal aliens in a foreign country, and the shame of their constant abuse intimidated them into silence. What would their family and friends think of them if they discovered the truth? Most of the girls adjusted. They obeyed their captors to win better conditions. Some aided their tormentors, subjugating other women to climb the ladder of oppression. Had Katya been one of those?

But Anastasiya refused to submit. She clung to what remained of her dignity. Her eyes glazed over in the mirror. She wouldn't last much longer. Eventually, they'd kill her, or she'd take her own life.

A long shard of the cracked mirror hung loose. The jagged edge was as sharp as a knife. Was today the day?

Outside, Vlad swore. Two loud bangs exploded behind her, vaporizing her desperate thoughts. She spun around to face her doom. But the door didn't burst from its hinges. Instead, a deadly silence thickened the air. What had happened?

"Hello?"

Nobody responded. *Is this a trap?* Would Vlad pounce on her as soon as she unlocked the door?

An acrid burning stench reached her nostrils.

"Is anybody there?"

The stillness gnawed on her nerves. She turned the key, and the bathroom door swung open.

Anastasiya clapped her hands over her mouth to stifle a scream. Vlad lay on the bed and stared at the ceiling. Two bullet holes bore into his forehead. She inched toward the exit, but he didn't shift his gaze. *He's dead.* Had an impatient John shot him?

This is your chance. Run! Leave this place and never look back.

But she didn't escape. Not yet.

A large envelope lay by the door. The label read: Anastasiya. Inside, she found her passport and four thick wads of fifty-dollar bills. How was this possible? Who had helped her? A pink business card fell to the floor. A single, cryptic word in Latin letters adorned the front. *BFF.*

From the Author

Hi there and thank you for reading!

I hope you enjoyed FRIEND LIKE ME as much as I enjoyed writing it. (Amy, I'm sorry for making your life so difficult!)

What to do next?

- Help other readers discover books they'll love - **leave a review**.

- Download my free short thriller, THE INTRUDER, available exclusively on my website: **jamiemillen.com/friend**

- Read the Claire Wolfe thriller series, starting with **YOU DID THIS** ("A sister's worst nightmare. A homicide detective's destiny").

I'd love to hear from you! Email me at jamie@jamiemillen.com. Let me know where you're from and what you thought of the book.

Enjoy your reading and stay awesome.

~Jamie

Acknowledgments

Behind every novel there is a long line of very talented and supportive people.

My team of awesome beta readers provided valuable comments and corrections. They are: Maura Bauwens, Heather Bryant, Lynn Lujan, Candice Lutz, Jennifer Medina, Roger Proctor, Roxx Tarantini, Billie Wichkan, and Kai Wills.

My excellent editor, Emmy Ellis, made the novel shine.

Teresa Collins, my trusty and talented proofreader, ensured the final manuscript is error-free and ready for publication.

I thank you all from the bottom of my heart.

~ Jamie

About the Author

Psychopaths. Stalkers. Killers.

Jamie Millen writes about the people you hope never to meet in real life...but probably already have.

If you enjoy crime thrillers packed with nail-biting psychological suspense, unforgettable characters, and breathtaking twists, you've come to the right place.

Visit **JamieMillen.com/friend** to download free stories, sneak peeks, advanced chapters, and more.

Printed in Great Britain
by Amazon

36237076R00189